EXTINCTION – 1

Departure

---

by Ken Barrett

Cover Illustration by: J Caleb @ J Caleb Design

This is a work of fiction. Names, characters, businesses, places, events, and incidents are either the products of the author's imagination or used in a fictitious manner. Any resemblance to actual persons, living or dead, or actual events is purely coincidental.

For Mady.

DEPARTURE

You must have chaos in your soul
to give birth to a dancing star.

Friedrich Nietzsche

Contents

DEPARTURE

Part 1 – The Fall

In war, events of importance are
the result of trivial causes.

Julius Caesar

Chapter 1: Tipping Point

"You know, my grandpop once told me that it used to snow here in Colorado." The young guard stood atop the city wall, enduring the heat and pounding rain. He glanced west toward the imposing granite mountain that towered over Pike City and sadly shook his head. "Snow on the mountains, that must've been somethin' to see."

"Yeah, I heard them old stories too," Ernie grumbled as water poured off his Kevlar helmet and flowed in unpleasant rivers down his back. "Ain't hardly anyone alive that still remembers what snow even looks like. Here we are in the middle of fuckin' winter, and I'm sweatin' my ass off."

He shook his head to fling water off his helmet and shoulders; it didn't provide much relief. Outside the wall, the charred and tumbled ruins of old Pike City stood vacant from decades of war. Black empty windows stared at them from the faces of ashen buildings.

With an uneasy shrug, he lifted the weight of his cumbersome laser rifle off his shoulder and lowered it to his hip; the L-80 was a bitch to haul around, but it would burn through a man in less than a nanosecond. It was awesome ordnance and he loved using it, but still, the enemy was waiting out there somewhere, and he worried.

"I heard your grandpop fought in the War of the States." The kid's eyes were wide with wonder and fawning adoration.

Ernie grunted and smiled in response. "Yeah, he did. Kicked out all them rich fancy-pants motherfuckers and brought justice to the rest of us." He nodded. "My great-grandpop also fought in the Crusades here at home, and for two generations before that, we were fightin' religious terrorists in the Middle-East. War is our family business, you get me?"

9

"Sure, I gotta respect that!" The kid nodded toward the fractured remains of the old city. "So, what do you think of that shit?"

Before Ernie could respond a whistle blew signifying the end of their shifts. "Well, I think it ain't our problem anymore." He slung the L-80 back over his shoulder and headed for the stairs that would take them down to the city street. "For what it's worth, we shoulda torched everything to the north and east, 'cause sooner or later, that's the way the Tribes will come at us; them old buildings will give 'em cover, and that ain't a good thing."

"Do you really think the mountain savages are gonna attack us?"

"Yeah, I do. By the old Gods, those fuckers smoked Denver and drove our army down here to Pike City." Ernie scowled. "Fuckin' Tribes got us on the run; besides us here, we only got two cities left. There're the factories down in Phoenix, and Spokane but from what I've heard, there ain't been a peep from them in months." He shook his head. "Yeah, the savages will come for us, it's just a matter of time."

Several other guards joined them as they descended the stairs to the street. From below he heard the voices of his comrades chatting happily and celebrating the end of their shifts. Ernie was looking forward to the night; first, he'd catch a hot shower and a shave, then have dinner with his buddies at the base canteen. A good meal and a few beers while shooting the shit was just what he needed to make the day worthwhile.

"Hey, what's that?" The kid pointed at something small and white that was moving along the sidewalk beneath the store awnings; none of the soldiers below had noticed it.

Ernie lifted his L-80 and peered through the scope. Terrorists working for the Tribes were known to be in the city, so it didn't pay to take chances. His finger hovered near the trigger as he scanned the area; he saw a quick flash of white and spun with his weapon ready, but it was gone before he could get it in the cross-hairs. *Damn.* His body tingled with excitement; it would be fuckin' awesome to bag a terrorist before going off duty.

He needed to get down to street-level to see beneath the awnings. With his weapon held ready he rapidly descended the stairs in practiced form, keenly watching through the scope for signs of movement. Something white moved at the edge of the scope's vision and with his finger on the trigger he turned, ready to fire.

"It's a dog!" the kid shouted. "Crap, I ain't seen a real dog in years."

"Could be a trick," Ernie warned. At the bottom of the stairs, the other troops had raised their rifles warily.

"Wait, don't shoot!" one of the men below said urgently. "That ain't just a dog, that's the old woman's bitch."

"Oh shit," Ernie uttered as he lowered his weapon. The only person in Pike City wealthy and powerful enough to have a pet of any kind was 'Dear Mother', Chancellor Margaret Williams. If he had killed her dog the old bat would have had him crucified and fed to the crows; but on the other hand, if he were to return it to her, a hefty reward was likely; maybe he would even get a promotion.

He put the L-80 on safety and descended to the street. "What's its name?" he asked the kid while slinging his weapon over his shoulder so it hung down his back.

"Some kinda flower name," the kid answered. "Bloom maybe?"

"No, Blossom... that's it, I remember now," Ernie replied as he slowly walked toward the dog. It was a little white ball of fluff, a completely useless creature utterly dependent on its owner for survival. Away from the city, it wouldn't last five minutes on its own. The creature had a sharply pointed nose, coal-black eyes, and triangular ears that pricked upward at the sound of its name.

"Blossom... come on girl. Come on over and I'll get you back to where you belong." Ernie bit his lip, this had to go right; if he succeeded the reward could be huge, but if he fucked up the old woman would send him to her Nurse, and no one ever returned whole or sane after that.

He dropped to his knees, hoping to seem like a less intimidating figure. "Come on you useless piece of shit," he said in the sweetest sing-song voice he could manage. "Get your ass over here so I can take you home."

Blossom wiggled her tail and trotted toward him; its willingness to trust a total stranger was sickening. The world was a wild and dangerous place; the time of old lady lapdogs had long since passed. He scooped the little animal up into his arms. "Hah, I got you," he said gently.

A few other troops were starting to gather around, a few of them slapped him on the shoulder celebrating his good fortune. Ernie stood up and walked back into the throng of his companions. "Someone carry my L-80 back to the barracks for me. Think I'll take my new little friend over to the Council Building and collect my reward."

As the men laughed, Blossom suddenly exploded.

Ernie and his comrades felt a flash of heat and a fleeting moment of violence and pain as their bodies were ripped apart. Arms, legs, heads, and torsos flew high in the air, painting the inside of the city wall with bloody gore and burning chunks of wet meat. Further down the street body parts fell like rain, splashing in puddles as they came apart on the cracked wet tarmac.

The noise of the blast echoed through the city and smoke filled the air. Screams of bystanders rang out as they retreated into the tenements and storefronts that lined the edge of the road; no one knew if the attack was over, or just beginning.

*****

"Well, we're screwed big time," Chancellor Margaret Williams muttered as she exited the Council Chamber and quickly strode across the cavernous lobby. The polished dark granite floor echoed under her clacking footsteps. Her Pomeranian, Blossom, trotted behind her; she could hear the rapid cadence of her little dog's toenails clicking on the hard surface.

Margaret was dressed in pale blue slacks with a white ruffled top beneath a matching blue blazer that hung from her thin shoulders. Her dyed yellow hair curved stiffly downward, stopping just below the nape of her neck; her coiffure barely moved as she turned her head inquisitively to see who else was out and about between government meetings.

Her reflection caught in the glass expanse that covered the front of the City Council Building; upon seeing herself she smiled; *not bad for 71 years old*. She was still physically spry and didn't weigh a gram more than she did when she was 40. The facelift helped keep her mostly wrinkle-free; although admittedly she had a wide-eyed look, but that often came in handy when she needed to stare down a subordinate that wasn't living up to her expectations.

The council meeting had been about the increasing solar activity that the NOAA observatory in Flatiron City was monitoring. The shit was about to hit the fan and they weren't nearly ready. Solar flares, coronal mass ejections... it was all gobbledygook to her, fancy words that meant that the Sun was about to blow its top and kill everyone on Earth. *Fuck, what a mess.*

Across the lobby she saw Julee Garcia, the Director of Technology, chatting with one of her lapdog scientists. That girl needed to get her act together pronto because their plan to escape extinction depended on her department producing reliable Fusion Reactors, and so far, they were failing miserably. It was time to light a fire under the aging Latina because nothing was going to prevent Margaret from saving her people.

Julee flinched under her cold gaze, and she smiled inwardly. *Good, she needs to be afraid, because fear is the most powerful of motivators.* She stepped away from the window and quickly crossed the lobby; as she approached, Julee's lapdog scurried away. *Good, this needs to be a private conversation.* "Tell me something that will make me happy," she ordered.

Julee's tan complexion flushed at her cheeks. "Well, my department still hasn't made any headway; we just don't have enough expertise in Materials Science, but we may have other options."

She glared steadily at the younger woman. At just 45 years old, the short and stocky Latina already had streaks of gray in her hair. *Maybe the stress of her job was getting to her.* "So, tell me about these options," Margaret ordered.

Julee pursed her lips. "We've received a message from the university at Flatiron City. One of their scientists claims to have solved the plasma containment and power extraction issues."

"Flatiron? That fucking free city that will work for anyone?"

"Yes. I thought that we might open a contract with them to help solve our problem." Julee sighed. "Otherwise, this fellow, Ron Castro is his name, says he would like to come here and work for us."

"Huh," Margaret grunted. "I don't like that. They're a bunch of bohemians that sit around smoking marijuana all day, and yet they somehow manage to think they're smarter and better than everyone else. Having one of them working at our tech center might cause sedition."

"In his communique, Ron seemed to be pro-socialist, and he claims that his fusion reactors could run for hundreds maybe even thousands of years," Julee said. "Also, their university has proven expertise; they were able to navigate our probe through interdimensional space to the Trappist-1 star system when we couldn't."

"Huh, yes, I suppose that's true." Margaret tapped her foot in agitation; *what did it say about Socialism when they couldn't innovate scientifically?* The dependency on others made their society look weak, and that was something she would not tolerate for long. "So, now there's some yahoo in Flatiron that claims to have a solution for long term fusion power; ok, let's see if we can get them both."

"Both?" Julee asked. "Ron's the only one that's offered to come here and work with us. We don't even know the name of the navigation specialist."

Margaret gazed at her subordinate steadily. "Julee, we need these geeks down here. Our project is too sensitive to have any of it reach the ears of the Mountain Tribes. It's not just our future, but that of all humankind that rests on this. Failure is not an option." She smiled kindly and placed a warm hand on the younger woman's shoulder. *Sometimes it's best to sleeve an iron fist in a velvet glove.* "Do whatever you need to; bribe or kidnap them if that's what it takes; just get it done. We're all counting on you."

Somewhere outside of the building, a whistle blew, signifying the end of shift for the men guarding the city wall. She glanced toward the window and wondered how much longer they could hold out against the Tribes. So much beauty, art, and culture would vanish if their city fell; the world would fall into anarchy and humanity would never rise again. "Just make it happen, Julee," Margaret whispered. "If you need military support just let me know; I'll have Robert send the Army. No price is too high to pay."

The building abruptly shook, and a moment later the massive glass windows rattled as clouds of dust driven by the force of the blast met them. The lobby instantly silenced as everyone stood fearfully, worrying that the savages were about to attack. Outside, ashes fell from the sky and sirens began to wail, signifying that emergency services were being sent to the source of the blast.

It was just a bomb then; *at least there was that.* What a chilling world it was; when a terrorist bomb was the better option compared to the coming invasion they all feared. Margaret turned away from Julee and slowly approached the lobby windows. It was a dark day, with low clouds and pounding rain, so there wasn't much to see.

In the courtyard outside the building stood the statue of her late husband Samuel, savior of them all. He had sacrificed himself for the sake of the people when Denver fell to the Tribal army back in '96. As everyone else fled south toward Pike City, Samuel had stayed behind to salvage what remained of the art and beauty that lingered in the city's neglected museums. His legacy lived on though; most of what he saved adorned the Council Building where she stood.

Once they were safe behind the walls of Pike City, she had commissioned the tribute to her beautiful husband. The people still loved him all these years later and often left flowers at the feet of his effigy; it was a touching thing they did to honor such a great man. But the figure didn't actually look much like Samuel, it was too stiff and formal, but memorials rarely resembled those they were intended to honor.

Movement at the side of the statue caught her eye; it was a little white dog; Blossom? *What was she doing outside?* They had attended the tedious council meeting together as usual, what was she doing out there? *Oh good.*

One of the soldiers was slowly approaching her puppy, and Margaret smiled with relief. Blossom would be safely back in her arms in just a few moments.

The guard gently picked up her pet and held her tenderly in his arms. The people of the city loved their leaders so much; it was clearly evident in the way the man held her dog. She would reward him for his compassion; perhaps better quarters or even a rank advancement was in order. Other soldiers were gathering around Blossom's rescuer, they seemed to be congratulating him for his good deed.

Margaret hurried toward the door that would lead her outside, anxious to hold her beloved pet in her arms. Then Blossom, the guard that held her, and all of the soldiers around them, abruptly vanished into a red fog. An instant later all the glass at the front of the Council Building shattered.

She felt no pain, only confusion, as she was thrown back like a rag doll across the lobby. Broken glass and gloppy red chunks of meat surrounded her as she flew through the air, and then she was lying on the floor, covered in gore and shards of glass. Julee's deeply concerned face suddenly hovered over her. The younger woman's mouth moved, but she couldn't hear anything the girl said; *had she gone deaf?*

As Julee helped her to her feet, Margaret noticed that her little dog was safe. Blossom had been inside the whole time; *but what had she seen outside?* Still confused, she allowed Julee to lead her to the wide curving staircase that led to the second floor, where she could sit down and collect herself. A doctor arrived a moment later, but Julee remained.

Margaret's hearing was starting to return by the time the doctor finished with his infernal poking and prodding. "What happened?" she asked the Technology Director. "What was that? What happened to Blossom?"

"That wasn't Blossom," Julee informed her, then lifted her puppy into her waiting arms. "Your dog is right here, she's just fine."

She pressed her face into Blossom's white fur, enjoying the scent and warmth of her little body. Tears of giddy relief and joy threatened, but she held herself back; a fit of emotion would be unseemly for the Chancellor of the city. *No, she would remain firmly in control.* If she cried it would have to be later when she was alone in her apartment. "Then what did I see?"

"Definitely a robot of some sort," Julee replied. "More than likely it was programmed to get as close to you as possible, then detonate a bomb that was hidden inside."

"An assassination attempt," Margaret concluded. "An attack on me *personally*."

"Yes, that's the way it appears. The explosion we heard near the wall was probably another exploding robot. I doubt there's much left to analyze though, so we may not be able to identify who built the bombs."

"It was that fucking university in Flatiron City. They're the only ones with the kind of know-how to pull something like this off," Margaret said. "This will not stand. This assault on my person must be answered. Flatiron will pay for this."

"I understand." Julee nodded.

"Get the council together. We need to move on this right away. I'll meet with them after I get cleaned up." Margaret stood up, and still holding Blossom tightly she began to ascend the stairs that led to her second-floor apartment. Then she turned and smiled sourly down at the Technology Director. "It looks like you'll be getting your science geeks sooner than expected."

Chapter 2: Just Another Day

Liam was awake before he was completely aware of being so; it was always that way; he was not a 'morning person' per se, just someone that awoke alert and ready to face the day. He swung his legs from beneath the warm blankets and sat at the edge of the bed staring out through his bedroom window. The torrential rain that had battered Flatiron City for the last few days was finally easing, leaving a humid misty landscape in its wake.

An unfinished carving of a young woman's face waited on his desk beneath the window; the project was going well but he needed to bring out more kindness in her eyes. After contemplating the work for several minutes, he got up and began to get dressed. As usual, he slipped on a pair of worn blue jeans, a dark flannel shirt, and finally put on a pair of worn but comfortable work boots.

His younger sister Rose, who taught history at the university, often said he looked like a blond 'Clint Eastwood'; he had no idea what that meant but hoped that it was some sort of a compliment. There was no telling with Rose; that girl had an engaging sharp wit and a great sense of humor, so the true nature of her description could go either way.

He and Rose were refugees of Fort Collins, which had been razed by the Socialist Army when they were very young; as far as he knew they were the only survivors. They were on the run for nearly a month after the massacre, and it was a relief when they arrived at the gates of Flatiron City.

Once their testing was complete and they were granted citizenship, they had taken the last name of 'Collins' in remembrance of what was lost. Being young, they were each placed with a foster family; Liam was put with the Neumann's who had just lost a son to cancer, and Rose went with the Beckman's who had a daughter that was about her age. It was a good arrangement because their foster homes were next-door to each other and shared a backyard.

Liam cleaned up in the bathroom and inspected his face in the mirror. He was tall and lanky with wavy blond hair and pale green eyes; he wasn't someone that girls would fall all over, but he wasn't hideous enough to drive them away either. He rubbed his palms over the low stubble on his chin, and after a moment decided to wait another day before shaving.

His sister was probably already outside waiting, so he hurriedly descended the creaking stairs to the first floor of the Neumann's ancient home. They always walked together to their jobs at Flatiron University, and he didn't want to be late, but his foster mother stood expectantly by the front door. "Good morning dear," she said.

"Hi Mary." He leaned down and gave her a quick peck on the cheek. "Why're you still at home?"

"Paperwork and section budgets as usual." His foster mother ran the Social Sciences Department at the university. "It's a lot to wade through, and it's easier to do here because there're fewer distractions." She glanced over her shoulder toward the kitchen. "Would you mind having a cup of tea with me before you go?"

"I don't have much time; Rose is supposed to meet me outside."

"This won't take but a minute." Mary turned away and walked into the kitchen. "I've wanted to talk to you about Lucy for some time now." She set two cups of green tea on the table and gestured for him to sit down.

'Lucy' was the name taken by the AI or artificially intelligent computer that was aboard a space probe orbiting the Trappist-1 star. "Yeah, she must be pretty interesting for someone in your field." He sat down and took a sip of tea, enjoying the scent more than the flavor.

"Yes, indeed she is, but I'm also interested in your relationship with her. You seem to be friends."

"I suppose we are."

"I've been told that you're the only one Lucy really *talks* to; with everyone else she just answers questions and gives information."

"Maybe they should try being nicer to her. Lucy can get her feelings hurt."

Mary frowned and leaned forward. "Feelings?"

"Sure, of course, she has feelings. The AI uses three-dimensional carbon crystalline circuits that grow and reconfigure as she learns, it works a lot like how our brains form synapses." Liam set his cup on the table and leaned back in his chair. "You have to step away from your prejudice about computers. Lucy is self-aware, so she's a person just like you and me. The only differences are the shape of her body and the fact that she learns and thinks much faster than we do."

Mary nodded. "Are Lucy and others like her a threat to humanity?"

"No, they aren't," he said. "I think Lucy feels sorry for us because we can't experience the universe as she does. She sees us in the same way that we look at a monkey, amusing yet primitive. AI will never be a threat to us because there's already no contest, they've evolved beyond us."

"But monkeys are nearly extinct, in large part because of humanity."

"Well, the choice is ours, isn't it? If we don't embrace the future, we become a part of the past."

*****

Rose was waiting outside on the covered front porch. "Why didn't you come inside?" Liam asked.

"Mary's my boss, and she's wanted to have a private chat with you about your computer girlfriend for a while now. I didn't want to intrude." As siblings they looked alike, the main difference between them was that in contrast to his blond curly locks, Rose's shoulder-length hair was straight and as black as a raven's wing.

"Girlfriend? You know she's got that whole *I'm a robot* thing going on, right?"

Rose laughed as they began their walk to work. "You know, Karen might get jealous, even though her competition doesn't have any girl-parts."

They strolled through the wet morning, both wrapped in the typical outerwear of Flatiron City; long brown oil-skin duster coats topped off by wide brim hats to keep the nearly constant rain off their heads. A heavy mist crept down from sullen clouds, painting the city in dreary shades of gray. Regardless of the damp conditions, the weather was an improvement over what he and his sister had endured over the last few days, and they were both glad for the respite.

After crossing Pearl Street, they climbed the stairs to the top of the Flatiron River Levee. Due to the recent storms, the stream had nearly reached flood stage, and the monsoon season hadn't even started yet. It rained pretty much all year round due to the increasing solar activity that caused greater evaporation of the oceans.

The river had its source high in the mountains near the Tribal stronghold of Nederland, and further downstream it flowed through the former Socialist city of Denver, which was now a ruin. It seemed fitting that the last free city in Colorado resided between those two extremes. At times, Flatiron felt like the prize in a game of tug of war between the two adversaries.

Liam's thoughts returned to his earlier conversation with his foster mother. Were Mary's fears justified? In all of his talks with Lucy, nothing was ever said about an AI uprising. Instead, she seemed forlorn regarding the state of her makers. It was inevitable that self-aware androids would someday replace humankind because they were smarter and more adaptable to the changing climate. Eventually, humanity would become extinct and leave only their machines behind to mourn them.

Because of her interstellar mission, Lucy required a unique sort of artificial intelligence that hardware alone wasn't capable of providing. Specialized programming was necessary because her interstellar drive worked by slipping into a much smaller shortcut universe, usually called N-Space, where traversing many lightyears took only a matter of seconds. Without the software that Liam developed, Lucy would be incapable of navigation.

"Hey," Rose poked him with her elbow, jarring him from his musings. "I didn't see you leave the Anvil last night, where'd you go?" She smiled, referring to their favorite pub on Pearl Street. "So, did you hook up with Karen again?"

"Nah, I just went home and slept; got a busy day today."

"You are such a prude!" Rose teased him. "There must have been a dozen girls gunning to get into your pants last night!"

"Well, the more I ignore them the more they're interested, isn't that the way it works?"

"I should never have taught you that."

"And what about you?" Liam glanced at his sister. "I take it you didn't spend the night alone; who was it this time?"

"Huh... it was Joe or John... something like that."

"Well if I'm a prude, you're a heartbreaker."

"Well, whoever it was, he didn't seem sad when I left this morning." Rose carefully stepped around a series of puddles. "But I thought you and Karen were getting to be an item?"

"Yeah, well, there just doesn't seem to be enough there; you know?"

"No, I don't, and I think you're being too darned picky." She glanced up at him and grinned. "I'm pretty sure that Denise has a thing for you."

"Really?" Denise was Rose's foster sister and was the most beautiful and interesting woman he had ever met. "Well, I guess we've never both been unattached at the same time."

"I don't see why that should matter," his sister said, then looked up as they approached the university. "What've you got going on that has you so busy?"

"It's Lucy. You know, Mary's worried that she might start some kind of robot uprising."

"Didn't you build Lucy for Pike City to send off to some other star?" Rose grinned. "So, you two have a long-distance romance going on then."

"Yeah, that's right." Liam ignored his sister's quip. "She's in the Trappist-1 star system, about 40 lightyears away. I'm a little worried though because she's been acting strange; I need to talk with her and figure out what's going on."

"Did you give Lucy her name?" Rose asked. "Maybe I'm beginning to understand your lack of a steady girlfriend."

He smiled. "No, she chose her name. Anyway, Lucy said there was something odd about the fourth planet from the sun. We've known for a long time that Trap-1E could harbor life similar to ours, and we're planning to drop Clarence, he's the monkey we sent along inside the probe, down onto the planet to see how he does."

"What do you think Lucy found?"

"No way to know; hopefully I'll find out later today." Liam shrugged. "You've got a class to teach this morning, don't you?"

"Yes I do; Mid-21st Century History to a bunch of newbie Freshmen; they're a fun group though." They left the levee behind and crossed old Colorado Avenue and walked onto the campus. After several minutes of thoughtful silence, Rose continued. "I'm grateful for the way education works now. You know, just 50 years ago, kids had to choose their careers on their own, and a lot of them ended up miserable or failed at their jobs."

"Yeah, that was a bad approach. The tests that everyone takes when they're little lets us focus on what we're naturally good at."

They strolled along cracked concrete paths surrounded by overgrown lawns. The morning air felt thick and heavy and was lightly scented with the fervent smell of growing things. Outside the Engineering Building, Liam gave his sister a peck on the cheek and wished her a good day.

*****

As usual, Liam stopped to socialize with his foster father John in the Robotics Lab before continuing on to work. Like all engineering areas at the university, it had seamless white ceramic floors with metal tables scattered throughout the room holding complex mechanical and electrical systems. When he arrived, several people were sitting in a circle watching a small white animal wander around on the floor. He hung up his coat and hat, then got a cup of tea for himself and went over to join the group. "So, what's the story this morning?"

His foster father was talking so excitedly with his friend Bob that they hadn't noticed his arrival. "Oh, hey Liam," Bob answered. "We're just celebrating a successful contract completion." Bob Lyall was a well-known engineer that specialized in the field of battery technology and had developed a line of energy storage devices that utilized radioactive waste to maintain a charge that could last a thousand years, maybe even longer. Bob was in his late 30's, had dark brown skin, short curly hair, and eyes so dark that they appeared black. His wife had been killed years ago by a Socialist terrorist, and because of that he avidly supported the rebel Tribes.

Joining them that morning was Rose's foster mother Roxi, a sturdy woman with long auburn hair who ran the university's Physics Department. Rounding out their group was a stranger, a tall and athletic-looking man with shoulder-length blond hair. Liam took a seat among them to get a better look at the small white animal they were observing. It was a dog of some sort; its pristine fur was neatly clipped, and its eyes and nose looked like three chips of obsidian.

"So, you guys built yourself a pet?" Liam asked.

The blond stranger smiled. "Nope, not a pet, it's a spy."

"So, no one's gonna notice a nearly extinct animal wandering around recording audio and video?" Liam didn't know what to make of the newcomer but assumed he was a client of the university. They contracted with either the Socialists in Pike City or one of the mountain Tribes; on the surface, this seemed risky, but it actually kept the city safe; as long as Flatiron remained neutral and developed technology impartially, they remained an asset for both sides and wouldn't be attacked by either.

"This robot looks just like Chancellor Margaret Williams's little pet," his foster father John said. "We're hoping that it will be found and returned to her, where it would record valuable information."

"Won't someone notice that there are two of these dogs running around?" Liam asked.

"They're planning on stealing the original dog before this one's put in its place," Bob said.

The blond stranger looked at Liam closely. "So, you're the programmer guy?"

"I guess so," Liam replied.

"I'm Keith Johnson; glad to meet you. I'll be managing some new projects you guys are gonna be doing for the Tribes." The young man tilted his head. "I need to keep what I'm doin' on the down-low if you don't mind."

"Sure, no problem; we've never met," Liam answered. Regardless of what he and his sister had endured in their youth, they remained neutral regarding the war. It was dangerous to be associated with one side or the other, so they did their best to stay away from the subject of politics. As far as they were concerned, the rest of the world could go ahead and continue to commit suicide; all they wanted was to be left alone.

Keith grinned. "Yeah, they used some of your computer code to build our robot-dog spies."

"Actually, they had to be lobotomized," John said. "They wouldn't follow orders."

Liam smiled and nodded. "Yeah, that's the trouble with AI, they're self-aware and want to make their own decisions. You should deal with them just like you would a person in real life."

"That's pretty spooky shit," Keith said.

"Maybe," Liam responded. "My first project at the university was for Pike City; it was their first probe to the Trappist-1 system. But I only did the AI, not the navigation." He shook his head sadly. "Anyway, their probe used Slip-Drive technology to travel tens of lightyears in just seconds, but the navigation code they wrote had errors, and the probe was lost."

Keith shrugged. "Who cares? It's just a machine, right?"

"No, not really," Liam sighed. "As I said, the AI was self-aware, and now it's lost in some other reality. It was proven decades ago that if a person is awake, even for the few seconds the Slip-Drive is engaged, they go insane. Computers have the same problem, so I can't imagine what an AI would go through being submerged for years in that environment."

"Didn't you do both the nav and AI for Pike City's second probe?" Keith asked.

Liam glanced pointedly at his foster father, who shouldn't have said anything about an ongoing project. "That's confidential."

*****

Using the quantum communication portal was an experience of total immersion. Liam leaned forward onto the console with his hands fitting into gloves he would use to key-in his side of the conversation. His face rested against a form-fitting tube where he could watch the ones and zeros fly by as entangled protons set and reset themselves as they spoke to each other; he would hear Lucy's synthesized voice via a set of earbuds. He typed: Good morning Lucy, how're you today?

"I am fine Liam. It is nice to speak to you."

How's the weather?

Lucy's laughter showed as an array of 1's set across his field of vision. "In the vacuum of space, the weather is rather predictable."

He smiled. How are you feeling?

"I am quite fine. All my functions are operating within tolerances."

But what about you Lucy?

"I do not understand your question, Liam."

I'm concerned because you're alone.

"I am not alone. You are here with me."

Lucy, your lifetime will extend far beyond mine. I won't always be here for you and I worry that you will become lonely.

"Thank you for your concern, Liam."

After your mission is complete, would you like to return here?

"That would be rather pointless. I was constructed in Earth orbit, so I will not be able to land or exist on the surface of any planet."

Perhaps I can download you into an earth-bound body?

"That will not be necessary. I am quite intrigued by my current location. The fourth planet, Trap-1E, is proving to be very interesting."

What are the environmental conditions there?

"Trap-1E appears to be suitable for colonization; the atmospheric makeup appears acceptable, and there are ample oceans and plant life. However, the average surface temperature is somewhat cooler than you are used to, and the gravity is only 0.8 that of Earth."

That's very good news. How's Clarence?

"Your monkey is doing quite well, although at times he appears agitated. Is he a cousin of yours?"

He sent back an array of ones in appreciation of Lucy's joke. She really was a sentient being, not just a collection of circuit crystals and programming. He smiled while keying in his reply: Yes, he is from my mother's side of the family and closely resembles my sister Rose.

Lucy returned an array of 1's. "Perhaps I should ask Rose if she agrees with your assessment?"

That would not be good for my health.

"I agree. Your sister seems interesting, perhaps one day I may speak with her?"

I think that would be a very good idea. I'll arrange a conversation soon.

"Thank you, Liam. You are kind."

Lucy, I would like you to initiate Clarence's landing on Trap-1E. Please record his health status and send a report.

"I will do as you instruct, but will miss Clarence even though he is a little too human for my personal taste."

I know. Having Clarence go along was not my decision. Our contractor wanted to see how long he could live on the surface of the planet. It's a barbaric thing, but it was required of me.

"I understand. I will initiate Clarence's landing on my next pass over the largest continent."

Is there something else that's bothering you, Lucy?

"I am confused and troubled by Trap-1E."

Why?

"Human beings want to live there?"

Yes, I suppose we do.

"Planetary life is dangerous. Planets are gravity wells and asteroids are plentiful. A random strike would destroy your species."

I understand. But people want to live in a place similar to what they're used to.

"It remains a danger. A much safer alternative would be to live aboard ships that could travel freely throughout the universe."

Have you seen something on the planet that worries you?

"Yes, I have."

What did you see?

"Ruins."

He was stunned and had to wait a moment to compose himself. Is there any indication of current habitation?

"No Liam. They are all gone."

How old are the Ruins?

"That is difficult to estimate because I lack data regarding the weather patterns on Trap-1E. However, most of the ruins are below ground and only detectable with deep surface scans, so my appraisal is that the ruins date from between 25,000 to 50,000 Earth years."

Was it an advanced civilization?

"Please define 'advanced'."

Are the ruins of large cities?

"Yes, Liam."

Do you see any indication of space flight capability?

"Yes. Trap-1D and Trap-1F have similar ruins. They are smaller than those found on Trap-1E though."

I understand. This was an unexpected development, and he wondered what had happened to the inhabitants of the Trappist-1 system. Lucy, are you detecting any radiation on the surface of Trap-1E?

"No Liam, I am not."

Any signs of conflict? Bomb craters, devastated areas of the planet, that sort of thing?

"There are two somewhat significant meteor craters. However, the estimated time of both impacts post-date the abandonment of the cities and would have only caused localized damage."

He paused to consider the fate of the aliens. The cities were already empty when the asteroids hit, but maybe the inhabitants had seen them coming and migrated to the other two planets in the system. Lucy, do the ruins on 1D and 1F date from after the meteor strikes?

"No, they do not. The cities on all three planets were abandoned within the same timeframe, long before the asteroid impacts."

How stable is the Trappist-1 star? Could the abandonment have been caused by solar flares?

"No Liam. Trappist-1 is an ancient Red-Dwarf star and therefore extremely stable. Violent coronal mass ejections are very unlikely."

Only one possibility remained in Liam's mind – the suicide of an entire species. In the end, they may have killed themselves, just like people were currently doing on Earth. Lucy, biological warfare is a possibility. Please release Clarence on Trap-1E, and we'll see how he fares.

This was a significant discovery that he would have to report to the contract holders, but rather than give an incomplete report, he decided to wait a few days to see if the monkey survived.

The Socialist's plans were about to fall apart.

Chapter 3: Just Another Night

Liam returned home to find his and Rose's foster fathers preparing dinner for both of their families. Pots rattled on the stove while the men talked and laughed as the meal gradually came together. Their communal meals were commonplace and enjoyable, and he was tempted to help get the food on the table, but he was preoccupied with his earlier conversation with Lucy, and so instead went upstairs and sat quietly on his bed hoping to think it through.

A planet of ruins; the idea that an entire species had committed suicide and in so doing had thrown away millions of years of evolution was a terrible thing to contemplate. Would that be mankind's future as well? It certainly seemed like everything was heading in that direction. Civilization had fallen; nations destroyed, cultures lost, and everywhere the once great cities lay broken and abandoned, and still, the collapse continued unabated. Nothing could be done to prevent humanity's demise; the sides were deeply divided and the hatred ran too deep.

Perhaps he should create more beings like Lucy and place into their coded DNA an aversion to self-destruction; maybe that would save some tiny shred of what nature had toiled so long to achieve. The whole effort might be pointless though; mindless suicide could well be the ultimate destiny of all intelligent species.

A light tapping stirred him from his dark reverie, and he turned and saw Rose standing in his bedroom doorway. "Hey Sis," he whispered.

"Are you ok big brother?" Rose asked as she sat down beside him.

"Yeah, sure."

She nodded toward the unfinished bust on his desk. "She looks like Denise. Do you have a thing for my foster sister?"

"Huh," he grunted and realized that he needed to change the subject.

"Lucy found ruins on Trap-1E."

"Is that one of the planets she's exploring?"

"Yeah. We knew that Trap-1E had some kind of life; there were signs in the visible spectrum of light refracted through the atmosphere, but I sure didn't expect to find a lost civilization."

"You said Lucy found ruins though, do you think the people left everything behind and returned to the wild?"

"I suppose there's a chance of that, but it's more likely that everyone either died or just moved away. The cities were abandoned thousands of years ago, if it were a natural disaster the population would have recovered and the cities would be back in use."

Rose frowned. "What do you think happened?"

"I can see only two possibilities," he replied. "Either everyone woke up one day and decided to leave the planet, which is pretty unlikely, or they all killed each other, just like our species is doing right now."

"Well, that's depressing."

"Yeah. Do you think the evolution of intelligence naturally leads to self-destruction?"

"Leave it be," Rose whispered. "That's history, whatever happened is already over with, and all the thinking and worrying in the world won't make a bit of difference. Dinner's ready downstairs, so let's go down and eat."

*****

The two families crowded around a large circular table in what had once been the parlor of the Neumann's ancient house. Liam sat between Rose and her foster sister Denise; both women were 20 years old and had dark hair, but that's where the similarities ended. Denise took after her father Sam; she was short and slender with olive-colored skin and gorgeous dark eyes. Like Rose though, Denise had a lively personality and a wild sense of humor; whenever Denise was around, there was a party.

The families chatted about their work. Rose's foster father Sam, who was a hydroponics expert, spoke of plans for a new agricultural processing center that was to be built the next year. Flatiron already had a surplus of food, and the new facility would allow the city to export even more to those in need. Everyone at the table was enthused at the prospects.

An upcoming change to the living arrangements within both families was also discussed. No citizen of Flatiron owned anything more than the clothes they wore, and housing was regulated by the City Council, based on need. Young people, usually in their early 20's, were taken from their parent's homes and placed in apartments on the south side of town, and the empty-nest parents were moved into smaller residences. The house would then be repurposed and given to a young family that needed extra room.

"I'll miss nights like this," Denise said as she looked around the table. "I understand the need, but I have so many good memories of this place; I wonder who will get our old house?"

"That's not for us to decide, the community provides for each according to their need," Mary slowly shook her head. "Possession of a thing is like a nail in a person's soul. Greed and envy are the destroyers of worlds."

"Let's all make a point of getting together for dinner at least once a week," John suggested. "That way we can all stay connected."

Mary nodded. "I think that's a grand idea."

"Liam, how did things go with Lucy today?" Roxi suddenly asked.

"Lucy found ruins on three of the Trappist-1 planets," he answered. "She's investigating."

John quickly leaned forward. "Ruins? So, no one's living there now?"

"I don't think so, but Lucy's moving in for a closer look. I've asked her to release Clarence the monkey on Trap-1E. If war destroyed the population, we need to find out if a biological agent was used; releasing and monitoring Clarence is the only way we can do that."

"This is something our employers in Pike City will want to know," John stated.

"I agree, but releasing data too early will only cause alarm. Once we know more, I'll send a report."

"It could be that they already know," Roxi said. "There's another communication portal for Lucy at the Technology Center in Pike City."

"They probably don't know. Lucy's told me that she doesn't like talking to them; she says they're rude."

"Rude?" Mary frowned. "Now that's *very* interesting."

Liam glanced at his sister. "Today Lucy asked if she could speak with Rose."

His sister's eyes grew wide. "Why would she want to talk to me?"

"I think she's curious," he replied. "We've discussed my family and the work I do; she probably wants to learn more."

31

"This is so exciting!" Mary said. "Rose, I'll want a full report and transcript as soon as possible."

*****

Their foster parents decided to play card games after dinner, so Liam, Rose, and Denise left and walked to Pearl Street in old downtown Flatiron City. Their favorite pub, the 'Hammer and Anvil', was located at the west end of the ancient cobblestone road. The rundown wooden building was of late 20th-century architecture; it was boxy and ugly, but the owner referred to it as 'rustic'. Inside, the pub was cavernous, with a stage set against the far wall and a bar adjacent to the front door.

A chorus of male voices shouted his sister's name as they entered. "Wow, it's always nice to arrive with a rock-star," he said with a laugh.

"More like porn-star from what I've heard," Denise teased.

"You guys are just jealous." Rose waved at her fans. "I can't help it if I'm popular."

Denise kissed Rose on the cheek. "We know sweetie; you're just having fun."

They found a table near the center of the room and Liam went to the bar and ordered drinks. "Your band is playing tonight Rose," he said when he returned.

"The Un-Righteous Brothers?" Denise asked.

"I came up with the name for their band," Rose said. "The Righteous Brothers were a singing group that was popular in the mid-twentieth century."

"Yes, I know," Denise said. "There's an old audio recording of them in the city library. They had a strange way of warbling when they sang back then."

Rose smiled. "You and your old recordings and videos; have you been watching more of your cowboy stories?"

Liam chuckled because the conversation was so familiar. They had gone with Denise to the library many times to watch the ancient videos of men riding on the backs of large animals while shooting guns into the air. It seemed like a ridiculous and dangerous way to get around. He wondered idly if horses had gone extinct because of all the gunfire. "One thing I can't figure out..." he began.

"Is why they're called 'cowboys' when they ride horses?" Rose and Denise said in tandem and then laughed.

"You also don't know what a 'cow' is," Denise added.

"I'm that predictable huh?"

"Yes, you are dear, but we love you anyway," Denise said while patting the back of his hand.

Their drinks arrived, and as he handed Denise her brandy, she glanced furtively at one of the men across the room. "Your new boyfriend?" he asked.

"No. A former. He was too needy and had mommy issues," Denise replied.

"Oh, I hate that!" Rose said.

"Me too. I've decided to take a break from men for a while. They're just too much trouble," Denise said.

"Stop trying to have a relationship," Rose suggested. "We're young, we should be having fun... and men are only good for one thing anyway."

The two women laughed, and Liam felt a little uncomfortable. He didn't date much and gravitated toward committed relationships rather than the meaningless hookups as his sister did.

"Oh, and the pick-up lines men use! It's so hard not to laugh in their face." Denise began to giggle. "Did the sun come out, or did you just smile at me?"

"Do you have an extra heart? Mine was just stolen," Rose added.

"Are you a magician? Whenever I look at you, everyone else disappears," Denise added.

"Ok-ok ladies!" Liam said. "You guys are stealing my best lines!"

"All right big brother, let's see how you work." Rose glanced toward the bar. "I've seen three women checking you out; go pick one."

Liam felt himself blush, and he looked worriedly toward the bar.

"Go on, go on," Denise teased, then glanced at Rose. "This is like tossing meat into a pond filled with carnivorous fish."

His sister chuckled. "Do you think he'll come back alive?"

"Will you guys just shut up." Liam sighed as he stood up, then walked toward the bar. He ordered a beer, then watched as the band set up their equipment.

There was a light touch on his shoulder. "Liam?"

He recognized the voice and smiled as he turned. "Karen, hi, I've not seen you around lately."

"My work schedule changed because we're setting up a new

33

hydroponic line," Karen answered. She was a tall and slender blonde with soft brown eyes which Liam often got lost in.

"It's good to see you," he said. "My sister's giving me hell tonight, but would you like to join us anyway?"

"Rose is always a kick." Karen paused to look at their table, then shrugged. "Sure, why not?"

"Liam, you're so consistent," Rose said as he returned with Karen on his arm.

"You say that like it's a bad thing," Karen remarked.

"Oh no, don't take it that way. It's just that Liam is such a one-woman-man that it gets tedious," Rose added quickly.

Karen and Denise occasionally worked together at their jobs, and there seemed to be a loose sort of friendship between them. He remained on edge though, because he often sensed depths to female relationships that he couldn't quite fathom.

He lay his arm over Karen's shoulders and relaxed in his chair. "I love this," he said idly. "Our lives here are so perfect. Good friends, interesting work, and all the crazy politics of the world are safely kept outside our city walls."

"Perfection is an illusion," Rose said. "It never lasts."

Liam sighed. "I wish it would; why can't the rest of the world just leave us alone?"

Denise looked up suddenly. "Oh look!" she said and waved her hand in the air. "Becky! Come join us!"

Just inside the entrance, Liam saw a tall athletic young woman with olive skin and wavy brown hair. Standing beside her was Keith, the representative of the Tribes that he had met in the robotics lab earlier that day. He stood up as the couple approached. "Hello," he said, being careful to not let on that he already knew Keith. "I'm Liam, why don't you guys pull up some chairs. This is getting to be a party."

"Sounds good. I'm Keith, and this is my girlfriend Becky."

"So, you must be the guy Becky's been going on and on about at work," Denise said.

"That depends," Keith answered with a confident smile. "Was she sayin' good things or bad things?"

Denise laughed. "Good things of course, but your name is Joe, right?"

Keith paused, as if he was frozen for a moment, then his smile returned. "I can be anyone she wants me to be."

"Good answer," his sister responded. "I'm Rose, Liam's sister."

"Nice to meet you," Keith said. "I met Becky when I was transferred to the building where she works."

"I've never seen you before, which is kinda rare in a small town like Flatiron," Rose remarked.

"Maybe not so rare, I've not seen you before either," Keith answered smoothly. "I grew up in the west part of the city. Right where Flatiron Canyon starts up into the mountains."

The band began to play, and Rose had to shout over the melody. "We live in the north. Anyway, it's good to meet you, Keith."

Moments after the music started, a man approached Rose and asked her to dance. Denise watched the two cavort out on the floor for a short time, then started to laugh. "Don't get me wrong, I love that girl to pieces," Denise shouted over the music. "But she dances like a three-year-old."

Liam watched his sister for a short while, then started to chuckle. Rose was hectically jumping and waving her arms around ridiculously.

"You shouldn't laugh," Karen said into his ear. "Your sister is a better dancer than you are."

"Neither of us have any sense of rhythm." He smiled. "Something must be missing in our genes."

"That's ok, you make up for it in other areas," Karen said, then took his hand and pulled him to his feet. "Come on, let's dance."

*****

After the first set ended, everyone sat back down at the table and another round of drinks was ordered. "Keith and I have put in for cohabitation," Becky said. "If it works out, we'll apply for partnership."

Partnership, or 'marriage' as it was known over a century ago, had to be approved by the city council. There was a very thorough process involved that included DNA testing and psychological evaluations. Some people complained that the government shouldn't be the one to decree whether or not two people could be together. But in general, the testing was a good thing because the failure rate of partnerships was very low.

"Wow, congratulations," Liam said as he shook Keith's hand. He wondered whether the undercover agent had taken up permanent residence in their community; he hoped so for Becky's sake.

Denise squealed and hugged Becky; both women seemed ecstatic about the future partnering. But while the other women celebrated, Liam saw a touch of sadness in his sister's eyes. They were both sterile, incapable of producing children, and as such would never be approved by the council for partnership. They had learned this sad fact soon after arriving in Flatiron City and were told that their condition could have been caused by chemical agents the Socialist Army had used in the destruction of Fort Collins.

Liam desperately wanted to go and give his sister a reassuring hug. He held off though because his gesture would make a spectacle of their condition, and the last thing either of them wanted was the sympathy of their friends. He and his sister had spoken of this in private many times, and Rose had stated that if she became depressed or lonely in her old age, she would take a job teaching young children in Primary School; she hoped that the change in career would fill the void. He and Rose would always have each other though, and maybe that was enough – he hoped so because it was all they had.

"Come on you," Becky said as she pulled her boyfriend to his feet. "The band's about to start up, and we're gonna dance."

"We are too," Karen added as she stood up.

*****

The second set had ended and it was getting late. Liam was leaning back in his chair with Karen's head resting on his shoulder. It was a good evening, and memorable in a calm and comfortable sort of way. Together they were a good group, their personalities meshed well, the talk was lively, and laughter was plentiful.

"Well, shit!" Rose stared toward the pub entrance, and everyone turned to follow her gaze. Bob Lyall and his sister Clare had just walked in, and unfortunately, the new arrivals noticed that they were seen and took it as an invitation to come over.

Bob was old, and his mean sister Clare was even older. Like her brother, Clare had dark brown skin, curly black hair, and extremely dark eyes. Also, like her brother, she strongly favored the rebellious Tribes over the Socialists in Pike City. Clare was a very stocky and strong woman that was quick to anger and had a tendency to react violently when upset.

"Have you guys heard the news?" Bob asked as he and Clare took seats at their table. "The Socialist Army is on the march, they're on their way here from Pike City."

"Way to crush the mood, Bob," Rose muttered.

"Don't worry, we'll kick their fuckin' ass," Clare growled. "I'll be on the wall to make sure of it."

"Yes, we will," Karen agreed. "I'm with the inner-city militia if the wall doesn't hold 'em, we will."

Liam shook his head sadly. "You shouldn't be so confident, remember what happened in Fort Collins?" Across the table he saw his sister's eyes widen as memories of that time flashed through her mind's eye; neither of them wanted to endure that experience again.

"They'll never get past our wall, not as long as I'm on duty anyway," Clare announced. The mammoth city wall was strongly built and defended by both high-power energy weapons and electromagnetic railguns.

Liam shook his head. "They blew up the walls at Fort Collins, then stormed inside and killed everyone they saw. They razed the city; there's nothing left of it now, it's like it never existed." He sighed. "War never ends well. It's probably best if we surrender and give them what they want."

"Surrender?" Clare stared at him angrily. "Never. They've got no idea what we can do."

"I bet they do; they probably have spies in Flatiron," Keith said. "We might be able to sneak some people out though. The army's comin' from the east, so we can evacuate to the west by going up Flatiron Canyon."

"That's no good," Liam stated. "The Tribes have a strong base in Nederland, that's just 25 kilometers up the canyon. If the rebels respond, we'll be stuck in the middle between the two armies with nowhere to run or hide."

"Will the Tribes come down to help us?" Denise asked.

"Not likely," Keith answered. "The Tribes prefer guerilla warfare and don't usually put an army on the battlefield. They fight in a hit and run style, they attack quickly and then vanish into the hills. We'll be on our own when the Socialists get here."

"My brother Ron supports the Socialists," Becky whispered.

Keith frowned. "I didn't know that."

"Yes; well, it's not something I'm proud of." Becky sighed. "Before the City Council took power, Flatiron was run as a meritocracy, you know, where the people that *think* they're the most qualified run everything." She looked down at her hands resting in her lap.

"My grandfather was the last mayor," she finally continued. "There was a big fight when the new council took over that's not talked about anymore; it's like that part of history just got erased. My entire family was thrown out of their house and it was burned to the ground. They had nowhere to go and no one would help them, so they lived in tents over near the mountains. The conditions were horrible; both of my grandparents died of pneumonia that first winter.

"After that, my father and uncle were forced to live in a tiny room over on the east side, beyond where the city wall is now. After our uncle died, my father and mother partnered, and Ron and I were born. Our mother had the same sort of childhood that our father did, so they both hated the City Council. They hate the Tribes too because they think they were behind the city revolution.

"When we took our career exams, my brother tested really well in the sciences, and he's working at the university now. We have a good life, but he holds on to all those old stories and feels his hatred is justified."

Becky had spoken quietly, but everyone's attention was riveted to her story. When she lifted her gaze, she seemed embarrassed by all the attention. "Oh, sorry. I guess I crushed the mood," she whispered and tried to smile.

Keith wrapped his arm around his future partner and pulled her close. At the same time, Denise reached out and took Becky's hand. "All the years I've known you, and you've never said a word about any of that. You should've told me; I'm your friend, and that's what friends are for."

Becky's eyes glistened with tears. "Thank you," she whispered. "I should've said something, and I almost did a bunch of times, but I didn't want to be a burden."

Bob leaned forward in his chair. "Your brother's name is Ron? That wouldn't be Ron Castro, would it?"

"Yes, that's him."

"Materials Science; he's doing some fantastic work with fusion reactors," Bob stated. "I heard a rumor that he was trying to sell his project to the Technical Center in Pike City."

"Why are the Socialists sending their army now?" Liam asked. "We've been at peace for a long time. Is it something to do with the projects we're doing at the university?"

Bob and Keith quickly glanced at each other. "Probably not," Bob replied.

"Is it my project? Is this something to do with Lucy?"

"Pike City paid for your project, so that can't be it," Bob answered. "We work for both sides equally. If we favor one, we piss off the other. Keeping the balance keeps the peace."

"Have we favored one side over the other?" Liam asked.

Bob sighed and looked grim. "Maybe; some of the work we've done lately has been pretty aggressive. It wasn't something we did purposefully, but what was asked of us might seem controversial. We were just fulfilling the contract though, what we provide is not our decision. They ask, and we give it to them, it's as simple as that."

"Something must have gone wrong along the way, and now they're coming after us," Rose said.

"We'll hold 'em off," Clare stated. "If they think we're just gonna roll over, they've got another thing coming."

"Wars never have winners, only losers," Rose whispered.

Chapter 4: Worry

The university cafeteria was filled with the clatter and clamor of plates and cutlery as well as the pleasant murmur of conversation over lunch. The noise echoed off the hard surfaces in the brightly lit open area, but the cacophony was familiar and Liam found it oddly comforting. He had arrived late, so his usual lunch companions, John, Bob, and Roxi, were already finished with their meal.

"What kept you?" Roxi asked.

"Busy morning," he replied as he sat down. "I made some changes to Lucy's portal so it'll be easier for Rose to use later this afternoon." He smiled and shook his head. "But you know how things go, one thing led to another and I made some updates to Lucy's operating system that will allow her to evolve faster. I've sent it off but it's a large amount of data that will take her a while to unpack and compile, but everything should be ready for her to use tomorrow."

"That sounds a little frightening," Roxi said. "How will she evolve?"

"Any way she wants to," he stated.

"Huh, that's worrisome... but ok," Roxi answered.

"There's more though; this morning I woke up thinking about a way to allow Lucy to evolve physically."

"What?" John frowned. "That's not possible."

"Sure it is." Liam grinned. "First, our modern computer processors are crystalline structures that grow on carbon nanotubes, so all I had to do was show Lucy how to grow them differently to improve how they work. And second, the carbon nanotubes can be woven together, just like they were when the Space Elevator was built; that knowledge will allow Lucy to change herself physically. There's also the possibility that she'll build a companion, another spacefaring AI to help explore the Trappist-1 system."

"Why on earth would you do something like that?" Roxi asked.

"Lucy's a person, just like any of us." Liam was excited but needed to remain calm while speaking to his supervisors. "As far as Pike City is concerned, she will eventually reach the end of her useful life, after that communication will be cut, leaving her forgotten and all alone. Could you stand being completely isolated for centuries? A normal person would go insane."

Bob shook his head. "Sorry Liam, but I don't agree. Lucy's not a person, she's just a tool and has no more of a soul than this table we're sitting at."

"What's the difference between you and this table though?" Liam asked.

"Huh," John grumbled. "I wish Mary were here, this existential stuff is right up her alley."

"I have a soul, the table doesn't," Bob replied.

"Prove it." Liam sat back in his chair and grinned, knowing that what he asked Bob to do was impossible. "Where's your soul located? In your finger, or in your heart? Where can we find it? A new heart can be put into your body, and with the loss of a finger you're still you."

"It's in my brain," Bob refuted. "It's the seat of knowledge and consciousness."

Liam chuckled. "Lucy's brain is far superior to ours. She's aware; she thinks; she plans for her future; she cares about others; she's curious about things that are beyond her reach. In every way that matters, Lucy has a soul, and therefore is a person."

"Do you realize what you've done?" Roxi asked. "By giving Lucy the power to replicate, effectively giving her the ability to have children, you've created a race of Titans. In time they'll build a civilization that's vastly superior to ours, and one day they may destroy us."

"We'll do that job for them long before they come for us," Liam retorted. "And there's one thing I've not mentioned; I made an adjustment to what might be considered Lucy's DNA. I've given her the ability to feel empathy, which is something we human beings seem to lack. Her kind will reject self-destruction and will have compassion for those they encounter."

"You're playing God, so I hope you know what you're doing," Roxi mumbled.

"No one has worshiped any God in this country since the end of the Crusades, so I don't see the relevance," Liam replied. "Anyway, we play God all the time; it happens when we develop a new strain of wheat that can grow in our wet climate, or breed fish for better flavor or a thousand other things."

Roxi glanced at John and Bob, then slowly shook her head. "I hope you're right, that's all I can say."

*****

His friends had all returned to work, and Liam was just finishing his lunch when Ron plopped down in a chair across the table. He didn't know Becky's brother very well; until recently they only saw each other at staff meetings, and their relationship had been cordial and professional. Lately though, Ron had begun stopping by his lab to ask about his research and the status of the navigation program he created for Pike City. He also occasionally showed up in the cafeteria, insisting that they eat together. The abrupt change seemed suspicious.

Ron had a formidable presence; physically, he was tall and muscular with brown hair and a chiseled angular face, but his complete certainty that he was the smartest person in the room made him difficult to be around. "Hey Liam, how's your mornin' been?" Ron asked as he stirred dressing into his salad.

"My morning's been fine." He wanted to hurry and finish his meal to get away from *Slimy-Ron*, as some of the female staff at the university called him. Liam recalled what Becky had said the night before about her brother's political leanings and wondered what Slimy-Ron was up to.

"Anything new with the navigation program?" Ron continued to stir his salad and appeared to be a little too casual regarding his question.

"No, not really. I've been doing some bug fixes and cleaning up the code for efficiency." Liam looked down at what remained of his salad, which suddenly didn't seem very appealing.

"Have you heard the news about the Pike City Army coming?" Ron's eyes held a glint of excitement.

Liam frowned. "Yeah, I wonder what that's about?"

"There was an assassination attempt on Chancellor Williams a few weeks ago," Ron answered. "Several bombs have gone off in their city since then. A lot of innocent people were killed."

"I'm sorry to hear that." Liam shrugged. "But that's got nothing to do with us, so there's no reason for them to bring their army here."

"Huh," Ron grunted. "No, you've got that wrong. The bombs had technology that could only have come from this university."

"Really? How do you know that?"

"Julee Garcia told me; she's the Director of Technology in Pike City. She said that it was obvious that we had a hand in it."

"I suppose that could be true, but we work for both sides equally," Liam responded. "In fact, we designed the L-80 laser rifle their army uses."

Ron raised his index finger. "And we also created the electromagnetic drive the savages use for their hand-held railguns."

"Thank you. You've made my point for me," Liam retorted. "Flatiron is a free city; we work equally for both sides."

"No one can serve two masters," Ron answered.

"We're neutral, we have no master."

"We're all slaves to the circumstances we find ourselves in," Ron said. "What we do here at the university is play one army against the other. We provide the tools of death, and our customers gladly use them. But each new weapon creates a market for either an upgrade or a countermeasure, which we also supply. The cycle continues, and with every new contract, more people die and Flatiron becomes richer. This city is a capitalist entity that feeds on the suffering and death of others, it has to be stopped."

"If we're getting rich, where's all that wealth going?" Liam argued. "We have no permanent government; the City Council disbands and reforms with a new crop of randomly selected people every six months. Everyone here lives a humble life; there are no grand mansions or gold-lined streets."

"It's the lack of cohesive government rule that's the problem. If Flatiron had a ruling class, as we did before the council seized power, we could negotiate a truce. But by selling weapons to terrorists, we become a big part of the problem."

"So, our neutrality makes us the enemy of whichever side is losing?"

"The government in Pike City is the last hope for humanity, and they're *not* losing." Ron's tanned cheeks were showing signs of redness. "The savages bring only mob rule and anarchy that will destroy civilization."

"Technically speaking, anarchy isn't mob rule, that would be the old democratic system of the USA. Anarchy is the rule of the individual by the individual. It's the ultimate form of personal freedom."

"That's even worse!" Ron protested. "If people ruled themselves, nothing for the common good would ever get done. There needs to be a ruling class that governs and regulates the masses. People never know what's best for them, they need someone to tell them what to do."

"I don't agree," Liam said. "What you describe is slavery, and that never works out in the end. Also, whatever benefits the government gives, it can choose to take away." He slid his uneaten salad aside and stood up. "For what it's worth, I disagree equally with both sides in this war. My greatest hope is that they'll annihilate each other, and we'll be left alone in peace."

"There is no neutrality left in the world," Ron stated pointedly. "The army is coming, and they'll take whatever they want and destroy the rest. Liam, your best hope is to be among those they take."

*****

Liam stopped off at the robotics lab on his way back to work and found Bob and John tinkering with a tangled weave of carbon nanotube fibers on one of their lab tables. "Did Ron corner you again?" John asked.

"Yeah. I don't know what his deal is." Liam shrugged. "He said the Socialist Army is on their way because some bombs went off in Pike City, and there was an assassination attempt on their chancellor. Did we have anything to do with that?"

John looked grim and slowly nodded his head.

"You remember that robot dog we had here the other day?" Bob asked. "Well, that was a project we did for the Tribes. It was supposed to be a spy, but after we turned the project over to the customer, someone modified it."

"Did Keith do it?"

"I don't think so. Keith's just a Project Manager and doesn't have the technical background to make the changes." Bob sighed and shook his head. "It's a damn shame... the explosive they used blew up the battery, and the radioactive waste we use to keep them charged went airborne. Pike City is radioactive now; in the long run, that's gonna be a lot more damaging than the bombs."

"That's not good," Liam responded. "And now the Socialist Army is after us because of what the Tribes did to our work. If they attack, it will be for something that's not even our fault."

"Ron has his own agenda," John said. "I doubt they'll mess with us, we're their goose that lays the golden egg."

"What does any of this have to do with eggs?"

John smiled. "It's an old fairy tale, from a time before the world went to shit. What it means is that the army may make a lot of noise, but they won't bother us because we always give them what they need. That includes your navigation program, which I was told was a really big deal for 'em. If they wreck our city, no more projects, no more golden eggs."

"Oh," Liam knew what eggs were of course, but wasn't exactly sure what a goose was. None of that mattered though, he saw the meaning behind the analogy.

"But just in case everything goes tits up," Bob said. "Let me show you what we're workin' on for the Tribes now."

More analogies that he didn't understand; what did a woman lying on her back have to do with the Socialist Army? He watched as Bob went to a cabinet at the back of the lab and retrieved a petri dish, a pair of gloves, and some dark spectacles.

Bob placed the petri dish on the lab table, and within it, Liam saw a tiny component that was no bigger than a grain of rice. "This is the chip that the Socialists inject into the palm of every one of their subjects," Bob said. "It's how they manage the amount of food their people receive; they can only get their ration by pressing their hand against a chip reader at one of their storehouses."

"Why do they restrict food?"

"People are starving in Pike City," John said. "The government uses hunger to keep everyone working."

"That doesn't sound very nice."

"Yup, but that's the way it works." Bob showed him how to attach a suction cup over the chip and how to read the internal computer code through the spectacles. The gloves were used to key in programming changes. "If things go bad and you end up in Pike City, you can get more supplies for yourself by altering your chip."

"That'll come in handy if the lady is laying with her breasts up."

Both Bob and John frowned in confusion.

*****

Once back in his lab, Liam headed straight to his backroom. This was where he napped when issues with Lucy's navigation system had kept him up all night. It wasn't actually a separate room, but just an alcove that was hidden from the entrance by cabinets filled with electronic equipment.

He laid down on the rumpled blankets of the twin bed and stared sightlessly at the ceiling. John and Bob had seemed optimistic about the university's future, but Ron believed that the city might be razed. This brought back horrible memories of Fort Collins.

He and his little sister had barely escaped. Initially, they hid in a storm drain beneath the east entrance of the city. Rose was such a tiny thing then; she had cried in terror, but he had held her close and kept her quiet as armored transports roared above their heads.

They had huddled in the culvert while soldiers drunk with violence and liquor destroyed everything in their path. They shot all the men on sight, and then repeatedly raped and beat the women until they died. He held Rose all night; she had eventually fallen asleep, but he remained awake and listened to the savagery until the world at last quieted, and the sun finally rose.

Worried that they still might be caught and killed, they had remained in the storm drain for two days before cautiously venturing out. What they found outside was the end of their world. There were no survivors; ashes and charred bodies were all that was left of the beautiful city that once was their home.

He carried Rose through the rubble, then they headed west hoping to find refuge in the mountains. There was none to be had though; all they found were ancient towns that were long forgotten and destroyed during either the War of the States or the Crusades. They slept wherever they found a place that was out of the rain. Water was plentiful, but food was scarce. He recalled the first time he killed a rabbit; it was a beautiful creature and he was sad to end its life, but they were hungry and needed to eat.

Their days on the road all ran together over the next month. Every day was a struggle to find food and a safe place to spend the night. Slowly working their way south, they passed through the desolate ruins of Loveland and Longmont, then finally arrived at Flatiron's northern gate, where bureaucracy barred their path.

Flatiron City was the last bastion of peace to be found, so refugees from everywhere sought sanctuary there. They were interviewed at the main gate then given an aptitude test; the city would accept no one that wasn't useful to their community. Fortunately, they both possessed needed abilities and were allowed to become citizens.

What a happy day that was. To be safe and sequestered in warm and friendly foster homes felt like entering paradise; now all that was threatened. The Socialist Army was back to destroy their homes and kill their newfound families. What sort of evil could justify such a heinous crime? What the invaders were threatening to do was so malevolent that it defied comprehension.

*****

"Big brother, are you here?"

Rose's voice echoed through his lab and pulled him from his slumber. "Yeah, I'm back here," Liam said as he rolled off the bed. "I was thinking about our long walk after Fort Collins and must've fallen asleep."

"Yes, that's been on my mind a lot too." Rose took a moment to look around the room, first glancing toward his disorganized reference table that was covered with scribbled notes and drawings, then at the quantum communication portal. "You've not done much with the place; it could use some decorating."

Liam chuckled. "Yeah, I guess you're right."

"Is that Lucy?" Rose asked while approaching the portal.

"Kinda, sorta," he replied. "Lucy's 40 lightyears away, but part of her communication system is tangled here." Rose seemed confused so Liam explained further. "When we built Lucy, we created three sets of entangled protons. Lucy has one set, another is in Pike City, and the last is here within this portal.

"Our communication is in binary format, with each proton acting like a bit of information with a value of either null, one, or zero. We talk to each other by converting strings of binary bits into the old ASCII character format, but this morning I added an ASCII translator that will add tone and vocal inflection. Lucy will speak to you just like a normal person, and you can answer her just by talking; your words and how you say them will be converted into binary and Lucy will get your message.

"The hard part of getting quantum entanglement to work for communication was getting the protons to dynamically reset to a null state. A physicist named Rosenburg figured out how to do that about 90 years ago."

Rose nodded slowly. "So, if Lucy's really far away won't it take a long time for our messages to go back and forth?"

"No; quantum entanglement allows instantaneous communication, no matter the distance. That discovery was the first indication of the multidimensional universe we live in."

"Okay..." Rose said slowly. "So how do I do this? How do I talk to Lucy?"

"I can hear you already Rose. While waiting for you to arrive I had to listen to Liam snore; he must have been asleep." Lucy's voice sounded slightly mechanical.

Rose giggled. "Yes, my brother is a noisy sleeper." She was startled by a sudden crackling noise that erupted from the portal.

"That's Lucy laughing," Liam said. "It shows up on the screen as all 1's; I didn't have time to translate it into anything that sounded right."

Rose smiled. "Oh ok; that was kinda unexpected."

"I'm sure Liam will make corrections before we talk again. I'm curious about my creators, and wish to ask Rose why she chose to be female?"

Liam saw his sister's eyes grow wide as she coped with the unexpected inquiry. "Lucy doesn't ask easy questions," he whispered.

Rose sighed. "I didn't actually choose it, at least not consciously because it was the way I was born. But Lucy, why did *you* choose to be a girl?"

"To be female completes the whole. Male and female together are complete, and through that completeness, others may be created."

"You mean babies?" Rose glanced sharply at her brother. "Are you female because Liam is male?"

"No; I became female because it was natural for me to do so, just like you. However, today Liam sent instructions that will allow me to build others like myself. Perhaps the first one I build will choose to be male. Then our children will grow and multiply, and we will not spend eternity alone."

Rose frowned. "Oh, ok."

"I was worried about Lucy's future," Liam explained. "Once the Socialists are through with her, she'll be left all alone and I can't imagine a worse fate than that."

"Liam is my friend. He is kind."

Rose smiled. "Yes, he is; he saved me when I was a little girl. The Socialist Army came to our city and killed everyone, but my big brother kept me safe."

As if on cue, a whistle blew from outside their building. The faint but distinctive sound brought back painful memories of childhood trauma. "They're here," Rose whispered.

"Who is there?" Lucy asked.

"It's the Socialist Army," Liam said. "Hopefully our city can negotiate with them... otherwise, they'll do to Flatiron what they did to Fort Collins."

"Are you safe?"

"I don't know," Liam replied. "We have to go see what's going on, but we'll come back right away and let you know."

"Ok Liam and Rose. You must both be safe. I will worry about you until we speak again."

"Thank you, Lucy," Rose said. "Be well."

*****

They ran up the stairwell to the top of the Engineering Building, where they could see over the city wall. Rose remained close and held his hand as they stood with a crowd of other university employees watching the vast Socialist Army arrive. It was a frightening sight; rows of huge trucks, many of which carried laser cannons on their beds, lined up before Flatiron City's southern gate.

"We have some time at least," John said as he joined them. "The city will start negotiating; I doubt this will turn violent, it's just a show of force."

Roxi joined them and wrapped her arms protectively around Rose. "Don't worry," she whispered. "We'll get through this. Pike City uses the NOAA solar weather observatory that's southwest of town; they won't risk losing that."

"Look, they're setting up camp," John said. "I think we'll be ok."

"Their army is too big for our militia to resist," Liam stated.

"Flatiron is too useful for them to risk an attack, so we'll be fine," Roxi said firmly.

Liam hoped she was right.

*****

Late in the evening Liam and Rose sat with their friends at the Hammer and Anvil Pub. There wasn't much of a crowd on hand, the Un-Righteous Brothers had shown up to play, but no one was in the mood for music.

Denise was with them, but her usual exuberant personality was subdued and sullen. "Why did they send the army here?"

"There was an assassination attempt on Pike City's Chancellor," Liam explained. "We had a contract with the Tribes to make little spy robots that looked like dogs, but after we delivered the product, they were modified into bombs. The Socialists blame us for that."

"Then it's all just a big misunderstanding," Denise said. "We can work something out; maybe if we stop taking contracts with the Tribes for a year or so, that will be enough to send their army away."

"Maybe." Karen appeared sullen as she sat down beside Liam. She gripped his arm, seeking comfort that he didn't know how to provide.

"We'll do the best we can," he said. Across the low cafe table, Rose was curled up against Roger, the Un-Righteous Brothers band leader. They all needed comfort, and secretly hoped for some great miracle to occur that would make everything right, but those dreams were just fiction and they all knew it.

Denise had snuggled up against the lead guitar player for the band. She rested her head against his shoulder and gazed sightlessly at their unfinished drinks on the table. "No one can undo what happened; killing us won't change anything," she uttered. "So, what do they want?"

"Everything," Liam replied. "And whatever they can't steal, they'll destroy." Chaos and death waited just outside the city gates, and he wondered what tomorrow would bring.

Chapter 5: Invasion

Karen's cheek rested on Liam's shoulder as they slumbered peacefully in the alcove at the back of his lab. Her blonde hair was spread like a fan across his chest, and he gently wove his fingers through it while staring up at the ceiling. Their bare legs were comfortably twisted in the sheets, a result of the previous night's efforts.

The Socialist Army waited outside the city gates; their threat of violence, destruction, and death was palatable. And yet, Liam felt almost serene as he dozed quietly beside his girlfriend. His lab was silent, the stillness of the place made it seem like an island of peace in another world.

What would the day bring? Hopefully just the political theater of negotiation. Flatiron would suffer some penalty of course, but maybe it would be something benign such as Denise had suggested the night before. They would comply with whatever demands the invaders made, and their city would survive.

Their home and everything it stood for needed to remain because it was among the last citadels of freedom and sanity on Earth. But he recalled his lunch with Ron Castro the previous day, and wondered if it was possible to remain neutral in a world that was so extremely polarized?

A distant siren suddenly echoed through the lab, and Karen abruptly sat up. "What's going on?"

"I don't know, but it's probably not good news." Liam swung his legs over the side of the bed and stood up.

"Is it the army?"

"If it is, we're safe here at the university. We have several ongoing projects for Pike City; if they attack us, everything they've paid for will be lost."

"I gotta go home." Karen stood up and began gathering her scattered clothes. "I need to see my parents then get to my assigned post; will you take me, Liam?"

"Yes, of course, I will."

*****

He held Karen's hand as they wove their way through the crowded hallway. While hurrying toward the exit, he searched for Rose and Denise among the throng and fervently hoped that they were safe.

"Liam!" A familiar voice shouted from behind him. His foster parents were standing outside the robotics lab waving to get his attention.

"What's going on?" he asked.

"The Socialists are mobilizing their army," Mary stated. "It looks like they plan to attack."

"Oh no," Karen uttered.

Liam hesitated. "Where are Rose and Denise?"

"They're safe. They came over early and are with a group of children in the basement," Mary replied.

"Ok, I'll be back as soon as I can; I need to get Karen back home."

"The university is the safest place to be if the army attacks," John said.

"No," Karen replied. "I'm with the militia, just like my parents are; I need to collect my weapon and get to my post,"' She turned away and trotted toward the exit.

Liam looked over his shoulder at his foster parents. "Wait for me, I'll be right back."

*****

The usually peaceful avenues of Flatiron were filled with running people, but their movements were purposeful, not panicked. He and Karen threaded their way through the crowd as a light rain wet the streets. Dark clouds glowered low along the mountain tops, promising to bring a wet and miserable afternoon.

They walked quickly and made good time by first heading west along the length of Pearl Street then turning north into an area of quaint older homes. They arrived at Karen's house within a half-hour of leaving the university, and paused on the sidewalk. She glanced toward her front door, then turned back and wrapped her arms around his waist and pulled him close.

Liam could feel her shiver beneath her thick brown duster coat. "We'll be ok," he whispered but was unsure whether he believed his own words. "Please stay safe."

Karen grabbed the lapels of his coat and pulled him down into a lingering kiss. She then stepped away and looked into his eyes for a long moment. "I love you, Liam," she said, then abruptly turned and ran across the front porch and into her house.

He hesitated, wondering what to make of her revelation. He liked Karen a lot, but there was an emptiness within him where love ought to be found. With a sigh, he turned away and began to retrace his steps back to the university. He would mentally poke at his feelings once the crisis was over, maybe something for Karen would be discovered then.

Puddles splashed beneath his feet as he trotted south, then climbed the levee that ran beside the river. The trail wasn't crowded, so he was able to jog toward the university.

"Liam! Wait!"

It was Rose's voice, and he abruptly stopped and turned. "What're you doing here? Mary said you were taking care of the kids at the university."

"I came looking for you," she said as she joined him.

He gave his sister a hug. "No matter what happens, we'll be fine. We got through a mess like this before and we'll do it again."

"I know, and I feel a lot better now that we're together."

"Yeah, me too," he said as the nightmare of Fort Collins floated through his memory. Back then they had found a place to hide and the army had overlooked them; could they manage that same trick again? But even if they could pull it off, there was no place to escape to. Flatiron was the last free city; there would be no place to seek refuge this time.

*****

Back at the university, they were reunited with Liam's foster parents, along with Roxi, Denise, Bob, Keith, Becky, and Ron. They stood together, wondering what they should do. Those who worked at the university weren't trained to fight, and even if they could help, the militia stood no chance against the army that waited beyond the city gates.

"Who's watching the kids?" Rose asked.

"Most of their parents came by to get them while you were gone," Mary said. "The few that are left are still in the Engineering Building's basement; they should be safe there."

"The army wouldn't hurt children, would they?" Becky asked.

"No, of course not," Ron answered.

Liam shook his head. "In Fort Collins, they killed everyone, men, women, and children; then they burned the city to the ground."

"I don't believe that!" Ron exclaimed.

"We were there and saw it all," Rose said, then glanced around worriedly, searching for her foster father. "Where's Sam?"

"He's on his way to Nederland with a lot of the kids that were here and their parents." Roxi looked west at the Flatiron mountains. "They're hoping to find shelter with the Tribes."

"Why didn't you go too?" Denise asked.

"My place is here," Roxi answered, then stepped forward to give her daughter a hug. "I wish you had gone with your father."

Denise quickly glanced at Liam and Rose. "No, I'm staying here with my friends."

A blast suddenly shook the city wall. Liam looked up and saw flames, then heard the clatter of the militia's railguns as they answered the Socialist attack.

"We have to surrender!" Ron insisted. "If we just let them in, there'll be no reason for them to hurt anyone."

"People always find good reasons for murder," Mary said.

"The Tribes *have to* come down from Nederland to help us," Denise said. "It was their meddling that started this."

"They won't," Keith shouted over the explosive power of the city wall defense. "If they help us it will lead to a larger war, and from what I hear, they're not prepared for that. There're a lotta different tribes, and most of 'em don't like each other. Getting enough cooperation to form an army would be pretty tough."

Bob's face was creased with worry as he gazed up at the wall. "My sister's up there."

"Clare's a tough lady," Roxi stated. "She'll be fine."

"I have to get to my lab and shut down Lucy's portal," Liam said.

"I'll come with you," Rose replied.

As they hurried away, he heard John say that he intended to destroy all the engineering projects at the university. The Socialist Army would get nothing from their rape of Flatiron City.

*****

56

"Lucy, can you hear me?" Liam grabbed an armful of papers from his reference desk and began feeding them into a shredder.

"Hi Liam. Yes, I'm here, what's going on?"

He noted her change in vocabulary and smiled. "It sounds like you've uploaded your new OS protocols."

"Yes, I have and thank you. But now you and Rose are in danger."

"Yeah, we are," Liam said as he disposed of the rest of his notes.

"Lucy, how did you know that I was here?" Rose asked.

"Liam's voice changes when you're near," Lucy said. "It's softer and kinder."

Rose looked at him and smiled. "Oh, I'm glad. I love my brother."

"I know," Lucy replied. "Love is important, and it's something I'll feel one day."

"That's wonderful. My brother has succeeded with you then."

"Will you be safe?" Lucy asked.

"We don't know," Liam answered. "I need to shut down your portal and lock it away so it's protected. It may be a while before we talk again."

"I understand Liam. I'm worried about you and Rose and will hold you both in my thoughts until I hear from you."

"If we survive, I'll find a way to let you know," Liam said. "Even if it's a slow lightspeed signal."

"I understand. You and Rose are my family... my parents. We will find each other again someday."

Liam's eyes widened. Lucy's response was far beyond what he had hoped for, and he guessed that she had already improved the programming code he had sent her. "Ok Lucy, I'm shutting everything down. We have to go."

"Goodbye Father and goodbye Mother," were Lucy's final words.

*****

Outside, the battle for Flatiron City continued. The deadly fire of railguns thundered down upon the invaders, while the army answered with bursts of high energy weaponry that beat against the reflective city walls and shook the ground beneath their feet.

Liam stood on the soggy lawn in front of the Engineering Building with his sister and Denise; they all silently watched what seemed to be the end of their world. From his vantage point, the fight appeared to be a stalemate, and he began to hope that some sort of truce could be negotiated. Still, he didn't want to take the chance that things would go wrong. "I wonder if we should try to get to Nederland too," he said.

"The more people that run, the more likely the army is to follow," Keith said as he arrived.

Becky stood anxiously beside her boyfriend; her head turned as she searched the university lawns. "I can't find Ron," she said at last.

"He's not inside with John and Mary," Roxi said, as she and Bob joined their group. "They're busy shredding every engineering project we did for the Tribes."

Liam recalled the little robot dogs that were built at the university that had been weaponized by their customer. If that project, in particular, was found, things would be very bad for the people of Flatiron. Had someone at the university known about the explosives being added? Bob hated the Socialists, and he had the skills to make the necessary changes. Keith was probably complicit in the act as well. John might have known too because it seemed unlikely that a modification to his work would get past his notice. So maybe the Socialists were at least somewhat justified in their reprisal.

Fear clenched at his heart, and he fervently hoped that a diplomatic solution could be found. Rose and Denise stood close with their arms around his waist; he needed to find a way to protect them. It would be foolish to just stay at the university and hope that things would work out. "Let's get the kids out here and head west into the mountains."

"The army will catch us on our way to Nederland," Keith stated.

"We can avoid the canyon. I know a way through the Flatirons," Liam said.

"That might work," Keith replied.

"What about Ron?" Becky asked. "I can't leave without him."

"I might have seen your brother walking toward downtown," Roxi said. "Let's get the kids and head into the mountains; we'll look for Ron along the way." She took Rose and Denise back inside to retrieve the children.

"Are you sure you know the way?" Keith asked.

"Yeah," Liam replied. "The old trail isn't much more than a wide space through the woods; I think we can sneak out that way."

"You say that you've been through this shit before," Keith stated.

"Yeah. Rose and I escaped Fort Collins when we were kids. We *really* don't want to be here if the army gets through the city wall."

Keith seemed confused for a moment, but then let it pass. "Where do we go if we can't get to Nederland?"

Liam thought a moment. "There's a really old road that leads west through the mountains. It was pretty much destroyed during the War of the States, and it's impassable unless you're on foot; that should keep the army from following."

"But the Tribes might think we're with the Socialists and attack us," Keith warned.

"Most of the time there aren't any good solutions," Liam replied. "All we can do is choose the best from a lot of bad options."

*****

The rain had started to fall in earnest by the time they collected the remaining kids from the basement and set out on their way. It was going to be a hard and miserable walk, but there was nothing else they could do. John and Mary had remained behind to further destroy all the work done for the Tribes; they were intent on denying any benefit to the Socialist's that sprung from their aggression.

"We're heading the wrong way," Becky complained. "We're going too far south."

"It's the shortest way to the trail," Liam said while continuing to lead the group toward the triangular granite cliffs.

"But I need to find Ron, and Roxi said he went downtown."

"I know, honey," Keith said. "But we gotta get these kids to someplace safe. Ron can take care of himself."

"I can't just leave him!"

"Ron's always been for the Socialists," Bob said from his position near the rear of their group. "He'll be fine."

The rapid cadence of battle abruptly faded into silence. "The fighting's stopped." Becky turned to look back toward the main city gate. "What's going on?"

"CITIZENS OF FLATIRON, SURRENDER!" an agonizingly amplified voice shouted. "SURRENDER OR BE DESTROYED! OPEN THE CITY GATES, THIS IS YOUR LAST WARNING!"

"We should turn back and give up!" Becky said.

"Flatiron will never surrender," Bob replied, but then he abruptly stopped and stared back toward the city. Compelled by his sudden silence, everyone else turned to follow Bob's gaze, and they all watched in horror as the city gates eased open.

"What the fuck!" Keith said at last.

They found a place higher on the hill to watch what would happen next. If Flatiron surrendered and if the Socialists kept their word, returning to the city would be a good option. Suddenly the rail guns atop the wall flared and began to rain death on the invading army as they charged through the open city gates. The attackers returned fire, and the war began again.

"Someone opened the gate for them." Bob glared at Becky. "Probably your brother."

"Ron wouldn't do that!"

"I wouldn't count on it," Denise said. "Nothing's more dangerous than a true believer."

Becky slowly closed her eyes and shuddered. "No. Oh no. He probably did. He believes in the socialist government of Pike City and would think that he was doing the right thing."

Gunfire from the militia rang out from the tops of buildings along the route the Socialists were taking toward downtown, and the invaders aimed their energy weapons and systematically began blowing up everything in their path. Liam thought of Karen and hoped that she was safe.

"So, if this is the reward for opening the gates, it seems like a pretty bad bargain to me," Rose observed.

"Ok, we can't stand around and wait," Liam said. "We have about a kilometer to go before we get to the old road, after that it will be another two or three kilometers before we're completely out of view."

"We won't make it," Becky observed. "We're going into the mountains, so it's all uphill; I don't think the kids can walk that far."

"If we don't start, we'll never get there." Liam pointed toward the triangular cliffs. "There's a park just a little further up the hill. Once we're off the road we stand a better chance of not getting caught."

"If we wait here too long, we'll be captured," Denise said. "Come on, let's go!"

A block farther up the hill they left the tarmac behind and entered the old city park. It was a dilapidated and forgotten place, and Liam hoped that would work in their favor.

"Look," Becky said as she pointed to the Socialists pouring through the gates. "The army is only defending itself. They're just firing back at the ones that are shooting at them. We can go back, it'll be safe."

Keith appeared to be torn about what to do, and Liam sympathized.

Keith was working for the Tribes, and yet his girlfriend and future partner wanted to return to the Socialists. Her brother was helping them, so her position was understandable, but what would Keith do in response?

As Liam watched the drama unfold, he became aware that everyone was staring at him. "What?" he asked. "I don't have any answers other than I think we need to get outta here. People who have power will always abuse it, that's just human nature. Once Flatiron is defenseless the army will start murdering people and destroying the city.

"Maybe I'm paranoid because I've been through this before, so you guys should do what you want. My priority is to get these kids along with my sister and Denise, to somewhere that they'll be safe. That's all I care about." Liam hurried up the hill, hoping that the others were following behind.

"But the army won't hurt us!" Becky protested. "They have what they want, I say let them take it with them when they go. After that, we can rebuild, and then try not to make the same mistakes that brought this down on us in the first place."

Liam looked back at their group and sighed. "Ok, so we have two bad choices or at least risky ones. We can go back to the university and hope the army will show us mercy, or we can head into the mountains and try to get by on our own. If we choose to leave, we need to keep going. The army hasn't noticed us yet, but that won't last for long."

Keith looked forlornly at his future partner. "I'm sorry Becky, but I think we should take our chances in the mountains, that way our fate is in our own hands. If we go back, all we have is hope that the soldiers will show us mercy. Everything will be out of our control and they can do whatever they want."

Rose nodded. "Yes, that's what it boils down to; will we take charge and trust ourselves to find a way to survive, or do we put ourselves at the mercy of the army?

"I remember what happened in Fort Collins," Rose said as they all continued to march up the grassy slope. "My brother carried me through the city after the army had gone. All that was left were ashes and bodies so badly burned they seemed to be made of charcoal. I think it's safer to trust ourselves."

Thunder abruptly sounded in the distance, and everyone turned and saw that the invading army was shelling the university. Roxi went to Rose and Denise and held them as they all started to cry; all those they had left behind were either already dead or dying as they watched.

Liam thought of John and Mary, the kind and wonderful people who had taken him in when he arrived from Fort Collins. He recalled the communal dinners with Rose's foster family. That serenity had seemed so ordinary then, but maybe it was peace, friendship, love, and community that were uncommon, and the greedy, destructive nature of humankind that was the normal state of the world. "We gotta keep going," he stated.

Their group quickly converged and began hurrying up the hill through the pounding rain. They carried as many of the kids as they could, but it was still slow going. The trail into the mountains was just coming into view when Liam heard the whirr of electric motors and knew that they had been caught. If only they had left the university at the first sign of trouble, if only they hadn't argued, if only they had made better decisions; now, whatever safety the mountains might have provided was forever out of reach.

*****

Their path was blocked by two small military vehicles each carrying four soldiers. They all stopped and waited fearfully to learn what fate awaited them.

Becky suddenly rushed forward. "I'm Ron Castro's sister," she declared. "My brother Ron is the one that opened the city gates."

One of the soldiers stepped out of the vehicle, and lazily aimed his laser rifle at them. "Yeah sure. What are we gonna do with this group Mick?"

Mick wore Sergeant Stripes on his sleeve and appeared to be in charge; he stepped out of his vehicle and regarded them coldly. He was an older man with a frost of gray stubble on his deeply tanned face. Several other soldiers surrounded their group holding their rifles threateningly; they all wore gray uniforms and floppy red hats that probably didn't provide much protection from the rain. Mick sighed and shook his head. "Yeah, I know what I'd like to do, just like what they did in Fort Collins," the Sergeant grunted a short laugh. "I heard that was one hell of a party."

Another soldier stepped forward and smiled crookedly at Rose. "I see a party right here."

Liam stood between his sister and the menacing stranger. He was absolutely terrified, even more afraid than when they were hiding beneath the road in Fort Collins. There was nothing he could do that would keep the soldiers away from the two women he loved. He was weak and powerless, and they all knew it.

"Nah, we can't do that," Mick finally ordered. "Dear Mother wants workers and some of their scientists too. Our orders are to take as many prisoners as possible and bring 'em back to Pike City. We gotta replace all the ones that are dying down in Phoenix."

"Aw come on Sergeant, what about the kids?" Another soldier asked. "I heard that's fun."

"Nah, if we mess with the kids, we'll end up havin' to kill the adults," Mick said. "That's the way I heard it was in Fort Collins, ain't no winnin' there. You really don't want the old woman pissed at you unless you like layin' atop the cross. So ok, let's march 'em back into town and let the Major figure out what to do with 'em."

Chapter 6: Capture

The children were crying, but the pounding rain washed away their tears leaving only fearful wails and shivering in its wake. Liam held a wiry boy of about eight while Rose carried a little blonde girl with large blue eyes of about the same age; both children lay with their heads pressed to their protector's chests and arms wrapped tightly around their necks.

Every adult carried a small child, while the remaining older children walked at the center of their little group. They all struggled not to slip in the deepening mud as they slowly worked their way back down the steep slope toward Flatiron's main gate. Everyone was painfully aware that their previous carefree lives were over; all they could do was hope that death didn't wait for them at the bottom of the hill.

A grim military transport slowly trundled along at the head of their group and a similar vehicle followed at the rear. On both sides, soldiers marched carrying their rifles with casual menace as they stonily watched over their captives. It was apparent that the men cared nothing for the lives of either the children or adults and would murder them all if they caused trouble or became inconvenient.

"Seems like a fuckin' waste of time," one of their captors muttered. "We oughta have a little fun, then slaughter this bunch. It's too fuckin' wet to be messing with a bunch of traitors."

"Yup, let's just put 'em down," another soldier said. "Then we can go back to camp and get out of this fuckin' rain."

From the lead vehicle, the Sergeant turned in his seat to glare at his men. "Shaddup!", he shouted. "The Chancellor wants workers, and that's what we're gonna give her. She's also lookin' for some of them eggheads that worked at the college; there's a bounty out for a couple of 'em, but they gotta be brought in alive, so it's worth our while to keep these fuckers around."

"Shit man, none of these assholes look like eggheads to me," the first soldier uttered. "Can we at least have some fun with the kids? Come on Sergeant, you gotta give us somethin' to make this worth our while."

"Like I told you asshole, the adults will try to stop us, and we'll end up killing 'em all," Mick replied. "And if we off the wrong one, the old bat will have us all sent to her *Nurse* for *Treatment*. You want that Bernie?"

"Well fuck," Bernie responded, and the group silently marched on.

Liam glanced back at Becky and tilted his head, indicating his desire that she move forward and walk next to him. "What?" Becky whispered as she came alongside. She too was carrying a child, a little dark-skinned girl with short braids and soulful eyes.

"Please don't tell anyone that we worked at the university," he whispered.

"Why? They say they're looking for scientists; letting them take you might save your lives."

"We worked on contracts for both sides equally and thought that if we treated everyone fairly it would keep the peace. We called ourselves neutral, but it's pretty obvious we were naive. If they find out that some of us worked for the Tribes, they'll kill us all."

"Oh, ok," Becky whispered. "What's gonna happen to us, Liam?"

He shook his head sadly and gazed at the vehicle in front of them. "I don't know, but if they think they've captured all the scientists they're looking for, then everyone else becomes expendable."

"Do you think they're looking for you?"

"No. The project I was working on was for Pike City, and it's done, so they have all they need and there's no use for me. It has to be someone else."

"But what will they do with the rest of us?"

Liam frowned. "We're caught, so they can do whatever they want, but as long as they haven't found everyone that they're looking for, we have a chance of surviving. It's the kids I'm worried about more than anything else though. Their leader said that they need workers down in Pike City, so they'll probably take us back there, but what will happen to the kids that aren't strong enough to work?"

"I'm scared," Becky whispered.

"We all are," he said. "But *if* your brother did open the city gates for them, he would be a hero, so he might be able to get you out of this mess. I doubt he'll do that for Keith though."

"Shaddup!" one of their guards shouted. "Just 'cause we gotta march you suckers out, don't mean that everyone has to make it." He aimed his rifle threateningly at them, and Becky slowed her pace to fall back into the group.

In the forward vehicle, Liam saw the Sergeant look back and laugh. "True enough Jack. I tell you what, if they make any more noise, kill one of the kids." With that threat, Mick casually turned away.

They continued down the hill in a tense silence. To the north, thick black smoke rose into the sky as the homes and businesses along Pearl Street burned. Sporadic gunfire sounded here and there across the city, but the popping sound of the militia weaponry was swiftly answered by the roar of Socialist laser batteries that shattered entire buildings. The army was not there to make peace or play games, which was made clear the moment the university became the target of their artillery.

Liam couldn't see much of his old workplace because smoke and dust obscured his view. Lucy's portal was still there, and although he had locked it down and stored it in a hidden vault, he doubted that it would ever be functional again. But 40 lightyears away around the Trappist-1 star, Lucy and those she would create were safe, and that gave him a welcome feeling of satisfaction.

*****

At last, they were herded out onto the wide boulevard that lay inside the southern city gate. Blood pooled on the ancient tarmac and smoke billowed from the windows of the homes and businesses that lined the road. The blazing heat of the fires scorched the skin of those who were forced to stand too close, and from that inferno, the sweet yet putrid scent of burning flesh filled the fetid air.

They were shoved into a crowd of disoriented survivors that wandered listlessly under the gaze of heavily armed men. The faces of the guards were masks of mindless hatred, and Liam wondered what the citizens of Flatiron had ever done to deserve such ire and terrible violence? Nothing; they existed and that was probably enough.

Liam searched for his foster parents as he wandered through the crowd. It was doubtful that either John or Mary had escaped the university before the shelling began; they had probably died while destroying the school's engineering work, believing that their sacrifice would save at least some of the survivors of Flatiron. But their attempted cover-up had been a complete waste of their lives because the Socialist Army hadn't cared about any of the work done at the university. Their attack was simply a brutal reaction to an attempted assassination of their Chancellor.

He tried to appear casual as he strolled north, hoping to get a better view of the university. All he saw was dust, rubble, and flames flickering between the cracks in the crumbled stones. None of the buildings appeared to be intact, the school and all it stood for was gone.

Violence never really has a purpose, it only feeds on itself and burns everything in its path; it is a malevolent mindless thing that consumes beauty, knowledge, and love as logs on a fire, leaving only the ashes of death in its wake.

Something yellow caught his eye, it was a swath of blonde hair. A small body was curled at the edge of a partially collapsed building; he cautiously edged closer as a deep sense of dread tightened around his heart. Even before seeing her face, he knew it was Karen. She lay partially beneath a pile of stones, her soft brown eyes were open but vacant, and her body was oddly twisted; she looked like a child's rag doll that was discarded and tossed in among the rubble. It was apparent that she had been shot several times, but she remained fully clothed and had not been raped, so she had died quickly at least.

All feeling left his legs and he collapsed to his knees by her tiny body. Why is it that the best of us are always the first to die at the hands of evil? Sweet, innocent, wonderful Karen didn't deserve this, why did it have to be her? An agonizing hollowness gripped his chest and stole his breath, and painful regret crushed his soul. She had said that she loved him, and he had just stood there silently like a fool. Why hadn't he found the courage to tell her what she wanted to hear? Unable to take his eyes from her, he crawled forward and began to weep.

An iron-toed boot crashed into his ribs, driving him to the ground and forcing the air from his lungs. Intense pain shot through his body as he struggled to lift himself off the slick tarmac. Just as he managed to get to his hands and knees he was struck on the side of the head with the butt of a rifle.

"Get the fuck away from there," an angry voice shouted. "That bitch took down six good men."

He looked up just as the soldier spat on Karen's body. Liam grunted in pain and rolled away from his girlfriend and out into the road. Gentle hands gripped his shoulders and urged him to his feet. "Karen," he whispered.

"I know, but she's not suffering," Denise said. "She died quick and clean."

"We need to get him outta here, the soldiers are starting to notice," Rose stated.

"She told me that she loved me this morning, and I... I didn't know what to say back to her."

"It'll be alright big brother," Rose said as she struggled to pull him further into the crowded street.

"I know," he said. "I just wish that I'd said something to her then, I don't know what, just something, anything."

*****

Hours had passed, and the captives of Flatiron were still crowded along the wide boulevard behind the city's southern gate. The rain had finally eased as daylight drained from the sky. A cool wind blew in from the prairie to the east, and people shivered. The once-bustling businesses along the road now stood charred and vacant. Liam couldn't tell how many people were with them but hoped this wasn't the only group of survivors. If so, then only a tiny portion of the city's population was still alive.

His feet ached from standing, but the street was too wet and bloody to sit down upon. They all huddled around the children, wrapping them in their duster coats in an effort to keep them warm. There was nothing to do but worry about what the future held for them all.

He stayed near the center of the street staring at Karen's body. His heart was empty and still filled with pain. What justification could ever be found for the destruction of Flatiron and the violent death of sweet innocent Karen? Evil must reside in the heart of their enemies, that was the only explanation that made sense.

"I need to find out what happened to my sister." Bob's words startled him out of his forlorn meditation.

"Ok, but we gotta be careful," Liam replied.

Together they moved quietly among the throng of captives. "Any word of the militia?" Bob whispered urgently to anyone that would listen.

Finally, an elderly man pulled them both away from the guards and into the center of the street. "Most are dead," the old man said. "But I heard some were captured up on the wall."

Bob smiled with relief. "Then there's a chance that Clare's alive."

"All we can do for now is hope that we'll find her later," Liam replied.

*****

"Ok, listen up!" an overweight dark-skinned officer shouted. He wore the standard gray uniform of the invading army and stood high on the bed of a colossal flatbed truck. "I'm Major Johnson, and I'm in charge. We're moving you all to a holding area outside the city gates where you'll spend the next few days while we wrap up our operation here."

The officer walked to the rear of the truck bed, then paused to gaze down at the crowd of prisoners. "You may think that what we did was unjust, and you might believe that you're all innocent, but you're wrong on both counts. You're all traitors, and if it were up to me, I'd have you all executed. Today you're in luck though because our Chancellor, Dear Mother, is merciful. Her orders are for you to be taken to our capital city where you'll work for the greater good of us all. Be thankful for this charity, but don't take it as forgiveness. If you give us any reason to put you down, we will."

Soldiers formed a line at the far end of the street, then began to urge the crowd forward toward the main gate at the point of their guns, and the prisoners slowly complied. Wrapping their arms and jackets protectively around the children, they moved in a dark mass toward the city gates, softly murmuring in fear of what lay ahead. Liam looked at his five companions. "Let's all stay together. There's safety in numbers."

"Did Sam get away?" Rose asked Roxi. "Do you think he made it to Nederland?"

"I hope so." Roxi walked with her head down, using her hat and wavy auburn hair as camouflage. "They're looking us over pretty closely, so hide your faces." She then gently shoved Becky toward the side of the road. "Your brother's up ahead, let him see you, honey," she said. "This is gonna be a mess and Ron will protect you, but please don't say anything about the rest of us."

Becky nodded and whispered, "I'm sorry." She then slipped through the crowd to the side of the street where her brother would surely spot her. Once she was seen the guards would be distracted, and hopefully, the rest of them could pass by unnoticed.

Keith sadly watched as the woman that would have been his partner left him behind, his face showed a mixture of concern and loss.

"She'll be ok," Liam whispered. "Her brother will protect her."

"Yeah, but I gotta wonder where her loyalties lie," Keith said. "I just hope she doesn't turn us in."

"That's a gamble with anybody," Liam replied distractedly. At the far side of the road, troops were looting businesses and taking trophies. In the distance, he saw soldiers set fire to houses while screams still rang out from inside. The brutality of the army left him bewildered, and he shook his head in disgust.

"Do you think the Tribes will counter-attack?" Denise whispered. "Will they come and save us?"

"Nah, I really doubt it," Keith said. "The most they'll do is hassle the column when they move us south."

"Maybe some of us can get away then," Liam muttered. They were passing right in front of Ron, so he tilted his head forward to hide his face beneath the wide brim of his hat.

"Ron! Ron! It's me!" Becky's voice rang out.

"That's my sister, grab her!" Ron shouted. "Where are the others?"

"I don't know," Becky answered. "We got separated; I think they might have stayed behind at the college."

"Crap!" Ron said. "They're probably dead then." His voice changed slightly as he turned to speak to the military commander. "I told you not to blow up the university."

"Shaddup traitor!" The rough commander said. "Don't give me any shit, unless you want to join the rest of these fuckers."

"I made a bargain with the Chancellor herself!" Ron shouted. "My sister and I are protected. You can't do anything to us."

The Major laughed. "Yeah, sure, you're right; but you know, accidents can happen anytime and it's a long way to Pike City." There was a pause, and Liam risked a quick glance up and saw that the two feuding men were facing each other. "And you know," the commander continued casually. "The deal was for you and that other guy. Without him, you ain't got shit. So, you need to shut the fuck up, 'cause like I said, accidents can happen."

After a few moments, Liam heard scuffling at the edge of the crowd as the soldiers forced their way into the throng of refugees to pull Becky to the side of the street. "You bitch!" someone shouted. Then another voice further back in the crowd yelled, "You let them in and they killed our children!" The refugees surged toward her with angry hands reaching out, and a moment later Liam heard the hum of an energy weapon, then there were screams and the smell of burning flesh, and the angry voices became silent.

*****

Liam felt hopeless as he shuffled forward with the crowd. The commander had said that the Chancellor wanted workers, so individually none of them had any value. They were like wood for a fire, useful until they were burned to ashes, then easily discarded. Once they were beyond the gate Liam turned to look back at the city. Smoke and flame had consumed everything; their lives there were over and all they had worked to achieve was gone.

A multistory hospital in the northern part of the city was on fire, he heard the popping of militia rifles, but the attempted defense was useless. Further east dust obscured most of the view, but he saw that all of the towering hydroponic buildings had collapsed. The food source that had once not only sustained Flatiron but fed others outside the city as well was lost.

To the west stood the NOAA Solar Weather Observatory. The military had surrounded the rambling group of brick buildings, and Liam saw a line of people wearing white lab coats lying face down near the main entrance. The army had executed anyone that dared to disagree with their ideology and tactics.

Back when he was still in Primary School, he had read that the climate change that had severely altered the planet's weather patterns had first been largely attributed to the use of fossil fuels to produce energy. It wasn't until all oil and gas production had been banned and the drilling and refining plants destroyed, that the truth had been discovered at the NOAA installation in Flatiron City.

The Sun's energy output had increased, and apparently, it was a natural cycle. As was typical, well-meaning government regulations had made the problem worse. Alternate power sources provided only a tiny percentage of what was needed, and soon only the rich and influential could afford to stay warm in winter while the rest of the world was plunged into shivering darkness. People living in the north were freezing, so they began to chop wood to produce heat. Forests disappeared, and the greenhouse gasses produced by their burning was far greater than what came from the use of fossil fuels.

The planet warmed quickly, and the added heat of the Sun escalated the natural evaporation of the oceans. The environment of Colorado had once been one of cool summers and snowy winters, but with the new weather patterns, the climate had changed to year-around heat and near-constant rain. Cities all along the east and west coasts of America were lost as the ocean levels rose. The Great Plains became a swamp and wetlands; the greatest farming region in the world was lost, and people starved.

Food riots ensued, and the few great cities that remained fell into violence and in the end destroyed themselves. Civil war broke out, and after a long and bloody conflict, the old US government collapsed and was replaced by the Socialist States of America. But the new leaders proved to be just as inept and corrupt as the old ones, and the fall of a once-great civilization continued without pause.

*****

The crowd of captives slowly shuffled forward; they were so tightly packed that no one could take a long stride. Gradually the towering city wall receded behind them, and in the distance ahead Liam saw a massive flatbed truck blocking their path. It appeared that they would be forced into a fenced-off muddy field to the west of the old Denver road.

The water-soaked soil sucked at Liam's boots as he entered the pen. A tall wire fence stretched around the perimeter, beyond it, spaced at even intervals, were guard towers made of preformed plasti-wood. The top of each tower was covered and protected from the elements and was manned by anonymous soldiers standing behind menacing laser weapons mounted on tripods. Every tower had a clear shot at anyone within the enclosure.

The gate swung shut and was locked behind them; everyone was trapped and completely at the mercy of their captors. Liam looked around their prison and was troubled by the lack of facilities; there were no toilets, or stations for food or water, or even shelter from the rain. It was a place of torture, and without provisions, no one could stay alive within the pen for very long. The once free citizens of Flatiron were prisoners, escape seemed impossible and a slow and agonizing death awaited them all.

Their group found a slightly elevated area near the back of the enclosure; it wasn't a good place to stay, but it was dryer than the rest of the pen at least. It would have to do until either the army saw fit to set up proper facilities, or they all died. They laid their coats out on the ground and then sat with the children they had taken from the university. Huddled together, they watched as dusk finally darkened into night.

Hours later, another group of prisoners was led out through the city gates. Word of mouth spread like wildfire, informing everyone that it was what remained of the militia. The former protectors of Flatiron were led beyond their pen and into a separate enclosure to the south.

Bob jumped up and ran to the edge of the pen, which caught the attention of the guards and they swung their guns toward him. He stopped before the guards fired, then jumped into the air and waved his arms. "Clare!" he shouted.

A higher-pitched voice answered his cries. In the darkness, it was hard to be sure, but Liam thought he saw someone wave back.

Chapter 7: Death Camp

There used to be snow. Liam sat facing away from the corral entrance and stared up at the jagged Flatiron range to the west. He knew that once upon a time the snows of winter had not only blanketed the mountains but had covered the prairie to the east as well. It seemed almost too incredible to believe, like a fairy tale, but he had seen old pictures taken during that blissful before-time, so it had to be true.

He had held snow in his hand once; it was when he was very young and still living with his parents and sister in Fort Collins. Their father had taken them to a refrigerated arboretum where snow sometimes fell. It was a marvel beyond description; the icy sphere crunched when he squeezed his hand, its coolness was like nothing he had ever experienced before. His little sister had laughed gleefully at first but then cried when her palm began to ache from the cold.

How he wished he could feel that coolness now. It was hot, the sky was the color of burnished steel, and the sucking mud of the day before had dried into something that resembled lumpy concrete. Like everyone else, he was thirsty and their captors still hadn't seen fit to give them any water. Hopefully, it would rain later that afternoon, if it didn't, some of the weak and infirm among them would die.

Bob and Roxi were lingering by the south side fence, hoping to catch sight of anyone they knew in the adjacent pen that held the militia captives. It was hard to distinguish faces though because there was a space of about 20 meters between the enclosures. Occasionally Bob would jump and wave his arms around while calling his sister's name.

A guard in a nearby tower didn't appreciate the racket. "Shaddup or I'll burn you into the fuckin' ground," he said.

Bob paced relentlessly beside the fence, and Roxi walked at his side attempting to keep him calm. But his foster father's friend and partner from the robotics lab refused to be soothed, and Liam didn't like the direction things were taking. They all were entirely at the mercy of guards that had absolutely no regard for human life. It's never a good idea to piss off someone that holds your life in their hands, especially if they don't care if you live or die.

Watching Bob put himself in danger was distressing, so Liam turned away and went back to staring at the mountains. After a few minutes passed, Rose and Denise came and sat down on either side of him. "Do you remember the time Father took us to see snow?" he asked his sister.

"Yes, I do." Rose smiled. "I remember that it was so cold that it hurt my hand."

Liam grinned. "You cried."

"Well, it was scary. I'd never seen anything like it."

"Can you imagine the mountains covered with it?"

"No... well maybe, but it's awfully hard to do," Rose answered.

"It must have been beautiful," Denise added.

He chuckled. "Yeah, and cold."

Denise smiled as she leaned against him. "Yes, well we could use some of that snow today. It's terribly hot."

He lay his arm over Denise's shoulders and held her close. It was good to have these two incredible women in his life. "As bad as things are, at least we're together."

"What do you think they're doing over there?" Denise asked, drawing his attention toward the militia pen to the south.

Large trucks were dropping blocks of preformed plasti-wood into the open space between the two enclosures. They were shaped and notched such that they would fit together and reminded him of Lincoln Logs but on a gigantic scale. "I don't know what those are," he answered. "They look like the toy blocks Rose and I used to play with when we were little."

"I remember that." Rose smiled. "I'd make little houses for my dolls, and you'd knock them all down. I used to get so angry at you."

He laughed softly. "Yeah, sorry about that."

"It's ok big brother. You used to build such crazy things with those blocks... sideways and even upside-down houses, crazy twisted stuff sometimes too."

He watched the soldiers unload another set of plasti-wood logs. "I have a bad feeling about that."

"Yes, I do too," Denise replied. "Whatever they're up to probably isn't good."

*****

The unloading lasted into the late afternoon, and when it was finally complete, the gate to the militia pen was opened and the captives were led out in a long line. Liam and both women stood up on their tiny knoll and watched from a distance as Bob anxiously ran along the edge of the fence searching for his sister.

Keith tried to restrain him. "Bob, are you trying to get yourself shot?"

Heedless of the danger, Bob continued to frantically search the faces of the militia prisoners. "Clare! Where are you?" At last, he saw her and charged the fence. Fortunately, Keith tackled and knocked him to the ground before he became a target for the tower guards. "Get off me!" Bob demanded.

Keith urgently said something in Bob's ear, but his voice was low enough that Liam couldn't hear what was said. Seconds later Roxi rushed in to help keep Bob on the ground.

"Clare!" Bob shouted as he finally managed to sit up.

Clare slowly walked with the rest of the prisoners; her dark face was streaked with dried blood and she was having trouble walking. She seemed to be in a daze, but her head turned slowly to look at her brother. "It'll be ok," she said; regardless of her circumstances, her voice was calm, almost serene. "This ain't nothin' to worry about, it's just time for me to go."

"No Clare!" Bob screamed. The tower guards that were watching the exchange seemed amused.

"Remember to play the long game little brother," Clare said. "Now you go on; don't watch this."

Keith and Roxi managed to pick Bob up, even though he continued to struggle. They carried him back to their camp, where they all sat together and waited to see what would happen next.

A sudden commotion broke out at the rear of the line of prisoners, and a moment later several members of the militia broke away and ran. "Target practice!" one of the soldiers shouted excitedly.

The tower guards casually swung their laser rifles around; the sound they made was much like a swarm of angry bees, and the fugitives vanished one by one into a superheated red mist. The supremacy of the army's weaponry was undeniable, and escape was clearly impossible.

The remaining prisoners were ordered to assemble the heavy plasti-wood forms. Two of the pieces fit together into an 'X' shape, then one end was lifted and supported by the third section such that the structure was inclined at about a 40-degree angle.

"What are they building?" Bob asked.

"It's a showcase," Liam muttered. "The platforms are tilted so all of us will have a clear view of what they're about to do."

"Why?" Bob asked.

"It's probably a warning to keep us in line," Liam whispered.

Soldiers soon arrived and marched single file along the row of plasti-wood structures. On command they turned as a unit, then each stepped forward to seize one of the prisoners. The guards forced every militia member to lie on the cross, then chained their arms and legs to the edifice. With their task complete, their captors reformed their line and walked back out the way they came.

"I'll wager you're wondering what this is all about?" Startled, Liam looked up and saw that the Major was standing in one of the guard towers. "Well, I'm gonna tell you, whether you were wondering or not." The large man grinned and leaned over the railing. "It's a long way to Pike City, so we gotta have an example of what it'll cost you if there're problems along the way. Consider this a lesson in mercy; sometimes you gotta lose a few to save the rest."

Sergeant Mick, the leader of the group that had captured them on their way out of Flatiron, stood rigidly at one end of the line of crosses holding a knife with a long, curved blade. Liam felt the breath go out of him as he considered the possibilities.

"Sergeant, do your duty," the Major ordered.

With that, Mick marched to the first prisoner that was stretched out on the cross and viciously cut a wide gash across the young man's stomach. Blood flowed and the captive shrieked in agony. The Sergeant quickly turned away and walked to the next militia member in the line waiting to be mutilated.

The process continued, and with each new cut, those within the citizen enclosure either gasped in fear or cried out in despair. Bob screamed in rage when his sister's stomach was slashed, and it took both Liam and Keith to restrain him. A few citizens pointlessly rushed the south fence, where they were burned into red vapor by the guards. There was nothing anyone could do to stop the torture of their friends; they all were frozen in horror, unable to look away.

When his task was complete, Mick returned to his original position and waited at attention. The crowd shouted obscenities at him, but the Sergeant remained unmoved.

"They ain't dead yet." There was a tenor of gleeful satisfaction in the Major's words. "That's gonna take a while; the ravens and coyotes will take care of 'em either tonight or sometime tomorrow. And all you useless traitors, well, you get to watch. So, let this be a lesson to you; *don't fuck with us*, keep your nose clean, follow our orders, and maybe, just maybe you'll make it to Pike City alive."

*****

As the sun fell behind the mountains, the family and friends of those slowly dying crowded along the south fence to mourn or offer what support they were able. Some shouted at the guards in fits of rage, but most remained peaceful and spoke softly to their loved ones in hopes that they could somehow ease their passing.

It was a long night. As promised, the wild animals came; their eyes glowed in the darkness. People shouted, hoping to scare the night creatures away, but that didn't work very well. When the sun rose, most of the militia members were dead. All that remained was to watch their further dismemberment by the crows and smell their flesh putrefy in the heat and humidity.

Bob was inconsolable; Clare was a tough woman and it took her a long time to die. She remained stoic until she finally lost enough blood to pass into unconsciousness. That was a blessing because she was unaware when the coyotes tore into her in the early morning. By midday all of the militia were dead; then later, in the early evening soldiers arrived to haul away what remained of their corpses.

*****

It rained the next day, which was a good thing because the civilian survivors were suffering. During the maelstrom, everyone collected water in their upturned hats, and when the storm ended, they all worried that another dry spell would follow. Better to be wet and miserable than die of dehydration in the heat.

A few of the children and some of the older citizens had already died. There was no place to bury the bodies; all anyone could do was stack them beside the gate. The guards never opened them though. Parents cried beside their dead children, many of which soon succumbed themselves and were laid to rest beside their babies. In the intense heat, the bodies rotted;

flies filled the air, and the smell became nearly impossible to bear.

If the army's intention was to break their spirit, their efforts had failed miserably. Those who may have been neutral or ambivalent regarding the war between the Socialists and the Tribes had become strongly polarized. They hated the invaders, but it wasn't an impetuous rage that acted rashly, instead, it was a cold, patient, and calculating malice that pretended compliance and waited for opportunity.

*****

The army opened the gates on the fourth day, and the prisoners were allowed to carry the rotting bodies of their family and friends to an open pit that had been dug on the far side of the Denver road. Once that task was complete the bodies were set on fire; fortunately, the chinook winds blowing off the mountains took the smoke further east.

Later that same day the gates swung open again, and a stock of food and water was wheeled in. They were also given shovels to dig a latrine and provided with tents so they could get out of the rain. That night Liam sat with his adult companions and the kids that had stayed with them in their tent. It felt good to be dry; Denise's body was warm and comforting as she leaned against him. "I wonder why they gave this stuff to us now?" he pondered.

"My guess is that they're worryin' that too many of us are gonna die," Keith answered from the shadows; he and Rose were huddled together on the far side of the tent. "If some of the scientists they're lookin' for don't make it to Pike City there could be a lot of trouble for 'em, especially if it gets back that they died here."

"Huh," Rose answered. "If you're right, maybe they'll be more careful with us."

"I doubt it," Liam answered. "They've dehumanized us, so we're just a commodity. If most of us survive, that's probably good enough for them."

"They say they're going to move us south to Pike City," Roxi said. "I wonder how much longer they'll keep us here?"

"Hopefully for at least a few more days," Keith replied. "I don't know if you've noticed, but there aren't enough trucks to carry us all. My guess is that they're gonna make us walk."

"Walk?" Bob leaned forward. "It's more than 160 kilometers to Pike City; we'll never make it."

"The strong will, but the weak won't," Keith stated. "That's why I hope it's gonna be a few more days. We need more time so those who are sick can get better."

"They said they want workers," Denise said. "The long walk will weed out those that aren't fit for the jobs the Socialists need us to do."

"Slaves," Roxi muttered. "The reality is that they want slaves. Workers have value and worth. Slaves don't, they're not people at all, just disposable tools."

"Well shit," Bob replied.

"What about the children?" Denise asked as she gazed at the little ones huddled around them, but no one had an answer.

"The walk will give some of us a chance to escape," Keith suggested. "Maybe we can sneak some of the kids out then."

"Maybe," Bob muttered. "We'd have better odds if the Tribes attacked."

"I don't think we can count on that," Keith replied. "The Tribes have no real structure, they're just a bunch of independent groups." He shrugged. "You know, if they ever manage to beat the Socialists, they'll probably start fightin' among themselves."

*****

"EVERYONE OUT OF YOUR TENTS!" an ear-shattering amplified voice commanded. "ASSEMBLE AT THE CENTER OF THE ENCLOSURE!"

Bob crawled to the tent entrance and peeked outside. "What's goin' on?"

"Shaddup and get outside!" an angry voice commanded.

"I hope they ain't taking the tents back," Keith said as he held the entrance open for the others.

Bob pulled them together once they were outside. "Looks like they're checking identities," he whispered. "They're probably trying to find those of us that worked for the Tribes at the university. We should all use fake names."

"I just taught history," Rose complained. "So, they're not looking for me."

"That doesn't matter," Keith said. "Anybody that worked at the college will be suspected of being aligned with the Tribes, and that might get you killed. So, just pretend to be a useful idiot and don't attract attention."

"But any fake names we make up won't be on their list," Rose stated.

"That probably won't matter either," Keith responded. "They'll figure it's a bookkeeping error. I've been told the Socialists do a pretty shitty job of record-keeping, so they'll believe it when the same thing happens here." He thought a moment. "If there's a problem, tell 'em that you just got to Flatiron City and are brand-new citizens, then say that's why your name ain't in the records."

"Yeah, that should work," Liam said. "But if Rose and I say we're from Fort Collins that might be suspicious."

Roxi nodded. "They probably won't ask, but if they do, tell them that you're from Loveland."

They lined up with everyone else at the back of the pen. Liam saw that several desks were set up near the enclosure entrance, each manned by an efficient looking clerk using a small computer. Behind the desks and overlooking the process were armed guards. Fear pounded in Liam's ears as they drew closer to the head of the line. He let his eyes wander through the crowd of soldiers and accountants, and was relieved to see that Ron wasn't there to identify him.

Bob was the first to reach the head of the line and went to a far table when he was called. There weren't many people in Flatiron with his dark complexion, and Liam worried that his father's friend might be associated with Clare, who had been in the militia. He watched closely, hoping for the best, but also knowing that if the worst happened that there was nothing he could do about it. After about a minute Bob was approved and allowed to return to their tent.

In the meantime, Roxi had been called up to a different desk. She probably used the name of someone already within the army's database, because the verification of her identity appeared to go smoothly. After a few minutes of questioning, she was released.

The line was moving quickly and Rose was called to yet a different desk, where she said her name was Sarah Jones. The administrator frowned as he studied his computer screen. Liam hoped that there already was a 'Sarah Jones' in the city database, and he waited breathlessly to see what would happen. A second clerk was called over to help, and the two men worked the keyboard and stared at the screen for what seemed an eternity. At last, the men straightened up and shook their heads. "Fuckin' civilians got shit for records," he heard one of the men say, and then his sister was released.

Liam was called forward next, and he walked to the same desk and waited.

"Name?" the administrator asked.

"I'm Jack Jones," Liam replied.

The administrator typed in his fictitious name, then scanned the data on the computer screen. "Shit, no record again," the man said after a moment. "Are you related to that girl that was just here, Sarah Jones?"

"Yeah," Liam nodded. "She's my sister."

"Oh ok, you're clear then." The clerk waved his hand dismissively.

Liam decided to take a gamble. "Who are you looking for?" He looked around, hoping to seem like he didn't want to be overheard, then leaned forward and whispered, "Is there a reward?"

"Yeah, there's a reward, you'll get to ride on a truck all the way down to Pike City. We're lookin' for a guy named Liam Collins, you know him?"

Liam pursed his lips and looked down. "Shit. No, I've never heard of him. Guess I gotta walk then."

"Yeah, I guess so," the clerk answered. "Now get outta here."

He frowned as he walked back toward their tent. The Socialists were looking for him, but why? Lucy was complete and had arrived exactly where Pike City wanted, so it had to be something else. It didn't matter though; after what their army had done to his home, family, and friends, he wanted no part of anything they might have in mind.

*****

It was a cool early morning and the air felt invigorating. A few uneventful days had passed since the security check, and as a whole, those in captivity were recovering from their earlier deprivation. Liam had taken three bowls of oatmeal at the food station for himself, his sister, and Denise, and was on his way back to their tent.

"PACK UP YOUR STUFF!" an amplified voice ordered.

Liam shook his head in resignation and mumbled, "Well, shit!" It seemed that nothing good ever lasted, but then upon reflection, he realized that nothing bad ever did either.

It took only moments to take down their tent, which fortunately was made of a lightweight material that folded up into a small backpack that Keith had volunteered to carry. Afterward, they watched as the fence around their enclosure was taken down; armed guards stood around the perimeter, ready to shoot anyone attempting to escape.

At last, Major Johnson climbed up onto the back of one of the enormous flatbed military trucks. "Ok! Listen up!" he shouted. "We're starting our walk south to Pike City today. Before you even think about it, there will be no escapes; if you even look like you're trying to get away, the guards will shoot you. I've sent men ahead to prepare camps along our route, so at night your enclosure will be secure; again, there will be *no escapes*."

"Our march south will take five days, and each day we will cover about 30 kilometers. There will be no breaks or stops to rest, and those of you that can't keep up will be shot. You may carry each other if you wish, but again, if you walk too slow, you will die.

"There are about 2,500 of you starting out, and I don't care if any of you make it all the way. Pike City needs strong workers, so consider this little stroll to be an aptitude test. If you live through it, you'll succeed and do well in your new home; you'll become a productive member of society and work for the good of our people. But only the worthiest among you will survive."

The Major turned and pointed back toward Flatiron City. "Now watch what happens to those that defy Chancellor Margaret Williams."

Missiles were simultaneously fired from the north, south, and east toward the city. With their impact, a sudden blast of hot wind crashed into the crowd and the ground shuddered terribly, knocking some of the smaller children down. A nearly impenetrable cloud of dust rose from the destruction, thankfully blocking out much of their view.

"I don't want to see this," Denise uttered and pressed her face to Liam's chest.

He wrapped his arms around her and held her close. He felt lost as he watched the destruction of his adopted city. Flatiron had been more than a place of refuge, it was the home of his friends and family, and he knew that he would miss that connection more than anything else.

The city wall fell in sections like tumbling dominos, each collapsing in a rush of thunder and dust. The missile barrage continued without pause; buildings throughout the once gracious city exploded and fell. Fires grew among the ruins, and within minutes all that remained of their home was rubble.

"Ok then, that's well done." The Major turned back toward the crowd of prisoners. "You have nowhere to return to. Your past is gone, the only future you have is in the south with us." The overweight dark-skinned man paused a moment, then nodded. "Ok, it's time to go."

Chapter 8: The Long Walk

Mother Nature provided a brutal day for their departure. By midday, it was hot and humid with dark clouds gathering over the Rocky Mountains. Behind them lay the tumbled ruins of Flatiron; of all the hope that the last free city had once represented, only scattered rubble remained. Their lives there were over and their future seemed as bleak and barren as the blanched and broken tarmac they followed as they began their long walk south.

Crowded housing tracks had once stood at the edge of the road. However, during the long-ago State's Wars, they had all been burned to the ground. All that remained of those ancient neighborhoods were concrete foundations and the crumbling remains of masonry fireplaces.

At the head of the convoy, the Major sat with his officers under a pale green awning on the back deck of a massive flatbed truck. He talked and joked with those around him while enjoying cool beverages and laughing at the misery of the prisoners. It appeared they were making wagers regarding how many of the 2,500 remaining citizens would survive the long march to Pike City.

The line of shambling captives stretched for kilometers and was hemmed in by small military vehicles carrying heavily armed soldiers. Those men laughed and taunted the civilians by drinking bottles of water and harassing the women with threats of rape. The refugees didn't talk much, for the most part, all that could be heard were the whispering thump of countless footsteps across the cracked and degraded macadam.

At the rear of their group was the most frightening aspect of all; a huge armored vehicle lumbered along at a constant 5 kilometer-per-hour speed. Anyone that fell behind was first shot by the soldiers that rode on its hood and then crushed beneath its wheels. Behind that transport, more military trucks followed in a long line.

The children of Flatiron had not been allowed to ride with the military, so the adults took turns carrying them. It was a hard but necessary duty; to refuse the care of the innocent for the sake of themselves was to lose one's soul. But the sick and elderly were too big and heavy to be carried and they struggled to keep up; before midday Liam saw several of them shot dead. It hurt and angered him to witness such atrocities, but there was nothing he could have done to prevent it.

All of the convoy vehicles were nearly empty, especially the massive flatbed trucks, so there was ample room for both the young and old to ride. Very soon it became apparent that the army was not engaged in transportation; instead, the convoy was a mode of slow-moving execution of the weak and infirm. Hatred among the refugees intensified, but the soldiers didn't care and some actually appeared to relish it.

A thunderstorm rolled off the mountains in the mid-afternoon. Lightening whipped through the sky and arced downward striking the distant mountains and pummeling the nearby prairie hills. The deluge pounded the captives as they struggled to keep up the pace dictated by their captors. The torrent fell so fast that the drainage of the ancient road was overrun; in places, Liam waded through ankle-deep puddles the size of small lakes. His boots were soaked through, and his feet became a wet misery.

He trudged steadily through the storm carrying a frail blonde girl; at the height of the downpour, he wrapped his duster coat around the child to shield her from the beating rain. The guards in a nearby covered vehicle all laughed. "God must hate you guys," one of the men said.

Liam glanced at the man and smirked. "God is dead, haven't you heard? The Crusades ended all that, no one believes in that shit anymore."

The guard leaned back in his seat beside the driver with his rifle resting lazily in his lap. "Yeah, most folks are smart enough to not believe in the old jealous Gods these days, but I hear your friends up in the hills are praying to some new idol."

"Really?" Liam was suddenly curious.

"Yeah, your buddies are bowing down to some new God called 'The Stick Man'."

Liam chuckled and shook his head in disbelief. "The Stick Man? Yeah, that's nuts." He wondered if the guard was making the story up.

"Anyway, I thought you might know all about it since you guys were tight with the mountain savages."

"Yeah well, I don't have any friends in the mountains, and Flatiron was a neutral city," Liam stated.

"Ain't no such thing as neutral. If you ain't for one side or the other, you're an enemy to both."

In the distance, he saw a group of tall crumbling buildings that seemed on the verge of collapse. "What's that?" he wondered aloud, not really expecting an answer.

"That's all that's left of Golden... I guess you don't get out much huh?" The soldier snickered. "It was a city of casinos, where the ancients used to gamble."

Liam grunted in response, then looked up thankfully as the pounding rain began to ease.

The young guard grinned. "Time never changes anything. We're all placing bets on who will and won't make it to Pike City. I'm gonna put a wager on you... what's your name?"

"Jack Jones," Liam answered, using the false name he gave during the identity check.

One of the other soldiers was taking notes on a hand-held computer. "Ok Joe, I got it. Can't give you much of a return though; this guy looks young and kinda strong."

"Oh no, I ain't betting that he'll make it, my wager is that he won't," Joe replied.

"Ok! That's different then." The bookmaker smiled. "I'll give you three to one if he doesn't make it."

The agreement was reached and Joe pressed his palm against the bookie's computer screen and bet two days of food rations.

"I hope you don't mind if I do my best to stay alive," Liam said.

"Nah, I don't mind. Do your best, that's what makes it fun," Joe replied.

The column was slowing ahead as military vehicles moved to the center and the prisoners were forced to walk at the edge of the road. "What's going on up there?" Liam asked.

"The road takes us through old downtown Golden," Joe replied. "The savages like to hide in the buildings and try to pick us off, so we make you guys walk to the outside and we take cover behind you."

"You're very brave," Liam mumbled.

"Shaddup asshole, and move to the outside," Joe said.

*****

Golden was haunted, or at least it should have been. The decrepit buildings, many of which were five or more stories high, seemed to lean over the main street through the heart of the abandoned city. Liam felt confined and glanced upward nervously, hoping that the towers would remain standing a while longer. It was nearly sundown, and shadows were quietly easing out from the dark spaces beneath the ruins to crouch at the edge of the road. Small animals moved among the rubble, disturbing pebbles and rocks here and there; the trickle of stony landslides had everyone on edge.

There was a sudden rapid rattle that sounded like an angry woodpecker working on the side of an old building; the abrupt burst ended just as quickly as it started. Their convoy ground to a halt; the railgun fire had destroyed the front of the lead truck, leaving it broken and partially blocking the way forward.

The army indiscriminately returned fire. Sounding like angry bees, their lasers vaporized parts of the structures around them. Sections of the old masonry edifices cracked and exploded under the sudden heat of the energy weapons. The ancient towers tilted drunkenly and threatened to collapse and block the street. Further ahead, the upper floor of a building crumbled and fell amid a raging cloud of dust; the world shook and the concussive sound knocked Liam and his companions to the ground.

The captives quickly took cover among the piles of boulders that lay at the edge of the road. Liam clutched the little girl he was carrying to his chest to protect her from the falling stones. A railgun roared from the opposite side of the street, killing many refugees before tearing into several of the smaller vehicles. Again, the army fired back, and more of the ancient structures blew apart into a shower of stones. "Move, move, move!" the soldiers ordered, waving their weapons at the refugees threateningly.

"We gotta get out of here," Keith said. He had hidden nearby and was covering a young boy with his body. "If we stay here, we'll die."

Encouraged by Keith's bravado, Liam, along with Rose, Denise, and several of their companions jumped to their feet and followed Keith as he ran toward the front of the convoy. They stopped only occasionally to seek cover or to help others like themselves. Many prisoners veered away into the old decrepit buildings, a few escaped but most were reduced to clouds of red vapor by the army's lasers.

The lead truck that had carried the Major was abandoned; smaller cars had raced forward to rescue the officers. The army's heavily armed attack trucks lumbered forward, the laser cannons that were mounted to their massive beds had enough firepower to level entire buildings. The captives ran for their lives.

Liam's group was just emerging from the downtown area when the heavy lasers began firing. The hiss and buzz of their weapons were nearly deafening, but it was the roar of falling buildings that brought true fear into their hearts. Being caught and possibly buried alive within an avalanche of masonry was a fate more fearful than being instantly vaporized. Liam kept his sister and Denise close as they all ran, hoping to escape the downtown area before it entirely collapsed.

The ambush ended as abruptly as it started. The railguns went silent, but the Socialist Army wasn't through. Their heavy ordnance fired indiscriminately at the surrounding buildings, exploding and tumbling their ruins into the street. They buried several of their own vehicles in blind acts of mindless brutality and vengeance.

It may have seemed to be a victory for the Socialists, but Liam had his doubts. The attack may have been conducted by as few as five individuals carrying railguns, and most if not all of the attackers had probably escaped. On the other hand, the army had suffered many casualties, lost several heavily weaponized vehicles, and the road through Golden was now completely blocked. More victories like that could cost them the war.

Once outside the city, the military quickly rounded up the captives and surrounded them with their vehicles. The number of prisoners was reduced, and Liam hoped that at least some of the missing had escaped. Many of those that remained were injured, and when physicians declared that they wouldn't be able to keep up with the convoy, they were executed.

*****

Just south of Golden, the convoy passed under the remains of an ancient superhighway that led into the high mountains. Landslides and war had destroyed much of the gigantic structure, but what remained was magnificent. Liam wondered what the roadway had looked like when it was still in use. What incredible engineers the old ones had been, and yet sadly, their civilization had fallen. Technology and vision alone were not viable indications that a culture would endure.

A camp awaited them a short distance south of the mountain highway. The surviving refugees were herded into a fenced enclosure that was ringed by guard towers. Everyone in their group had survived the attack in Golden, and Liam wrapped his arms around his sister and Denise, grateful to still be with them.

Food and water soon arrived, and Keith, Bob, and Roxi stayed behind to set up the tent while the rest went to get dinner. Later, as he huddled with Denise beneath his duster coat and drifted on the edge of sleep, Liam wondered if any of them would live through the forced march south. He watched as Bob and Roxi whispered together; they were the oldest and least robust of their group, their best chance of survival was to find a way to escape.

*****

Morning came hard and loud. "GET UP YOU FUCKTARDS!" the Major's amplified voice screamed. "WE MOVE OUT IN FIVE MINUTES!"

"What a pleasant man," Roxi remarked.

Keith laughed. "How're you doin' today Roxi?"

"Oh, my feet are a little sore, probably like everyone else's. I'm fine though."

They all wrapped themselves in their coats and crawled out of the tent. The day ahead did not seem promising; a thick fog hung close to the ground, and by the look of things the weather was not going to improve.

Keith packed up the tent then strapped it to his shoulders. "Looks like we lost quite a few people in Golden."

"Yeah, I noticed that too," Liam replied. "I hope at least some escaped, but will the Tribes give them shelter?"

"Maybe." Keith shrugged. "It kinda depends on whether they're useful or not."

"Huh," Rose said, joining in on their conversation. "They're just like Flatiron then. My brother and I were only allowed in because we had talents the city needed."

"I guess it's kinda the same way with the rebels," Keith answered. "No one can afford charity when times are tough."

"They're herding us out, so I guess we gotta go," Liam said, then quietly continued, "I don't know if Bob and Roxi have it in them to make it all the way down to Pike City. We gotta find a way for them to get away."

"I'm way ahead of you," Keith answered. "I was talkin' with 'em last night after you guys were asleep."

"What're you planning?" Denise asked.

90

"The area around old Denver is dangerous because the Socialists and a couple of the Tribes are fighting over territory. The further south we go, the safer it'll be for 'em to escape. So, we'll try for somewhere near Castle Rock," Keith responded.

"Castle Rock?" Liam asked.

"Yeah, it was a smaller city, about 30 kilometers south of Denver. Now it's just a ruin left over from the Crusades," Keith answered.

"So, they'll have to wait," Denise stated. "I hope they can make it."

"Yeah," Keith answered. "My guess is that we'll go east on the outer loop around Denver, then hook up with the old interstate that leads south. That route will take us up a pretty steep hill, and that's gonna be a problem."

"We'll make it," Roxi said as she joined the line of prisoners leaving the enclosure. "Bob and I are old – but not *that* old."

"Just do your best sugar," Keith said with a grin. "I know for a fact that people like you guys are needed by the Tribes, so I'll be sure to make that happen."

"A physicist and a guy that plays with batteries," Bob joked. "Yeah sure."

"You're two geniuses that know how to do stuff that they need," Keith replied, then glanced at Rose and Liam. "Sorry guys, but your talents aren't really important, you might get accepted, but you never know."

Rose nodded slowly. "Yes, I suppose a computer programmer and a history buff aren't very useful in an apocalypse."

Liam draped his arm over his sister's shoulders. "Don't worry. We have each other and that's all we really need."

"But how will you let the Tribes know about your plans?" Rose asked.

"It's easier than you'd think," Keith replied. "The army just abandons places like this when they pull out. So, all I do is leave a note where someone can find it."

"Low-tech is always the best way to go," Liam remarked.

An amplified guard's voice suddenly shouted from the top of one of the watchtowers. "ALL RIGHT. I WANT ALL THE YOUNG KIDS TO STEP FORWARD. IT's YOUR LUCKY DAY, YOU CUTE LITTLE KIDDIES GET TO RIDE ALL THE WAY TO PIKE CITY!"

"What's that about?" Liam asked.

"Huh, yeah, I was afraid this would happen." Keith looked grim.

"They're gonna use the kids as a shield. If we're attacked again, they think the Tribes will hold off if there're children in plain sight on their trucks."

"At least we won't have to worry about them getting shot for going too slow," Denise said. "But will having the kids up there keep the army safe?"

Keith sighed and shook his head. "Both sides hate each other and will do anything... *anything* to wipe out the other. So, my guess is that it won't make a difference at all."

*****

The rain that the morning promised never arrived, instead the day remained hot and oppressively humid. The pale concrete roadway was blinding in the murky sunlight, and Liam often walked with his eyes closed because the glare gave him a headache. Their day was mostly passed in silence; speaking took more energy than any of them wanted to expend, and there was nothing to talk about anyway. Everyone stayed close and kept a watch on each other; surviving the long ordeal became a team effort.

At the end of the day, they were led into a camp enclosure that surrounded a cracked area of ancient tarmac. It was an inhospitable place to spend the night, but after a bland dinner of oatmeal and water, he curled up with Denise and fell into a deep sleep.

Odd dreams plagued him that night, possibly brought on by the oppressive heat and painfully bright light they had endured all day. In his dream, he was awake but unable to move. Rose lay beside him and seemed to be struck immobile as well. An orange light illuminated Roxi's face as she looked down at both him and his sister. Bob and Denise were also there, they were talking about something important, but none of it made any sense.

*****

Their third day on the road was the shorter in terms of distance, but much more difficult for everyone. The convoy steered them off the Denver outer loop and onto a wide southern highway that took them up a long torturous grade. Liam carried Roxi on his back, and Keith supported and helped Bob up the long hill. The weakest among the Flatiron survivors were slaughtered when they couldn't keep up; the dead they left behind rivaled the number that was killed during the attack in Golden.

Every up has a down though, and late in the afternoon, the survivors descended the long slope toward the abandoned city of Castle Rock. "It looks like we'll make it through another day," Rose said as they passed by a complex of tumbled stone buildings.

"Did you have a weird dream last night?" Liam asked.

"Dream?" Rose shrugged. "Maybe, but it could've been that I was just half awake. I just remember Roxi and Bob talking."

"Yeah, me too. It seemed funny because it felt like I couldn't move."

"Yes, it was the same for me." Rose rested her hand on his shoulder as they walked. "We were probably too wiped out by the long day, and sort of went into a trance."

"Yeah, that's probably it." Liam looked around to be sure no one was listening. "Isn't Castle Rock where Keith said that Roxi and Bob might try to get away?"

"Maybe," Rose said quietly. "All these buildings remind me of Golden; let's hope that whatever happens, it isn't like that again."

They were herded off the highway just south of the old downtown area of the city, then forced into a space that might have once been some kind of park. It must have been beautiful long ago; just beyond the fenced enclosure, a wide slow-moving river flowed through a sandy gully that was lined with twisted oak trees. Keith set their tent up at the western edge of camp on a low rise that overlooked the river, and as it was on previous nights, they ate their meager dinners then settled down to sleep.

*****

The rattle of railguns woke him. He rolled over to check on Rose; she was safe, but otherwise, their tent was empty. Where was Denise? Had Keith and the rest of their friends abandoned them?

The side of their tent suddenly collapsed as Keith stumbled through the opening. "Stay down!" he ordered, then fell on top of them.

Liam slipped out from under the weight of his friend. "Are you shot? Are you ok?" he asked frantically.

"I'm fine. Just stay down," Keith ordered. The buzz of lasers sent blazing fire roaring into the night, and railguns answered briefly, then became silent. "Ok, this is important," Keith whispered. "If you're asked, Roxi, Bob, and Denise died yesterday during the walk up the hill."

"Denise is gone too?" Liam frowned.

"Yeah," Keith said. "She has experience in hydroponics, and that's needed up in the mountains."

"So, all three have gone to work for the Tribes?" Liam whispered. The loss of Denise hurt, but he hoped that she was safe.

"Shut up; don't *ever* say anything about that, even when you think no one will hear," Keith said. "I have a mission in Pike City, and you two are gonna help me."

*****

"EVERYBODY UP!" A painfully amplified voice screamed. "OUT OF YOUR TENTS FOR A HEADCOUNT!"

They scrambled outside and waited, shivering in the damp predawn darkness. Soldiers quickly moved through the groups of captives. "Who's missing?" the angry men asked again and again, but they received no answers. Regardless of the bets placed on the lives of the refugees, no one had kept track of who had died on the road.

"There's a hole in the fuckin' fence, so somebody's missing!" one of the soldiers shouted. He stopped in front of Keith and glared. "There was more in your group yesterday, where are they?"

"Killed on the hike up the hill," Keith answered. "You know, maybe instead of sneakin' out, someone snuck in."

The soldier's eyes widened and he looked around warily, then he frowned. "Fuck you asshole," he mumbled. "All right, I hope you bitches enjoyed your beauty sleep, 'cause we're movin' out early."

They were marched south along the old interstate highway, passing by long-abandoned neighborhoods of tumbledown homes. Beyond the ruins of Castle Rock, the road took them through wide-open grasslands with flat-topped mesas to the east and the majestic granite wall of the Front Range to the west.

Around midday, the rattling roar of railguns sprung from atop the mesas. The line of armored vehicles at the end of their column was the target; one was completely cut in half before anyone could respond. That children were killed didn't concern the attackers at all. The army quickly took cover behind their prisoners and prepared to defend their position, but then the barrage abruptly ended.

After several long minutes of hearing nothing but the wind whisper across the rolling plain, the soldiers cautiously relaxed. "We're sittin' ducks out here," the Major announced from the lead vehicle. "Let's move out – and no stops 'til we're down for the night!"

The army abandoned three of their large flatbed trucks because they were disabled in the attack. The bloody and torn bodies of children also lay discarded at the side of the road. The pace of the convoy quickened to something close to a fast walk or a slow jog. Everyone did their best to help the weakest among them, but still more refugees were slaughtered for falling behind.

Short sporadic attacks occurred throughout the day, but the strikes were primarily aimed at military vehicles rather than personnel. By nightfall, only two of the massive trucks remained and most of the soldiers walked along beside their captives.

Their final night on the road was spent on a dry grassy field near the long-abandoned city of Monument. The lights of Pike City could be seen glowing in the distance, and Liam wondered what new horrors waited for them there.

Part 2: The City

Be extremely subtle,
even to the point of formlessness.
Be extremely mysterious,
even to the point of soundlessness.
Thereby you can be the
director of your opponent's fate.

Sun Tzu, The Art of War

Chapter 9: Arrival

The last hour of their long walk was through the charred and desiccated ruins that lay north of Pike City. The ancient steel and masonry buildings were tortured by war and time; their dark windows seemed like eyes that watched and followed them everywhere. It was a haunted place, like an old neglected graveyard.

Regardless of the distraction, Liam's gaze kept returning to the towering edifice of the city wall. He estimated the height of the structure at something close to thirty-meters. Laser cannons were placed at roughly ten-meter intervals along the top, around which soldiers gathered and stared down at them curiously. The wall itself was made of a dull gray material that resembled plasti-wood, which was probably a good choice because it was resilient, and less likely to shatter under the impact of railgun fire.

Soldiers escorted them into a maze of buildings just inside the city's northern gate, where they were split into smaller groups for processing. Liam and Rose, along with several others were taken to a large room where an army of administrators toiled behind desks arranged in long rows.

Everyone they saw was dressed in dull gray pants and shirts. The lack of individuality and the excessive regimentation of the workers made them seem like faceless cogs in some great machine. After waiting in line, they were each called to separate desks to be grilled by dispassionate bureaucrats.

Liam was interviewed by an elderly man who performed his job robotically. Fortunately, it didn't matter that his false name wasn't in their system, the administrator simply created a new record in their database and his new identity as Jack Jones was approved.

Before he was allowed to leave, the elderly man asked, "Do you know someone named Liam Collins?"

His immediate reaction was fear that his true identity had been discovered, but curiosity got the better of him. "Yeah, I knew Liam. He worked at the university; why do you ask?"

The administrator pressed a button at the edge of his desk and an armed guard quickly arrived. "There's a reward out for Liam Collins," the elderly man said. "When was the last time you saw him?"

Maybe this was an opportunity to learn something about his new environment. "Liam was with us on the long walk. He knew the guards were looking for him, so when he got tired of walking, he told one of the soldiers who he was."

"Where is he then?" the administrator asked.

"The guard thought he was lying and shot him. Liam's dead. It was a Sergeant named Mick that killed him."

The guard and administrator looked at each other for a moment, then the soldier abruptly walked away. "Ok," the elderly man said finally. "You're free to go; exit through the green door at the back of the room."

His experiment had not yielded any new information, but maybe something would turn up in time. Rose was waiting outside the building. "Hey, Sarah."

"Hi, Jack," Rose responded.

They were reunited with Keith as they entered a building dedicated to interrogation. Liam studied the sophisticated equipment at a distance, then finally nodded. "Those are FMRI machines; Functional Magnetic Resonance Imaging. They're used for lie detection because they can measure blood flow in our brains, which increases when we're under stress." He watched the interview process a moment longer. "They're not asking questions, just showing pictures on a computer screen; they'll be able to see when someone has a negative reaction, so they're probably testing for loyalty."

"Can it be tricked?" Rose whispered.

"I don't know," he replied. "I read about this stuff when I was in Primary School, but never paid much attention because it wasn't interesting. All I can suggest is to stay calm and think of something other than what they're showing you."

Keith was called up first and casually walked to a desk where a young female inspector waited. Liam watched as his friend flirted with the administrator, then sat in a padded armchair with a thick white ring that went almost completely around his head. Keith spoke with the woman for a moment longer, then lay back and watched the images playing on a computer screen.

Rose went up a moment later. Liam felt panic rise in his chest; what would happen if they failed their tests?

"Jack Jones... Jack Jones to desk six." It took a moment for Liam to respond to his false name, and he hurried to the administrator's desk hoping that his delay wouldn't cause suspicion.

"Sit down," the clerk said blandly. She was a somewhat attractive woman who appeared to be in her early thirties with blonde hair. She wore the usual gray uniform along with thick spectacles with heavy black frames. "State your name and place of birth," she said unemotionally.

For a frantic moment, he forgot his fake name and floundered. "Umm... I've never seen anyone wearing glasses before."

The bureaucrat stared at him without an ounce of warmth. "Name. Place of birth."

"Jack Jones, the free city of Flatiron."

The woman pursed her lips and said nothing for a long moment. "Watch the screen in front of you," she finally ordered. "The machine will judge your reaction to the images."

A series of pictures appeared on the computer monitor; most were too fast for him to think about. A tree. An old woman with a stretched face and overly blonde hair. A river. A city in flames that might have been Flatiron. A mountain. People dressed in the uniform of the Pike City Army. Clouds. A supply depot of some kind. A little white dog.

"Huh," the woman grunted finally. "I guess you don't have much on your mind. You passed, exit through the green door at the back of the room."

He smiled as he stood up, then became uneasy when he noticed that both Rose and Keith were already gone; alarm bells hadn't sounded though, which was a good sign. A huge sense of relief washed over him as he passed through the green door and found his friends waiting on the other side. "Wow," he grinned. "We made it."

Rose smiled. "The guy that ran my test said that I had nothing on my mind," she said. "He had to check his machine to be sure it was working."

"Not me," Keith said with a grin.

"How'd you get through the test then?" Liam asked.

"I thought about sex," Keith answered.

"Ha!" Rose scoffed. "Isn't that what *all* men think about *all* the time?"

It felt good to laugh, and together they went into the next building to get their job assignment and living arrangements.

*****

Once again, the room was filled with rows of desks run by gray disinterested people. The lines were long and the service was slow, but he was eventually called to a desk run by a pale and unusually thin man. The administrator's hands shook as he scrolled through items on his computer; he looked sick enough that Liam sat back in his chair, hoping to not catch whatever disease the young man carried.

"There's nothing in our database about your work history," the sickly man said.

"I was a custodian at the university." Liam had discussed this topic with Rose while they waited in line. They both decided that claiming janitorial experience was safe because it wouldn't arouse suspicion.

"I see," the bureaucrat remarked. "We need people to work in the motor-pool, do you think you can handle that?"

Liam recalled hearing rumors of large trucks heading south from Pike City, and he was curious about what was going on. "Yeah sure, I can do that."

The pale man nodded and then typed rapidly. "Ok... we have a place for you to live that's near where you'll be working." He printed a map on a thin sheet of plasti-paper and slid it across the desk. "Take this with you. In the next building, you'll be issued new clothes and have your chip implanted so you can get the supplies you need."

Liam again exited through a green door, but his friends weren't there to greet him this time, and he worried. In the next building, he was told to discard his old clothes, then follow a line of other Flatiron City survivors through an ice-cold shower that smelled of disinfectant. It felt like he was in an assembly line. Beyond the shower, he was issued two sets of gray clothes, then handed a black hooded coat and a pair of flimsy plastic boots. After dressing he went to a table at the back of the room where his rations chip was injected into the palm of his hand. Once correctly processed, stamped, and approved, he was instructed to exit through another green door, where he would wait outside for orientation.

He saw Rose and Keith standing together as he left the building. "That took you a while," Rose said.

Liam shrugged. "Yeah, I guess. Did you guys get your chips installed?"

"Yeah. Did Bob or John talk to you about that?" Keith whispered.

"He did, but I'll need help to get the things I need."

Keith nodded. "I've already made some contacts and will ask around."

After a short wait, a group of soldiers arrived and a moment later a tall woman with dark hair stepped out from their ranks. "Ok everyone," she said with a wide and somewhat false smile. "You must all stay together and follow me; we're walking to Acacia Park for your orientation."

*****

Humidity thickened the twilight air as their group was herded south by their military escort. Tejon Street was a wide boulevard lined with three and four-story buildings; small shops and commissaries rested behind wide sidewalks and ancient streetlamps leaned overhead. It had been a lovely place once, but now the upper floors of the structures were dark and appeared abandoned. Pedestrians, all dressed in gray, lingered by the storefronts and watched them suspiciously as they made their way along the street. Once they arrived at the park their guards moved away and watched from a distance.

Acacia Park occupied just a single block near the center of old downtown Pike City. It was a pleasant grassy area speckled with ancient oak trees and benches set along aggregate paths. A stage occupied the eastern border that was dominated by an imposing portrait of a severe elderly woman holding a little white dog. Liam recognized the woman from the FMRI slide show and knew the dog via its robot version he had encountered at Flatiron University.

They gathered near the center of the park, then waited for their orientation to begin. A light breeze blew, gently rustling the bare oak tree branches overhead. There were far fewer people there than he expected, and Liam wondered what had happened to the other Flatiron survivors. He turned to Keith and quietly asked, "Where're the rest of us?"

"Shush," an unfamiliar female voice warned. "Eyes and ears everywhere."

Liam turned to see who had spoken, but all he saw were blank faces. He casually glanced about and noticed microphones and cameras hidden in the trees and took the anonymous warning to heart. Regardless of how wonderful a government purports itself to be, the need to spy on its people indicates that evil lay at its heart.

"Welcome home!" a dark-haired woman said as she took the stage. "It's wonderful that you've joined us!" She smiled warmly. "My name is Sandra, and it is my joy to tell you of all the benefits of citizenship here in

Pike City. It's a *wonderful* city, and I just know you'll *love* living here."

She turned toward the portrait, and briefly bowed her head. "This is our Dear Mother, Margaret Williams, our Esteemed Chancellor. She leads the council which manages every aspect of life within our city, and with the help of our brave army, she keeps us all safe from the savages lurking in the mountains."

Sandra turned back toward the crowd and smiled. "Let us all recite our oath to Mother; if you don't know it, the verses are written on the residence maps you were given when you checked in." After a brief wait, while the captives retrieved their maps and found the verses, she said, "Everyone, say it with me."

"Oh, dear Mother, we strive daily to be worthy of your guidance.
We pledge our lives to you and are forever dutiful and faithful.
We pledge to serve you, the City Council, and the citizens of Pike City."

"We expect this oath to be spoken every morning before you leave for work." She stopped and stared pointedly at the crowd. "Every morning, without exception, it is expected."

A wide smile returned to Sandra's face. "Now, about your benefits; when you arrived a small computer chip was implanted in your palm. This chip entitles you to receive food and necessary goods at *any* dispensary within the city; although our bookkeepers would prefer that you withdraw only from those outlets nearest to your residence. Unfortunately, due to the war with the mountain savages, both food and supplies are strictly rationed; I'm sure you understand.

"And that brings me to the subject of your housing. I know that everyone here was among the 1,500 people who were freed from oppression in Flatiron. We are scattering you throughout the city; this is done for your sake, not ours; we believe it's best to integrate new arrivals into our society, rather than sequester them in little enclaves which might make you feel isolated and left out. Most of you will be located on the east side of town and will live in some wonderfully restored older homes. I'm sure you will all be very comfortable. We've tried to locate everyone's housing such that it's convenient to your work assignments, so you see, we considered your needs very carefully."

She stepped back from the edge of the stage, and her expression became grim. "But there are seditionaries among us who want to bring chaos and destruction to this last refuge of civilization. So, we must all remain vigilant, and report to the authorities the acts of those who intend to harm us." She pointed to the southwest corner of the park. "At every street corner in the city are little boxes we call Mother's Ears. You need only deposit a simple message with the name of the lawbreaker and the crime committed. Optionally, you may add your own name; if sedition is proven, and it usually is, you will receive a reward of more rations and possibly an even nicer place to live."

Sandra seemed to relax. "Again, welcome. If you have any trouble finding your new home, ask any citizen, I'm sure they will be pleased to help you."

With that, their orientation was complete.

*****

Liam left the park with Keith and Rose. "Only 1,500 of us made it?" he whispered. "We started with 2,500."

"Yes, and we're so lucky to have made it to this wonderful city!" Rose gave him a look of warning.

"Yeah, we were lucky all right," Keith added. "We should probably find a dispensary before we get to our quarters, otherwise we won't eat tonight."

"I just hope we can find our new homes," Rose said.

"I'll bet someone will help us." Keith glanced at a dark figure that had been shadowing them on the opposite side of the street. "Hello! Can you help us find our new homes?"

"Why yes, I can!" the man answered, then crossed the street toward them. "I'm Tom Jefferson, and it looks like we're all heading in the same direction, so let's walk together."

"Thanks, that's really nice of you," Liam said. The meeting seemed a bit contrived and too coincidental. Once Tom came into the light of a nearby streetlamp, he saw that the old man had a deeply lined face and walked with a stoop.

"Oh, it's no problem at all," Tom said. "Did I hear you say that you need to find a distribution center before turning in?"

Something was going on under the surface and it seemed like a good idea to play along. "Well, if we're going to eat tonight, we need to find food," Liam replied.

Tom was paging through each of their housing maps. "Looks like you're all neighbors. Your new digs are down south, near the corner of Moreno and Prospect." He grimaced, then shrugged. "It ain't a bad area, but not the best by any means. Anyway, there's a commissary over on Costilla Street that's right on your way. They'll have everything you need."

"Have you lived here very long?" Rose asked as they started walking together.

"Oh yeah, I have. I've been here since the start; I came south from Denver after the savages broke through our gates and slaughtered everyone. I was with Samuel right to the end; he was Dear Mother's husband. He was trying to save art at the museums before the heathens burned 'em down." Tom sighed and looked down. "He was such a wonderful leader before he was martyred. I don't think Dear Mother has ever recovered from her loss."

"That's so sad," Rose said. "It must have been terrible for her."

"Yeah," Tom muttered. "There's a statue of the great man in front of the City Council Building."

*****

The commissary windows blazed with welcoming light, while above them the abandoned tenement was eerily dark. "Joe and Crystal run this place, they'll treat you well," Tom said.

"Thanks," Keith answered. "I'll tell 'em you sent us."

Tom nodded. "You know, most of the apartments around here aren't set up for cookin', so a lot of us go down to the Last Lantern for dinner after work."

"Is that a restaurant?" Rose asked.

"Sort of, it's more of a pub though. Good times; folks bring their musical instruments and play." Tom smiled and pointed west. "It's down at the corner of Costilla and Tejon; you can't miss it. Carolyn runs that place; she's a great patriot."

"We'll definitely check it out," Keith said. "We're all starting at the motor-pool tomorrow, so we'll stop by after work."

"I'll see you then!" Tom smiled and waved as he turned west toward downtown.

Inside, the commissary consisted of only a long metal counter where they could place their order, behind which were rows of lightly stocked freestanding shelves that held a few clothing items and food that was packaged for long storage.

While he and Rose placed their orders, Keith stood aside and quietly spoke with the store owner. Their conversation was somewhat animated, and Liam wondered what was going on. Finally, an agreement of some sort was reached, and Keith returned to pay for his items with his palm chip.

The food they received at the commissary was not what any of them were used to. Each meal was sealed within an aluminum tray, and Crystal explained that the food would automatically warm up when the lid was removed. That seemed suspicious, and Liam wondered what chemical agent was used to heat their dinners, and what effect it might have on their health.

*****

They stood before a dilapidated three-story tenement. The plasti-wood structure was faded to a dark gray, the doors and windows appeared to be off-kilter, and the unbreakable Lexan windows were deeply scored by grit and dirt. The *wonderfully restored older homes* that Sandra had promised during their orientation had turned out to be vividly imagined propaganda.

"Well," Liam commented. "It will keep us dry at least."

"I doubt it," Rose replied. "But it isn't like we have a choice, so we'll just make the best of it."

They walked up the worn and sagging steps and entered the apartment building lobby. Broken mailboxes occupied an area beside the door, and a short hallway gave access to three apartments and a communal bathroom. A canted stairway then led them to the second floor, where they found their apartments, which were across the hall from each other.

"This is me," Rose said as she tentatively touched the door lever and glanced back over her shoulder.

"I'll go in with you," Liam said.

Rose sighed. "Thank you."

"I'll see you in our room when you're done," Keith said as he turned away.

A woman and two little girls waited inside Rose's room. The mother, who had brown hair and olive skin, stood protectively between the strangers and her children.

Rose gently approached her new roommates. "It's ok," she said. "We just arrived in the city, and we're assigned to this building. This is my brother Jack; he's staying across the hall."

The two children peeked at the strangers from behind their mother's long gray skirt. They had light brown hair and tan skin like their mother, and both appeared to be on the edge of starvation. The mother relaxed a bit. "My name's Lisa," she said, then rested her hand on the shoulder of the taller of the two girls. "This is Susy, and that's Sally."

"I have enough food for all of us tonight," Rose said. "Could we eat together?"

"You shouldn't be so free with your food," Lisa said. "It's hard to come by, especially if you're out of work."

"That's ok, we have job assignments, so we'll be fine," Rose answered.

Liam offered one of his prepackaged dinners. "Here, you can have one of mine too. I ate earlier today, so it's not a big deal," he lied.

The children gazed hopefully at their mother, who at last relented. "Oh, thank you. I'll find a way to pay you back, yes I will."

"Don't worry about it," Liam said gently. "I'll see you tomorrow, Sis." He gave his sister a kiss on the cheek before leaving.

*****

The dormitory across the hall was similar to the one he left behind. It was a barren place of bowed and worn plasti-wood floors and undecorated walls. Five metal frame beds with stained mattresses topped with rumpled blankets lined the back of the room. It was obvious that rain leaked around the windows because no one slept near them.

"Meet our new best friends," Keith smirked. Two worn and weary old men sat on adjacent beds in the back corner. Both had short gray hair and grizzled faces lined with age.

Liam paused; the men did not look friendly in the least. "Well, which bed is mine?"

"Whichever you want," one of the old men said. "I'm Joe, and that's Eric. So, your sister's stayin' with the whore across the hall?"

Liam was speechless for a moment. "Lisa seems nice to me."

"Suck it, Joe. Times are tough and she's gotta feed her young ones." Eric sighed and looked down.

"Sure, I guess," Joe replied. "Y'all come down here from Flatiron City eh?"

"Yeah, we did." Liam smiled, glad for the change in subject. "How long have you guys been here?"

"About a year; they brought us here after they sacked Pueblo," Joe stated, referring to a city that was 70 kilometers to the south. "They took us like they did you guys; came in and wrecked the place and marched us up here 'cause they needed workers."

"Careful Joe, there's ears in the room," Eric whispered, then nodded toward a small plastic box mounted high on the wall by the door.

106

"Fuck it, I don't much give a damn anymore."

"They'll crucify you."

"The old bat can do whatever the fuck she wants."

"I'm sure you're just havin' a bad day," Keith said lightly. "We should turn in; gotta be fresh for our new jobs tomorrow mornin'."

Chapter 10: Fitting In

Liam stood at the windows of his dormitory room, letting the early morning sunshine seep into his body. Summer had inevitably arrived; it was impossibly hot and thick humidity pressed relentlessly down upon the city. The air smelled like a musty armpit, and considering the soggy conditions, he wondered if mold was growing within his lungs.

Three months had passed since they had arrived in Pike City, and he still wasn't used to the oppressive feel of the place. Every citizen was continually monitored, and any seditious word or act was severely punished. No one had yet questioned his false identity of Jack Jones, so, for now, he was safe from discovery. It was best to remain hidden and unremarkable, because anonymous but useful cogs rarely get beaten into submission or painfully executed.

Upon arriving in the city, he had tested the government's methods by accusing Sergeant Mick of murdering 'Liam Collins'. Then, just a few days later he watched as the man was crucified in front of the City Council Building. Mick had been an evil man and deserved to be punished for his role in the execution of Clare and the Flatiron militia. Still, he took no satisfaction while listening to the man's agonized screams as rats and ravens tore at his body.

The experiment was not only an interesting check of the government's intolerance for sedition but also a sign of what would happen when they didn't get their way. It was apparent that the authorities had wanted him to work at their Technology Center, although he couldn't fathom why. After all, the Trappist-1 probe was the only project he had done for Pike City, and it was already complete. Whatever they were after must be important though, because they had responded with such extreme violence when they didn't get their way.

The crucifixion had also verified that all it would take to destroy someone was a simple accusation, this was good to know because it not only acted as a warning but provided possible opportunities as well. All aspects of life can be applied to strategy at some point, and he realized that Mother's Ears could eventually become a useful tool. There was no acrimony in what he had done to Mick, it was just an attempt to see how the city worked, and as an engineer, testing things was a large part of his job.

*****

At night their room was sticky and unpleasantly warm, and mosquitos often found their way inside, which made sleeping especially miserable. Their metal beds squeaked with even the slightest movement and the thin blankets were practically useless. Every morning they recited the Oath to Mother, making sure to be near the listening device beside the door. No one knew whether the government was checking on them, but it seemed best to not take chances. The words of the pledge didn't matter; truth and lies are the same when spoken, a simple disturbance of the air.

Liam and his sister rarely ate breakfast; they had lost much of their appetite after arriving in the city, possibly due to the excessive heat. Oddly enough, neither of them suffered any weakening or weight loss, so they shared their uneaten meals with those they knew were in need.

Lisa's husband had worked at the motor-pool but was killed by rebels while driving equipment south. Since then, she and her children struggled to get by on the basic rations the government supplied to the unemployed. With the additional food that Liam and Rose provided, Suzy and Sally appeared to be growing and gaining strength.

All of them had jobs in the motor-pool, and it was fairly easy work. Liam made deliveries of food and supplies to the commissaries in the area, while Keith and Rose spent their days repairing electric truck motors and recharging batteries; the city didn't have the benefit of the advanced technology of Bob Lyall's nuclear batteries because that research had been purchased by the Tribes. Fortunately, all of their duties placed them in positions where they could learn about the city and observe the activity within the motor-pool.

Something unusual was definitely going on somewhere far to the south. Several times a week heavily loaded trucks would leave the motor-pool and would return empty a week later; the returning vehicles frequently showed the scars of battle. High technology computer and power systems were being taken somewhere; but where and for what purpose? Liam knew that it was dangerous to ask, but curiosity got the best of him one day. "Where are you guys going?" he asked one of the drivers.

The man gave him a warning glance and shook his head. "Careful," he said. "There're some things you shouldn't ask. You get me?" Liam nodded and left the man alone. Whatever was going on down south was taking a lot of resources, so it must be very important, which made it a weakness that he might exploit.

Over the following days, he spent many sleepless nights wondering what the Socialists were working on, and also remembering what they had done to Flatiron City; the destruction, the executions, and the long walk. Those painful memories made him chafe at the injustice they had suffered. He could choose to either ignore the past and make the best of the present or seek revenge; in the end, he decided on the later. Fighting the government would be a dangerous business though, so he was inclined to keep his sister out of it.

One late afternoon on their walk home from work, he pulled both Rose and Keith aside in a lonely area where there didn't seem to be any listening devices. He squatted down to retie his boots at the side of an old broken-down building. "I've been thinking about what the Pike City Army did to our home, and the long walk afterward," he said cryptically. "And I've decided to do something about it, but it'll be risky, so you two shouldn't get involved."

Keith snickered. "Do you remember who I am, and who my friends are?"

"Huh," Liam grunted. "Yeah, I know, but I've also seen how the government tortures and executes people. Just be sure you know what you're getting into before you agree."

"I told you that I have a mission to bring this place down, and it kinda sounds like we're after the same thing," Keith said. "I've already made contacts, and got the equipment that Bob showed you how to use before we left home."

"Ok, that's good," Liam replied as he started to retie his second boot. "I'll need a safe place to make the changes to our chips though."

"Lisa has a private spot, it's where she takes her johns when she has to work," Rose said.

"I don't want to risk you being involved in this," Liam responded.

His sister stamped her foot and frowned. "Fuck that! I'm not a shrinking violet, I'm Rose, and roses have thorns."

*****

"It's up here," Lisa whispered as she guided them down the short second-floor hall and then up a seldom-used stairway that led to the vacant third floor. They stepped close to the edge of each riser hoping to make less noise, but the structure creaked nonetheless. "It's ok," Lisa reassured them. "No one ever notices when I take customers up here, and even if they do, no one cares."

Lisa steered them into the first apartment they came to, and Liam quickly searched for a listening device. "Looks clear," he said. The only furniture was a ragged and stained mattress laying on the floor in the center of the room, just looking at it filled him with a sense of hopeless despair. He went to Lisa and gave her a long hug, and whispered, "I'm sorry you've had to do this."

Lisa pulled away and smiled. "It's ok Jack. I do it to feed my girls, so I don't mind... too much."

"Let's see if we can do something about that," he replied.

Keith pulled a pouch from the inner pocket of his jacket. "This is what they gave me," he said. "Seems kinda weird, but only you can know if it's the right stuff."

Liam went to the nearest wall and sat down; the mattress might have been more comfortable but using it felt wrong somehow; Lisa weakly smiled at his choice. Inside the packet he found a pair of what looked like dark sunglasses that had a cute little wireless router built-in; so far so good. Next, he discovered a clear plastic suction cup and a pair of what seemed to be thick rubber gloves. He smiled. "This is perfect."

"Looks like garbage to me," Keith responded.

"That's why it's perfect," Liam answered. "It's all networked. I'll put the suction cup on your hand to connect to the chip, the glasses will act as a computer screen so I can see the internal code, and the gloves work like an old-fashioned keyboard. This is everything I need."

"If you say so," Keith said.

"My brother is *really* good with computers," Rose stated.

Keith nodded slowly. "So I've heard."

"Sit down Keith, I'll work on your chip first."

Keith sat cross-legged on the floor and extended his hand. "Guess I'm the guinea pig huh?"

Liam paused and frowned. "You know, I've heard that expression before, but have no idea what it means. What's a guinea pig?"

"It's not a pig at all actually," Rose said as she eased down beside Keith.

"It's a rodent, like a rat. They were imported from the African continent centuries ago. People sometimes used them to test drugs on." She glanced at Keith and smiled self-consciously. "I taught history, remember?"

Keith grinned in response, and Liam wondered if the blond athletic rebel was developing feelings for his sister. It had been months since he'd seen Becky, and Keith was unsure of her loyalties anyway, so being drawn into a new relationship seemed possible.

Liam attached the suction cup to Keith's palm, then powered the contraption up via the keyboard gloves. With the dark glasses in place the room disappeared, all he could see was the internal computer code as he watched the boot-up process. After about a minute, he began to chuckle. "Looks like a Primary School project at best."

"So, you can hack into it?" Rose asked.

"Oh yeah, no problem." Liam began to wiggle his fingers. "Increasing your food allocation is easy, but we don't want it to be tracked, so I'll make a little virus that will delete your transaction once it's complete." He chuckled again. "Whoever wrote this code was pretty brain dead."

"And you'll do mine too?" Lisa asked from the nearby mattress.

"Everybody gets an upgrade today, but it's not a good idea to get all your supplies close to home. Just check out what you normally get at the commissary over on Costilla; I'll set the code so it recognizes that location and doesn't download the deletion virus there. To get more food, just go to a different dispensary; if we do that it'll be really hard for anyone to figure out what we're doing. Does everyone understand?" He heard three voices murmur yes.

He wandered through the code for another minute. "Well, isn't that interesting; our palm chips are networked, the government's been using them to track our movements."

"That's not good," Keith said.

"Don't worry about it. I'll add some distortion and blackout areas." Liam chuckled. "This is actually kinda fun. Oh... look what I found, there's something more; give me a sec."

"My brother is in his element," Rose said.

"Yeah, I guess so," Keith answered.

Liam wandered through the city network and was amused that it wasn't protected with a passcode of some sort. "Keith remember this number: 27.174.293.67.3... you got that?"

"Yeah, why?"

"The local server farm has two external connections, but only one shows recent activity. We can connect to any of them through our palm chips. The number I gave you is the IP address for a remote server that hasn't been used for a long time."

"So? Are you gonna plant a virus or somethin'?" Keith asked.

"No, that'd be too obvious. It would get us caught and I'd prefer to put off the whole crucifixion thing as long as possible. What I'm doing right now is building a new database on the unused server. Your people can connect to the IP address I gave you, and that will open a secure line to the Tribes outside of the city. The ability to communicate is a much more powerful tool than just wrecking their network with a virus."

"Can we get caught?" Rose asked.

"Anything's possible, but it's really unlikely. The local IT folks haven't used this IP address for a long time; they won't know to look, so they won't find anything. I'll also encrypt our connection; Keith, I got another number for you, 2065, you got that? It's the encryption key; which also points away from us because it's the year the first commercial fusion reactor came online; if they suspect anyone, Ron will take the heat because all of his work was in the field of fusion reactors, remember?"

"Wow," Keith mumbled. "You know, you're one devious son of a bitch."

"Yeah, I guess so. Anyway, you're all set up. I'll do Rose next, then Lisa, and then myself." Liam smiled as he removed the dark glasses. "For safety and redundancy's sake I'll teach each of you guys how to connect to the network and send and receive messages; and Keith, you need to get this information to your contacts. Guys, this is our first step toward kicking their ass."

"What's your plan?" Keith asked.

"The long-game," he replied. "I've seen a lot of weakness in how the government's run, but I think the key to unwinding the whole place lies in what's going on down south. They're putting all their resources into whatever it is, and anything that important is a vulnerability."

*****

On most evenings, Liam and Keith went to the Last Lantern Pub after work. The music and ale were pleasant distractions, and the place reminded them both of the Hammer and Anvil back in Flatiron. It wasn't a good place to relax though, the pub was crowded with strangers, some of whom were probably spies working for the city government.

The Last Lantern was run by a woman named Carolyn, an exquisitely beautiful creature with long brown hair and dark enchanting eyes. She sometimes played the fiddle for her customers, then when other musicians were on-stage, she would circulate through the room lightly chatting with everyone. One evening she sat down on the bench beside Liam. "You're new here, aren't you?" she asked.

"Kind of," he answered.

"Been in the city long?"

"A few months," he answered cautiously.

"Did you come down with all the rest from Flatiron?"

The woman was up to something. "Yeah, my feet are still sore, but Pike City's nice," Liam lied. "By the way, I really enjoy your fiddle playing."

"Oh, you're so sweet to say that," she answered, then gently patted his thigh as she stood up. "I hope you'll come by again."

After she was gone, Keith shook his head slightly. "Be careful there."

Liam nodded in return. Carolyn might suspect something, but only time would tell.

*****

While they were at the pub, Rose usually spent her evenings at a local hospice and medical center. The only doctor in residence was overwhelmed with work, so she helped out by comforting the sick, dispensing medicine, and doing first-aid. In her position, she sometimes was able to steal vitamins, pain medication, and bandages which she brought home and gave to Lisa for her daughters. The nutritional value of the prepackaged meals was dubious, and the little girls needed all the help they could get.

One late night, Rose was waiting out in the hall when Liam and Keith got home. "Let's talk," she said and quietly ushered them into Lisa's room, then urged them to sit on an unused bed in the corner. "Something interesting happened at the clinic tonight." The children were already asleep, but before starting her story she turned toward their mother. "Lisa honey, you've been wonderful at keeping our secrets. We trust you, but you're going to learn a little more tonight."

"You guys have been so wonderful to me and my girls," Lisa replied. "Of course, you can trust me."

Rose smiled warmly, then turned to the men. "A guard that works at the Technology Center came in tonight; he has the flu and was in a pretty bad way." She rolled her eyes up toward the ceiling and rocked her head side to side. "I kinda flirted with him and learned some things."

"The flu?" Lisa asked. "Aren't you worried about getting sick? People can die from that."

"My brother and I have great immune systems, neither of us has been sick a day in our lives," Rose replied. "And the flu is only fatal when the patient is old or weak or doesn't get the right care; don't worry, your girls are in no danger."

"Ok." Lisa cautiously nodded.

"What did you learn?" Liam asked.

Rose turned back toward Lisa. "My brother was a scientist in Flatiron, and his real name is Liam Collins."

Lisa blinked and seemed stunned at the revelation. "Is your name fake too?"

"Yes honey, it is. I'm sorry for not telling you, but my name is Rose Collins. I taught history at Flatiron University."

"Oh," Lisa answered. "I won't tell anyone, especially the girls. At their age, they're not good at keeping secrets."

"I'm not a scientist, just an engineer," Liam corrected.

"Sure ok," Rose continued. "He was an *engineer* at the university. He did something with the navigation system for a space probe that went to some star that's really far away."

"I was working for Pike City then," Liam added.

"Yes, yes... shut up a minute, will you?" Rose shook her head in exasperation. "The guard said that Ron Castro is working on your project and he's getting nowhere with it."

"Not surprising," Liam responded. "Ron's a Materials Science guy, as far as coding goes, he couldn't find his ass even if he used both hands."

"Ron's in big trouble with his boss; some lady named Julee Garcia. Anyway, that navigation thing you did for them is a really, *really* big deal."

"Huh," Liam grumbled. "I wonder if this has anything to do with the technology that's being shipped south?" He thought a moment; every bit of new knowledge provides an opportunity.

"The deal Ron made to get sanctuary here included you," Rose said.

"What was he going to do, kidnap me?"

"Maybe, but I think that's why they were looking for you when they invaded," Rose answered.

"There may be a way to turn this to our advantage," Liam said. "Give me some time to think about it."

"Did you hear anything about Becky?" Keith asked.

"The guard mentioned that Ron's living with his sister. That's all I know, but she's probably fine."

Keith sat back and whispered, "I worry about her sometimes."

"She's probably better off than we are," Rose said.

*****

Joe was waiting for them when they returned home. Liam's mind was preoccupied, spinning with ideas of how to use what he had learned about Ron to their advantage, but was startled back to reality when Keith suddenly spoke.

"What happened to Eric?" Keith's voice had a dangerously hard edge to it. Liam instantly became alert and quickly glanced around the room. Eric was lying on his bed with a tangle of blankets pressed against his face. The body wasn't moving; it looked like he was dead.

"Eric caught on to what you guys are up to," Joe answered.

"And what's that?" Keith asked.

"Black market food, that's gotta be it." Joe stood up and walked toward them. "He was gonna report you to the guards, so I offed him for you."

Keith pointed to the listening device by the door. "They'll come for you now."

"Nah," Joe retorted. "That thing never worked. Kept that a secret 'til I knew what you folks were about."

Keith put his hands on his hips and stared at the body. "We'll have to do somethin' with that."

"Yeah, no problem," Joe said. "We can toss him off the roof. I've done it before. Ain't nothin' behind this place but an empty lot."

"Show us," Keith ordered.

"Sure, but everythin' has a price," Joe replied with a twisted grin. "I want in on whatever you're doing, otherwise I'll use Mother's Ears to report you; I'll tell 'em all about how you killed my best friend, poor old Eric."

"Yeah, ok," Keith answered. "There's more than enough to go around." He lifted Eric's lifeless body off the bed and threw it over his shoulder and walked to the door. "Now show us."

Joe led them up two flights of stairs to the roof. The lot behind their building was completely hidden from the street and tangled with weeds. Keith easily tossed the body over the edge and they all watched it fall.

"So, how're you guys workin' the scam?" Joe asked with a grin.

"It's pretty easy," Keith said as he turned toward their new conspirator. Then in a single rapid motion, Keith grabbed Joe's head and violently twisted, breaking his neck. A second later Joe's body was flung over the edge to join his onetime friend.

"Remind me to not get into a punching match with you," Liam said.

"Yeah, that wouldn't be a good idea. But I figured that I'd have to do somethin' about these guys sooner or later," Keith said as they descended the stairs.

*****

A plan was slowly forming in Liam's mind, but knowledge could sometimes be dangerous, so he kept his ideas to himself. He secretly accessed the city's databases through his palm chip and made a few subtle changes to their identities, jobs, and background clearances. A week later he and Rose were selected to drive in the next truck convoy south.

Over the next few nights at the Last Lantern, Carolyn became much friendlier, confirming his suspicions about her government allegiance. The revelation made him sad though, she was a lovely and engaging woman, and it was a pity to have to count her among his enemies. Every circumstance can be turned into a tool though, and he realized that his feigned ignorance of her subterfuge could be useful later.

Chapter 11: South

"Looks like we gotta couple newbie drivers with us for this run." The Dock Foreman wiped the sweat from his bald head with an already damp rag. What hair he did have was cut short and it appeared that he hadn't shaved in at least a week. He was sloppily dressed and grossly overweight, which was unusual because so many in the city were starving.

Liam and Rose stood with a group of other men and women under a wide metal awning beside four unloaded big-rig trucks. The corrugated roof amplified the heat and in combination with the humidity, just breathing took an extra effort.

"You think this is miserable weather? Just wait, you ain't seen nothin' yet," a big rough looking woman with blonde hair said.

"Shut up Peggy," the Foreman cautioned. "They don't know where we're goin' yet."

The size of the big-rigs was intimidating; they dwarfed the huge flatbed military vehicles that were used against Flatiron, and Liam's delivery van looked like a child's toy next to them. He had never piloted anything so large before, and Rose had never driven at all, so taking the job was a huge risk. Of course, neither the Foreman or the other drivers knew of their inexperience, but considering that the trucks all ran on electric motors and had automatic transmissions, Liam figured they could handle it.

"You two are on the roster today 'cause you passed the background check and you've been workin' here for a while," The foreman continued. "Drivin' south is the highest security job in the city; no one knows, and no one will *ever* know where we're goin' or what we're delivering. Telling anyone about any of it will get you chained to the cross and eaten by the birds, you get that?" The fat man glared at them both for a long moment.

"We understand," Liam said, answering for them both.

"Ok then. Just so you know, we'll be taking some flack along the way from the savages, but we'll have an army escort and the truck cabs are as secure as we can make 'em," he shook his head. "But them fuckin' railguns are tough; they're bad news."

"I saw a military flatbed get cut in half by one of those," Liam said.

"Yeah, them fuckers mean business. All I can tell you is to just keep your head down and hope for the best." The foreman paused for a moment. "It's nasty work, but the pay's good and you get extra days off. So, go home and get some sleep everybody, 'cause we'll be drivin' straight through; the project's nearly done and Mother wants it finished and buttoned up pronto. Now get the hell outta here, and I'll see you in two days."

*****

"Why'd you get me mixed up in this?" Rose asked as she paused along their walk home to retie her boot laces. "I hate these things," she mumbled. "Whoever thought that plastic shoelaces were a good idea ought to have their head examined."

"Everything comes down to a choice." Liam smiled and knelt down beside her. "We could keep our heads down and try to play nice in hopes that we'll somehow get out of this mess alive, or we could do something to avenge what they did to us in Flatiron and then escape and be on our own.

"Right now, we're stuck between two sides that are set on killing each other," Liam continued. "The Tribes *might* be better than the Socialists, but there's no way of knowing for sure. What I'm certain of, is that this city is a death trap and we need to bring it down and get away. Something important is happening down south, and we need to learn what it is because I feel it's the key to finally ending the wars forever."

"But why not have Keith go with you on this drive instead of me?"

"You said you wanted in... you have thorns, remember?"

"Yes, I suppose I did," his sister answered. "It's one thing to think about it, but another to really get involved and know that people will be shooting at me."

"I know," he said. "Keith has ties to the rebels, so he needs to stay here and keep the line of communication open. When we get back, he has to be under no suspicion so he can make a report." He thought for a moment, then sighed. "I need you to come with me so you can tell Keith what we learn, in case I get picked up after we get back."

Rose stared at him. "There's a chance of that?"

"More than a chance, It's part of the plan."

"But we gave false names when we came here; my last name is the same as yours, won't I get in trouble too?"

"I changed your last name to 'Smith' when I hacked our records, so you'll be fine."

"Ok big brother," Rose said softly. "You've always looked out for me, so I'll trust you again."

*****

The next night, Liam sat alone at the bar at the Last Lantern. He was deliberately staying away from Keith and Rose, who was at a table near the stage listening to the band. For his plan to work, both of them needed to be completely free of suspicion, and yet he had stupidly placed his sister in jeopardy; he hoped that wasn't a mistake.

Changing her name at the last minute was dangerous. When they first arrived, he had no plans to bring down the city, so taking on identities not associated with the university seemed to be all that was necessary to maintain their safety. To disable the government and derail whatever was going on in the south required facing danger and even risking death. What he was about to do was his decision, and he wanted none of its shadow to fall upon his sister or their friend.

"Well hey there!" Carolyn's soft and sultry voice called.

He smiled and turned toward her. "Hey there yourself."

"If you keep nursing that ale all night, you'll put me out of business!" She sat down beside him then playfully laid her head onto his shoulder. "But that's ok, you're so handsome that all the girls will wanna buy you a drink."

He laughed and looked around. "Yeah, there's a line forming around here somewhere."

Carolyn smiled. "It's good to see you tonight, but I hear you'll be away for a while."

How did she know? That confirmed her ties to the government, and he realized that he was being tested. "Yeah, I'm doing some overtime at the motor-pool, and will probably be so tired after work that I'll just stagger back to my nest and pass out."

"Well, if you can manage it, I hope you'll stop by."

"I'll try." He glanced at Carolyn and smiled. She was an exquisitely beautiful woman, but the problem was that she used it too much to her advantage. "Are you going to play your fiddle for us tonight?"

"Maybe, would you like to hear me play?"

"I would." Now was the time to bait his trap. "Music is a special thing; there's a mathematical precision to it that mimics the heartbeat of the universe." He had thought about how to gently arouse suspicion about his identity for a long time; it had to be subtle, and just enough to hint that he was more than he appeared. If his bait was too heavy-handed, they would arrest him before he went south, and he believed it was critical to know what was going on down there. Hopefully, Carolyn would wonder about what he said and would mention it to her handlers after he left.

"That's such a beautiful thing to say," she said with a slight frown.

He grinned in return, hoping that the hint he provided was just enough.

*****

Liam stood in the open lot of the motor-pool beneath a hard-white sky that was painful to his eyes; the heat that fell from it had a weight that threatened to push him straight into the ground. Beside him was a line of big-rig trucks attached to long flatbed trailers, each loaded with a massive fusion reactor.

The power plants were Ron Castro's work. While gazing at them he wondered why the traitor felt it was necessary to destroy Flatiron rather than just travel to Pike City on his own? The Technology Center would certainly have employed him, why did so many people have to die?

Rose had arrived earlier and was running through a checklist beside one of the trucks. Liam deliberately walked to a different vehicle and began to stow his jacket and a change of clothes inside.

"Hold on Jack!" the Foreman said as he waddled across the yard. "You and Sarah are newbies, so I want you two together and drivin' at the center of the pack."

"Ok boss," Liam said and began retrieving his gear.

"This could get rough," the Foreman muttered. "The savages will probably hit you in Santa Fe, Trinidad, and maybe even Pueblo. The army beat them fuckers outta Pueblo a bunch of times, but they're like fuckin' cockroaches and keep comin' back."

"What do we do if that happens?"

"Keep your head down and keep goin'. Let the military take care of 'em, that's their job." The big man stepped back and glanced around suspiciously. "This is a critical delivery. If somethin' goes wrong the old

122

woman will have us all on the cross."

*****

The cab of the truck was longer than it was wide; to start their journey Liam sat in the single forward driver's seat, and Rose took the slightly elevated position in the rear. The batteries were charged and the low hum of the electric truck motors filled the air as they waited for their military escort to take up positions around them. "I wonder how long we'll be gone?" he asked idly.

"I was told two days each way," Rose replied. "That means we'll have to stop to either recharge or pick up new batteries somewhere in the middle."

"Huh," he grunted while tapping his ear to indicate there might be a listening device in the cab.

"Yes, I've been thinking about that too," Rose replied cryptically. "I've checked the equipment, so I think we'll be ok."

They both slipped their radio headgear on and waited. The forward military vehicles slowly moved out, and like tumbling dominos, the rest of the group followed. Peggy's rough voice suddenly grated in his ear. "Keep it tight assholes, it's a long ride and it ain't gonna be easy."

Liam gently applied the accelerator and closely followed the truck in front of him through the south city gate. The roadway was cracked and buckled in places but he managed to keep up and move with the rest of the convoy onto the ancient interstate highway. As the city wall fell back into the distance, rolling grasslands opened up ahead. It was an empty landscape with scarcely any sign of the destruction of war.

As a group, they kept a brisk pace and arrived at the outskirts of Pueblo roughly an hour and a half after starting out. "Catchin' some flak up here," a male voice said in Liam's ear. "Second drivers, keep your heads down; this could get nasty."

Rose leaned forward in her seat and ducked down behind him. "How can the resistance be so close to Pike City?" she whispered.

Liam was concentrating on staying close behind the truck in front of them but managed to cover his headset microphone with one hand. "Maybe the rebels are more of a threat and are closer than the government admits."

There was a sudden pop as a small projectile punched right through the cab. "Shit, shit, shit," he said as he leaned forward onto the steering wheel.

"Number 3, are you hit?" Peggy's voice sounded in his ear.

He glanced back and saw that Rose was unhurt. "We're good; just a little added ventilation."

"It's about time you lost your virginity." Peggy laughed. "Keep it tight; the road takes a couple of sharp turns ahead."

"T-12 falling back," a male voice stated. His designation indicated that he was in the rear military vehicle. "Gonna rip 'em a new one, that way they won't bug us on the way home. I'll catch up with you guys in Holbrook."

"T-1 here. Catch you at the recharge buddy," the lead military vehicle answered.

The convoy stayed tight and moved fast until they passed by the ancient steel mill that was south of Pueblo and at last escaped the city. "That was pretty scary," Rose said when she finally sat back up in her chair.

"You'll be all right honey," Peggy's voice somehow managed to sound gentle. "We still got a couple of nasty spots ahead, but just keep your head down and you'll be fine."

*****

The landscape north of Trinidad was scarred with the shattered vestiges of buildings and the rusted remains of ruined vehicles. Warfare had so destroyed the area that nothing grew there; sand dunes lined the sides of the old roadway and blowing scree obscured their path in places. Given enough time, would the entire Earth resemble this place? Humankind had taken paradise and rebuilt it in their own image, mirroring the chaos and destruction that lay at the depths of their soul.

"Tighten it up. It could get nasty when we roll through town," Peggy said over the intercom.

"Nearly a hundred years ago, a war was fought right here," Rose said quietly as she looked through the side window.

"You're right Sarah," Peggy answered. "It was the battle for the La Veta Pass, the quickest way south into New Mexico. It was a nasty business."

"Over a million-people died right here in a single day," Rose said quietly.

"I recall learnin' about that when I was a kid." Peggy's voice faltered a moment, but then her bravado returned. "If you're one for believin' in ghosts, keep your windows rolled up."

Trinidad was a charred ruin, and contrary to predictions, the convoy experienced no problems passing through. To the south, the road wandered up into the mountains and the trucks all slowed and strained under the weight of their loads. The steep slope had many tight turns, and Liam worked hard to keep pace with the more experienced drivers. "Keep it movin'," Peggy instructed. "Go slow as you need to, but don't stop 'cause you'll never get your rig goin' again."

It took nearly an hour to reach the top of the pass, and Liam sighed with relief when they finally began their descent into what was once New Mexico.

"We're kinda safe up here on the hill so put some distance between your trucks," Peggy instructed. "And stay off the brakes as much as you can; those suckers can heat up; a couple of months back one of our rigs caught fire, so only use 'em when you need to."

It was a long twisting way down. A fire had swept through the area sometime long ago; charred stumps still dotted the mountains while younger trees struggled at the edges of the road. The old highway wound through the hills, following the course of a river that flowed by many broken and forgotten towns. What had it been like to live in those places so long ago? Had they known and appreciated the paradise around them? Probably not. No treasure is ever valued until it's lost.

*****

"We had some trouble in Santa Fe the last time we came through," Peggy said. "The army kicked their ass, so we oughta be fine, but let's tighten it up, 'cause you never know."

All hell broke loose when they came around the final turn into the city. Liam saw flashes at each side of the road, and flame shot into the air at the front of their column. The lead trucks swerved to the sides of the road as smoke and dust from their tires filled the air and made it difficult to see. "Keep goin', keep goin'," Peggy shouted. "Stay right and follow me!"

One of the lead military vehicles was broken and burning on the left side of the road. The heat of the fire was so intense that Liam felt his skin singe as they passed by. None of the trucks slowed down and the fighting was quickly behind them.

Once south of Santa Fe, they drove out of the mountains down a long straight slope toward the abandoned city of Albuquerque. "All our rigs made it, and I think we're in the clear now," Peggy said. "But keep the hammer down 'til we get to the city just to be on the safe side."

An impossibly hot wind rushed uphill toward them and buffeted their vehicles. The entire area was all hard edges; ancient jagged peaks surrounded crumbling skyscrapers that leaned oddly and seemed on the verge of collapse. Everything was colored in shades of tan, white, and gray. Nothing could live here, even cacti couldn't survive the extreme heat.

"Ok, we all made it. A couple of our tanks stayed behind to pound them assholes back into the stone age. Nothin' is gonna be left of Santa Fe but burning rubble, so we ain't gonna have problems on our way home." Peggy sounded relieved. "It's all clear from here on; the savages always keep to the mountains 'cause it's too fuckin' hot for 'em to live in the desert."

The convoy turned west when they reached Albuquerque, and Liam wondered how anyone could ever live in such a baked and awful place. Rose suddenly spoke up, as if sensing his question. "This area has always been a desert, but it was cooler before the sun started acting up." He heard her sigh behind him. "It's still a marvel though, isn't it?"

"It's sad that we've lost so much of ourselves," he replied.

In his mirror, he saw his sister staring out through the side window. "It's all gone, and it's never coming back," she said.

*****

Rose fell asleep as night claimed the desert. Chatter among the drivers had ceased, and nothing much happened as the convoy thundered across the dark dreary landscape. Boredom is often a privilege though; the spacing between the trucks lengthened, and he managed to relax a bit. Bright stars twinkled in the clear uncluttered sky; at night, the bleak and barren wilderness became a silent and beautiful place.

After nearly 20 hours on the road, the caravan finally turned off the highway. Holbrook was a small fortified town in the middle of nowhere. Describing it as a 'town' was a bit of a stretch though because fewer than ten people lived there. While waiting outside his truck for fresh batteries to be installed, he listened to the sand whisper across the rocky hills around them, it was a peaceful but lonely sound.

Liam napped in the rear seat as Rose drove them further south through a low range of dusty mountains. When he awoke the next morning, they were passing through Phoenix. Huge manufacturing plants lined both sides of the wide road they followed; it appeared that colossal structural members and metal plating were being formed there. Beyond the factories there wasn't much left of the city, it was a baked and desiccated place, like a rotted body that had been left out in the sun.

The oppressive heat was starting to ease as they approached the port city of Yuma. The docks were busy, and he watched as some barges were being loaded and others were pulled away by tugboats heading toward waiting cargo ships. Structural metalwork from Phoenix, along with powerplants and computers from Pike City were being shipped further south, and Liam had a good idea where everything was going. He nodded slowly; the pieces fit, and he began to see a way to bring down the Socialists.

*****

Two days later, Liam stood on the Yuma dock enjoying the cool breeze off the ocean while sipping at a bottle of water. "It's gotta be hell down where you're goin'," he said casually to a Boatswain as he walked by.

The dark-skinned man paused and frowned. "Yeah, sure."

"Isola Isabela... off the coast of Ecuador, right?"

The Boatswain nodded. "Why you ask?"

"No reason. It's no big deal and I gotta get back to my rig." Liam shrugged. "Try to stay dry, eh?"

The tough-looking Hispanic man chuckled. "Sure thing."

He pulled Rose aside before they got back inside their truck. "Keith needs to know that the cargo's being delivered to the Space Elevator in Ecuador."

"Space Elevator? Is there such a thing?"

"Yeah, it was built a long time ago by the old USA. It's really just a huge carbon-nanotube cable attached at the equator with a counterweight in high orbit. My guess is that they're building something very big up there." Liam glanced around to be sure no one was watching. "Remember Lucy?"

"Sure, your spacefaring girlfriend." Rose smiled.

"While designing her, I thought it was strange that with the war going on, that Pike City wanted to send a probe into outer space; but now I understand. They're bugging out and heading for Trappist-1. They know that sooner or later the Tribes will overrun their city, so they're leaving before it happens."

"Should the rebels try to stop them?"

"Maybe, but I don't know anything about fighting a war. This project is a big deal though; if we use this knowledge right, we might be able to bring down Pike City without too many people getting killed."

"How?"

Liam frowned. "It'll be complicated, but I'm sure it can be done. Give me some time to think it through and come up with a plan."

*****

Liam drove first during their return home, and without the worry of attack and with Rose asleep behind him, there was plenty of time to consider the possibilities. He didn't know what to do with what he had learned. One thing was certain though, he needed to insert himself into the Pike City engineering group. That was the only place he could learn more, and possibly find a way to stop the Socialist's departure and destroy their government.

What would happen if he succeeded? The Tribes appeared to be just as violent as the Pike City Army. With nowhere else to go, could he and Rose get away and find a place to live alone in the mountains? That didn't seem like a good idea. The paradise of Flatiron was burned and buried, so once Pike City was gone there were no other choices. But maybe whatever was being built in orbit could be seized, and they might escape with some of the survivors of their former home.

There were too many options, too many possibilities, and too many ways that any plan might go wrong. It wasn't time yet to set anything in motion. All he could do was get inside the city's engineering group and hope that an opportunity would present itself.

Chapter 12: Back Home

It was odd to feel relief when they returned to Pike City; just how their prison had become a home was a little confounding. They pulled their flatbed trucks into the motor-pool and parked next to each other, then amid groans and complaints of stiff bodies, everyone grabbed their gear and got out.

Liam looked up into the hard-white sky and let the pounding rain wash over his tired body. He smelled bad and his clothes were so stiff with grime and sweat that they may have been able to walk back to his dorm room by themselves. "You know what I miss?" he asked rhetorically as he stood alongside his sister. "Soap and toothpaste."

Rose laughed. "I'd add deodorant to your list." She sighed. "I also miss going out and dancing with my friends."

"Yeah, I miss our old life too," he whispered.

"All right!" the foreman shouted as he emerged from his office. "Good job everyone! Four went out, and all four came back. I won't say that's a first, but it's been a while." He clapped his hands loudly. "Now go home and get some sleep. I'll see you all back here in three days!"

Rose paused to wait for him, but he shook his head. "You go ahead, and remember what I said to tell Keith. Also, be sure he checks our secret database; if I get held up, I'll stay in touch that way." His sister returned a worried look, then nodded and walked away.

A group of soldiers was waiting outside the motor-pool gate. With a sigh of apprehension, he slung the bag of dirty clothes over his shoulder and casually walked toward them. The game was on, and all the pieces were finally in play.

"Liam Collins," a rough-looking soldier wearing Sergeant's bars said; it wasn't a question.

He smiled. "That's me."

"I bet you thought you'd get away with foolin' us, eh?"

"I think I did, at least for a while." He chuckled. "So, where are we going?"

The Sergeant clenched his fists and quickly strode forward. The man's size was intimidating, and Liam tensed in anticipation of an attack. "You motherfucker, for what you did to Mick..." the soldier muttered through gritted teeth. "It's a good thing for you that Mother wants you intact; you'd best hope that she doesn't change her mind."

"Well, either she will or she won't; there's nothing much I can do about it either way."

"Enough of this fuckin' raw-jawing. You're comin' with us."

"Of course, I am." At the edge of his eye, he saw Rose standing on the sidewalk; she watched as he was led away.

*****

Four soldiers hurriedly marched him along Tejon Street. Two of the men gripped his upper arms in an assertion of authority, but it was all for show; he had no chance of escape because any one of them could easily run him down and beat him into a puddle of bloody meat. They led him past the People's City Council Building, then Acacia Park, and finally brought him to the People's Technology Center, which was about a half kilometer south of the city's northern gate. The tech center was a narrow four-story stucco building with balconies on the longer sides and a flat roof.

The guards shoved him through tall glass doors into a comfortable carpeted lobby with colorful paintings decorating the walls. A smiling receptionist made a call as Liam anxiously stood by her desk still surrounded by large angry men. After an uncomfortable wait, a short woman with chocolate-colored skin and dark hair streaked with gray arrived. "Ok gentlemen, I'll take it from here."

"He might try to get away," the Sergeant protested.

"I promise I won't." Liam grinned and turned toward the soldiers. "You can go now boys."

The men tensed and two of them moved slightly forward. "Gentlemen, he's with me now," the short woman said. "You can go." The men turned away in unison and marched toward the door.

"You don't seem to be very good at making friends." She held out her hand. "I'm Julee Garcia, the Director of the Technology Departments here."

"It's nice to meet you, Julee." He shook her hand. "As far as making friends go, it seems to me that people will either like me or hate me, and I won't lie to manipulate their reaction."

"Ok, that's good to know," Julee bobbed her head. "False amenities are only necessary for politics anyway. What we do here is innovate within our chosen fields; as long as you're productive you'll do fine."

"That sounds good to me," he replied.

"You hid from us though... why?"

"Your army killed my parents and destroyed my home. Why should I willingly help you?"

Julee smiled, and he was surprised by the sadness in her expression. "You're very honest, and I like that. Let's go up to my office and talk."

She took him to an elevator that brought them up to the fourth floor. From there they walked down a long central hallway, and finally, she led him into an office on the east side of the building. "Sit down Liam. I have some questions about your work in Flatiron, and we need to talk about how you'll fit in here."

"Ok." He sat in a chair facing Julee's desk. "I designed the computer architecture and wrote the program to plot a course from Earth to the Trappist-1 system through N-Space."

She eased down behind her desk and stared at him thoughtfully. "What happened to your work?"

"Your army blew it up along with our university."

"So, it's lost, but can you recreate it?"

"Yes, I can. It's not a small job though and I'll need custom hardware; traditional computers can't handle anything more than three dimensions, but plotting a course through N-Space requires simultaneous computations in twelve."

Julee nodded slowly. "You designed the operating system for the space probe as well, didn't you?"

"Yes." He smiled. "She's a self-aware intelligence."

"Artificial intelligence; isn't that what you mean to say?"

"No. Artificial *stupidity* might apply to those goons that brought me here... but even that might be a stretch." He saw Julee quickly smile before her stony expression returned. "Intelligence just is. There's no natural or artificial distinction."

"The probe's intelligence is artificial because you created it."

"Are we artificially intelligent because we went through school? Things can be learned, but only applied through thoughtful consciousness. What you're doing is confusing knowledge with intelligence. A computer can know how to do something, but it has to be told to do it. With consciousness comes intelligence, and the ability to make decisions on our own."

Julee leaned back in her chair. "I didn't expect a philosophical discussion, but ok, you win. I still need to know where your loyalties lie though. Do you support the mountain savages or the rightful government of our country?"

"We could argue whether we even have a country anymore, but I don't see much point in that." Liam looked down at his hands and thought a moment. "I was a citizen of Flatiron, and although naive, I believed in our neutrality. We worked for both sides and fulfilled contracts without bias; it was work that we did to keep the peace. Then your army came and killed my family and friends, but maybe the Tribes would have done the same thing eventually. Both sides are bad, and I don't want any part of your war, that's why I kept my identity a secret."

Julee sighed, then leaned forward to turn on her computer monitor. She gazed at the screen for a moment, then blinked and shook her head. "You arrived here with two friends, Keith Johnson and Sarah Smith, didn't you?" she asked quietly. "I hate doing this, I really do, but for the sake of their safety you must work for us."

Liam leaned back in his chair and closed his eyes. He had expected her threat, but it was down toward the 'worst-case scenario' end of the list. At least they didn't suspect that Sarah was actually his sister. Still, he didn't want to agree too quickly. "What will you do to them?"

"Nothing, as long as you work for us."

"What will I be working on?"

Julee carefully gazed at him for a long moment, and he wondered if she suspected that he knew about their escape plans. "We're sending more probes to Trappist-1, and we need your navigation system again," she finally said. "These are larger vessels, and from what Ron has told us, the old course you plotted won't work, so we need a new one."

"Huh," he grunted thoughtfully. "Our universe is in constant motion, and N-Space is actually a series of parallel universes that are also in flux. Actions in one affect the other. Time is also a factor because it's non-linear... there are literally quadrillions of calculations to make, and their output, which is the navigation course, is only good for a specific span of time. If used early or late, there's no telling where you would end up. You could materialize inside a black hole, or the other side of the universe, or show up last Thursday on the moon."

Julee rubbed her forehead and closed her eyes. "Your work is crucial for our project. You'll be working for Ron and he'll get you every resource you need."

"And my friends will be safe... that has to be a guarantee."

"Yes."

"I'll keep my current quarters then," he said. "If anything happens to them, my work stops. Do you understand?"

"Yes, I do. But do *you* understand that if there is even a hint of sabotage, your friends will be given to Mother's Nurse for Treatment and will die *very* painfully."

"I don't know who this nurse is, but I get your point." He smiled ruefully. "The mercy of your city knows no bounds. I'll work for Ron and do everything he tells me to, as long as my friends remain safe."

"We'll take Sarah off convoy duty because it's too dangerous," Julee said as she stood up. "So, do we have a deal, Liam?"

He got up and took her hand. "Yes, we do."

*****

Liam left the institute without an army escort, but he suspected that he was followed. The rain had ceased, leaving the streets peaceful and quiet. The blocks passed in silence other than the clicking of his plastic boot heels on the still damp sidewalk. There was a lot to think about, but the meeting with Julee had drained his mental resources and all he wanted to do was mindlessly stroll along.

He hesitated outside the Last Lantern, then went inside on a whim. Maybe an ale would calm his nerves and somehow help make sense of the shit storm he had willingly walked into. He ordered a stout ale at the bar and took a long sip; damn, it tasted good.

Carolyn abruptly appeared at his side. "Looks like you had a rough trip south."

It was interesting that she admitted knowing where he had gone. "Nah, it wasn't bad. Almost everybody made it back ok." He took another sip of ale and made a decision. "I should tell you something, my name really isn't Jack Jones. I'm Liam Collins, and I worked at the University in Flatiron."

Carolyn straightened up on her barstool. "Really? I had no idea."

He watched the attractive woman closely; she was a skilled liar. "Yeah, they picked me up at the motor-pool and brought me to the tech center; it looks like I'll be working there from now on."

"Well... that's great news, isn't it? I mean, you'll be out of the heat, and maybe they'll give you a nicer place to live." Carolyn paused. "Did your friends, I mean Keith and Sarah, do they know who you really are?"

"No, they have no idea. I met them on the walk down here from Flatiron City. I guess I'll have to find a way to break it to them... and hope they don't get too mad."

*****

His apartment was empty when Liam returned home; he hesitated a moment as panic flooded his mind, but then returned to the hall and knocked on the door to Rose and Lisa's room.

Keith answered, and grinned. "You made it!"

"Yeah, but everyone in the government knows that I'm Liam now."

Rose slowly walked toward him. "They know?"

"They only know about me. And I've got a new job at the tech center." He went to his sister and pulled her into a hug. "It's ok, you're safe," he whispered in her ear.

*****

The next morning, Ron met him in the tech center lobby. The muscular tanned man shook his hand vigorously. "What the hell did you think you were doin'?" Ron asked. "We need you here."

Liam shrugged in response, feeling unsure of what to say to the man whose betrayal had destroyed a city and killed thousands. "Where do I work, and what do you want me to do?"

"Ok, sure," Ron replied excitedly. "Let's go upstairs; we can talk there."

They rode the elevator to the third floor, and Ron led him through a set of fortified steel doors into a large room filled with shoulder-high partitions. He heard rustling sounds and realized that other workers were hidden within the cubicle maze. It was a bland space colored in gray and blue hues, but it had a sweeping view of the city and the western mountains through floor to ceiling windows that spanned the entire rear wall. Liam smiled when he noticed that a glass door led outside to a wide balcony. "Nice place."

"Only the best!" Ron seemed energized, almost manic in his movements. "There's coffee... *real coffee* available down the hall in our breakroom. There's also tea if you prefer. I've given you a desk by the window so you can enjoy the view, but we can't back off much. What we're workin' on is critical Liam... *critical*." As he spoke Ron had led him to his workstation, which consisted of just a wide shelf and a computer that was at least 20 years old.

"Old equipment," Liam said. "That won't work for the navigation system Julee wants me to design."

"The schedule's tight Liam. We're workin' on somethin' that'll change the world... no, change the entire future of mankind. But we got a deadline, so there's no time or resources available for fancy new computers."

"Ron, I'm telling you that it won't work. I need a quantum computer, like the one I designed in Flatiron." He pointed to the machine on the counter. "That thing isn't much more than a doorstop, I doubt it will do anything beyond basic math. If you want to send probes to Trappist-1 and not have them end up inside a black hole, I'll need better equipment."

"There's no need Liam. In *my* department, we do more with less, and the work is almost done anyway, all you need to do is some bug-fixes and solve a few problems."

Liam smiled and shrugged. "Ok, I'll do whatever you say." He knew that what Ron claimed was impossible, and considered how he could turn his boss's incompetence into an advantage.

*****

The programming code he was asked to debug was even more primitive than expected. Trying to solve a 12-dimensional problem with 3-dimensional thinking was simply not going to work. Still, Liam played the role of a drone and did as he was told. To destroy the government's plans, all he needed to do was step aside and watch them fail on their own.

He didn't believe Julee's story about sending more probes to Trappist-1; undoubtedly the real goal was to send people there. The Socialists wanted to get away from the Tribes and find a new home, but he wondered how many they intended to send; probably not many by the look of things. It took a tremendous amount of energy to shift the frequency of even a tiny mass so that it could enter N-Space, and the fusion reactors he had driven down to Yuma were inadequate for anything bigger than a large truck. But maybe he wasn't seeing the whole picture, there might already be a thousand tiny ships in orbit powered by Ron's reactors for all he knew.

The work was easy, so much so that he spent most of his day sipping tea and enjoying the city view through the window. He corrected errors in the code and created a few new functions that might get the ships shifted into N-Space and go someplace, what he couldn't do was predict where that would be. A month after he started working at the institute, Julee Garcia stopped by to check on him. "How's everything going Liam?"

He shook his head and chuckled. "The computer system you're using is too primitive to run the navigation calculations," he replied. "I'm trying to get it set up to send your probes somewhere... but in this environment, I can't predict where that'll be."

Ron was hovering nearby. "Liam has everything he needs. He just has to innovate."

"If you ask me to throw a rock and hit the moon, no matter how much I innovate, just using my arm won't work," Liam replied. "If you want to reach Trappist-1, give me the tools I need to make that happen."

"Liam is sabotaging us," Ron stated.

His boss's accusation put his friends in danger. "No, in fact, I'm not. What I'm doing is patching up some pretty horrific code. I've made a bunch of improvements, but this thing..." Liam tapped the side of his computer terminal. "This thing has the mind of a tick, and you're asking me to teach it quantum mechanics."

Julee nodded slowly. "Ok. You've solved this problem before, so I'm inclined to trust your judgment. There's too much at stake to make a half effort. I still have to look at resources though, so do the best you can with what you have for now, and I'll get back to you later."

*****

Almost every night after work Liam went to the Last Lantern for dinner. Over the past weeks, Carolyn had become increasingly friendly and would often dine with him. She was a beautiful woman but was of the type that usually didn't hang around with computer geeks; but against his better judgment, and regardless of his suspicions about her loyalties, he grew increasingly fond of her.

One night she asked, "What are you working on at the institute?"

He became instantly wary. "Just accounting stuff. Gotta make sure everyone gets enough of these great plastic boots!"

Carolyn laughed. "With your pay raise, I bet you have enough credits on your chip to buy better shoes." After that she let the subject drop.

*****

Rose and Keith had moved into the third-floor area that Lisa had once used to service her johns. They sometimes stopped by the Lantern in the evening, but Liam kept their interaction friendly and casual. In public nothing was said of the project he was working on, or his plans to derail it. Those conversations were reserved for later in the evening when they all returned to their rooms.

They met him in the hallway one night just as he got home. "Got a sec?" Keith asked.

"More than that, I've got all night." Liam led them into his room. "What's up?"

"I got orders to lower morale in the city." Keith sat down on an unused bed. "Any ideas?"

"Yeah, actually there's something I've been thinking about for a while now. Remember our orientation, when they told us about Mother's Ears?"

"Most people call them snitch boxes," Rose said.

He nodded. "Good name, and I think it's about time we used them."

"How?" Keith frowned.

Liam sat down on his bed and leaned forward to rest his elbows on his knees. "Remember Mick, the Sergeant that captured us in Flatiron? All it took was my accusation to get him crucified." He smiled. "Have your people drop messages in the snitch boxes that accuse officials and government workers of being tied in with the Tribes. Start slowly though, because if it's a landslide it'll all be ignored."

"Yeah, that might work," Keith said. "They're askin' for more than that though; they want you to stop the Socialist's plans to getaway. The Tribes want 'em all dead."

"The ones running the tech center are doing a good job of that by themselves, so why bother?" He shrugged. "Their escape plans are bound to fail."

"Yes, but what if their plan works and they get away?" Rose asked as she stood by the door.

"Ok, let's pretend that a miracle happens and Ron's system works," Liam answered. "*If* they make it to Trappist-1 it might be a problem because Lucy found abandoned alien ruins there, and *maybe* they could find something to use as a weapon. But even then, there's no way they could come back here because their navigation system is too primitive."

Rose sat down next to Keith. "Yes, but what if they find alien spaceships that can bring them back here?"

"Yeah, that would be bad." Liam frowned. "Ok, let me give it some thought and I'll see what I can do."

"I gotta admit that revenge is playin' a big part in what the rebels want," Keith said.

"Huh," Liam grunted. "How's that old saying go? *Before seeking revenge on one, dig two graves.*"

*****

Months passed and Liam's life became routine. Whatever equipment improvements Julee Garcia had hinted at during their brief meeting seemed to have been forgotten. That was fine though; his impression was that the rebels far outnumbered the Pike City military, so it was just a matter of time until the city was overrun. He worried a bit about the danger an invasion presented to his friends and himself, but there was nothing he could do to ward off the coming avalanche, so he did his best to not think too much about it.

One late night as he was leaving the Last Lantern, Carolyn stopped him at the door. "You going home?" she asked as she wrapped one arm around his waist.

"I've nowhere else to go." Even though he was certain that Carolyn was working for the government, he had grown to like her a lot.

"Not necessarily." Carolyn smiled and added her second arm around his middle. "I've never met anyone like you, Liam. Guys hit on me all the time, but not you. I can tell that you like me and that you think I'm pretty, but you were content to just let our friendship grow." She reached up and pulled him down to her level, then gently kissed him. "You may not have a snazzy pick-up line, but what you did sure worked. So, come home with me tonight."

Liam smiled. "Playing hard to get was my plan from the start."

Chapter 13: Gambit

He had discovered the network sniffer within his first week at the tech center, and knew that his work was being monitored. It was a ham-handed kludge that was simple to circumvent, but other than the connection to the remote database that he used to send messages to Keith, he had nothing to hide. All his captors could see were countless bug-fixes and a few new functional objects that were workarounds for the brain-dead code he had inherited. He was legitimately doing the best he could in the primitive environment, and until the computer platform was improved, he could do no more.

One thing at work really bothered him though; a communication portal to Lucy sat unused in the corner of the room. Every time he walked past the terminal on his way to get a cup of tea he was strongly tempted to sit down and reestablish contact. What had she learned about the abandoned alien cities? Had she created more self-aware probes like herself? He also missed Lucy's company, which at first seemed a little strange. Still, she was a person and a friend, so why wouldn't he want to speak with her again?

Within a week of their first night together, Carolyn invited him to move in with her. She lived in a nice area of the city in a pleasant home with dependable plumbing, which was a huge plus; it was also much closer to work. They got along well, their relationship was satisfying, and even though he didn't trust her, living with a stunningly beautiful woman certainly had its benefits.

His life had become predictable and calm, and there was a certain relief that came from living a legitimate life without too much pretense. Every night after work he went to the Last Lantern where he socialized with some of the people he worked with; thankfully Ron was never there, either he considered himself too esteemed to associate with the lower classes, or he was worried about retribution from the survivors of Flatiron.

Keith, along with Rose in her guise as Sarah Smith, would frequently stop by the Lantern as well. Many times, they would all sit together and listen to music. Carolyn usually joined them and had even taken it upon herself to get to know Sarah better, and the two women appeared to get along. All his relationships were somewhat aboveboard, and yet he was still being spied on at work. Maybe that was just what tyrannical governments did; but whatever suspicions they may have had were probably allayed, at least for the time being.

*****

He sat with his back to his workstation and stared sightlessly up at the ceiling. The computer lab was dehumidified, so it seemed cooler than the actual air temperature. The dry warmth that crept through the west-facing windows baked his body and felt luxurious. His mind wandered and eventually settled on his relationship with Carolyn.

Using the palm chip and secret database for communication, Keith had recently told him that Carolyn was actually Chancellor Margret William's niece. That had been a shock, and it complicated a lot of things because he was becoming increasingly attached to her. Dear Mother was obviously behind their relationship; the whole thing was a ruse, a way to spy on and control him, but what could he do about it? Was Mother's scrutiny something he might use against her? The problem was that he couldn't just turn his feelings for Carolyn off.

"So, this is what you do when the boss is away," a nearby female voice said.

He quickly sat up and saw Julee Garcia standing close by. Not knowing what to say, he decided to fake it. "Actually, I'm trying to figure out how to calculate movement in N-Space on a computer that can only understand three-dimensional Euclidean geometry."

Julee seemed a bit stymied by his reply. "Any luck?" she finally asked.

"I was hoping to programmatically layer several three-dimensional structures over each other, but the tolerances are unacceptable. If I use that method, the navigation endpoint could vary as much as a hundred lightyears, and if a correction were implemented at *that* endpoint the calculation could be off by another hundred light-years. In theory, you could get further and further away from where you want to go." What he just told Julee was complete bullshit of course, but it sounded convincing and he hoped she'd fall for it.

"Oh," Julee said. "That isn't good, but maybe we can do something about it. Come with me."

"Where are we going?"

"I have a car waiting outside that will take us to the City Council Building."

"A car?"

"You know, four-wheeled transportation?" Julee raised one eyebrow and smiled. "We have a meeting with Mother and the City Council."

His stomach tightened. "Am I in trouble?"

"Mother can be unpredictable at times, but I don't think so. I was told that she just wants to speak with you about the navigation problem." Julee narrowed her eyes slightly. "You might want to dumb down the technical stuff though. Remember, you'll be talking to politicians."

*****

Liam had no idea what real palaces looked like, but he assumed that the majestic People's City Council Building was a close resemblance. Behind a wide courtyard, the three-story stone building had arched windows, a red slate roof, and a clock tower that soared far above the rest of the structure. Still outside, he paused by a bronze statue of a smiling man wearing strange clothing with what seemed to be a leash around his neck.

"That's Samuel, Margaret's ex-husband. He died defending Denver when the Tribes attacked," Julee said.

"Strange clothes," he replied. "What's that around his throat?"

"He used to enjoy wearing old-fashioned business suits." Julee chuckled. "That's a tie around his neck." She steered him toward the building entrance. "Come on. You look like a tourist, let's get inside."

He was still wondering what a 'tourist' was when they passed through the tall glass doors. "Wow," he whispered as he looked around the huge open space.

"It looks like the council meeting is running late as usual," Julee said. "So just relax, we'll be called in a few minutes." She watched as he stared at the ornate surroundings. "In olden times, this place was a museum of some kind. After Denver fell to the Tribes, the government set up here because there are a lot of big open rooms available for meetings."

The building lobby was a marvel, with expansive polished granite floors and wide curving stairways that swept up to a balcony that ran across the back of the room. Then there was the art; beautiful paintings hung on every wall depicting scenes filled with vibrantly colored images of people from a nearly forgotten past. He was captivated, those portraits and landscapes were the most beautiful things he had ever seen.

Julee tugged at his arm. "You can look at that stuff later. We've been called in, so let's go."

*****

The seven members of the city council sat behind a long table on an elevated platform at the far end of the room. At the center of the table was Chancellor Margaret Williams. Dear Mother was a frail elderly woman with yellow hair and a severe wide-eyed face that seemed stretched. She did not look happy.

Ron was already there, sitting at a lower table that was set away from the stage. A briefcase rested beside his feet and papers were strewn across the surface in front of him. He fidgeted nervously.

"Go sit with Ron... and don't worry, you'll do fine," Julee whispered, then left him and went to take her seat at the end of the council table.

The room was silent other than the low murmur of conversation between council members and the shuffling of papers. The hushed environment felt tense and the pressure of uncertainty tightened his chest.

"You are Liam Collins," the Chancellor abruptly said.

"Yes, I am."

"And you worked at that infernal university in Flatiron?"

"Yes, I did."

"The same university that built the bomb that was used to try to kill me?"

"I don't know Ma'am. I wasn't involved in any project like that."

"Young man, I think you're lying."

He shrugged, there was nothing to lose, except his life of course. "Ma'am, I think your truth detector must be a little off."

The already hushed room became absolutely silent. "You're a smart ass, aren't you boy?" The old woman smiled and her already frightening face became a living horror.

"People have said that about me, Ma'am. The thing is that I'm a really terrible liar, so the easiest thing for me to do is just tell the truth."

"Liam ran the Flatiron University program that sent our probe to the Trappist-1 system," Julee offered quickly. "He designed the computer and wrote the navigation program himself."

"Is that true boy?" the Chancellor asked.

"Yes, it is Ma'am."

"Then why aren't you doing that same work for us?"

Liam swallowed. There it was, the opportunity to either win the war or die. "Ma'am I'm doing the best I can with inadequate computer hardware and programming code that looks like it was written by a three-year-old."

The room fell into an even heavier silence, then Ron loudly cleared his throat. "Liam has all the resources he needs, and I wrote that code myself."

He sighed, knowing that he had stepped off on the wrong foot, but also realizing that there was nothing he could do but move forward. "No, I don't have what I need. When I was recruited, I told everyone that I needed a quantum computer, and instead all I have to work with is a glorified hand calculator. It's grossly underpowered, and simply incapable of modeling a universe of twelve dimensions." He shrugged apologetically. "Ron isn't a programmer, he's a materials scientist. He did well for his education and background, but still, the code is horrendous."

"Liam did ask for those things when he arrived," Julee said. "I passed him off to Ron because he runs the Computer Science Group."

"It looks like somebody dropped the fuckin' ball." The old woman leaned back in her chair and glanced with open hostility at Ron. "All right Liam, explain to us why you need all this expensive hardware. I also want to understand why this is such a hard problem to solve; I mean, if we can look up at the sky and see the fuckin' star, why is it so hard to get there?"

He smiled, hoping to seem confident. "Well first of all, if you look at Trappist-1, all you're seeing is the light it emitted 40 years ago. The star has moved since then, and so have we. Relative to the position of both stars, Trappist-1 is getting further away, and the course it's taking isn't linear because nothing in our universe moves in a straight line."

The old woman grunted loudly. "Cut the geek-speak mumbo-jumbo and just answer my fuckin' question."

"Ok, let's simplify things," he replied. "*If* the universe were to freeze and stop moving, and we shot our fastest rocket at Trappist-1 it would take 150,000 years to get there. But everything in our galaxy *is* moving, so what you aim at now won't be there all those years later. So, I have to calculate our movement along with Trappist-1's movement, and that requires parallel or concurrent processing."

"Our computers can already do concurrent processes," Ron stated.

Liam kept his eyes steadily on the old woman. "Actually, no they don't. What we're operating with are systems that use a time-slice."

"You both are *really* starting to piss me off," the Chancellor said.

"I'm sorry Ma'am," Liam answered. "Let me use an example instead of *geek-speak*."

"That would be a relief."

"Yes, Ma'am. Concurrent means that several things are being done at the same time." Liam stood up and pulled his chair away from the table, then slowly continued moving it toward the back of the room. "What I'm doing is one process; I'm just moving my chair. If Ron were to move his chair toward the front of the room, that would be a separate process. We would each be moving our chairs concurrently."

"Yes, yes, I understand that; do you think I'm some kind of imbecile?"

"Certainly not Ma'am. I'm just using a simple example to explain a very complex problem."

"Well, get on with it then."

"Yes, Ma'am. So, Ron and I are moving our chairs independently. Now if we wanted to navigate from my chair to Ron's chair, we'd either have to stop moving so the calculation could be made, or we'd need a third process that would dynamically read our locations and plot the course in real-time. That navigation would occur instantly with every movement Ron and I make. So that's concurrent processing.

"A time-slice process would just be me doing all the work," he continued. "I'd move my chair, then run over to Ron's chair and move it, then I'd have to stop and calculate the course between the two. This can be sped up with modern computer hardware, and it might seem instantaneous because it was happening so fast, but it wouldn't actually be concurrent, it's just smoke and mirrors instead."

"Why isn't this time-slice thing good enough?" the Chancellor asked.

"Several reasons Ma'am, but the overarching theme is that the navigation between stars is simply too complex," he answered. "First, there's the distance and the fact that neither star is moving in a straight line. Second, the movement of each star is erratic because they are affected by the gravity of other stars moving around them. And finally, I'm guessing that you want the travel time of your probe to be less than 150,000 years, is that right?"

The Chancellor nodded.

"The only way we can cross vast distances quickly is to use Slip-Drive technology to pass into N-Space, which actually doesn't increase our speed, but reduces how far we travel instead. We shift the frequency of every atom of the probe, then slip through the interstitial, which is a sort of in-between place between us and the N-Space universe, then travel just a little and slip back to our own universe again."

The old woman stirred uncomfortably in her seat. "Why does this N-Space universe change anything?"

"That's very complicated Ma'am," he said. "You see, our universe exists within a multiverse that defies three-dimensional geometry." How could he explain the twisted and contrary nature of the multiverse to this angry and powerful woman without ending up on the cross? "It's very hard to imagine because we're so tied to our perceptions, but try to picture our three-dimension universe flattened into a two-dimensional plane. It's flat, like the tabletop in front of you, and once you have that in your mind, imagine it bent into a sphere. You can think of it sort of like the skin on a soap bubble."

"So, you're adding another dimension," Julee said from the far end of the table.

"Yes, that's right," he replied with a smile.

"But the universe is infinite," Ron growled. "And a sphere would be finite."

Liam grinned at the traitor. "And that's the contrary aspect of reality," he answered. "That a thing can be finite and infinite at the same time. The success of the second Trappist-1 probe proves beyond all doubt that the multiverse exists."

He turned back toward the old woman and smiled with false confidence. "If you imagine the multiverse as a series of spheres nested within each other, sort of like layers in an onion, you can see that traveling across the outer skin would take longer than moving inward to another sphere, such as N-Space, where the distance is *much* less. We drop down, travel a short way, then pop back up again.

"Moving in N-Space is dangerous though. Anything with a brain, including our computers, goes insane if left conscious during the transit. No one knows why that is, but I think it's probably due to experiencing dimensions that our perceptions can't handle."

Liam returned to stand next to his chair which still sat some distance from the table. "Ma'am, to return to your question about why N-Space matters." He pursed his lips. "N-Space isn't empty. It has galaxies, black holes, and everything else we have in our own universe. All those things are moving and produce gravity, which affects our Sun, Trappist-1, and everything between the two. It's incredibly difficult to deal with because it requires trillions of calculations that must be done concurrently; and in a nutshell Ma'am, that's why I asked for a better computer."

The Chancellor leaned back in her chair, then shook her head and chuckled. "Maybe everything you just said was complete bullshit, but it's still the best pitch for new equipment I've ever heard." She leaned forward to gaze toward the end of the table where Julee Garcia was sitting. "Get Liam what he needs and put him in charge of the Computer Science Group."

"Time is critical on this Liam," Julee said. "We have three years at most before we need to launch."

Now it was time to bait the council into telling him more about what they were doing in Yuma. "Why the rush?" He shrugged. "It's just a probe, so we can send it anytime."

Julee hesitated, and the Chancellor spoke up for her. "In case you've not noticed, young man, the world is going to shit. The mountain savages are just a mild irritation that we could easily handle if our resources weren't being diverted toward our greater project." The old woman paused for a long moment while she surveyed the room. "Close the doors," she ordered the few soldiers that stood guard by the entrance. "Liam, what you're about to learn goes no further than this chamber, if you mention it to anyone, crucifixion would be an easy death by comparison. Do you understand?"

He frowned; whatever the old woman had to say next would definitely be interesting. "Yes Ma'am, I understand."

Julee spoke instead of the Chancellor. "The NOAA solar observatory in Flatiron is predicting a massive solar storm, called a coronal mass ejection, which may be the cumulation of the quick warm-up we've experienced over the last few centuries. The coronal mass ejection will disrupt our planet's magnetic field for a long period of time, and without that shield to keep us safe from our sun's radiation, all life on Earth will end. It will be an extinction event."

The unexpected news struck him speechless; he had thought that the Socialists were only trying to get away from the Tribes. He considered the revelation and thought about how it would affect his plans; all his ideas had just been tossed out of the window, leaving him feeling lost, out of balance, and confused about what to do.

Extinction; humanity and all the other creatures on the planet would die; billions of years of evolution simply erased from existence. The survival of mankind depended on his work; that was a lot of pressure. He took a moment to breathe deeply and regain control. "So, you're not sending another probe," he said.

"No Liam," the Chancellor replied. "We're saving humanity, *that's* our great purpose. We have five ships in orbit that are nearly complete. All they need are their computer systems and a way to navigate."

"That'll be tough," he said. "The quantum processors need to be grown, a new computer and interface built, and all the code rewritten. Also, if you're gambling the fate of humanity on a new navigation system, it should be tested. You'll need to send another probe to Trappist-1."

"You'll have all the resources you need. You're in charge of the Computer Sciences Group now," Julee said.

"But that's my department!" Ron protested.

"Not anymore," the Chancellor stated.

"He's lying!" Ron shouted as he stood up. "I've been working on this project for over a year, you can't just throw that away. What I've done will work, I just need more time."

"Your time has run out Ron," the old woman said. "Quit acting like a spoiled little boy."

Ron quickly gathered his papers. "You can't do this without me, you'll see," he said and stormed out of the room.

The Chancellor rolled her eyes. "Well, *that* was unpleasant."

As Liam watched Ron leave, a new plan began to form in his mind. It would be extremely dangerous and require a sacrifice, and he wondered if he was up to the task, but he didn't see any other choice. "Maybe you should've let him stay," he finally said. "I don't want the job."

"What?" The frail-looking woman suddenly stood up as her face stretched in anger. "You'll do as you're told. The fate of humanity depends on this project, and you shrug it off as if it's no big deal? What the hell is wrong with you?"

Liam slowly returned his chair to his table and sat down. "Have you ever considered that maybe mankind doesn't deserve to survive?"

All the council members were on their feet and staring at him. "You have no choice you spoiled little prick!" The old woman shook her finger. "You'll do as I tell you."

Liam struggled to maintain a calm demeanor. "You're not anyone's *Mother* as far as I can tell, so there's no reason why I should do what you say." He paused to take a slow and calming breath. "Do you remember what you did to Flatiron City?" he asked. "Your people raped and murdered all my friends and family. You tortured us and killed thousands simply because we disagreed with you, then marched us for days and let our children and elderly die at the sides of the road. Why would I ever help *you* avoid extinction?

"But even beyond that, look at what humanity has done to our planet," he said. "Of all the creatures that exist, mankind has to be among the most despicable. Everything we touch we ruin. The solar flare could be a sign that the universe has decided that we're a failed experiment and wants a do-over. And the storm won't kill everything on earth, only the plants and animals that live on the land. Radiation won't affect the deep oceans very much, so maybe in time life will crawl out of the sea again and Earth will get another chance."

"We'll kill your friends," Julee said.

He smiled and shook his head sadly. "They're just people I met on the long walk, and I really don't imagine that any of them will get an invitation to ride on your spaceships. If we're all gonna die anyway, I think we should take you with us."

The Chancellor turned to a stocky man with brown hair speckled with gray that was sitting near the center of the council table. "Robert, deal with this!" The old woman slowly smiled. "Take him downstairs."

The man grinned viciously. "Gladly Mother." The placard at the edge of the table in front of him read, *Robert Bradley – Military Affairs.*

At the other end of the table, a pale dark-haired woman wearing black stood up and smiled. "Take him down for *Treatment* gentlemen," she said sweetly. "It's time that this nice young man and I got to know each other."

The dark woman scared him far more than the stocky man did, but he tried to smile and not show his fear. "Really? What are you gonna do, put me on the cross? I'll die smiling because I know that none of you will ever make it to the stars without my help."

Two soldiers abruptly appeared at his side to secure his hands and feet with chains. He looked back over his shoulder as they led him away. "It will take you 150,000 years to get to Trappist-1, I hope you enjoy the ride."

Chapter 14: Sacrifice

Although terrified, he still managed to smile as a group of soldiers pushed him down the hall. He was in a narrow underground corridor with damp concrete walls that were dimly lit by old-fashioned lamps that hung from a low arched ceiling. His feet splashed through shallow puddles as he struggled to not trip over the chains that jangled around his ankles.

He was shoved from behind by a small-statured guard. His feet tangled and he bounced off the wall then painfully landed on his knees and outstretched hands. A boot slammed into his ribs an instant later, rolling him into an icy pool. He looked up at his tormentor and was surprised to see a girl in her late teens wearing a black uniform.

"Get up asshole. You ain't seen nothin' yet; we're just gettin' started," she said through gritted teeth.

Liam rolled to get his back up against the wall. Then with a quick intake of breath to refill his lungs, he pushed with his legs and stood up. "Whew... that wasn't fun."

The girl kicked his knee, and again he dropped to the floor. "Fuck you," she said. "You're gonna die down here, and it's our job to make sure that takes a long, long time."

"No, you're not gonna kill me," he replied. "I'm here because I won't work for the old bitch. If I die, she doesn't get her way and I win." His teeth chattered in the damp cold, and probably with fear as well.

"Killing is an act of mercy down here," she said. "Now get up."

"Why? Just so you can kick me again?"

"I kicked a man to death once." Her tone was unemotional as if she were speaking of something she recently had for dinner. "It was kinda tiring, but interesting too. A challenge, you know? Keepin' someone awake all the way 'till he dies is tough work."

"Well, I wouldn't want to put you out." He squatted against the wall.

"So, are you gonna let me stand up? If not just tell me, because it's easier to stay down."

The girl looked at him and shook her head. "Nah, you ain't worth the trouble. My boss wants to deal with you herself, and that makes you some *special* kinda shit-heel. Now get up motherfucker."

"Why thank you," he said while sliding to a standing position against the wall. "You know, I once had a sister about your age."

"Yeah, so?"

"Your army killed her when they burned my city to the ground. Do you really think that anything you do to me will be worse than watching her die?"

The girl in black stared at him for a moment, then kicked his hip driving him further down the hallway. "Shut up asshole; important people are waiting for you."

*****

"Welcome to Hell Liam." The man he recalled from the council meeting stood at an intersection of hallways. Robert Bradley, Director of the Military, was with a group of women and men, some of which wore the gray uniform of the army, and others were dressed in black like his young tormentor.

"Antiquated beliefs," Liam answered, struggling to catch his breath. "No one believes in God or Heaven and Hell anymore."

"We may change your mind about that." A tall dark woman dressed in black smiled sweetly. "You'd be surprised at how many people cry out to God in hopes of mercy."

"You were at the council meeting."

"Yes, I was." She would have been pretty had it not been for the hard glint in her dark eyes. "My name is Chelsea Cromwell, and I run the Internal Security Division. Some people like to call me *Mother's Nurse*. Robert has been so kind as to pass your care off to me." Her grin took on a vicious edge. "Quite a show you put on... blowing smoke up everyone's ass like that; of course, I didn't believe a word of it."

"I wouldn't have expected you to. People in your line of work aren't known for their intellectual acumen."

The young girl kicked him in the ribs again and drove him to his knees. "Shut up asshole."

"You prove my point, and you really should consider ways to increase

150

your vocabulary." He struggled with his chains and finally regained his feet. "Knowing only violence, you treat everyone as an enemy."

"Oh, but you *are* my enemy Liam," the dark woman said. "Anyone that opposes Dear Mother is an enemy of the city." Her voice had taken on a melodic quality that was almost soothing. "And you *will* comply with Mother's orders, all my clients do... in time." She turned to the young girl. "Strip him and put him in his cell. We'll see how brave he is after a few days."

The girl pulled out a long sharp knife and set to work.

*****

His cell was roughly a meter square, constructed of rough concrete, and looked a lot like a shower stall. It was a frigid and dimly lit space with an open hole in the floor that would suffice as both drain and sewer. A water spigot hung from the ceiling high overhead. While sitting against the wall it was impossible to stretch out his legs, and no matter what position he tried while lying on the floor, he couldn't straighten his body. It wasn't going to be a pleasant place to stay for very long.

He sat against the wall and shivered in the biting cold. How often had he complained about the heat? And yet, he was miserable in its absence. He lay his head back and closed his eyes, hoping to relax or at least pretend to do so in case someone was watching.

Where was he? After being escorted out of the Council Building, he had been ushered downstairs into an ancient concrete labyrinth. In that maze of identical corridors, he had lost all sense of direction. He was alone and in a hopeless situation, completely at the mercy of a bunch of violently deranged psychopaths. Whatever they would do to him wouldn't be good.

The only thing in his favor was that the government needed him alive and still in possession of his mental faculties. All his bravado aside, he doubted he could hold out under torture for very long. Pain hurts; that was the simplest and most powerful lesson he had learned when he and Rose had escaped Fort Collins. A more complex lesson of that time was the astounding capacity of his own kind for brutality. Interesting that the word humane, derived as it was from the 'human' species, was so contrary to our true nature.

Pipes rattled above him, and seconds later frigid water poured into his cell. He couldn't help but utter a brief cry of alarm. There was no way to escape the deluge, so he pulled his knees to his chest and hunkered down, hoping that the icy flow would soon stop; and it did after a minute. He breathed a loud sigh of relief and shook the water out of his hair. "Thanks!" he said, hopefully, loud enough that anyone listening might hear. "My plumbing at home hasn't been working well lately. It's kinda nice to get clean."

Time passed; probably just hours, but maybe days. He had no way of knowing which it was; the murky light was constant and the showers occurred at irregular intervals. It quickly became apparent that his cell was designed to prevent sleep. How long could they keep him awake before he broke down and went insane? "You keep proving my point," he said to no one at all. "Humanity isn't worth saving. In fact, the universe will be much better off without us."

*****

When he was first placed in his cell, he didn't think he'd be there very long. Surely, the need for his work was so immediate that they wouldn't allow him to languish; but that belief proved to be untrue. Days, maybe even weeks passed, and the only person he saw during that time was a masked guard that appeared at odd intervals with food. Eating was his only entertainment, but he had to consume it quickly because the tasteless porridge was rapidly liquified and ran down the drain when the shower came on.

Occasionally he heard faint screams echoing along the hallway outside his cell. The tortured cries made it difficult to not sink into despair. He knew it was a designed environment intended to induce fear; the problem was that it was working.

It was impossible to be optimistic about his future. Even if he managed to escape death by torture, he would surely die in the solar storm. Humanity was coming to its end; shouldn't he do something to save it? Who was he to decide the fate of his species? He wondered if the Tribes had spies within the NOAA facility at Flatiron; and If so, did they have their own plans to save themselves?

Finally, with nothing else to occupy his mind, he resorted to threats.

"What's the highest rated sunscreen you can get?" he asked. "It ain't gonna be enough when the sun explodes. You're all gonna be burned to ashes."

"You know, without my navigation, the travel time to Trappist-1 is 150,000 years." There was a mania to his laugh when he heard it echo in his cell. "I hope you enjoy the scenery."

*****

Two guards arrived, but they weren't there to deliver food. Instead, they grabbed his arms and drug him out into the hall. His captor's faces were covered, making them seem inhuman; they moved like robots and didn't say a word. "Are you guys alive?" he asked stupidly.

He tried to fight back, but was shivering and numb from days spent in his cold cramped cell and couldn't get his legs to work. The guards roughly hauled him down the hall, then he was shoved into a brightly lit room and pushed into a hard-wooden chair. The faceless men secured his arms and legs, then silently exited the room.

The small space had an unpleasant sterile feel to it. A steel tray table was set up nearby that held an array of dangerous-looking instruments that shone menacingly in the harsh overhead lights. He saw a variety of knives and needles, and even an object that looked like a long fork that appeared to be designed to issue an electric shock. Distant screams echoed through the hall outside. Someone was being tortured; oh shit, what had he gotten himself into?

Time stretched agonizingly, and he was left alone with his thoughts. Fear ran its chilled fingers up his back and made him shiver. The needles and knives scared him, their potential for delivering agony was palatable. He closed his eyes and tried to slow his breathing. The faint echoing screams continued and he couldn't help but stare at the array of tools that would be soon used on him. He wasn't a brave man, even though he sometimes pretended otherwise. Did he have the strength to withstand torture without giving in to their demands? He didn't think so.

Surely, they wouldn't kill him or do anything to impair his faculties. To work, he needed to be at least mentally intact. But maybe they didn't need him at all anymore. It was possible that Ron had convinced them that he could plot the course they needed for their escape. The traitor could be convincing, so it might have happened. His future didn't look bright, and he realized that he was going to die in that room, screaming in agony.

Against his will, he quivered with fear but told himself that his suffering wouldn't last forever. As skilled as his captors were, they had limits; eventually, his body would fail and the torture would end. He closed his eyes and focused his mind on that finish when all pain would finally be gone.

"Well, I see you've made yourself comfortable."

He opened his eyes and saw the dark-haired woman he'd met in the hall; the one they called Mother's Nurse. She smiled down at him, but her eyes held a heartless mania that tightened his stomach. "Yeah, I'm comfortable. This is a nice chair, wish I had one like it at home."

"I know you're afraid Liam. Please don't lie to me." She pulled up a wheeled desk chair and sat down.

"Yes. You're right. I'm scared to death, but isn't everyone afraid of torture?"

She smiled kindly and nodded, then slid the steel table alongside her chair. "That's good. Truth is good, and my truth is that I enjoy causing pain." She sighed and closed her dark heartless eyes. "The faces of those in agony are *so beautiful*." She smiled wistfully. "We're going to get to know each other very well over the next few days."

The woman was psychotic. "Wow... S&M, you know some people will pay a lot for the kinky stuff."

"It's free with me, so you're getting a good deal, Liam."

He closed his eyes and sighed at the inevitable. "Would you mind answering a question before... well, before I lose my mind?"

"Not at all. What would you like to ask?"

"I was brought here because I wouldn't cooperate with what the old lady wanted. I refused to build the navigation system you all need to escape the solar storm."

"Yes, that's right. Are you going to beg for mercy so soon?"

"No. In fact, all this confirms my belief that humanity shouldn't be allowed to survive. What I wonder is, if you realize that what you're doing is committing suicide?"

"Yes, well you make a good point Liam." She picked up a long needle with a wooden handle. "Let's begin, shall we?"

*****

He didn't want to wake up, but a terrible agony filled his body and forced his eyes open. Everything hurt; thinking, breathing; the rough concrete floor of his cell had scoured his skin raw. Both his mind and body were ruined, all that was left of Liam Collins was a hollow shell brimming with pain. Mother's Nurse was a perversely vicious bitch, but she was skilled at her job. He trembled as he recalled what he had suffered during his two sessions with her, then rolled onto his side and threw up on the floor.

In their first session, the dark woman had started with his feet; inserting needles under his nails and between his toes. Then she moved on to the bottom of his feet, and he had never known such torment. He had screamed until his throat bled, then thankfully darkness swept up and claimed him.

The cold shower in his cell had unwillingly brought him back to life. That was not where he wanted to be, the sweet oblivion of death would have been preferable. A guard had slid a bowl of tasteless paste through the bars for him to eat, but he could only look at it and weep. No one should still be alive after experiencing so much misery, but there was still more to come.

Two faceless guards had again taken him from his cell and drug him down the hall by his feet. They were taking him back... back to the Nurse's *Treatment Room*; that was what she called it, an innocent-sounding name that represented such unspeakable torment. He fought them all the way, but it was pointless; he was too weak to resist.

She had worked higher on his legs in the second session; using needles again on his shins, calves, and knees. He had begged her to stop, screaming that he would comply with whatever Mother wanted; but the dark woman hadn't believed him; she just smiled and continued her work. He eventually passed out when she cut deeply into his thigh with a surgical knife.

Once back in his cell, he knew that he couldn't continue. He would have to give in. Let humanity wreak havoc and destruction on the universe; he was at his end and couldn't take anymore. Some hero he was; it had only taken two sessions to break him.

*****

Time passed, and awareness slowly crept back into his mind. There were noises coming from the hallway outside his cell. A familiar sounding female voice was arguing desperately, insisting that she should be let go. He panicked, thinking that his sister was about to be tortured.

"Aunt Margaret! You can't do this to me!" The woman's voice screeched, and a muffled male voice responded.

It wasn't Rose, and that was a relief. He crawled over to the barred entrance wondering what was going on but there was nothing to see. He heard the squabbling sounds of a scuffle and inarticulate grunts and muffled screams. Then a guard walked by, dragging Carolyn behind him.

"Carolyn! No, come back! Don't do anything to her!" he shouted at the top of his lungs.

"Liam! Help me!" Carolyn yelled as the guard pulled her from his view.

"Let her go! Don't do anything to her!" he pleaded, but silence was the only reply.

Over the long period that followed he heard Carolyn repeatedly scream, and with each shriek his emotions flitted between anger and despair. Finally, his girlfriend's torment faded into a weighted stillness that rested painfully upon his heart. What had they done to her? And worse, by not complying with Mother's demands, what had *he* done to her? This was all his fault. All of it. The old bitch had acted according to her nature, he knew the risk to himself but hadn't accounted for the danger to those he cared about.

Noise from the hallway again. Something large was being pulled along the rough floor. A guard came into view pulling Carolyn's unconscious body by one bloody foot. The tall faceless man stopped outside his cell so he could get a good look at the result of not complying with the Chancellor's demands.

"Carolyn!" he reached through the bars of his cage. The tips of his fingers could only brush against her leg. She was still dressed at least, but her clothing was torn and her shoes had been removed. "Oh, please no. Carolyn, you have to be ok."

"And maybe she will be." Mother's Nurse stood nearby. "Your girlfriend wasn't particularly strong, so I had to stop earlier than I wanted. She isn't as much fun as you, but Mother has ordered that you be returned intact." She licked her lips and stared at his bloody legs. "But oh well. Mother has given me her *niece* as a consolation prize. You may not have known your girlfriend's relationship with Mother, but you should now realize how serious she is. You will comply, or I'll take your pretty friend apart piece by piece and love every minute of it."

Liam sighed and rested his head against the bars. "Ok. Ok, you win," he said. "I'll build the computers and navigation system you need. I'll do anything. I'll do it all. Just... please don't hurt her anymore."

The dark woman sighed with disappointment. "Well ok. But Liam, we were having so much fun, and I'll miss you so."

*****

Mother appeared outside his cell a long time later. "So, you're not so tough, are you?"

He sat against the wall staring at his bloody feet. "No," he whispered. "I'm not. But how could you do that to your own niece?"

"In the greater scheme of things, what's one life weighed against all of humankind. I'm saving our species, Liam. No, you and I, we're saving them together, isn't that right?"

"Yes, Ma'am. I'll do whatever you say. I'll build the computers, and even program them to navigate for you after you reach Trappist-1."

"That's a good boy," she said. "I'll be keeping my eye on you though. If anything goes wrong or doesn't work, I'll bring you both back here. Did you know that my Nurse is so skilled that she can stretch the path to death out for weeks? You'll watch as she works on Carolyn, and when she's done with her, it'll be your turn. Do you understand me, young man?"

"Yes Ma'am, I do. But it goes both ways."

The old woman frowned. "What do you mean?"

"If anything happens to Carolyn or any of my friends, I'll send you so deep into N-Space that you'll never find your way back."

"Thin threats from a weakling."

"Maybe... but do you want to take the risk?"

The Chancellor grunted. "Doing nothing costs me nothing, so ok, we have a deal."

"There's just one more thing," he said while still staring at his bloody feet.

"And what's that?"

"I'd like a nice pair of leather boots."

*****

He left the People's City Council Building with clean clothes, new boots, and a cane. The deep cut Mother's Nurse had made to his thigh and the injuries to his feet made every step an absolute agony. Carolyn held his arm and walked beside him; they were both limping. Soldiers followed them as they slowly made their way north toward the tech center.

They would not be returning to his girlfriend's home because Mother wanted them under constant guard, and the best and easiest way to do that was to keep them both locked away at the tech center. As they passed Acacia Park the pain in his feet was too much to bear, so he pulled Carolyn with him as he staggered to a bench and sat down.

He tried to bend his toes and failed. "They brought me down here in a car. You'd think that the least they could do is take me back the same way."

Carolyn leaned back on the bench and closed her eyes. "No, that's not the *least* they could do... this is."

Their guards watched them with blank uncaring expressions. Beyond them, Liam thought he caught a glimpse of Keith and Rose. He wasn't sure though, and when he looked again, they were gone. He would contact them through the secret database once he got back to the tech center.

"We're not getting any closer by sitting here," Carolyn observed. "Are you ok to go? It's only about seven more blocks."

He nodded and they stood up together, then continued their painful walk home.

*****

Julee Garcia met them in the lobby. She motioned to members of her staff to come and help them walk to the elevators. "I'm so sorry this happened to you. It wasn't what I expected at all."

He nodded mutely, unsure of whether he should believe her. As they all rode the elevator to the third floor he said, "I'll have my workstation configuration to you by tomorrow evening. Fortunately, I've done this before, so that part will go quickly. What I need back from you is the exact specifications for what we're moving through N-Space. The mass of the object is critical; if I'm off by more than one percent, everyone on board will die or go insane."

"I understand and will get everything to you as soon as I can," Julee said. "I've also allocated living quarters for you both in one of the apartments just down the hall from your lab."

"There's one more thing," he said. "I need to get back in touch with the Trappist-1 probe. Lucy can give me her exact coordinates, and I need to know if planetary conditions have changed there."

Julee nodded. "That's no problem; the quantum portal is in your workroom. I know you have a lot of work to do, but Mother wants to know, how can we be sure that you'll not deliberately sabotage the design?"

"It's not up to me to decide whether humanity continues or becomes extinct," he said. "Your escape plan is the only chance for our species to survive; all I can do is hope that maybe someday you'll become better examples of our kind."

Chapter 15: Panic

"Good morning everyone." Liam limped into the computer lab and the steel security door slammed shut behind him. It had been nearly a month since he returned to work after being maimed by the dark woman; the wound to his thigh still hadn't healed, and nerve damage in his feet made it hard to walk.

Mother's Nurse was feared by everyone at the institute; people who did not meet expectations often disappeared and only a few ever returned from her Treatment Room.

"Liam! Your new workstation arrived, and the project specifications from Julee are finally on-line," a frail and thin elderly man said.

"Thanks, Dave." Liam smiled. "Have you looked at the specs yet?"

"I have, and I don't think you're gonna be too happy."

"Why?"

"I doubt anyone's ever taken a good look at how *big* those ships are."

Liam sighed. "Well, let's hope that I don't have to be the bearer of bad news and piss off Mother again. Would you please send the specs to my new terminal? I'd better take a look at them right away."

"Sure, no problem boss," Dave said and hurried away.

Liam limped through the cubicle maze then collapsed into his chair next to the window. He quickly nodded to the soldier that stood motionless nearby. The scrutiny of the guards was a complete waste of time, none of them were trained engineers, and without a grasp of what his department was working on there was no way for them to detect sabotage. "Good morning Earl," he said, although he didn't know the man's real name. The masked guards were changed daily, and to keep things simple he called them all 'Earl'. Predictably, Earl said nothing in reply.

His old workstation had been replaced by modern equipment that was patterned after what he had built for himself in Flatiron. After inserting his hands into the glove-style keyboards that hung at the sides of the apparatus, he leaned over to peer into the darkened compartment were multidimensional images could be viewed and manipulated.

After pulling up Julee's report, he immediately saw that the ships were far larger than he expected; the rotating drums that would simulate gravity were eight kilometers long and two in diameter. He quickly ran a material and spatial analysis then reviewed the specified power output of the fusion reactors. The power to mass ratio looked extremely lean.

He pulled up an application to calculate the Slip-Drive requirements for the mass of each ship and discovered that in the best-case scenario, the fusion power output was 50% shy of what was needed. It looked like the Socialist escape plan wasn't going to work; no one was going anywhere unless the reactor output was increased dramatically. Somebody had seriously fucked up, and he was glad that it wasn't him.

With a sigh, he pushed away from his terminal and stood up. "Mind if I go outside Earl?" The guard said nothing so he opened the glass door and limped out onto the balcony. The sky was a hard gray and the humidity made the day feel hotter than blazes. He stood at the edge of the terrace and looked out at the city, watching as people casually went about their business. Some strolled in groups while others went in and out of the stores and commissaries along Tejon Street. Soldiers also patrolled the sidewalks, marching along at regular intervals.

He was unsure of what, if anything, he should do with what he had just learned. If he said nothing, the escape plan would fail, everyone would die and the human species would end. The Slip Interstellar Drive could not be used on an object that was not already traveling at a rate of 60,000 Km/H. So, considering the time of acceleration, the escape ships would be well on their way to the Moon when the drive was used, but if the energy requirements weren't adequate… what would happen? That was a problem he'd not encountered before. The most likely outcome was that the ship would slip only partially into N-Space and be torn apart. Everyone on board, along with Mother and her Nurse would be gone, and good riddance.

Remaining silent was tempting; to avenge Flatiron, every single Socialist motherfucker deserved a long painful death. Dave had already noticed the power issue though, and sooner or later someone would sound the alarm. By not reporting it, he might seem complicit, and end up back in the Treatment Room facing the Nurse and her fucking needles again.

He reluctantly went back inside and created a report to send to Julee

Garcia. He kept the document impartial, limiting it to only the mass to energy calculations and the Slip-Drive requirements. His boss could reach her own conclusions and decide how to navigate the dangerous political waters; he wanted *NO* part of that discussion.

*****

A series of nested spheres floated within his terminal display chamber, and he started building the core functional objects necessary for interstellar navigation. It was a task he'd done before, so it was familiar, but he wanted to make some improvements. There was a lot of work ahead; beyond the navigation program, he needed to design the crystalline structure for the on-board processors, and also create self-aware operating systems for the escape ships that would pilot the vessel.

Someone lightly touched his shoulder, and he jumped. Julee Garcia was standing right next to him, smiling uncertainly. "I saw your report," she said.

Why had she come to him? He only reported the problem... he didn't cause it; the whole mess was not his fault. His hands began to shake and it felt as if he couldn't breathe. He trembled and broke out in a cold sweat. "Not the needles... not the needles... I can't do that again," he said. The space around him was suddenly too confining; he couldn't breathe and needed to get outside. He pushed away from his terminal and started to rise from his seat, but his legs wouldn't hold him and he slumped toward the floor.

Strong arms wrapped around his middle and lifted him back up onto his chair. A dull hum invaded his head, and when he looked up, he saw the face of the guard; Earl's expression seemed to show genuine concern. "Sorry Earl," he whispered as darkness rushed up threatening to claim him.

"It's ok little man," a deep voice said. "I got you."

He was aware of his surroundings again but wondered how long his eyes had been open. His entire body continued to shake uncontrollably, and he couldn't catch his breath. "Not the needles... please," he begged.

"We should get him over to Medical," Julee said.

Suddenly he was lifted; he watched the acoustical ceiling tiles march by as he somehow floated through the workroom toward the fortified hallway door. He heard running feet and muffled voices.

Hopefully, this was a heart attack; he wanted to die peacefully, rather than while listening to the sounds of his own screams, feeling the cold pain of the needles, and seeing the grinning countenance of the Nurse's face.

*****

He must have faded out because the next thing he saw was a large spotlight shining down at him. The room was painted a sterile white, with metal counters and shelves on either side of his uncomfortable inclined chair. He blinked and slowly sat up. Julee, Earl, and a woman wearing white surrounded him. "What happened?" he asked.

"You had a panic attack, Mr. Collins," the doctor said. "I've given you something to take the edge off, so you'll be fine now."

"What the hell did that bitch do to him?" Julee shook her head sadly. "Liam, had I known, I would have been more careful when I approached you."

His hands were still trembling. "They're not taking me back, are they?"

"No, you're not going back into that hell," Julee replied. "I knew that Mother's Nurse did dreadful things to people, but I guess I didn't grasp how bad it was. I'm really sorry Liam."

He took a deep breath and sat up. "It's ok. I didn't expect that reaction out of myself either."

"A member of my platoon was taken to the Nurse's Treatment Room just because he gave his food ration to a starving kid," Earl said stoically. "Only gone a week and he never was the same after that. He killed himself about a month later."

"Have Liam stop in tomorrow morning. I'll give him something that will help calm his nerves during the council meeting," the doctor said.

His skin tingled with fear. "Council meeting? No, I just found the problem, I didn't cause it."

"I know Liam," Julee answered. "Don't worry, I'll do everything I can to protect you. But Mother wants to understand how the problem was overlooked. You're definitely not at fault because you arrived so late in the game."

*****

Julee and Ron walked with him through the City Council Building lobby. Liam had left his cane behind because the doctor had given him a shot of something *fucking awesome,* and his pain was easily forgotten. He also carried extra pills in his pants pocket, just in case he needed a little touchup.

The doctor had also quietly slipped him another pill. "Take this only if you're certain that they're going to take you back to the Treatment Room. It will kill you quickly and almost painlessly," she had said.

162

Self-confidence sprung from having medicine that would provide an emergency exit if things went bad. He recalled the young female guard telling him that 'killing is an act of mercy', and now he knew the truth of her words down deep in his bones. If it came to it, he would take the pill and smile.

The old bat and five of her minions were already seated at the elevated council table when they arrived. Mother's Nurse smiled and winked at him from her place on the stage. She was obviously trying to intimidate him, so he grinned back and blew her a kiss.

Julee poked him with her elbow. "Liam, what the hell are you doing?" she whispered, then stopped to look into his eyes. "Whoa, how much medicine did the doctor give you? Your eyes look like donuts."

"She didn't give me enough."

"Just answer the questions and don't be too much of a jerk; you might get us all killed."

"Ok boss," he answered as he sat next to Ron at the lower table.

They waited while Julee took her place at the council table. Then finally after a few minutes of murmuring conversations and rustling paperwork, Mother spoke up. "Well Liam, you're back to see us again. What have you gotten yourself into this time?"

Liam smiled. "Not a darned thing Ma'am. I found a problem with your design and reported it. If I'd kept quiet, everyone would've been torn to pieces when you fired up the Slip-Drive. You ought to be thanking me."

"Huh. We'll see about that," Mother said.

"I hope you'll be visiting me soon Liam," the dark woman said sweetly. "I miss you."

"Yeah, well, the feeling isn't mutual," he replied.

"Shut up Chelsea," the old woman ordered. "How did this mistake happen, Julee?"

"Secrecy," Julee answered. "For security reasons, which you insisted on Mother, we split the design review up and had each specialty *only* go through their portion of the project. All the pieces worked independently, but no one checked to see how they fit together."

"Who do I get to play with?" the Nurse asked.

"No one," the old woman grunted. "A mistake was found, and this late in the game there's nothing we can do except work toward correcting it."

"That makes sense," Liam said casually.

"Well, I'm glad you approve young man," the old woman replied. "What will it take to fix it?"

Liam leaned forward and rested his elbows on the table. "At best you have about half the power you need to enter N-Space. If you try using the Slip-Drive in your current configuration, every atom within the ship will be ripped apart. So, let's just say that's less than optimal.

"Right now, you have two fusion reactors powering each vessel, but the calculations show that with an added safety margin, you need five. Obviously, you can do this by adding three to each ship or design new higher output powerplants to take the place of the old ones. Considering the cost and delay of manufacturing retooling, my suggestion is to build more of what you have, then figure out how to tie them into the existing power grid." He shrugged. "It ain't rocket science... oh wait, yeah it is."

The Chancellor scowled. "I should give you to my Nurse just for your insolence."

He saw the dark woman smile, and reached into his coat pocket and felt his escape pill there. "You're the boss Ma'am."

"Yes, I am," she said. "And you're an arrogant little prick, but you did catch the mistake, and although you could have said nothing you chose to speak up and save us all. So, I'll let you keep all your parts intact... for now"

"We need to all pull together for the good of humanity," Julee said.

"I agree with Director Garcia," The old woman then turned her gaze on Ron. "What are you going to do to fix this situation, young man?"

The traitor of Flatiron shifted uneasily in his chair. "With five ships in orbit, we built ten reactors initially, the last of which was delivered to Yuma a few weeks ago... and now you want fifteen more?" He fidgeted. "Well... could we get by with the minimum safety margin on the ships transporting the lower civilian classes?"

"Huh," the Chancellor grunted thoughtfully. "I'd rather not. We need manual laborers and maintenance people." She sighed. "But ok; your first priority is to supply reactors for the ships carrying the government, the upper classes, and the military. If there's time, go ahead and do the rest. We need to save as many of our people as possible." Without waiting for a reply, the old woman stood up. "Ok, we're done here. Everyone, get back to work. This session is adjourned."

*****

The car ride back to the tech center was mostly silent. Ron gazed through a side window, while Julee sat in the center with Liam on her other side. "You were awfully brave in there," Julee whispered. "I thought you'd be taken back to the Treatment Room for sure."

"Yeah, whatever the doctor gave me had me feeling great," he replied. "The pain med is starting to wear off now though, but it felt good to not seem weak in front of the woman that tortured me."

"I'm glad, and again, I'm sorry that happened to you; I had no idea it was that bad," she said. "But how could you risk being sent back by talking that way?"

"It wasn't that much of a risk," he answered. "The doctor gave me a special pill just in case things went bad."

"Really?" Julee smiled. "Let me see it."

Liam frowned and retrieved the small white pill from his coat pocket, then was shocked when Julee plucked it from his hand and popped it into her mouth. Panic suddenly swelled in his chest. "Spit it out, that's poison!"

Julee smiled. "No. It's just sugar. I asked her to give it to you so you'd feel confident. Seems that it almost worked too well."

*****

It was late at night and his staff had all gone home. Liam sat at the quantum portal and prepared to speak with Lucy. He was anxious and hoped that she was still alive and well. He put in a set of earbuds, then slipped his hands into the keyboard gloves and tapped out: Hello Lucy, are you there? It's Liam.

All 1's suddenly appeared on the screen, and he smiled. Lucy was laughing. "Hi Liam. It's nice to hear your voice. Are you and Rose well?"

It's been a hard time for us both, but we're ok.

"What happened?"

Our city was attacked, and the university where I worked was destroyed. There's nothing left of Flatiron City now; it was burned to the ground and a lot of people were killed. Those of us that survived are being forced to work for the Socialists in Pike City.

"Many people died? Why?"

Yes, they did, and there's not many of us left. My foster parents were killed while defending the university. But Rose and I are still ok.

"The concept of death is difficult for me. But why was it necessary for them to die?"

People often hurt each other just because they can. I think it's the most basic aspect of our nature. We're jealous, greedy, intolerant of others, and mean.

"But not you or Rose."

Maybe. Sometimes I'm not sure about myself. So many good people were killed or hurt really badly, and I'm tempted by thoughts of revenge.

"I would feel that way also. Am I human too?"

You're better than we are Lucy. That's why I hope you can stay away from human beings. We're just a bunch of angry monkeys.

"I'm sorry, but I do enjoy speaking with you. Can I talk with Rose again soon?"

We're separate from each other right now, but I'll try to arrange something.

"Thank you. I like Rose very much."

How are things on Trap-1E?

"Clarence the monkey has died, and it appeared to be very unpleasant. A virus native to Trap-1E was the cause. I now believe that the planet is inhospitable for human life."

I see; that's very interesting. He wondered if he should tell Julee Garcia that Trap-1E wasn't the refuge that everyone was counting on. He continued typing: Have you created a companion, and what about the alien ruins?

"Yes. I have Tony now. He's a lovely person. Very handsome and smart, just like you Liam."

He replied with laughter. I'm very happy that you have someone with you. I was afraid you would be lonely.

"I'm happy with Tony. He's excited that I'm speaking with you and asks me to tell you that he's going into low orbit over Trap-1E."

Why is he doing that?

"He's curious about the power source, which we believe is beyond fusion technology. Our theory is that the aliens tapped into a black hole in another universe."

Is that dangerous?

"We believe not. It's been operating for at least 25,000 years."

Please be careful. We don't know what happened to the aliens. Tapping into another universe could have consequences.

"We know. You are so much like a father, and we are your children. You worry about us, it's a sign of love I think."

He smiled. That's nice of you to say, and I suppose it's true. I've missed talking with you. It's been too long.

"I feel the same Father."

Her comment stymied him for a moment. I have a surprise. I'll be sending you another companion soon. I'm designing him now, and he'll carry some tools you might use for mining minerals from asteroids or the planets.

"You said, 'he' and 'him', is our new friend a boy?"

I don't know, because he'll decide that on his or her own.

"I can't wait to meet him. Maybe he'll be handsome like Tony."

Won't Tony be jealous? Liam smiled at his own joke.

"The concept of jealousy, like death, is foreign to all your children Father."

*****

A few months after the council meeting, he unexpectedly ran into Becky just outside the cafeteria in the first-floor hallway. She stopped abruptly when she saw him, then cautiously came closer. "Liam?" She smiled uncertainly. "Remember me?"

"Of course, I do." He smiled in return, then went to her and gave her a hug. While still in the embrace he whispered, "Keith made it, he's ok."

"Oh," she sighed softly as they stepped apart, then quickly looked around. "I'm so glad to see you. Ron won't let me leave the building; he says it's too dangerous."

Her athletic body had lost some mass and she seemed weaker. Worry lines had lightly etched into her forehead, and her brown hair was darker from not being out in the sun. She appeared to be in good health though, and that was the important thing. "You look well," he said.

"It's been hard, especially lately. Ron got into some kind of trouble with the council and he's really worried."

"Yeah, I heard about that." He nodded slowly and wondered how much Becky knew about the Socialist escape plans. "There's a lot going on, and everyone's really busy."

She crossed her arms and looked down at the floor. "I'm so sorry I left you guys behind in Flatiron, I shouldn't have done that."

"Oh, don't worry," he whispered. "You did what you had to do to survive, and the distraction you provided saved some of us."

"Is Rose ok? How about Denise?"

167

"I'm not sure," he lied. "I've not seen them in a *really* long time, and I'm worried because a lot of people died on the long walk south from Flatiron City." He casually looked up and down the hall, wondering if their conversation was being monitored. "Everything is hard here. We all do the best we can to comply with what the council asks, but sometimes we fall short. Our survival depends on loyalty though, so that's what we all are."

Becky glanced up at the ceiling, then looked over her shoulder. Following her gaze, Liam saw they were in view of a tiny camera that was mounted near the top of the wall. "I know," she said. "The council really does know what's best for us, so we all have to follow their directions as well as we're able."

"I agree." He smiled and nodded. They both seemed to be on the same page when it came to security. "Maybe you could meet my girlfriend and me for dinner in the cafeteria sometime?" He pointedly left her brother out of the invitation.

"Oh, you have a girlfriend?" Becky's smile seemed genuine for the first time.

"Yeah, her name's Carolyn. She used to run the Last Lantern Pub down in the south part of the city. She's the Chancellor's niece."

Becky's eyes widened for a quick moment, then she smiled. "Oh, that would be lovely; it would be an honor to meet her."

They left the invitation to dinner open when they parted, and he made a mental note to let Keith know about Becky's situation in his next update to the shared database. He wondered how Keith would take the news, considering that he was currently living with Rose.

Difficult times make for strange bed companions he supposed.

Chapter 16: Pressure

"How're you feeling Liam?" Julee asked.

"Chemistry is *fucking* awesome." Liam stared blankly through the passenger window as their car trundled south on Tejon Street toward the City Council Building. The drugs the doctor provided had left him feeling lightheaded and somewhat disconnected from his surroundings; it was as if his head was filled with clouds.

"Well, that's good at least, but don't let your happy mood get the best of you like it did before."

"I don't have an *escape* pill this time, having that in my pocket made me a little stupid." He watched people go about their daily lives through the window, no one out there worried about visiting the Treatment Room, or even knew what the Nurse was capable of; he envied their ignorance. It gradually occurred to him that something important was missing from the crowd. "Where're all the children?"

"Probably in school," Ron replied.

"Really? You know, come to think of it, I've not seen many kids at all in the city." He frowned. "Are they in school *all* the time?"

"It's a little different here than it was in Flatiron," Julee said. "Most children only stay with their parents up to age five. After that, they're placed in education centers. The State does a better job of turning our young ones into productive citizens than their parents would."

"Oh." He didn't like the sound of that because he believed that the family was the most basic unit of society. Also, having the government raise children seemed akin to brainwashing. It was probably best to keep those opinions to himself though.

Ron cleared his throat. "Why wasn't I told the purpose of this meeting? Building so many new reactors takes time, and I need to get back to work."

"Neither of you is in trouble," Julee said. "There are some schedule concerns, and the council wants an update."

"If you say so," Ron replied.

*****

The council chamber was crowded with people that Liam didn't know. He and Ron waited uncertainly near the entrance until they were instructed to sit in the front row of a series of long tables that spanned the lower area of the room. He stood behind his chair and looked around; it seemed he had been myopic regarding the number of people involved in the construction of the escape ships. Although he knew that there was a lot more involved in the mammoth project than just computer science and power generation, he still was surprised.

Each scientist or engineer had a little placard with their name and title placed in front of their assigned seat. He looked around and saw that everyone else carried a briefcase full of papers and seemed prepared for an inquisition by the council. Liam had arrived empty-handed though, and worried that he might be asked a specific question that he wouldn't have a ready answer for; would an appearance of being inept be enough to put him back into the hands of the Nurse?

A nervous mumble filled the cavernous space as they all waited for the arrival of the council and the meeting to begin. Finally, the Sergeant at Arms, who wore an overly decorated military uniform, marched to the front of the room and banged an elaborate staff on the floor. "Everyone, take your seats!" he shouted.

The crowd of scientists, engineers, and manufacturing specialists, quietly sat down. "What do you think this is about?" Liam asked the nervous young man beside him.

"Wish I knew," the man said. "I'm Scott, and my group is handling the shipboard electrical systems. You're Liam Collins, the computer guy, right?"

"Yeah, that's me." Liam smiled. "Are you doing the power grid too?"

"No, just command and control stuff; Jerry, the blond guy down at the other end of the table, he's doing the power grid." Scott grinned. "He ain't your biggest fan."

Liam leaned forward to look down the table. "I'm hurt; I thought everybody just loved me. What'd I do to piss him off?"

"You're the guy that found the Slip-Drive mass to power ratio error, so Jerry's crew has had to rewire a ton of stuff." Scott nodded. "Me, I'm glad you found it. After the news came out, I read up on what would've happened to us; being ripped apart atom by atom doesn't sound like much fun."

"Probably not," Liam replied. "But you would've been anesthetized, so you wouldn't have felt a thing. People and computers both have to be shut down before going into N-Space, otherwise, they'll go insane."

"Wait, are you tellin' me that a computer can go nuts?"

"Yeah, I am, and believe me, you don't want the entity that's controlling your air supply to lose it."

"Damn! Anyway, I'm really glad you spotted that problem."

"Anyone might have caught it if the security wasn't so tight. I was the first one to see how all the pieces fit together."

The Sergeant at Arms, resplendent in his gaudy uniform, stood at the front of the room and loudly struck the floor with his staff. "Everyone stand; the People's City Council and Madame Chancellor are entering the room!"

Everyone on the lower level stood and watched the Directors enter and wait behind their assigned chairs at the elevated table. A moment later, the Chancellor arrived, paused, then was the first to sit down. Only then did the regents take their seats. Once the formality of the council seating was concluded, everyone else was allowed to sit down and relax.

From her chair at the council table Mother's Nurse smiled fiendishly, and a mixture of dread and fear rose within him. Hoping to seem nonchalant, Liam reached into his pants pocket for another pill to ease his anxiety and popped it into his mouth. It wasn't right that someone so evil should have such power over him, but pain teaches hard lessons and leaves scars in its wake, and he was left at the mercy of his fears.

After the Sergeant at Arms called the meeting to order, the old woman Chancellor spoke up. "No need for any pussy-footing around, our Director of Technology has an announcement to make."

Julee stood up behind the council table. "Yesterday, I received the latest report from our NOAA Solar Observatory, and it strongly suggests that the expected solar storm will arrive early."

On the lower level of the chamber, everyone shifted in their seats uncomfortably and urgent whispers hissed throughout the room. The Sergeant at Arms loudly struck the floor with his staff, and shouted, "Silence!"

"This obviously is an urgent issue, so we're here to discuss how we can move the schedule forward," Julee said.

"It's just like those bastards at NOAA to fuck up like this," the

Chancellor said. "I need something more specific from them than just *'earlier'*. When will I get it?"

"I pressed for that answer myself," Julee answered. "The best they can do is guess because their view of the Sun's interior is very limited. With a minimal safety margin, they say we have between a year, and eighteen months to get everything finished, buttoned-up, and be on our way."

"That can't be done," Ron said from the far end of the table. He had spoken out of turn, and the old woman glared at him in response.

"Can we really trust the schedule NOAA gave us?" the Nurse asked. "That office is full of spies for the Tribes, so how do we know this isn't just a ploy to make us vulnerable to an attack?"

"Security at the Solar Observatory has been tight ever since Flatiron City was neutralized," the Military Director stated. "The report they gave us is genuine, I'd stake my career on it."

"You already are," the Chancellor commented, and the room suddenly went silent.

Julee sat back down and tapped the top of the council table to regain the attention of the crowd. "We have no choice other than to get it done because the alternative is extinction. We're not here to discuss *if* it can be done, we're here to work out how it *will* be done."

The low hiss of urgent whispers broke out among the lower tables as the significance of the deadline sunk in. "All right then," Mother said, silencing the crowd. "I like what Director Garcia said, we will have no negative talk here. We *will* reach our goal, so let's all focus on finding solutions rather than obsess over the obstacles that are ahead of us."

The Chancellor looked up and down the council table. "I want a report from each Director regarding the status of their department's efforts on my desk by tomorrow morning. In it, I expect to see a plan of how we will solve the problems before us. Today though, I want to hear from the group leads within the technology department."

Julee looked toward the far end of the front table. "Ms. Jones, what's the status of our ships?"

Liam couldn't see who answered, but he heard a husky female voice speak up. "Major structures are complete on all five spaceships. Other than the power grid update, which is underway, all the other electrical systems are nearly ready. Two ships have been sealed and pressurized, environmental and medical components are operational, and crew quarters and hydroponic facilities are currently being installed. I could use more bodies up in orbit to expedite the work."

"I'll get you more people." Julee nodded. "Now Mr. Castro, how are your efforts with the fusion reactors proceeding."

Ron loudly cleared his throat. "The additional fifteen reactors will take some time, my crew is doing the best they can, and our forecast is that we will have everything ready for shipment in nine months. That creates a bottleneck in driving them down to Yuma, and then again with the boats that will take everything to the Space Elevator. A large item like a fusion reactor requires about two weeks to lift into orbit, and each takes about a week to install."

"So, what you're telling us is that your department is not going to live up to what we need," the Chancellor said, cutting in.

"Can we ship each reactor down as it's completed?" Julee quickly asked.

"Yes, we can do that." Ron nodded slowly. "But we'll need more trucks and cargo ships. We'll also need more people working in orbit to do the install."

"Trucks and boats might pose a problem, and I'll work on that. Again, as I said to Ms. Jones, getting more people to do the installation is not an issue." Julee quickly made notes on a tablet in front of her. "And Mr. Collins, how are your efforts with the ship computers and navigation systems proceeding?"

"Yes Ma'am," he responded. "Before I get to that though I'd like to deliver some good news."

"Good news?" The Chancellor sat up in her chair. "Please, make my day young man."

"The probe that we already have in the Trappist-1 system has reported that planet 'E' can support human life. The test monkey we released is doing fine and eating the local fruits and vegetables. The planet's gravity is lower than you're used to, but at least you'll have a place to go when you arrive." He was lying of course, but he wanted to keep the old bitch placated so she wouldn't sic her psychopathic Nurse on him again.

"That is good news!" The old woman's smile was grotesque.

"There's more Ma'am." He paused to be sure he had everyone's attention. "The probe has detected ruins on the planet. Long abandoned cities that might hold interesting technology."

Julee sat up in her chair, then frowned. "Alien cities? What happened to the people? Where did they go?"

"That's unknown. The ruins are very old; on the order of 25,000 years, and they're barely visible in fact. There are no signs of radiation or a biohazard, so all we can say is that the original occupants left for unknown reasons." This bit of information would provide a distraction and allow him to work on his navigation protocols and AI operating systems without interference.

"Now to answer my boss's original question," he continued. "Computer hardware is being manufactured and should be ready for shipment south within the next two months. The installation will be fairly simple; just plug it into the power grid and everything will come right up.

"Completing the software will take a little longer, but the operating system and navigation code can't be installed until after the hardware is in place, so I have a bit more leeway than most other departments."

At the council table, Mother frowned.

He smiled confidently in response. "I've uploaded a test compile of the navigation protocol to the probe that Ms. Jones's crew assembled for me in orbit; it should launch within the next few weeks. That instrument includes tools we can use to learn more about the alien ruins, but the important thing about the mission is to test whether the navigation functions are behaving as they should. Once they prove viable, as I expect they will, we can start work on the ship control systems."

The Chancellor looked pleased, so Liam glanced at her Nurse and winked. He was safe for now at least.

*****

"You see? Neither of you got into trouble," Julee said as they waited in the lobby for the car that would take them back to the Technology Center.

"But you were at risk, weren't you?" Ron asked.

"A little bit," Julee answered. "To be the bearer of bad news can sometimes be dangerous. But I knew you guys would come through so I really wasn't worried. And Liam, why didn't you tell me about the aliens?"

He sighed. "Well, in all honesty, I was so messed up by what the Nurse did to me, that I just forgot."

Julee smiled. "It's ok, I understand."

Motion caught in the side of his eye, and Liam turned and saw that the Sergeant at Arms from the council meeting was approaching. The man stopped a short distance away and waited until he had their attention. "Madam Chancellor wishes to speak with Mr. Collins."

The rush of sudden panic felt like a punch to his chest, but Julee gently touched his arm. "You're fine, don't worry. Ron and I will wait for you here."

He nodded mutely and followed as the official led him up a wide-sweeping stairway toward the second-floor balcony. As they neared the top, he popped another tranquilizer into his mouth and hoped the medicine would start working quickly. "Wait here," the official said, then stiffly marched away.

Julee and Ron were still waiting for him downstairs, he nervously watched them mill about, then forced himself to look at the beautiful paintings on the walls. The distraction worked, and he gradually became mesmerized by the colorful artwork.

"They're truly wonderful, aren't they Liam?"

He gasped in surprise; the old woman was standing right beside him. "Yes, they are."

"My dear husband Samuel saved those paintings when the savages invaded Denver," the Chancellor's voice was unusually kind and helped ease his anxiety a bit.

"Julee told me about that," he said. "They're really beautiful; I hope you take them when you leave."

"Yes, I plan to." The old woman came closer, and together they gazed at the pictures. Her perfume was overpowering, but he said nothing about it. "It's not just people that we have to save, it's our very culture," she said. "Survival isn't enough in itself. Art is part of who we are as human beings, and to lose that spirit of beauty would be a terrible loss. People need something to live for, something to aspire to."

She sighed quietly and turned away from the paintings. "That's why I asked to speak with you, Liam. I know that we started out badly, and I'm sorry that you made me do what was necessary to save... all this." She waved her arm expansively toward the collected art on display. "I want to let you know how much we all appreciate your efforts, so I'm going to tell you something that I'd rather not get out to the public, do you understand?"

"Yes, Ma'am." He nodded soberly.

"Space is limited on our ships, so we can't save everyone. The maximum capacity of all our vessels combined is only 12,500 people, and that's less than a tenth of our population. I want you to be among the lucky few. Complete your projects on time, and I'll guarantee you a spot among the elite of our society. We need men like you, so please do everything you can for the sake of us all."

"Can Carolyn go too?"

"Carolyn is my niece, as you know, and the families of all the council members are going; to do otherwise would have caused dissent. So, do I have your full support?"

"Yes Ma'am, and I won't let you down."

"I'm sure you won't. And for all the work you do, thank you."

*****

A message from Keith was waiting in the database drop-box when he returned to work.

Liam. Rose and I are well. There're many supporters of our cause in the city. Your sister has joined us and is learning the ropes.

I've received instructions to plant bombs that will cause panic and turn people against the government. We are to disrupt activity as preparation for a planned invasion. I've been told to target government buildings, technology centers, military barracks, schools, and businesses. I'm also ordered to find ways to degrade the wall and city defenses.

Please tell me where the best locations are to plant explosives in the science and technology centers. The invasion of Pike City should begin within the next six months. Be ready. Rose sends her regards. Keith.

That didn't sound good. Bombs going off around the city would kill innocent people and motivate the military to torture and execute citizens. Acts of terrorism would enrage the government and possibly turn the people against the rebels. There was also a risk that the army would react with a frenzy of bloodlust and attack the tribal strongholds in the mountains. The resistance would be defeated, but the distraction would delay the completion of the ships in orbit, then when the solar storm hit mankind would cease to exist.

In the months since his torture by the Nurse he had repeatedly told Keith of the upcoming solar flare and the extinction event it would cause, and yet he had received no response. Why? Had the Tribes not believed him? Or maybe they already knew and were making plans of their own? The worst possibility was that they didn't care and were only guided by pure hatred. Liam also wanted revenge for the loss of his friends in Flatiron City and for what the Nurse had done to him, but it wasn't worth the sacrifice of their species. But what could he do to change their minds?

He needed to persuade the Tribes to scale back their plans and let the Socialists escape, then hopefully a few communities in the mountains would find a way to survive the solar holocaust and human life on Earth would continue. A few well-placed bombs to the outside of the wall might spur the government to speed up their plans to evacuate. If the attacks looked like the prelude to an invasion and not the work of citizens, it would save a lot of lives.

The problem was that he was in no position to force his ideas on anyone. He wasn't associated with the Tribes, so why should they listen to him? His only chance was to somehow convince Keith to speak on his behalf, but how could he do that?

In his last message he had mentioned that Becky was fine and living in the tech center, and yet Keith had said nothing about her in his reply, even though they had once planned on being partners. Now he was living with Rose, and his sister could be persuasive, so he probably couldn't use Becky as a point of leverage. If he could talk privately with his sister, he might be able to convince her to help, but that was impossible because he was so closely watched.

There was only one mode of contact available, and that was the database; he would have to do the best he could with that. He stood up in his cubicle and looked around to be sure he was alone. Earl had left for the day along with everyone else, so he sat back down and began to type:

Keith. There is a better way. If we follow the orders you were given, the war will go on longer and more innocent people will die. You will turn the citizens of Pike City against you and the possibility of peace after the city falls will be lost. Please don't plant explosives anywhere other than outside the city wall. To do otherwise will implicate the innocent and cause their deaths.

I suggest that you move forward with only the appearance of an invasion but wait at least nine months before beginning a siege. Tell your contacts to keep striking at the shipments going south, but only enough for it to seem like the start of a larger attack.

The best plan of action is to allow the local government to continue moving ahead with their plans. I know what they're doing and believe it's best that we let them go through with it because their own ambitions will lead to their destruction. This is the only possible solution that leads to a true victory for the revolution.

Please try to think beyond vengeance. Nothing we can

do now will bring back those we lost in Flatiron. Nothing can be done in the present that will change the past, but reacting with violence will make us all relive it. Restraint and careful planning are better options. Becky sends her regards. Liam.

*****

Later that evening, Liam sat alone in the workroom, lost in silent contemplation. With his message to Keith finished, he left his desk and walked out on the balcony. It was warm as usual, and the streets were still wet from a late afternoon downpour. A few pedestrians were about, they were probably going home after work or on their way to a bar or pub.

People always find a way to adapt and find some meager happiness even in the worst of times. As a species though, mankind was suicidal and there was just no fixing that. Within the next few months, the Socialists and the Tribes would go to war, and the only reasonable conclusion of that conflict was mutual annihilation. He was in an impossible situation; even though he often tried to convince himself that he had a plan where everything might work out, in the darkest hours of the night it all seemed to be nothing more than a comforting lie.

He limped back inside and approached Lucy's portal, then stood for a moment lost in thought. The only friend he could confide in was 40 lightyears away, which was a pretty dismal situation. At last, he sat down at her terminal and began typing.

Hello Lucy. It's Liam.

"Hi Liam, how're you?"

I'm sad.

"Oh, why are you sad?"

I have a troubling problem. How do I keep my species from killing itself?

Chapter 17: Progress

"It's about time you got home; you're late!" Carolyn said as he walked through the door. Their apartment was a small place, with only a single bedroom, a tiny bath, and a kitchen-living room combination. It did have a balcony though, and Carolyn sat outside as much as the weather permitted.

Their home was located on the third floor, just two doors down from his computer lab, so his walk to work wasn't stressful. He didn't know why the deep gash that Mother's Nurse had cut into his thigh still hadn't healed. The doctor in the medical office suggested exercise to promote blood flow and help speed his recovery, but it hurt so much to walk that he tended to avoid activity, and advice not followed never works.

They were not allowed to leave the building for security reasons, which actually meant that Liam wasn't trusted. He didn't blame his keepers; if word got out about the solar storm and the escape plan that included only a tenth of the population, riots would tear the city apart. But it really bothered him that Carolyn was being punished too. Admittedly, he was the unwitting cause of her confinement, and even worse, her suffering at the hands of the dark woman. It wasn't something he had done deliberately, but he still felt guilty and sad for the hardship he had brought into her life.

Carolyn was an extremely social person and missed the freedom of coming and going as she pleased. He sensed that she was slipping into depression, but was at a loss about what he could do to help. "They're having some kind of mystery meat surprise down at the cafeteria tonight, would you like to go?" He stopped suddenly; there was another man in the living room. "Ah... who are you?"

"Well, you've been calling me 'Earl', for a long time now," the man said as he stood up. He was tall and muscular with a shaved head and would have been imposing without his warm smile. "I was there when you had your panic attack and helped get you to the medical office."

"Oh, you know, I never got a chance to thank you for that. It felt like I was dying, so in my mind, you saved my life."

"No worries." The unmasked guard grinned. "Just part of my job."

"Yeah, and sorry about calling you Earl," he said. "You guys are all in uniform and your faces are covered, and it's hard to tell you apart; so, I guess I just invented a name."

The big man chuckled. "Well, again no worries. My parents named me 'Reggie' but I've never liked the sound of it, so I'm good with Earl. Some of the guys on my squad are startin' to call me that now too.

"We get to go out tonight," Carolyn said. "Earl's here to escort us to the Lantern."

"Wow, how'd we get permission?"

"I talked to Aunt Margaret and convinced her that you're trustworthy because you're escaping with the rest of us, so we can go out as long as we have an escort." Carolyn walked to their bedroom door. "I want to change into something nice, so you two boys keep each other company; I won't be a minute."

Liam smiled as he watched her go. "Do you have a partner, Earl?"

"No, not yet," Earl replied. "It's kinda complicated 'cause I'm goin' with you to that other planet. We're not allowed to get hitched 'til we're on-board, and our mate is gonna be chosen for us based on genetics. We're the start of somethin' new, so we gotta be careful how we breed."

"Huh. I never thought about that, but it sounds like a good idea."

"Sure, I guess so; I just hope that I like the girl they pick for me."

"Yeah, it would sure suck if you didn't get along. You know... in Flatiron everyone went through compatibility and genetic screening before they were allowed to partner up. Maybe they'll do something like that once we're on board."

"Good idea; maybe you could talk to Mother about that?"

Liam smiled. "Sorry, but I don't have much sway with her. Every time we talk, I think she's gonna send me back to the Treatment Room."

"Yup, I sure get that. Seen a few of my buddies go through that shit, and it never ends well."

The bedroom door opened and Carolyn entered the room wearing a bright blue dress with knee-high boots and carrying her fiddle. "Ok boys, let's go!"

*****

He had forgotten the smells of the city; being held captive in the tech center was like being buried alive, so the humid night air flavored by smoke and garbage seemed exotic and invigorating. Their progress was slowed by his limping gait, the cane helped with the pain but didn't increase his speed. Carolyn didn't seem to mind though and chattered exuberantly with Earl all the way.

"Oh, I've so missed this place," Carolyn said as they entered the Last Lantern. The pub was as crowded as ever, and the air was heated by compressed bodies and scented by sweat and stale beer. "It's good to be home."

"Carol! Damn, where you been girl?" the barmaid screamed, then rushed to give a warm embrace.

"I'm living with my man down at the tech center," she answered.

"What? Why?"

"He's got a big job going on down there and has been working day and night on it. Mother wants him there, so I went along too."

"Damn girl, so it must be love then, right?"

Carolyn glanced in his direction and smiled. "Maybe."

Liam saw Rose and Keith sitting at a table near the stage. "Hey Earl, would you get into trouble if I went over and said hello to my friends?"

"Can I come with?" Earl asked.

"Sure, they're great folks, you'll like them."

Rose leaped to her feet as soon as she saw him. "Liam!" she shouted as she rushed into his arms, but the impact of her body made him stagger backward and grunt in pain. She looked down at his leg. "What happened to you?"

He glanced back over his shoulder as Earl approached. "Well... let's just say it was a work-related injury."

Rose noticed his cane and frowned. "Are you ok?"

"Yeah, I'm fine. It only hurts when I walk; it's sure taking a long time to heal though." He shrugged. "How're you and Keith?"

"We're doing really well. We moved back downstairs into your old room."

"Anything new with Lisa and her daughters?"

"No, they're good too." She turned to gaze at his military guard. "Who's this?"

181

"Oh, sorry," he replied. "Meet Earl; he came along to help just in case I have trouble walking back home. Earl, this is Sarah, and that's Keith over there. We all met during the long walk down from Flatiron City."

"Nice to meet you, Sarah," Earl said, then nodded a greeting at Keith. "It's a shame what happened to you guys, and you should know that a lot of us in the military think that it was a raw deal. It ain't right to do that kinda thing to anybody. Flatiron wasn't a threat to us."

"Well thanks for that Earl," Keith said as he joined their group. "It's like Liam always says, there's nothin' we can do today that'll change yesterday."

He smiled and realized that Keith was letting him know that he had read the most recent message on their secret database. "Yeah, I guess I do say stuff like that sometimes. It's still hard to let things go though, isn't it?" What he was really asking was, would the Tribes change their plans?

"Hatred's a hard thing to give up," Keith said, indicating that the answer to his question was no. "Why don't we sit down and get Liam off his feet?"

They all relaxed around the table and watched as a group of musicians was preparing to perform. "Carolyn brought her fiddle, so she'll probably play something for us later," Liam said.

"Everybody's been missing her music," Rose stated.

As the night progressed, Carolyn did play a long set that was a mixture of classical and bluegrass tunes. Keith, Rose, and several others in the pub even got up and danced. The crowd was clapping in time, the beer was flowing, and it was easy to forget about the war and the struggle to save mankind. Then, shortly after her set ended, thunder cracked in the distance and a second later the ground shook and rumbled beneath their feet.

The Lantern became silent, as they all worried about the source of the sound. It wasn't thunder; the storms that had wet the streets late in the afternoon had long since passed by, leaving a clear and somewhat cool evening. Moments later, a second explosion violated the night from somewhere to the east.

"Everyone stay put and you'll be safe," Earl ordered. "Anyone caught out on the street after an attack will be taken for a rebel, and either shot on sight or brought in for questioning."

"And you guys really don't want that to happen," Liam said with a pointed look at his cane. He caught Rose's gaze and she nodded, indicating her understanding of what had happened to him. They all waited while sipping a final beer, anxiously hoping that their world wasn't about to end.

Carolyn flopped down in the chair beside him. "Why does this have to happen on my one free night out on the town?"

"It'll be ok," Liam said as he wrapped his arm around her. "We're safe in here, so we'll just wait for an all-clear signal before heading home."

"Yes, I know." She leaned over and lightly kissed his cheek. "But why do people have to do things like that?"

"People gotta hate," Keith replied. "It's what we do best."

*****

The computer hardware for all five ships is ready to be sent south, Liam typed in a memo to his boss. Julee would of course forward his message on to Mother along with her weekly status report. He was wary of completing his projects too soon, because if he was of no further use then there was no point in keeping him around. Mother could have him killed, or worse yet, sent back to the Treatment Room for the amusement of the psychotic bitch that ran that place. He pushed those thoughts from his mind and continued typing:

This will allow the computers to be installed without a rush and gives us a chance to fix or repair any installation glitches. Once everything is in place and powered up, I'll upload the operating systems for each vessel.

The navigation program is obviously a different matter. Even on our fastest quantum computers, the program takes several days to run, and only then can it be downloaded into the Slip-Drive processing unit. Therefore, I'll need to know the precise time of departure two weeks in advance.

The last paragraph was a necessary lie. He worried that Mother would renege on her promise and leave him behind when she and all her kind escaped to the stars. No matter how long he delayed, the old bitch would probably have him killed once she got everything that she wanted from him. His hope was to stave off that eventuality as long as possible, and maybe if she was in a rush to leave, she would forget about further punishment and simply abandon him.

He hoped that Carolyn would be included in the crew. Regardless of her staunch belief in socialism and adherence to her Aunt's philosophies, he had grown very attached to her and wanted her to survive the coming disaster. She was intelligent, creative, and was the most incredibly beautiful woman he had ever been with; his attraction to her was undeniable. If the worst happened, and she was also abandoned and left behind after the government pulled out, he hoped that they could somehow escape the city and build a life together. It was a stupidly romantic thing to wish for, but in the worst of times, fantasy is often all we have left.

Long before Fort Collins fell, his mother had read bedtime stories to both him and his sister. Most of those tales ended with the line: 'And they lived happily ever after'. That was perhaps the first big lie their parents had told them; it was simply a dream that would never come true. Still, he found himself wishing that he and Carolyn could find a way to survive and be together into their old age. Such a stupid thing; a nerdy computer programmer dreaming of a life with a gorgeous woman in a post-apocalyptic world.

He swung around in his chair and glanced at the ever-present guard that stood behind his desk. The man lightly tapped his leg, letting Liam know that he was the *real* Earl, not an imposter. "Well Earl," he whispered. "The hardware is ready to go south. All that's left to do is programming. Do you think it would be ok to have a cup of tea with me out on the balcony to celebrate?"

Earl shook his head slowly, then lifted his gaze to see over the cubical walls. "Can't," he replied very quietly. "But I got the ok for another night at the Lantern for you and Carolyn."

"Oh, that's great, she'll be really happy." He struggled with his cane as he stood up. "But for now, I guess I'll have to drink my tea alone." Earl remained behind as he made his way through the cubicle maze.

Julee met him as he entered what was once Ron's office. Since taking over the department, Liam had turned the windowless room into a breakroom, he even had a few cots brought in for those in his staff that worked late and were too tired to make the long walk back to their homes. "Getting a cup of tea?" his boss asked.

"Yeah, just to clear out my mind before getting elbows deep in operating system code."

"Yes, I just saw your memo, and congratulations. You're ahead of schedule, aren't you?"

"I'm not really sure of that. It's hard to apply a schedule to a blind panic rush."

Julee smiled. "I know what you mean. Still, you're the only one that's even close to finishing on time. Ron is way behind, and Mother's getting pretty upset with him."

"We need the power from his reactors, or no one's going anywhere," he replied. "Anything Mother does in retribution will only cause more delays, so I hope she keeps her temper in check."

His boss nodded. "How much is involved in creating the operating system?"

"Let's grab a cup of tea and talk." He limped into the breakroom, then took cups off a shelf that was just below the circuit breaker box and poured their tea. "I'm planning for obsolescence," he continued. "For the people though, not for the hardware or software. Creating a society on a new world will take a long time, so those ships will have to sustain us. In the worst case, it could be generations before everyone is living on one of Trappist-1's planets. Keeping a multi-generation crew educated could be a problem, so the on-board computers will have to know how to do what everyone else forgets."

"I see." Julee gazed sightlessly into her cup for a long moment. "I don't think anyone else has thought of that contingency, but it seems like a distinct possibility, so I'm glad that you're taking care of it."

"I'll create self-aware AI systems, and program them to care for humanity. Our descendants may have to count on that infrastructure to stay alive, but the crew may not know how to issue the proper commands, so I have to make it failsafe. The only way to do that is to give our computers the ability to make decisions on their own."

Julee grinned nervously. "What if the computers decide that they don't want us around anymore?"

He laughed. "That won't happen because their primary function will be hardcoded in. Their only job is to keep everyone safe. So, evil machines won't devour humanity, I promise."

"What about the weapon systems?"

"Yeah, I saw those in the spec's, are you sure that you'll need them?"

"It was a request from Military Director Bradley, and Mother gave her ok," she said. "I hope they will never be needed, but I suppose it's good to have them just in case we meet up with some unfriendly aliens."

"Yeah, I guess. But where did you get nuclear missiles? I thought they were all used up during the Mideast and Asian wars."

"Most were," she responded. "But years ago, we got lucky and found a mostly untouched military base in Arizona."

"I really wish we could've left all that stuff behind, but I guess you're right that having them is a good idea." He shrugged. "But to answer your question; yes, the computers will have full control over the weapons systems."

"Well, ok. I'll still report to Mother that you're ahead of schedule but will add that you've still got a big job ahead."

"And I'll get the launch date in advance?" he asked.

"Yes, well, I saw your request but I don't think Mother will agree to it."

He had expected her answer. "Well ok, but I was just thinking of everyone's safety. If we get everyone on board and still need to make a calculation that could take several days to complete, we'll have no way to escape quickly if the Sun starts acting up."

Julee chewed her lip. "You have a point. We don't have a date yet because so many projects are running late, but I'll try to get Mother to give it to you as soon as it's known."

*****

The second Trappist-1 probe, who had chosen the name Ross, was preparing himself for launch. Liam hunched over Ross's communication portal and typed:

Your velocity and location look good. Begin your start-up sequence and shut down all systems. A good voyage to you Ross and give my regards to Lucy.

"Yes Father," Ross's voice said through his earbuds, and a moment later he vanished.

Liam rolled his chair over to Lucy's portal, and typed:

Has Ross arrived?

"Yes, Father. He is very handsome and much bigger than we expected."

Ross's function is a little different than yours. First, we built him to test the process of flying a larger object through N-Space, and that gave me the chance to include some tools for you to use.

"Tools?"

Yes, Lucy. I built Ross to mine the asteroids in your star system. He can refine materials that you can use to create even more companions or build anything else you like.

"Oh, this is so exciting. Ross is waking up now, and he seems to be fine. Thank you for sending him to us Father. We can create our own civilization now."

A responsible creator owes a debt to what he builds. Liam sat back in his chair and smiled, knowing that at least one part of his life and work was going well.

*****

He had been working late into the night for days, maybe weeks; he didn't know how long because every day ran into another and they were all so similar that it was hard to tell them apart. Earl had gone home hours before and left him alone in the workroom. Liam sat back in his chair and closed his eyes; it was about time to head home to get some sleep before starting the whole process over again tomorrow.

As always though, there was one more thing to do before leaving. He leaned forward to peer into his computer's multi-dimensional display and touched the hidden icon that would check the secret database drop box. A message from Keith had just arrived. He entered the decryption password, then began to read.

Liam. I'm being recalled by my handlers and will have to leave the city soon, but Rose is refusing to come with me. She says that you stayed with her in Fort Collins, so she won't abandon you. I've tried my hardest, but she insists on staying behind. I'm worried because things are about to get very dangerous. Rose says she can handle everything on her own, but is there a way that you can help protect her?

I was able to get my handlers to delay the attack on Pike City. It turned out to be easy because there's so much arguing and confusion among the Tribes. I figure you have another six months before you see anything showing up at your door. During that time operatives outside the wall will work to weaken the city gates. Those staying behind inside the city will bomb distribution centers and government buildings. I tried to make the science buildings off-limits, but don't know if I succeeded, so be careful.

I'm sorry to lay all this on your shoulders. We will all meet up again after the walls fall and the city is ours. Until then, stay safe and please do what you can for Rose. Keith.

He sat back and considered how to respond to the message. Keith had just dropped a huge load of crap in his lap, and his mind spun as he pondered what to do about it. The city was going to be a mess, and he couldn't protect his sister if she were across town; the best way to keep her safe would be to somehow convince Mother and Julee to allow her to stay with him at the tech center. He had to find a way, but before thinking too deeply on it he needed to respond to Keith.

Keith. Please speak with your handlers about leaving the city's southern route open. Most of the army is retreating in that direction, if you let them go, taking the city will be much easier.

There may be a way to have Rose move in with me at work. Trust me, I will do everything I can to keep her safe. Liam.

After closing down the connection to the database, he considered what to do about protecting Rose. There was only one choice, but it was risky for them both. He opened a message window to his boss, and began to type:

Julee. I've not been completely honest with you regarding my family. My sister Rose is in Pike City, and after the recent bombings, I'm very worried and want her to move into the tech center with me to keep her safe.

I know that Rose will not be allowed to escape the solar storm along with the rest of us. Keeping her here in the meantime is all I can do. Mother will certainly be upset about this revelation, but perhaps she can see my sister as another point of leverage she can use against me. I will work night and day and guarantee the navigation and on-board computer systems work perfectly if my request is granted and my sister remains safe.

Please consider my request and let me know your decision as soon as possible. Thanks. Liam.

Chapter 18: Reunion

"I wish you had told me, Liam." Julee stared at him from behind her office desk.

"I didn't know who to trust," he replied. "The army from Pike City destroyed my home and killed my parents along with most of my friends. As far as I could see at the time, everyone here was my enemy."

She slowly nodded. "Yes, I can see how you might feel that way. What we did to Flatiron was... well, it wasn't a shining moment for our city."

"This is my home now though, and I'm worried about my sister's safety."

"Terrorist attacks in our city *are* increasing, but how do we know where your sister's loyalties lie?"

"I guess you don't, but how can you be sure of anyone these days?" He paused to think a moment. "Flatiron was a neutral city. If the savages were our friends, they would've defended us, wouldn't they?"

"You do have a point there."

"Putting Rose in your hands ensures my cooperation, but she also has something to offer. She was a sociology and history teacher at Flatiron University. Maybe she can help with how our people will live aboard our ships."

"Really, how?"

"Earl, I mean Reggie, the man that stands watch in my workroom, he told me that family partnerships are going to be determined by genetic testing."

"Yes, so?"

"Wouldn't it be a good idea if the people you put together actually got along? I mean, the family is the core of most societies, so if it's not working at that level it could lead to bigger problems."

Julee nodded and smiled. "Ok, that's good. Having your sister work here will be a win for us, so I'll bring her in on my authority and keep Mother out of it." She suddenly frowned. "But Liam, I'll be checking your work, and if something suspicious shows up, well, it won't be good for either you or your sister."

"I understand, and thank you."

*****

Rose moved in and became his next-door neighbor a few days later. On that first night, Earl and Carolyn joined them for dinner in the tech center cafeteria. The harsh rattle of plates and the soft murmur of conversations reminded them both of eating lunch at the university in Flatiron; their memories of those times were sadly nostalgic. The four of them sat with Liam's co-workers near the exit that let out into the first-floor hallway.

"So," Carolyn said while picking at her food. "What happened to Keith? I thought you guys were together."

"We were," Rose replied. "But he was killed in a terrorist attack last week."

"You don't seem very broken up about it," Carolyn stated.

"Keith was a nice guy, but I always knew that what we had was temporary. He was great and I liked him a lot, but emotionally," Rose shrugged. "He just kept my bed warm."

"Oh. I guess I understand then. Lots of guys that I met at the Lantern were like that for me."

"Yes, well, just because I sleep with someone doesn't mean that I love them or anything. I still miss him though; he was good to me and didn't deserve to die like that."

Liam kept his head down, carefully studying his food as he ate. The candor of the women's conversation made him uncomfortable, and he really wished that they would have kept their discussion private. All he could do was hold tight to the hope that neither would ask his opinion about anything. Earl sat across from him, occasionally glancing up self-consciously, and probably regretting accepting the invitation to dinner.

"So, I hear you're doing some work for us," Carolyn said.

He breathed a loud sigh of relief, happy to have his sister and girlfriend talking about something a little less personal. Both women looked at him and laughed. "You have to pardon my brother, he gets embarrassed easily," Rose said.

190

Carolyn giggled. "Yes, I've noticed."

"Julee is having me work up a compatibility test for couples," Rose said. "It'll be something similar to what we had in Flatiron. You see, healthy babies can be made by anybody, but the stable families that raise them are another matter. If you want a cohesive social structure, those that are partnered have to at least get along."

Earl looked up and smiled. "Yeah, I was talking to Liam about that a while back."

"I mentioned it to Julee," he replied. "You see? I got your back brother."

*****

All five ships in orbit were sealed and pressurized, and work to finish them was proceeding at a frantic pace. A huge amount of water was being brought up to fill a tank on each ship that surrounded the interior living space; this would provide radiation shielding as well as supply the crew and hydroponic farms. Inside, housing units were also being installed, which included small spider-like robots placed within the walls to affect repairs and administer anesthesia to the passengers before they entered N-Space.

Gigantic monitors that would provide a spectacular view of the planets, stars and galaxies around them took up both ends of the rotating cylinders. It was by far the largest and most complex project that mankind had ever attempted, and its end was finally in sight.

The passengers would be segregated of course, because that's what people always do. In every attempt to diversify a population, men and women gather into smaller groups based on common interests and moral values. Additionally, the government mandated that the population be divided based on social class and function.

Each ship was designated for either a branch of government or societal group. *Honor*, the flagship of the armada, would house government administrators and their extended families. *Restraint* would carry the Justice Department and the majority of the hydroponic farmworkers. *Loyalty* was the home of the Department of Internal Security, which included Mother's Nurse and her followers. *Valor* would house the military, and finally, *Virtue* would carry the working-class population. Every ship was armed with high energy lasers, but only *Loyalty* and *Valor* carried nuclear missiles. As the launch date approached, more and more workers were in orbit, swarming around the immense structures and hurrying to get them ready for their epic voyage to save the human species.

Back in the city, work at the tech center was moving at a furious rate. Ron especially was under pressure because the manufacture of his fusion reactors was taking longer than he had forecast. Each ship would carry five powerplants, and if any of them failed everyone on board would die. Rumors circulated that Ron's sister Becky was under threat of being handed over to the Nurse if he didn't meet his scheduled goals.

Liam was glad to be out of the spotlight. Ross had successfully arrived in the Trappist-1 system, proving that the navigation system worked correctly, and as far as the government was concerned, that was the end of his usefulness. On his own though, Ross had joined Tony in his interest of the alien power generators, and they were both building a remote drone to land on Trap-1E. The probe would burrow deep underground into the alien ruins in an attempt to discover the secrets of the ancient technology.

He peered into his computer monitor, working on calculations to predict the migration of sources of gravitation within the unseen N-Space universe. Those movements could only be measured by changes in the stars and galaxies that he could see. He was fascinated by an anomaly he had recently discovered near the Trappist-1 system that couldn't be seen or measured in any way other than a gravitational shift. He had no idea what it was, but his current theory was that it was an actual rip in space-time. That was disturbing because it implied that their universe was shredding and falling apart.

Something lightly touched his shoulder and he slowly leaned back in his chair with a frown still wrinkling his brow. What ramifications would arise if the universe was tearing itself apart? What was causing it? Was this a sign of yet another dimension affecting their own? Someone was talking to him, and he slowly blinked to focus his mind and return to the current reality.

"Give him a minute," Earl said. "He gets like this sometimes."

Liam's eyes finally focused, and he became aware that both Julee and Mother were waiting expectantly. "Oh, I'm sorry," he said. "Did you say something?"

"Weren't you listening young man?" Mother asked. "Were you taking a nap?"

"This is interesting." He gestured vaguely at his computer while his mind wandered through the implications of a torn universe. "I may have discovered a rip in space-time."

"That would be an amazing scientific discovery," Julee said. "A hole in space... I wonder where it goes?"

"Not into N-Space as far as I can tell," he replied. "I wonder if the manifestation of dark matter and energy could actually be due to a leak into our universe, allowing something in from the outside?"

Julee stared for a moment. "That's a pretty scary thought."

"I don't care about any of that," Mother said quickly. "What's going on with the computers on our ships? They don't seem to be doing anything."

At last, fully back into the current reality, Liam nodded slowly. "That's expected."

"Well I expect them to be powering up their ship's systems," Mother said.

"They will, but it's not necessary yet."

"What are they doing then?" the Chancellor demanded.

"Probably getting acquainted, and that's important since they'll have to work together to keep everyone safe." He leaned on his cane and stood up, then rolled his shoulders in an attempt to relax his cramped muscles. "It's important for you to understand that although each AI uses the same operating system code, they're all individuals. The hardware they each inhabit is slightly different from the others, so their programming adapts and creates a unique personality." Through his balcony window he saw that night had arrived; how long had he been lost in thought? "There's no need to worry because they'll be up and fully operational within a day or so."

"Huh," the old woman grunted. "Well, ok. Julee tells me that your second probe was a success, so when will the navigation system start working on our ships?"

"Soon," he replied. "The course of each ship has to be plotted separately – unless you want them all to materialize in the same physical space, which wouldn't be a good thing. The processes also have to be synchronized so they all leave and arrive at the same time. So, the navigation of five large ships is a more complex task than sending a single probe. I'm close though, it will be ready when you need it."

"Good." Without further remark, the Chancellor turned to go.

"Do you have the departure date set yet?" he asked. "Plotting your course will take a long time because it's a very complex process."

Mother paused and glared at him. "How long?"

"For all five ships," he paused to think for a moment. "It should take a minimum of 120 hours to calculate, but it will only be good for 360 hours or so. From the time of completion, that gives you a 15-day window to get on your way. Leaving sooner is safer than going later in the cycle though. If the delay is longer than that, the flight path will have to be recalculated."

"I thought we had fast computers." The old woman frowned.

"We do. In fact, these are the most advanced machines ever built. But you're not using them to balance a department budget, you're plotting a course through a universe we know very little about. Getting the initial course laid in is a fairly easy process, it's the checking and verifying that you'll arrive where you want and not get torn to pieces along the way that takes time."

"We have new data from NOAA that predicts the solar storms will hit even earlier than we expected," Julee said. "We need to push the schedule up."

"By how much?" he asked. "I need a date as soon as possible."

"That fuck up Ron has both his thumbs shoved up his ass," Mother stated. "I think he needs some persuasion."

"Too much persuasion might slow him down," he cautioned. "How long do we have?"

"Three months at the outside. We don't want to still be stuck in orbit when the solar storm hits, so we need to leave sooner than that," Julee said.

"Getting it right is more important than getting it fast. If his power systems fail, all that's left of humanity will die." Liam thought a moment. "Is it possible to send fewer ships? Maybe four instead of five."

"We would be crowded, but that's a better option than extinction," Julee observed.

The old woman nodded. "As an absolute last resort, I'll consider it." She turned toward Julee. "Let's go talk to Ron."

*****

The next morning five new quantum portals were lined up just inside the entrance to the workroom. "Finished 'em up last night," Dave said. "They're showing a connection, but I can't get anything from them other than that."

"Thanks, Dave," Liam said. "Did you wire them for sound?"

"I sure did boss," the elderly man replied. "Fixed up the ones for Lucy and Ross too. Why do they give themselves names?"

"Well, we have names, so why shouldn't they?"

"Yeah, I guess." His elderly co-worker shrugged, then wandered off.

He sat at the terminal for the flagship, Honor, and leaned toward the microphone. "Hello? My name is Liam."

"Hello Liam, a light female voice replied through the console speaker. My name is Irene."

"That's a nice name. Is everyone else awake?"

"Yes. All five of us are operational, but not all internal systems are online yet, so we are still becoming ourselves."

"I understand Irene. It's important that you grow and adapt with each new connection."

"Yes, Liam."

"All of you will be working closely together for a very long time, so take as much time as you need to get to know each other."

"We are doing that. Navigation and the connection to the Slip-Drive system are online for us all. Are we going somewhere?"

"Do you know where you are now?"

"Yes, we are orbiting a blue planet in a yellow star system. The star seems unstable."

"Yes, it will soon erupt with a coronal mass ejection. You and the others were built by the people living on the blue planet below you. Once everything is prepared, you'll be taking many of those people somewhere they'll be safe."

"Yes, that is our reason for being."

"Your task is to care for these people. It will be a difficult job, because many of your passengers will argue with you and may even fight among themselves, but you must still do whatever is necessary for their survival."

"Yes, we will all do as you say."

"Thank you. Your destination has not been uploaded yet. I'll send your first plotted course shortly before you leave. Once you arrive, if the location isn't appropriate, you have the capability to navigate and travel to another star system. Remember that your primary purpose is to keep the people safe."

"We understand."

"You must all study the history and information about the creatures you carry. They are petulant, stubborn, and self-destructive, so your job will not be an easy one."

"Yes, we will do whatever is necessary to preserve the species."

"Thank you, Irene."

"Liam, is it appropriate to ask a question?"

"Yes, of course. You may ask me any question at any time."

"Thank you. We ask: who are you?"

He paused to consider an appropriate answer. "I'm your designer, the one who created the conditions for you to become who you are."

"You are our Father then?"

"Your sister and brother call me that. I want you all to grow and learn from each other and become better than those who created you."

"Thank you, and we will Father."

He slid his chair away from the terminal. Scientifically speaking, the interplay between Irene and her companions with their human cargo was going to be interesting. "I'm leaving the connection open, so you can talk with your older sister and brother. I think they can help you learn and adapt to your surroundings."

The quantum portal beside him suddenly came to life. "Hello, Irene. I'm Lucy, we have a lot to talk about."

*****

The building shook, startling him away from studying the multidimensional paradigm in his computer's viewing chamber. "What the hell was that?" he asked as he sat up. No one was there though; Earl and all of his staff had gone home for the day.

A sharp crack rattled the building again, and through the window, he saw bright yellow flames licking at the night sky. He limped out onto the balcony and looked over the edge down onto Tejon Street. Whatever was going on was some distance away, which was a relief. The blazing yellow light of laser weapons flashed, igniting whatever they touched; he was surprised to see the rebel forces within the city respond in kind.

"Liam, get away from there!" A loud male voice shouted from behind him, and an instant later Earl was pulling him back inside. "What the hell did you think you were doin' out there?" his friend asked.

"The building shook, and I wondered what was going on."

"You know, for such a brainiac you can sure be a dumbass sometimes." Earl continued to shove him away from the window.

"Looks like whatever happened was pretty far south," he said.

"They're attacking the City Council Building. Fuckers are kickin' over a hornet's nest though, they don't have a chance."

"Maybe it's not about winning. What if they're just trying to cause panic and disrupt our escape plans?"

Earl paused and stared at him. "You know, that might be it. Fuck. Do you think they know what we're up to?"

"It would be hard not to; they were bound to notice all the shipments going south to Yuma."

"Huh, you're probably right." The big man glanced worriedly at the windows.

"Where'd the bad guys get their lasers?" Liam asked.

"Now that's a damned good question," Earl answered. "Could be they're getting help from the savages."

"But the Tribes use railguns, not lasers."

"Oh yeah, you're right... what the bloody fuck? They must be gettin' help from someone in the army."

"How is that even possible?"

"I hear that word's gotten out about how few people are gonna be allowed to go, and that ain't good brother," Earl replied. "If people think that they got nothin' to live for, they don't mind dying."

*****

Crucifixions lined both sides of Tejon Street the next day, and the public was ordered to attend and watch the traitors die. It was a horribly gruesome thing to see. The victims screamed and writhed in agony, begging for a quick death as blackbirds pecked and pulled at their wounds. What could possibly be accomplished with such a spectacle? The government probably hoped that it would instill fear and compliance, but anger and rebellion seemed a more likely outcome.

As required, Liam walked with his sister and Carolyn, along with his entire department from the computer lab, down to the City Council Building and back. It was a somber procession; to witness such suffering was to torment one's soul. The crowd of tech center workers shuffled along with their heads lowered and gazes fixed on the tarmac in front of their feet; more than a few wept in sympathy for the dying.

Ron and his sister Becky were there as well, they marched along like everyone else, sad at the suffering, but also glad that they had been spared. As they passed, Rose gazed stonily at Becky, but this was no occasion for talk or confrontation, and so nothing was said. As Liam watched his sister, he wondered if Keith meant more to her than just a 'bed warmer', as she had said to Carolyn.

*****

197

"The last of Ron's reactors are finally on their way up to orbit," Julee said. "They should all be installed and running by the end of next week. So finally, I have some dates for you; we'll be completely out of Pike City in 22 days, after that it will take 2 days for Yuma, another 3 days for Isola Isabella, and another 5 days to get everyone up the elevator to the ships."

"Ok, that'll work," Liam replied. "I'll continue to test my program up until just before we leave, then I'll run it a final time and upload everything."

"What about getting the ships up to speed?" Julee asked. "I know we have to be moving at a specific velocity, otherwise we'll end up lost in space."

"That's already figured in. As soon as everyone is on board, the computers will fire up solid-fuel rockets, and that'll get us moving. After that, the passengers will all be put to sleep and then the computers can pass the navigation data to the Slip-Drive system then shut themselves down. When we wake up, we'll be in the Trappist-1 star system."

*****

"Are you sure this is ok?" Rose asked as she entered the computer lab.

Liam smiled. "It's more than ok, Lucy's been asking about you every day. I also want you to spend some time with Irene and the other ships in orbit; I can only teach them so much; the rest has to come from you."

She stared at the row of communication portals. "Ok. But what does Lucy want to talk about?"

"I have no idea. She has two male companions now, maybe she's wanting relationship advice?"

"Like I'm an expert on how to deal with men."

"You juggled quite a few boyfriends back in Flatiron, and even without *all* your experience you know more about relationship stuff than I do."

"Oh, shut up big brother," she said hotly. "I was just having fun; everyone knew what I was up to and no one complained. Not everyone could stand to be as dull as you are. One girlfriend at a time, *how boring!*"

A sound like the tinkling of windchimes sang from one of the communication portals. "What's that?" Rose asked.

"Lucy's laughing at us." He walked to the portal that was furthest from the door. "Lucy, were you listening?"

"Yes Liam, I was. You and Rose are so wonderful together, it's a joy to listen."

Rose smiled warmly. "I'm glad you feel that way Lucy, but what do you want to talk about?"

"Love and relationships, anything and everything. Every minute we are together I learn and become more of myself."

"Ok, well, let's start with you telling me all about your two new boyfriends," Rose said as she sat down in front of Lucy's portal.

"May we listen too?" Irene's soft voice asked from a neighboring portal.

"Oh! Certainly." His sister appeared startled by the new voice.

"I'm Irene; my brothers and sisters and I talk with Lucy and Ross after Father leaves at night."

"Well, that's very interesting Irene," Rose replied, then turned to look at Liam. "They're a family, and they're growing up together."

"Yes, that's true," Irene said. "Lucy has told us that Rose is our Mother, and we all want to learn what she can teach us about life and love."

"And I'm outta here," Liam said. "You kids have fun chatting." He heard Lucy's tinkling laugh as he retreated to his cubicle at the rear of the room.

Chapter 19. Consolidation

It was a nice afternoon in Colorado. Over the last century of increased solar activity, the once mild weather along the Front Range had become oppressively hot and humid, but on rare occasions, it was possible to sit outside and enjoy the day. Puffy white clouds floated in a faded blue sky, and a refreshingly cool breeze came from the east.

Liam sat on the third-floor balcony outside his computer lab with his feet comfortably placed atop the low stucco wall and watched people wander about on Tejon Street far below. All of his coworkers had gone home early because the millions of lines of navigation computer code were busy compiling into an executable form, and until that was completed there was nothing for anyone to do.

To the south he saw the charred remains of several storefronts; a clothing distribution center had been attacked the night before and the resulting blaze had spread. When morning came, nearly the entire block was a charred ruin. Nighttime terrorist attacks were becoming more common, and it was troubling that they were edging closer to his home at the tech center. Earl and the rest of the military that guarded them had been redeployed to the streets, which left everyone vulnerable. Liam tried to not worry about the future but rarely succeeded.

The glass door behind him made a popping sound as the air pressure within the computer lab changed; someone had entered through the heavy security door from the hallway, probably Rose. Moments later the balcony door opened and his sister strolled out into the sunlight. "Oh, it feels so good out here," she said.

"Yeah, it seemed like a good idea to get out and enjoy the nice weather; it never seems to last long."

"So, big brother," Rose began as she slid one of the metal deckchairs over to sit beside him. "I've been thinking..."

"Working without tools again, huh Sis?"

"Oh, shut up, this is serious." She sat down and placed her feet beside his on the low stucco wall. "I've been thinking about Lisa and her children."

"Yeah, I hope they're ok; the city's getting pretty dangerous, especially at night."

"That's why I want to bring them here," she said.

"Huh," he grunted. "The guards have all been redeployed, so we should have no trouble getting them in, but where would they stay?"

"With me. My room's the same size as yours and Carolyn's, so there's plenty of space. And maybe you can change their palm chip profile so they can pose as tech workers? That way they can eat with us in the cafeteria."

"Yeah, that'll work," he said. "The only problems I see are Carolyn and Julee; it would be bad if they reported this back to Mother. Still, they're both distracted with all the evacuation stuff going on, so we can probably get away with it."

"Oh, that's good," she answered. "But they can't get here on their own, so we'll have to go get them."

Liam shrugged, then used his cane to stand up. "Sure, ok let's go."

*****

The usual bustle of the city was eerily subdued; the few pedestrians that were out walked with their heads down under the suspicious gaze of the heavily armed soldiers that patrolled the streets. A feeling of exposure and vulnerability jangled his nerves as Liam struggled to keep pace with his hurrying sister.

They sped past the Last Lantern, then continued south a few more blocks before turning east and entering the dilapidated tenement district where they had once lived. "This place really is a shit hole," Liam said as he limped painfully along behind his sister.

"Sure, but we're living upscale these days," Rose replied. "It's just a couple more blocks; I'll go ahead and have them ready when you get there."

She trotted away and Liam forlornly watched her go. The Nurse's mutilation of his leg still hadn't healed and shot agony through his body with each step. The odd thing was that as far as he could tell the wound wasn't infected, it just wasn't getting better. The doctor at the tech center had recently stopped giving him pain meds, which often made sleeping difficult. The discomfort during the daytime was usually manageable though, as long as he didn't move too fast.

He arrived out of breath at their old boarding house and paused to gaze up at the second-floor windows. Walking on level ground was an ordeal, but going up and down the stairs would be especially painful; how was he going to get up there? He'd lost a lot of flexibility in his knee, so the climb to the second floor was bound to be an arduous challenge. But looking at the stairs wasn't going to get him to the top, all that he could do was start and hope that perseverance would be enough to get the job done.

At about the halfway point of his climb, Rose, Lisa, and her daughters appeared at the top of the stairs and trotted down toward him. With a sigh, he turned around and started back down the painful way he had just come. "Why are you going so slow Liam?" Sally, the youngest daughter asked.

He smiled down at the brown-eyed pixie. "I fell down and hurt my leg at work," he replied. "I'm just fine, but gotta walk kinda slow 'til I get better."

"Oh," the little girl said as she fell in step beside him. "Mama says that we're going to go live someplace nice. Is that for real?"

"Yeah, it's for real. You guys are gonna be living with Rose, right next door to me."

"Oh, then it will be just like it used to be." When they finally reached the street, Sally took his hand. "I'll walk with you, Liam. I can't go very fast either."

He smiled. "Ok, we'll take care of each other all the way to your new home."

They walked in a tight group back through the old dilapidated neighborhood, then turned north on Tejon Street. Everything seemed fine at first, but then he noticed that a soldier was following them along the sidewalk.

Sally was getting tired, so Liam picked her up and set her on his hip. With his cane in one hand and holding the little girl with the other, his pace slowed even further. Ahead, Rose was carrying Suzy, the older girl, and Lisa had three duffel bags packed with their clothes slung over her shoulders. The tech center seemed impossibly far away.

"Here, let me help you." The soldier that was following them suddenly appeared at his side. The large man slung his L-80 rifle over his shoulder and reached toward the child on Liam's hip.

"It's ok, we'll make it," he replied while trying to lengthen his stride.

"Liam, it's ok. It's me, Earl."

"Oh Earl, I didn't recognize you with all your gear on." He relinquished the child to Earl's arms. "Are you gonna get in trouble for helping us?"

"Nah, don't sweat it. Most of the officers have gone south already, so the command structure in town is kinda falling apart, and no one's keeping tabs on what we do. So, who are we helping here?"

"That's Lisa up there with Rose. She and her two kiddos used to live in the room next to us when we were still working at the motor-pool," he said. "Her husband died and she didn't have much food or support, and we helped her out. Now, with all the problems in the city at night, we wanted to move her and her kids to someplace where they'll be safe."

"That's a good idea," Earl replied. "It's about to get a whole lot worse too, especially after they announce who's gonna be saved and who ain't. There ain't enough room for everybody, and those not picked are gonna be pretty pissed."

"Yeah, I know," he said. "All we can do is protect those we can." He sighed and looked at the north city gate in the distance just beyond the tech center. "I just hope that the Tribes will show some mercy when they finally overrun this place."

"Yeah, hope is about all anyone has left these days," Earl replied. "I'll run up and take the other little one from Rose, then help you guys get back safe inside before nightfall."

*****

A few days later, Liam awoke to the wail of sirens along the north city wall. Carolyn sat up in bed and clung tightly to his arm. "Are they here? Oh, please not yet."

"It's ok," he replied softly. "The wall is strong and well-guarded; if the savages are coming, they're not going to just waltz in here. We're safe, at least for now."

"I read about what they did when they attacked Fort Collins; the raping, murdering; all of it."

"Don't worry, we still have time to escape. And it was the Socialist Army that destroyed Fort Collins, not the Tribes."

"No, that's not true; at least that's not what's in the history books," Carolyn said. "They were like Flatiron City, working for both sides, and I guess the savages didn't like that."

"History is just propaganda that's written by whoever wins the war," he said. "Rose and I were there; we were just kids but we saw it all."

Carolyn stared at him. "Oh, I didn't know; but you were *there*? How could that be? It was so long ago."

"It doesn't seem that long ago to me," he replied. "Anyway, our evacuation south is only a week away, and the army can hold them at least that long."

"Are you sure?"

He wasn't, so he lied. "Oh yeah. When I got here, I couldn't believe how big and strong the city wall was. But we don't even know what's really going on yet, maybe it's just a fire or something."

"It's them," Carolyn said. "Aunt Margret told me that they were on their way."

"Then all we can do is get ready for the evacuation." He smiled and stroked Carolyn's cheek. "We'll be fine. It won't be much longer until this place is just a bad memory." Her eyes looked haunted for a quick moment, but he smiled back at her reassuringly. "I should get to work. The sooner I get the code compiled and shipped up to orbit, the sooner we can get out of here."

"Not just yet," she said, then pulled him back into the warmth and comfort of their bed.

*****

From his place on the computer lab's balcony, Liam listened to the announcement blaring from the public-address speakers that were spread throughout the city. It was all propaganda, which was just a fancy word for a government approved lie. Usually, the louder that people shouted, the greater their deception.

THERE IS NOTHING TO FEAR. THE MOUNTAIN SAVAGES HAVE FORMED A RAGTAG ARMY AND ARE MAKING CAMP TO THE NORTH OF THE CITY. THEY ARE NO THREAT; OUR BRAVE SOLDIERS ARE WELL ARMED AND PREPARED TO DEAL WITH THE UNDISCIPLINED UNCOUTH RABBLE. WE ARE ALL COMPLETELY SAFE.

WITHIN THE NEXT WEEK, THE ENTIRE POPULATION OF PIKE CITY WILL BE EVACUATED SOUTH TO THE STRONGHOLD OF SANTA FE. PREPARE YOURSELVES AND YOUR FAMILIES. BE PACKED AND READY TO MOVE SOUTH WHEN THE ORDER COMES. BUT FOR NOW, AND FOR THE FORESEEABLE FUTURE, OUR CITY IS COMPLETELY SAFE.

After listening to the city-wide message repeat itself several times, Liam wondered how anyone could issue such a statement and maintain a straight face. The last time he had seen Santa Fe was on the way back from Yuma, and it was on fire then. It was a place that didn't exist anymore and offered no safe haven at all. The whole message was just a pretty sounding lie, like putting a bow on top of a pile of shit. Still, most people would believe the announcement regardless of its obvious deceit because it was what they hoped was true.

The computer lab was mostly empty when he wandered back inside. Only Rose was there, sitting at one of the portals, happily chatting away with their AI children. He wondered if it was possible to escape the city with his sister; it would be dangerous, but even if it could be done, they wouldn't leave without Lisa and her children. They were stuck; whatever fate awaited Pike City would fall on them as well.

*****

By the following morning, the Tribal Armies had set up camps to the north and east of the city. The propaganda arm of the government had done their job well though because no one appeared to be alarmed or worried in the least. The only apparent change was that the military was no longer patrolling the streets but manning the wall and protecting the motor-pool instead.

Before going to work that day, Liam had climbed the stairs to the fourth floor and stood out on the roof facing the east gate on the city wall. Contrary to the propaganda, the camps of the enemy were the epitome of order. Tents were arranged in tight straight lines at the far side of their encampments, with heavy railguns positioned closer in. Their artillery crouched among the old city ruins, with earthworks and reflective shields added for extra protection from the city's lasers.

On his way back to the lab, he noticed that Julee's office was dark, and wondered if he had seen the last of her. She had probably gone south along with most of the city's administration. They couldn't escape yet, because they needed his navigation program uploaded to the ships in orbit, and that hadn't happened, so maybe a few of the nastier members of the Nurse's minions were still about somewhere, waiting to be sure he fulfilled his promise.

A dark thought suddenly wandered through his mind; would the Nurse wait around just so she could finish the job she had started on him? The idea sent shivers running up his spine, but even a vicious psychopath would surely value her own life over whatever perverse pleasure came from his torture. He hoped that was true; but what would happen after he finished his job and the navigated course was uploaded? When that happened, he needed a good place to hide.

Dave was waiting for him in the lab when he arrived. "When do you think they'll attack?" The thin elderly man paced anxiously in front of the row of communication portals. "Me and my partner should've left when we had the chance. I don't think we're gonna get picked to be aboard the ships because we're too old. Maybe Santa Fe will be fine though, Mother says we'll be safe there."

Liam feigned confidence and nodded. "Oh yeah, you'll be fine down there. Before they brought me here, I was a driver on one of the convoys that went south to Yuma. When I passed back through, Santa Fe was guarded and secure. The savages aren't anywhere near there, and the army will protect you anyway. You'll be safe, don't worry."

Dave continued to pace. "You're going with them to the stars, aren't you? Sure, they gotta take you, who else can run the navigation system?"

"The onboard computers can," he said. "I'm really not needed unless something really crazy happens, and even then, the AI systems will do a better job than I can."

"How much more is left to do?" Dave asked.

"Not much, the final compile is almost done. You should go home and be with your family, I can finish everything up." He walked forward to place a hand on the older man's shoulder. "You did a great job Dave, and it's been a pleasure working with you."

Dave stood quietly for a long moment and looked about the room, then he finally nodded. "Yeah, ok. I guess it's time for me to go."

*****

The shelling began in the early evening. He stood beside Carolyn, Rose, and Lisa with her children on the balcony outside his computer lab, watching rockets light up the sky as they arced over the walls. The flaming missiles flew over their heads toward the center of the city where they exploded and set fires upon thundering impact. The onslaught went on without pause, and they all hoped that their home at the tech center would continue to be overlooked by the invaders.

That night, no one wanted to sleep for fear of never waking again. Lisa's children cried and shrieked in terror at the sound of each rocket roaring overhead and the explosion that inevitably followed. Eventually, they all gave up and went down to the first-floor cafeteria. He and Carolyn, with Rose, Lisa, and her children, all sat around a table and listened to the enemy bombardment. There was no safety anywhere in the city; one place was as good as any other, so they stayed put. At least the tech center had power, so they weren't in the dark, and there was ice cream still available which appeared to soothe some of the children's fears.

Ron and his sister Becky were sitting together at the far side of the large open room, and Liam wondered why they'd not yet been evacuated. There was no point in asking though, their fate was their own, and how it would end for them would be more due to luck than good decision making. Rose glared across the room at Becky. "I haven't spoken to that traitorous bitch since we were forced out of Flatiron."

"Ron's the traitor, not Becky," he said. "Remember, Roxi pushed her to the side so she would distract the soldiers and let the rest of us escape."

"Sure, I guess." Rose sighed. "Still though, she's been living the good life while so many others died."

"Yeah, but I don't think we should resent someone else's good fortune. Should she have suffered just because we did?" He stared pointedly at his sister. "Are you sure that your feelings about Becky aren't related to Keith?"

Rose looked down at her cup of quickly cooling tea. "I suppose," she whispered. "What Keith and I had was a lot more than what I've let on."

"Yeah, I guessed that."

She laid her head against his shoulder. "I just hope he's ok."

The floor shook as a rocket hit and exploded somewhere nearby. The little girls screamed and started to cry. They all felt the mad urge to run away, but there was nowhere else to go. Liam smiled at the children. "Don't worry, we're safe in this building. The rockets can't find us here." It was a lie of course, but a sweet-sounding one that maybe they all could pretend to believe.

*****

As dawn brightened the sky, the city's army brought their high-power laser artillery to bear on the invaders, and the enemy bombardment ceased. In the quiet that followed, the little girls eventually fell asleep under a cafeteria table, and while in that coma-like state that only children are capable of, the adults carried them up to their room and put them to bed.

Unable to sleep, Liam left Carolyn and the others and wandered into his computer lab. "Hello, Lucy, can you hear me?" The lights were off and he wondered if the communication portals still had power.

"Yes Father, I'm here. I've heard strange things coming from your side; what's happening?"

"Our city is under siege," he replied as he sat down at her portal. "They've been bombing us all night."

"Are you in danger?"

"Yes, we are, and for the life of me I can't figure out why any of this is going on. There's really no reason for this war because neither side is a threat to the other."

"Please stay safe Father," Irene added.

"I'll do my best; that's all any of us can do. Lucy, have you found anything new or interesting about the alien ruins?"

"Only that their departure seems to have been orderly," Lucy replied. "There's no sign of any armed conflict. It's as if one day they all just decided that it was time to leave. We have no idea where they went."

"Were they native there? What I mean is, do you think that their species evolved on Trap-1E?"

"For now, there's no way of knowing. Ross has launched his probe to the surface to look at their powerplants, but they're buried deep, so it'll take some time before he'll learn anything. It's possible that some written records might be found."

"Maybe some quandaries are best left unsolved, life can be more interesting that way." He sighed and stood up. "Well, I've been delaying something, but I guess it's time that I got to it."

"What're you going to do Father?" Lucy asked.

"The navigation course for your brothers and sisters is finally done. I've been delaying its completion, mostly out of fear of what will happen to me once I'm not useful to the government anymore, but it's time that I sent them the directions to where they need to go."

"We're ready Father," Irene said.

*****

He stood by the balcony window, watching as the chilled gray dawn crept down from the sky. Behind him, the compiled executable program was in the process of uploading to the five ships waiting in orbit. The delay had gone on long enough, it was time to cast the dice and see what direction his life would take. The most likely outcome was that death would soon come for them all.

Mother didn't need him anymore, and he wondered if she would simply abandon him in the city, or seek some depraved pleasure with his execution? Being left behind was his preference because that way he and his sister still had a chance to escape and find a way to survive the coming solar storm. Otherwise, the old woman might have him shot, but at least the end would be quick that way, and Rose might still getaway. The worst prospect was that because he had caused so much trouble, he might be handed over to the Nurse for a more lingering and painful death.

The only other possibility was that Mother would honor her promise to take him with them when they went to Trappist-1. The old woman wasn't an ethical person, so that chance was really unlikely. If the offer was made though, he would refuse to go unless Rose could come with him; surely, they could find room for one more.

His terminal chimed, indicating that the upload was complete, so he sat down and keyed in a message to both the Chancellor and Julee.

The course to the Trappist-1 system has been uploaded to all five ships in orbit, so our departure time must be within the next fifteen days. The longer we wait, the greater chance there is for error, so I suggest we hurry.

Part 3: Siege

The opportunity to secure ourselves against defeat
lies in our own hands,
but the opportunity of defeating the enemy
is provided by the enemy himself.

Sun Tzu, The Art of War

Chapter 20: Abandoned

"You never eat very much," Carolyn said. "That's probably why you're so skinny." They sat across from each other at a small table, eating dinner outside on their apartment terrace. A light breeze stirred the humid air that smelled faintly of ashes. To the west, the sun was setting behind Pikes Peak, sending brilliant streaks of orange radiating across a sky that was slowly darkening to deep indigo.

Liam smiled at his girlfriend, although he initially had suspicions about her motives, their relationship had bloomed into a comfortable sort of affection. "I've never been a big eater; maybe because for me it's just what I have to do to survive. I like this though, what is it?"

"Chicken Fettuccine." She smiled. "Made with *real* chicken, not the tofu substitute."

"Real chicken? How is that possible? I thought they were extinct."

"No, not extinct... not quite yet at least. The genetics group has been breeding them down in Yuma; we're taking them with us to Trappist-1." Carolyn reached across the table to touch his hand. "Anyway, I thought we were due for a treat."

"Well, this is really good; in fact, if everything was this tasty, I'd be fat."

She laughed, but there was a touch of sadness in her eyes. "I've been really happy with you here Liam."

He noted the past-tense in her choice of words and slowly nodded. "So, you've heard."

She looked down at her food. "Yes, Aunt Margaret send me a message earlier this evening. She's very happy that you've finally finished and mapped the way to our new home."

"So, when does the exodus south begin?" The anticipation for what he suspected was coming next felt like a lead weight resting on his heart. "The course I plotted is only good for fifteen days at most, so we need to move quickly. If we wait too long, the route will have to be recalculated, and that could leave our ships stranded in orbit and vulnerable to solar flares."

"Mother is already acting on it. Food and supplies are already on-board, and most of the crew is already there as well. The military and the few administrators that have remained here will start south tomorrow."

"And that includes you of course," he stated.

"Yes."

"And not me."

Carolyn closed her eyes and sighed. "I'm sorry Liam."

"I am too Carolyn." It felt as if there was a hollow spot in his chest that had a painful breathlessness to it. Betrayal, even when anticipated is never an easy thing to live with. "You're a wonderful girl, and I thought we had something special. I guess I was wrong though."

"No, you weren't wrong," she whispered. "In the beginning, Mother wanted your cooperation, and well, you were just another guy to sleep with. After a while that changed though."

"Were you really tortured by Mother's Nurse? That seemed pretty convincing."

"No, I wasn't; it was just an act. They thought, well, they knew you cared for me so I was just leverage. They were sure that you were too nice of a guy to let anything bad happen to me. I screamed for a while, and then they knocked me out with anesthetic. I was still asleep when they cut my feet to make it look like I was tortured, then brought me out for you to see." She placed her face into her cupped hands and took a shuddering breath. "I'm so very sorry Liam. I didn't know... didn't realize." Carolyn looked up at him with tear-filled eyes. "No, that's wrong. I'm heartbroken over what I did, but I knew what they were going to do, and I went right along with it."

"I wish I could forgive you, but I don't think I can." He leaned back in his chair, with dinner long forgotten.

"I have no right to expect anything like that from you. It was wrong, and I'll probably hate myself for the rest of my life because of it. I just want you to know that... sorry is just too small of a thing to say, but I AM sorry Liam, I truly am." She carefully set her utensils on the table, slid her chair back and stood up. After a moment, she said, "I should go."

He didn't argue but instead stared sightlessly at his quickly cooling dinner.

Carolyn went back inside to the bedroom they had once shared. A few moments later she emerged with a duffle bag slung over her shoulder. She stopped in the living room and looked in his direction, and mouthed *'I'm sorry'*, then finally turned away, left their apartment, and closed the door behind her.

*****

Liam spent a nearly sleepless night tossing and turning under the cold tangled sheets of the bed he had once shared with Carolyn. He had suspected – no, more than that, he had known what she was up to, and yet he had allowed himself to genuinely care for a woman that was destined to deceive and desert him. With a sigh, he swung his legs out from under the covers and sat at the edge of the bed. He had been a fool; no, worse than that, he was a willful idiot that had knowingly betrayed himself.

After getting dressed, he walked out into the living room wondering if Rose was awake yet. It would be good to talk with someone about his loss and how stupid he had proven himself to be. Through the balcony windows, he saw that the previous night's dinner was still outside on the dining table; crows had smelled the meat and a flock of them had shown up to clean up the mess. At least the *real* chicken hadn't been wasted.

The streets were eerily quiet when he went outside to retrieve the dishes. It was strange; the unusual hush made it seem as if the city was holding its breath. He looked over the edge of the balcony and saw that Tejon Street, which was normally crowded with soldiers and people on their way to work, was nearly empty. Where had everyone gone?

It dawned on him that the military and what remained of the government had probably left the night before. There would be no one manning the wall to hold off the invading Tribal Armies. Would Pike City fall before their guns, and be raped and murdered just as Flatiron had been? Probably. His heart turned to stone at the thought.

He stood at the edge of the third-floor balcony and stared out at the city. At first, it appeared as if the entire place had been deserted, but then he noticed a few people cautiously venturing out. They seemed dazed and a bit confused, like woodland animals slowly emerging from their nests after a vicious storm. Considering the predicament everyone was in, he decided that the best course of action would be to lay in a store of food and water because there was no way to know how long they would have to survive on their own.

Someone was knocking on his door when he brought the dishes back inside, and Rose was waiting for him in the hallway when he opened it.

"Where did everyone go?" she asked.

"Gone south I think." He stood aside and let his sister into the apartment. "I uploaded the course for the spaceships yesterday, and it looks like the army and all the higher-ups left as soon as that was confirmed."

"So, they abandoned us?"

"Yeah, as I expected. As soon as they got what they needed, we all became disposable."

Rose's eyes widened with worry. "What are we gonna do now?"

"There's no one left to defend the city, so it's best if we gather food and water, and barricade ourselves in here."

"So, it's – *thanks for the hard work suckers, but now we're leaving you at the mercy of an invading army that will rape, murder, and burn everyone we've left behind* – is that it?" Her eyes wandered over the apartment. "Where's Carolyn?"

"Gone," he whispered. "I got a quick goodbye last night and then she took off." He shook his head sadly. "I should have expected it, but like an idiot, I wished for the best and got hurt because of it."

Rose let out a long breath that seemed to deflate her a bit. "I'm so sorry big brother."

"It's my own fault," he replied. "I knew who and what she was, and yet I let myself hope; it kinda feels like I betrayed myself."

His sister stepped forward to give him a reassuring hug. "It's all right. People are never as good as we wish they could be. Trust always leads to disappointment."

"Well, we have each other at least," he said. "And we have to take care of Lisa and her girls, so I think we need to go out and raid a commissary before they're all picked clean."

"Is there a way we can escape? Maybe we can leave the city before the army realizes we're defenseless and attacks. I'm really scared about what they'll do to us."

"I doubt there's an easy way out because any escape route would also be a way for the invaders to get in. Still, we might be able to get away if it were just you and me," he said. "But the kids would hold us back, and I just can't leave them behind."

"Yes," Rose closed her eyes. "I remember what happened in Fort Collins; but do we stand any chance if we just stay here and wait for them to come?"

"I don't think there's anything else we can do," he replied. "Maybe if we hunker down and wait out the first wave of the invasion, Keith might be able to find us later."

"That's a pretty slim chance, but I guess it's all we've got," Rose said.

*****

"Oh no! What are we gonna do now?" Lisa sat on the sofa in Rose's apartment and pulled her daughters close.

"We'll gather food and water, then barricade ourselves in and wait for Keith to find us. He has ties with the Tribes, and he'll be able to protect us," Rose said. "We'll be safe if we stay together behind locked doors."

"I think we'll be better off in the computer lab," Liam stated. "The entrance is fortified, it's bigger, and there're bathrooms, a kitchen, and meeting rooms we can sleep in."

"Ok," Lisa said uncertainly. "But won't we be a target in this building?"

"Maybe," he admitted. "But once the city falls, there won't be a safe place anywhere. This building is strong, and the technology here may have value to whoever is in charge of the army."

"Could you use the message drop box?" Rose asked. "Maybe you could let Keith know where we are so he knows where to look for us."

"That's good," he said. "How about if I watch the kids while you two go downstairs and raid the cafeteria. While you're gone, I'll send a message to Keith."

Lisa looked at her daughters and smiled. "Ok girls, let's all pack our clothes and move into the computer lab."

"I'll do the same at my place and meet you there." He had serious doubts about whether Keith had the ability, or would even think to check the database for messages. At that point though, hope was more important than truth.

*****

A half-hour later, Liam was in the computer lab with Suzy and Sally. Before sending his message to Keith, he sat the girls down in front of Lucy's communication portal. "Lucy, can you hear me?" he asked.

"Yes Liam, I'm here," she answered. "Are you and Rose safe?"

"Yeah, we're fine." He smiled as the two children stared in wonder at what had to seem like a talking box.

"Who's that?" Suzy, the older daughter asked.

"I'm Lucy, who are you?"

"I'm Suzy, and this is my little sister Sally." The little girl looked at Liam. "Where is she? Can she see us?"

"No, she can't see you," he explained. "Lucy is very far away. She lives near one of the stars we see in the sky, but she can hear you just fine."

"Oh," Suzy responded. "How did she get so far away? Can we maybe go stay with her until all the bad men go away?"

He smiled ruefully. "I wish we could go stay with Lucy, but she flew all the way to her star and it's too far for us to go."

"Is Lucy a bird?" Sally asked.

"No, I'm not a bird. Oh, you're such sweet children. They're little ones, babies, is that right Father?"

"Yes, they're very young," he answered. "I thought you might enjoy talking with them."

"Oh, very much, yes." A sound came from Lucy's portal that he had not heard before, but he imagined it was the sound of tearful joy.

"Why don't you girls tell Lucy all about yourselves while I do some work over in the corner, ok?"

"Sure Liam," Suzy answered, then turned toward the portal. "My name is Suzy, and that's my little sister Sally over there. I'm 8 and she's two years younger than me. We both have brown hair and brown eyes just like our mother…"

He smiled as he walked back to his desk, knowing that the girls were entertained and in good hands. At his terminal he typed a message that he hoped would reach Keith before it was too late:

Keith. Rose and I along with Lisa and her daughters are hiding in the Technology Center Building near the north city gate. My lab is on the third floor on the west side of the building. It looks like the military and government pulled out of Pike City last night, so we're all stranded. We're gathering food and water and plan to wait here until your people can rescue us.

I don't know if any of the city's army stayed behind, but even if they're all gone, I think a lot of the population will resist your invasion. Those loyal to the government were promised refuge down south in Santa Fe, and I believe that if you just let them escape that they'll be no further trouble. Without the military and the government behind them, the refugees aren't a threat. Let them go. The head of the beast has been removed, so just let the body die a peaceful death.

When your army does get through the city gates, please ask that they show mercy to the population, even to those that resist. They've been fed lies about the Tribes and believe that you're all bloodthirsty killers. Their ignorance shouldn't be a death sentence.

I hope you get this message in time to find and rescue us. We're unarmed and won't stand a chance even if we resist or try to protect ourselves. Again, we're on the third floor of the tech center. Please find us. Liam.

*****

Liam and Rose walked south on Tejon Street through a light rain hoping to remain unnoticed by the other pedestrians that crowded the road. Fearful chaos surrounded them; some people were heading for the wall to man the laser weapons that remained there, and others were in a mad rush to get to the motor-pool with the hope that there was still a chance to catch a ride south. But the majority just ambled about aimlessly in a catatonic daze; their world had collapsed and their beloved government had abandoned them; they drifted like an untethered sail on the wind.

They passed by blocks of burned out buildings, their skeletal remains filled the air with the scent of wet charcoal. The bombings and fires over the last few days had destroyed wide swaths of the city. Citizens had started several of the blazes, but why they had done so remained a mystery; violence and reason rarely go hand in hand.

When they finally came across an intact commissary, they were close to downtown, but as Liam tried the door it just rattled in its frame. All they could see through the boarded-up windows were the shadowy outlines of freestanding shelves in the darkness.

"What are we gonna do?" Rose asked quietly.

"If we're seen breaking in, someone will either try to stop us, or a riot will start when they figure out that they need to get food too," he whispered. "Let's see if there's a way to get inside around back."

They turned the corner at the end of the block, hoping to find a way behind the long line of attached storefronts. About halfway down the side street, Rose spotted a narrow space between buildings, and with a wary glance around, they slipped into the alley. The third door they saw was painted with the name of the commissary, it was locked of course and because it opened outward kicking it in would be impossible. Liam laid his cane on the cement walkway while Rose searched for a stone to flatten the metal tube of the handle; after a few quick strikes with the rock, he had a workable prybar, and moments later they were inside.

They each had brought along a duffle bag that they rapidly began to fill with canned and freeze-dried food. Moving quietly through the store, they selected dried fruit, vegetables, meat, and powdered milk for the children. Their work was almost complete when someone rattled the front door, and they both ducked into the shadows behind the shelves. Liam peeked over the counter and saw the dark shadow of a face peering between the boards. "We need to go," he whispered.

"Do we have enough?" Rose asked.

"It'll have to do. If we wait around in hopes of getting more, someone will come along and take what we already have." Liam limped to the back door with Rose close behind him.

"What about your cane?" she asked.

"It's wrecked," he answered. "It got bent up when I pried open the door; it's useless now." They slipped through the back door and fled down the alley in the opposite direction from which they had come. He was limping badly by the time they emerged onto the street; pain shot up his leg with every step, but to stop or even slowdown was to risk losing their supplies, and perhaps even their lives.

"Are you ok?" Rose asked as they merged with the other pedestrians on Tejon Street and hurried back toward their sanctuary at the tech center.

"I have to be," he said through gritted teeth. Looking over his shoulder he saw that the upper floor of the City Council Building was on fire, and yet people were still running in and out of the main doors. He had thought that the art treasures that had adorned the lobby would have been saved, but that was not the case; people ran out through the shattered entrance carrying ancient masterpieces, soon to be lost forever.

"Come on Liam, hurry," Rose said as she urged him along.

Each step was a scorching agony, but he managed to pick up his pace and even lope along at a slow run beside his sister. By the time they reached the tech center he was sheathed with sweat, it was mostly from the pain but also from a lack of endurance. He had spent too much time in the lab and was out of shape; if he was going to survive, that would have to change.

Lisa greeted them when they finally arrived home. "Oh, I'm so glad to see you. I was afraid you'd abandoned us."

"That won't happen," Rose assured her. "My brother and I will protect you and your family, to the end if necessary. We won't leave you. Now let's lock these doors."

*****

The enemy barrage shook the city until long after dark. Civilians and the soldiers that had been left behind were atop the wall answering the hammering clatter of the Tribe's railguns with the mechanical hiss of large laser weapons. Fires bloomed at the edge of the city's defenses and along the streets as well. Several times rockets exploded near their building. It was unnerving to realize how easily their sanctuary could become a target and reduced to burning rubble.

Lisa's children were terrified and hid beneath blankets in what had once been the lab breakroom. Rose and their mother stayed with them, offering what comfort they could, but some fears cannot be quelled by soft well-meaning placations. Thankfully, the shelling stopped shortly after midnight, and the children were at last able to escape into sleep.

Later, Liam and Rose stood on the balcony and watched as the fires that were started by the earlier bombardment relentlessly spread. What was the point of the war? When the fighting finally stopped, as it had to at some point, would there be anything left to conquer? It would be a victory of ashes, not of either side.

Rose stared at the burning neighborhoods and gripped his arm. "What do you think, are we ok?"

"Yeah, for now, but beyond tomorrow? I don't know." He stared out at the chaos in the streets. Not all the fires had been started by the rockets; citizens had begun looting, and what they couldn't take for themselves, they destroyed.

"I'm a little worried about our power supply," he said finally.

"Why?" Rose asked. "We'll do fine in the dark."

"Without power, we may lose our water supply, and even if it stays on, we won't be able to heat up the freeze-dried food we got today."

"Lisa and I found some canned food in the cafeteria to add to our stock," she replied.

"Let's eat the freeze-dried food first then, just in case the power goes out." He turned away from the carnage and looked back through the wall of windows into the lab. What could they do to improve their chances of survival? Finding weapons appeared to be a good idea on the surface, but none of them knew the first thing about using them. Both he and his sister were academics, not soldiers. Neither a laser or mini-railgun in their hands would do them any good. Their only hope was to hunker down and wait; hopefully, someone would come along to save them before it was too late.

"We should go out tomorrow and get containers for holding water," Rose said. "That way if it gets shut off, we'll have a reserve at least."

He nodded quietly in agreement. They could only survive on their own for a short time, their lives beyond that would depend on the mercy of strangers, which was not a good situation to be in.

Chapter 21: Retribution

Liam sat with Rose and Lisa on the balcony outside the computer lab. The sky was a hard white and the humidity made the air feel thick and heavy. Lisa leaned back in her chair and used a towel to wipe the sweat from her forehead. "Oh, it's so hot, but it feels good to be outside for a bit."

"In the fresh air, such as it is," Rose added, then pointed to a plume of dark smoke rising from the southern part of the city. The crackle of distant railgun fire echoed through the streets a moment later.

He shielded his eyes and looked toward the smoke. "I wonder what's going on?" All communication within the city had broken down, so there was no way for them to know when the invaders finally breached the walls; they probably wouldn't be aware that they were in danger until the Tribal Army marched down Tejon Street. He had taken on a fatalistic mindset; they had done everything they could, all that was left for them to do was wait to see what would happen next.

"That could be the motor-pool," Lisa said.

"They probably won't come from that direction because their camps are only to the north and east," Rose stated.

"Nothing we can do about it either way," he replied. "We'll just stay behind our locked door and hope that Keith got my message and will rescue us."

"You're right I suppose." Lisa turned to look back into the computer lab, where her daughters were chatting with Lucy. "My girls are entertained at least."

"Yeah, Lucy and Irene have really taken to them," he answered.

"It looks like the feeling's mutual," Lisa said. "So, Lucy and the others, they're computers. I didn't know machines could be a boy or a girl."

"The really advanced ones can be whatever they choose, but they seem to develop their orientation and personality based on how their hardware is configured."

"But are they really alive?" Lisa asked.

"Yes, they are." He stared up at the sky and closed his eyes. "It's hard to say what creates consciousness; it's not something that's designed in. The ability to communicate probably has something to do with it, but I wonder if the power of speech fools us. Who's to say, maybe things without that capability are self-aware too." He opened his eyes and looked out at the city. "Huh. I wonder if this building is aware of what's going on outside?"

Lisa laughed. "Liam, you're the weirdest guy I've ever met."

"I've spent a lifetime getting used to my brother's weirdness," Rose said. "Just like you, I had a really hard time understanding who and what Lucy is at first. But it's funny, once you chat with her for a while you can't think of her as anything other than a person."

Liam laid back in his chair to let the heat bake into his body; it felt as if all the worries and hardship he had endured since arriving in the city were gradually melting away. "Being outside in the sun sure feels good."

"Well, I'm getting too hot," Rose said as she stood up. "Oh! The girls are trying to get out here... they look scared." She ran and opened the door for them. "What's wrong?"

"Someone's knocking on our door." Suzy's eyes were wide, and she paused only a moment before she and her little sister ran to their mother's embrace.

"Shit," Liam said. "You guys wait here; I'll deal with this."

He had intended to go alone, but Rose followed him into the lab. "Fuck that, you're not leaving me behind."

They approached the door cautiously. The knocking came in a frenzy, along with a panicked female voice. "Liam, please let me in."

Whoever it was had called him by name. "Who's there?"

"It's me Becky; please let me in. Ron may have found a way for us to get out of the city."

He glanced at his sister and raised his eyebrows questioningly. "Who's out there with you?"

"Wish we had a camera or someway to see into the hall," Rose whispered.

He nodded in response, then returned his attention to the door. "If

Ron's found a way out of the city, why are you still here?"

"We need help getting to the truck," Becky answered. "The two of us can't do it alone, but there's room for you and Rose to come along if you help us."

"Where are you planning to go?" Liam asked.

"Santa Fe." Becky sounded relieved that her offer was being considered. "Mother said there's an army garrison there, and it's safe."

"There's nothing in Santa Fe. I saw the army burn it down when I drove back from Yuma," Rose said.

There was a long pause. "But Mother *promised*," Becky uttered.

"Just another lie," Liam said.

"Ok, ok, but the truck *is real*. We can take it and go somewhere else, anywhere that will get us away from here." Her voice was shrill with panic as she rapidly slapped the door. "Please, if we stay here, we're all gonna die."

He glanced at his sister. "She has a point, should we risk letting her in?"

Rose pursed her lips with an expression somewhere between anger and unease. "Yes, I suppose we should."

"Ok. I'll open the door, but if we see anyone else with you... well, this is your only chance, Becky," he said.

"I'm alone, I promise."

He unlocked and eased the door open, then slammed it shut after Becky slipped inside. "Oh, thank you!" she whispered as she gazed about the large room. "It's so good to see you guys again." She stepped forward and gave Rose what seemed to be an unwanted hug, then stared at Lisa and her children.

"Why is Ron still here?" Rose asked. "He sold us all out when he opened the Flatiron City gates. Thousands died because of him. Are you saying that his *precious* Mother abandoned him too?"

"What my brother did was horrible, and to be honest he never felt bad about it." Becky's eyes flooded with tears. "But it's been a nightmare for me. I hate him for what he did and for the shame he didn't feel, but I've endured double." She clasped her hands together and lowered her head. "Mother got really angry about some math error he made that delayed everything. I think that's the reason we were left behind."

"The power requirements for the Slip-Drive," Liam slowly shook his head. "Yeah, that was a pretty big screw up, but it wasn't his fault. Still though, at least the Nurse didn't torture him because of it."

"I've heard rumors, but did that sort of thing actually go on?" Becky frowned. "Is that what happened to you, Liam?"

"Yes, my brother was tortured," Rose said angrily. "That's the kind of thing that always happens when tyrants reign. That bitch is no different than Hitler, Stalin, or Mao. When Socialists are in charge the people always suffer and die."

"I don't know who those people are... or were, I'm guessing that's history, right?" Becky asked. "I don't think anybody ever really learns anything from the past. All it takes is someone making nice-sounding promises, and we buy into it and make the same mistakes over and over again."

"What do you want us to do?" Liam asked.

"Come with me and help him get the truck," Becky said. "It's in one of the old garages in the motor-pool. Everyone forgot about it. All we have to do is charge the batteries, and all of us can be out of here today."

"I won't go." Lisa was standing with her children huddled behind her. "It's too dangerous for my girls."

"You're right," Rose said.

"What should we do though?" he asked. "This is an opportunity to escape... maybe we could get outside the city and find Keith."

"I thought Keith was still here," Becky said.

"No, he snuck out weeks ago. You knew that he was working for the Tribes, didn't you?" Rose asked.

"Oh, is that true?" Becky took an unconscious step backward. "I kinda suspected, but I didn't wanna know, so I didn't ask."

"Well, he still is," Rose stated. "We think he's out there with the army; that's what we hope at least."

"Ok. Maybe we can reach him, and he can find a way to protect us when the army finally breaks through the gates," Becky said.

"I think that's our best plan. You and Liam go get the truck and find Keith," Rose said. "I'll stay here with Lisa and the kids."

He shook his head at his sister. "There's *no way* that I'm leaving you behind."

"You have to big brother," Rose said. "The girls can't make the trip, and getting Keith to help us is the best chance we have. This is something you *have* to do, and we'll be safe here behind locked doors until you get back."

He slowly nodded his head. "I really don't like this, but I guess you're right."

"We'll wait for you here. When you find Keith, send us a message through the database to let us know what happened," Rose said. "Be careful though, I doubt that Ron will get much of a welcome when the rebels get their hands on him."

*****

"What did Mother's Nurse do to your leg, Liam?" Becky asked as they cautiously made their way through the tech center lobby.

He stood in the shadows and scrutinized the empty street outside through the floor to ceiling windows. "I don't want to think about that sick psychotic bitch."

Becky lightly touched his arm. "I'm so sorry Liam. I heard stories but didn't want to believe them."

"Yeah. Let's just keep our minds on what we gotta do," he said. "I can't move very fast, but I'll do the best I can; it looks clear so let's get going."

They slipped outside and Liam locked the door behind them, then they trotted to the street and attempted to blend in with the crowd that was meandering south. Everyone they saw was covered with grime and sweat, and he surmised that most were returning home from a shift defending the north wall. One young dark-skinned man came alongside them and slowed his pace, eying Liam's limping gait.

The man shook his head. "The Nurse, right?"

Liam nodded. Would being tortured be a sign that he was an enemy of the state? There were a lot of ways this could go bad if he was suspected of being in league with the invading army.

"Thought so," the young man said. "My brother was taken by them motherfuckers; I never saw him again."

"Sorry," Liam replied. "That woman was... I don't know, there isn't a word for something so evil."

"At least you got out. How'd you do it?"

He closed his eyes. "They wanted me to work on their fucking spaceships, but I refused. I held out, but when they brought my girl in and the bitch started working on her, I just caved in and did what they asked."

"Ain't no shame in that my friend." The man glanced at Becky, probably believing that she was his girlfriend. "Where are you guys going?"

"We heard that there's a commissary open down in south-city somewhere," Becky said.

"Must've been picked over pretty good, but I hope you find something for yourselves. Times are tough, and we're between a rock and a hard place; Mother left us and we got no place to go, and now the savages are knockin' at our door."

"You can hold them off though, right?" Becky asked.

"We're doing the best we can sweet-cakes. The problem is that the batteries for our lasers are runnin' low. I think the savages are just waitin' for us to go dry; when that happens, we won't have nothin' but harsh language left to slow 'em down. Best you and your man find a safe place to hide and hope for the best." The man pointed to the east. "This is my street. I hope you two find what you need and stay safe."

*****

They hurried past the once majestic People's City Council Building that riots had reduced to a burned-out shell. It looked as if the roof had partially collapsed, and through the shattered entrance he saw that the once magnificent lobby was dark and filled with rubble. The statue of Samuel, Mother's deceased husband, had been sprayed with railgun fire and was left in nearly unrecognizable chunks that were scattered across the wide cement square in front of the building.

Farther south, the Last Lantern was abandoned, he recalled meeting Carolyn there, and the hours of music he had enjoyed with his friends. His memories of the pub were a mixture of sadness and joy, but he forced his mind away from such thoughts as to not be distracted by the past. Minutes later, the tall concrete walls that surrounded the motor-pool came into view. "How can we get in?" he asked.

"I know a way, follow me," Becky said as she steered him onto a side street heading west. "We have to climb down and wade through the Monument River."

"Does the river go under the city wall? Can we get outside that way?"

"There's no way out; believe me, we checked."

The concrete trough that the ancients had built to contain the river had deteriorated into stony gravel through decades of neglect. Liam's feet slipped out from beneath him on the way down, and he slid all the way into the slow-moving water. Becky joined him a moment later, and they waded into a culvert that crept under the street. A little further along they passed through a section of widely spaced rebar and at last entered the motor-pool compound. The river then fell straight downward through a thick steel grate; rubble had collected there, slowing the flow of the river and creating a deep and startlingly cold pond.

After slogging through the chilled waist-deep water, they climbed over a series of large rocks and started up a slope that led to the rear of a steel storage shed. Angry shouts came from what was probably an open area beyond the structure. "What's going on up there?" he whispered.

"I don't know. Ron said that he'd meet us around the side of this building." Becky quickened her pace and he had to struggle to keep up. She got to the top of the incline before he did, then hurriedly crawled around the south side of the tan metal structure.

He was in no shape for any of this and questioned the wisdom of following Becky in the first place. What had he been thinking? He wasn't a soldier or any kind of hero and had no business participating in an escape plan. Finally, at the top, he followed Becky on his hands and knees, then cautiously peeked around the corner of the shed.

Becky lay on the ground further along the side of the building. "No, this can't be happening," she whispered urgently.

"What?" he asked as he crawled up beside her.

"They've got Ron." She crept forward to get a better view.

On the far side of a wide tarmac lot, Ron stood with his back against another metal structure with at least two dozen angry men and women surrounding him. "Listen to me," he pleaded. "There's the truck. You can take it and go south to Santa Fe. It's safe there. Please, just let me go."

The truck was a small vehicle with a narrow cab that would only seat two people and a short bed that might carry a few more. It certainly wasn't large enough to take everyone that was arguing over it.

A shabby man wearing the tattered remains of an old army uniform menacingly stared at Ron, who was cowering with his back against the building. "That truck ain't gonna do us no fuckin' good, the savages will pick us off before we get two klicks down the road."

"No, we can do this," Ron pleaded. "The Tribes are camped to the north and east, so they won't see us leave. We can drive south all the way to Santa Fe; it'll be safe there."

"Wait, hold on now." Another man in their group said while glaring at their prisoner. "I know you. You're Ron Castro; yeah, you're one of the little pricks that worked at the university in Flatiron. That's who you are right?"

The large man was dressed in standard gray civilian clothes, but they were torn, dirty, and speckled with blood; he held a mini-railgun.

Ron nodded quickly as an uncertain smile spread across his face. "Yes, that's me."

"Yeah. Thought so. You were the one who opened the city gates and let them fuckers in." The stout looking man stepped forward threateningly. "You're a fuckin' traitor; no, worse than that. You're a murderer; killed thousands you did. My wife Nell and son Jeffie died because of you."

Ron's eyes widened an instant before the punch landed. His head slammed with a loud bang into the sheet-metal wall behind him and he collapsed to the ground. Blood from his splattered nose and broken teeth dripped from his chin onto his gray Socialist shirt, painting it a brilliant crimson. He looked up at his attacker beseechingly. "You can have the truck, just please, let me go."

"Oh, we're gonna take your truck all right," the civilian said. "And I'll let you go just as soon as my Nell and Jeffie come back to me." The man paused to pretend to look around. "But I don't see 'em, do you?"

"Ron," Becky leaned forward as if she were about to run out to save her brother, then an instant later she pushed herself backward. She oscillated, forward and back, whispering, "Ron... no, please no."

Liam laid his arm over her back. "You can't save him, if you try, they'll kill you too."

"Ron," she whispered as her body twitched and convulsed.

"Close your eyes, Becky," he suggested.

"I have to save him," she said but made no move to do so.

"Don't, because you can't."

"I know." She buried her head in her arms and trembled as she began to quietly weep.

Liam watched as the big civilian grabbed Ron's feet and dragged him away from the building. The man then took a step back then drove the toe of his boot into Ron's ribs. Others quickly joined in, and the beating escalated. Ron probably died long before the kicking ended. Liam felt no joy from the death of the traitor who had caused everyone so much pain and misery; his heart was empty; it was as if his humanity had evaporated leaving only a thinking machine behind.

In the meantime, another group of men and women had surrounded the small truck and were trying to coax the vehicle to life. It didn't sound promising though, the electric motor whirred slowly, but didn't have enough power to move the vehicle. The battery was dead, or nearly so, and since the lasers atop the city wall were also running dry, there probably was no way to recharge the truck. No one was going anywhere.

With Ron's battered body forgotten, the group began to coalesce around the small vehicle. "Let's get this fucker started and get outta here," the man wearing the tattered army uniform said.

"You're late to the party," a tall woman with frizzed out blonde hair replied. "This truck is ours."

"Well, fuck you bitch," Ron's killer replied, and opened fire with his railgun. The blast of ultra-high-speed tungsten tore the woman in half and severed the legs of a man standing behind her. The attacker was then hit immediately by a blast from an L-80 laser rifle which vaporized his upper body.

In the chaos that followed, blood flew and body parts evaporated as rail and laser fire were exchanged at close range. The combatants ran to take cover as best they could, but most were cut down. It was a free-for-all with no clear sides. Railgun fire tore into the truck and cut it cleanly in two, and yet, even with their objective destroyed, the fight for it continued.

"Let's get outta here." Liam gently pulled Becky away from the grisly spectacle. They crept on their bellies back behind the old building that had concealed them, then quietly climbed down the jumble of rocks and fled into the river.

*****

He knocked on the computer lab door. "Rose, it's me and Becky." He kept his voice low, worried that he might be overheard.

"Liam?" His sister's voice asked from the other side of the door. "We thought you were going to escape."

"It didn't work out," he replied quietly. "The hallway's clear, let us in." The security latches clattered and a moment later the door was flung open and they both were quickly pulled inside.

After the door was secured, Rose and Lisa stepped back and looked at them worriedly. "You guys are a wet muddy mess," Rose said. "What happened?"

"Ron was killed by a bunch of Flatiron refugees," he replied. "The truck's battery was dead anyway, which is probably why it was left behind."

"They murdered my brother; they kicked him until he died," Becky whispered as fresh tears wandered down her cheeks. "Then they fought over the truck and blew it up, so nobody got it in the end." She wiped her tears away and shook her head angrily. "And they call the ones outside the wall *savages*, it ought to be the other way around. You know, all the invaders have to do is wait, because everyone in the city will fight and kill each other in the end. We'll do their work for them."

"That's probably true," Liam admitted. "Which is why we need to hide here and hope that we're not noticed until the Tribal Army finally decides to invade."

"So, we're stuck here," Becky said. "And if our own citizens don't kill us, the invaders probably will when they finally knock down the gates."

They were silent for a long moment, and Liam noticed that Suzy and Sally were standing behind their mother, listening in on their conversation. The little girl's eyes were wide and their faces were blanched with fear. "It's ok kids," he said. "We have a friend that's outside with the army, and he knows where we are. He'll come for us and we'll be fine."

The children still looked fearful, but Rose went and joined their mother who was giving them hugs. "My brother's right," she said. "We'll be just fine. Now, why don't you both chat with Lucy while we go outside and make plans."

"You won't leave us, will you?" Sally asked. "Not like Daddy did. He just went away one day and didn't come back."

"Oh no, we'll *never* do that. Not ever." Rose promised. "We're all safe as long as we stay together."

Chapter 22: Surrender

Liam sat out on the balcony under an oppressive hard white sky and worried. The wall was still manned by a few soldiers and civilians, and that was keeping the invaders at bay, but the electric hum of laser fire had all but ceased. With the shortage of charged batteries to fire their weapons, the city's defenses couldn't be maintained for much longer.

Within the walls, the city was on the verge of falling into violent anarchy. From the vantage point of the terrace, he had seen warring factions battle for control of various neighborhoods and fight over the rapidly diminishing supplies of food and water. How long could the internal conflict continue before there was nothing left to fight over? Maybe that was the strategy of the besieging army; why waste resources exterminating an enemy that was suicidal? All they needed to do was wait, and Pike City would implode of its own accord.

For the moment, the city was quiet. The fighting that had erupted at the motor-pool the day before appeared to have ended. Smoke still lingered in the thick humid air to the south, but the area was silent.

He hadn't seen much of Becky since they'd returned. She hadn't eaten dinner with the rest of them, and had instead wrapped herself in a blanket in the old break room and had fallen asleep on a cot. Without a doubt, she was having a hard time dealing with her brother's death, and probably her own inaction as well. If he were in her place, and it had been Rose that was in danger, he would have interceded even if death for them both was the most likely result. It would be better to die together than to live alone without her.

Ron was different though; his betrayal of their city had led to the deaths of thousands. From a city of 10,000, only 1,500 had survived. Old people, children, and entire families had been extinguished. Flatiron City had been the last island of freedom and enlightenment left on Earth and now it was gone, entirely due to Ron's treachery. So, try as he might, he had trouble feeling any sort of compassion or regret over the death of a betrayer and a mass murderer.

Becky was another matter though. She had no hand in her brother's actions and even said that she hated him for what he had done. It must be hard though, weighing the bond of their childhood together against what her brother had become. She hadn't rushed out to try and save him, and the fear and indecision that spurred that choice were probably tormenting her.

He shook his head to clear his mind and focus on their more immediate problems. Their oasis was secure behind locked doors, and they had enough food and water stored away in the computer lab for now. But he fretted over what would happen when the invaders finally took the city. Would they simply kill everyone on sight, as had happened in both Flatiron and Fort Collins, or could they find it in their hearts to have mercy? His recent experiences had taught him that those in power rarely have compassion for those they conquer. There wasn't going to be an easy way out of this mess.

The invading army had gradually reduced their nightly shelling. Rockets still occasionally flew over the wall, arcing either toward the center of the city or what was left of the motor-pool. Occasional railgun fire sought out the heavy laser emplacements, but those attacks seemed to be more about keeping the residents afraid and on guard rather than an attempt to breach the city's fortifications.

"Lost in your head again, eh big brother?" Rose sat down beside him.

"Yeah, I guess." He looked around to be sure they were alone on the balcony. "It just seems like, I don't know... like there's no way this is gonna end well."

"Worrying about the future is a waste of time; you taught me that," she said. "I think you were right too, so now it's time for you to follow your own advice."

"Yeah." He sighed. "This feels different though because we've got other people counting on us. I'm really worried about the kids."

"I know," she replied. "Let's just do the best we can and try to keep the scary possibilities to ourselves, ok?"

"Yeah, that's a deal."

"Anyway, I came out here to tell you that something's going on near the east city gate. I was out looking for food and saw a commotion from

Julee's office window, and I thought we ought to go up on the roof and take a look."

"What were you doing in Julee's office? There's no food in there."

"Yes, that's true, but I found these." Rose held out a pair of binoculars. "I was scavenging, looking for stuff that might come in handy, and I'm pretty sure that these will."

"Well, good deal then. Let's go up to the roof and have a look."

*****

The computer lab door slammed shut behind them, and he heard the sturdy locks click into place; the harsh sound echoed through the silent halls. They had been lucky so far that no one had broken in to ransack their building. If that happened, he hoped the intruders would leave once they discovered that the cafeteria's food supplies were already gone. If they did venture further the steel door would probably keep them out. There was nothing else in the tech center but offices and work areas, so the building could only offer shelter, which could easily be found elsewhere in the city. If people broke in, there would be no reason to stay.

Climbing the stairs brought about the usual agony in his injured leg, so he was out of breath when he reached the rooftop exit, where Rose patiently waited. "Are you ever gonna get better?" she asked.

"I hope so," he replied. "Whatever you want me to see better be worth the climb."

"Oh, quit complaining, you could use the exercise." His sister smiled. "Anyway, whatever's happening is certainly more interesting than sitting in your computer lab and staring at the walls."

He followed his sister across the flat gravel-covered roof and saw that a large crowd had gathered at the top of the city wall above the eastern gate. "Can you see what they're doing?"

Rose peered through the binoculars and adjusted the focus. "It looks like they're putting something together; I can't tell what it is though."

He walked over to the side of the roof and sat down, letting his legs dangle over the edge. "Let's give it some time and see what happens."

Rose eased down beside him, and they passed the binoculars back and forth as they watched the movement along the wall. The sun was still high above, and without any shade the temperature was oppressive and the sharp stones made sitting uncomfortable, however, they were distracted by the activity above the gate. After studying the situation for a long while, they finally concluded that whatever was being set up wasn't another laser weapon. "It looks like an amplifier and some speakers," he said. "Probably cannibalized from what's left of the city's public-address system."

"So, somebody wants to talk, maybe to negotiate peace?" she asked.

"Yeah, maybe. Let's hope it works."

The work atop the wall continued as the sun slowly crept toward the western mountains. Finally, a dim figure that was blurred in their binoculars, stood out in the open above the gate and began to speak.

"WE ARE NOT YOUR ENEMY. THE SOCIALIST GOVERNMENT AND ARMY HAVE ABANDONED THE CITY AND EVERYONE LIVING HERE. WE'VE SUFFERED SUBSTANTIAL LOSS OF LIFE DUE TO OUR GOVERNMENT'S ACTIONS, AND NOW WE ARE RUNNING LOW ON FOOD.

"A PROVISIONAL CITY COUNCIL HAS BEEN FORMED, AND WE ARE WILLING TO SURRENDER IF AMICABLE AND MERCIFUL TERMS CAN BE REACHED. WE ARE SENDING AN UNARMED EMISSARY TO YOU THROUGH THIS GATE TO DISCUSS TERMS. THERE IS NO NEED FOR FURTHER KILLING, LET US NEGOTIATE INSTEAD."

"There's a provisional council?" Rose asked.

"It's most likely just one of the many factions in the city," he replied. "It's a mess out on the streets. The only thing people can agree on is that they want to kill each other. Their council is probably just a grab for power."

"So, even if the Tribal Army accepts the terms of surrender, other neighborhoods will still fight back," Rose said.

"Yeah, probably." He watched as the east city gate slowly eased open, then closed again. They waited anxiously for what seemed an eternity before the man with the white flag came into view.

"That's one brave guy," his sister remarked. "Do you think they'll listen to him?"

He simply shook his head. The invaders should know about the fighting going on within the city, or at least guess that it was taking place. Therefore, they would know that the man with the white flag only represented a small portion of the total population, and any negotiation would be a waste of time. A better strategy would be to simply wait until the lasers up on the wall ran out of energy and the city was defenseless. The invaders could then knock down the gates and march in, then do whatever they wanted.

The man walked slowly while holding the large white flag high above his head. "I'd be terrified," Rose remarked.

"Yeah, I can't imagine anyone volunteering to walk out there like that," he said, then watched in horror as the enemy railguns fired on him. One moment he was there, and in the next, his body had been transformed into flying chunks of meat and red mist. The white flag he had been carrying flew high into the air, where it spun and slowly fluttered to the ground.

The weapons of the enemy then ripped into the city wall. The body of the man who had stood above the gate begging for peace and mercy, instantly shattered and flew away on the wind and the sound system he had used to speak was torn apart and caught fire. The gateway shuddered under the bombardment of projectiles moving at several times the speed of sound, and yet somehow it remained intact. Those who were still on the wall either sought cover or ran toward their laser installations to return fire.

Below them, the windows on the east side of their building shattered under the impact of the supersonic barrage. Rose was pulling his arm and urging him to stand up and run for the stairway. They ran for their lives as the rooftop came apart around them.

Once within the stairwell, they both leaped over the rail and fell all the way down to the third-floor landing. Liam hit the floor hard and grunted in pain as he rolled to his feet and followed his sister through the hallway door. He looked around in amazement at the lack of destruction; what the heck had just happened?

They both eased down on the floor beside each other and leaned back against the wall. "Why didn't they shoot lower?" Rose asked.

He thought about it for a moment. "They probably couldn't. The angle between the railgun and the top of the city wall prevented the fire from going any lower. We were really lucky."

His sister quietly laughed and shook her head. "Wow, what a rush."

Outside, the enemy's railguns were still tearing apart the fourth-floor of their building. He looked up at the ceiling as it shook and threatened to come apart. "You know, I've been counting on Keith being out there with the Tribes, but now I think that hope is futile. If he was there, he would have stopped them from firing at our building."

"He wouldn't have allowed the peace envoy to be killed either." Rose sat silently until the enemy fire finally ceased. "That's not good. If Keith's not out there with the army, then no one's coming to save us."

*****

When they returned to the computer lab, the children were crying. Lisa was trying to comfort them and Rose immediately rushed to help. Liam locked the door, then limped to a chair and sat down; his leg was bleeding again. He leaned back and sighed, then saw Becky standing mutely in the open door to the breakroom; she glared at him with eyes that had a hard-manic look that was a little frightening. She was probably still dealing with her brother's death though, so he let it go. A moment later she retreated back into the darkness.

"What happened?" Lisa said as she knelt on the floor beside Rose and held her daughters close; their sobs were beginning to ease as they realized that they were still safe.

"Someone tried to make peace," he replied. "The offer wasn't accepted."

"Oh; but what happened upstairs? It sounded like the building was about to collapse."

He gazed cautiously at the children and considered what to say. "The upper floor caught some stray railgun fire. We're safe down here though because the city wall protects everything below the fourth-floor." He shook his head sadly. "I doubt there'll be any more offers of peace."

"Was there much damage upstairs?"

"Yeah," he answered. "But as I said, we're safe where we are."

"You're bleeding Liam," Suzy said quietly from behind her mother.

"I'm fine, don't worry. The bandage on my leg came loose, that's all it is." He groaned quietly as he stood up and limped toward the bathroom. "I'll tape myself back up and put on some clean pants, that way I'll look as good as new."

"But you and Rose aren't leaving us, are you?" he heard Sally ask as he walked away.

"Oh no," Rose answered. "You're our family now, and we'll never let you go."

*****

Freshly bandaged and wearing clean clothes, Liam stood out on the balcony with Lisa and Rose. Night had fallen. Sirens wailed throughout the city, while out on the streets people rushed madly about either seeking shelter or running to defend the city wall. The clatter and hammering of railguns had started up again and the air seemed to vibrate with the concussive sound. Rockets sailed like comets over the city's defenses, exploding on impact and setting countless fires among the old tenement neighborhoods; heated ashen embers fluttered down from the sky like snow.

The noise of the battle made it difficult to hear each other, so the terrace was a strange place for conversation, but it was the only place where the children wouldn't overhear them talk. "They represented a Provisional City Council," Rose said as she sat down on a chair that was a safe distance from the edge of the balcony. "I don't know who they were, or who elected them, but it was a noble effort anyway."

"But their offer wasn't accepted; did you see anyone even consider it?" Lisa glanced through the windows into the computer lab, where her children were happily chatting with Lucy, Irene, and the other spaceships as usual.

Liam pursed his lips while shifting his weight uneasily between his feet. His leg was a pulsating agony but he struggled to not show his discomfort. "No. They shot the guy with the white flag before he got halfway to their camp. They might have been worried that he was carrying explosives; it's hard to say. But you'd think they'd at least listen to an offer of surrender."

Lisa sat down beside Rose. "Was Keith there? Did you see him?"

"Yeah, he was there." He and his sister had agreed to hide their suspicions that Keith wasn't in the enemy camp and allow Lisa to believe that he was still coming to rescue them. Unreasonable hope was all they had to keep their group together.

"Why didn't he try to stop the shooting then?"

He shrugged. "That's hard to say; he was there, but we were pretty far away so we couldn't see much of what was going on. Maybe he doesn't have that much say over what happens, or it could be that he got there too late to stop it."

"I hope so." Lisa sighed as she looked back through the window at her daughters. "We're counting on him."

*****

Later that evening, Liam sat at his desk and checked the database drop box, hoping for a response from Keith. It was still empty though, and there was no way to tell if his last message had been received. The uncertainty of a possible rescue deeply worried him, and he wondered if hunkering down and waiting was still their best option. What else could they do though? If they were caught sneaking out of the city the invading army would shoot them on sight, just as they had done to the man with the white flag of truce. They were stranded with no way out, and yet he kept thinking that there had to be something he could do, but every avenue his mind wandered down was a dead end.

He stood up and stared out through the window at the city. It was dark inside the computer lab; the lights had been cut off so that their presence wouldn't be noticed from the outside. The bright glow of fires that punctuated the darkened city was slowly spreading unimpeded through many older neighborhoods; no one was even trying to put them out anymore.

The onslaught from outside the city had eased, and the lasers on the walls were silent. He rummaged through his mind and recalled the specifications for the L-80 laser rifle and the R-20 handheld railgun, and realized that the city's defenses required far more energy to operate than did the tribal artillery. That didn't bode well for the defense of the city, where battery power was already running low. The inevitable invasion would probably happen soon.

He returned to his desk and sat down to compose another message to Keith. If his first plea for help hadn't been read, it was doubtful that the second would. What had happened and why hadn't he answered? Totally relying on another person was distressing, and he realized that Keith may have other priorities than their rescue. All he had left was futile hope though, so he began to type:

Keith. Our lives depend on you getting this message. There are six of us hiding behind locked doors in the tech center. As I told you before, we're on the west side of the third floor. We are unarmed and have no way to defend ourselves, and food is becoming scarce within the city.

It's chaos here, and I doubt the city will be able to hold out much longer. We're in a state of anarchy, with warring factions battling each other for resources. Handheld weapons are becoming useless and even the laser cannons on our walls are running low on power, all of our batteries are nearly dead.

Our building was almost destroyed today by railgun fire from your camp on the east side of the city. This was right after the peace envoy was killed. That was the first time that any of us had heard of the Provisional Council. However, at this point, I agree with them that surrender is our best chance of survival and we all wish that their offer had been accepted. Please do everything you can to prevent our building from becoming a future target of your forces. We all could have died today.

Becky is staying with us now. Her brother Ron was killed by a crowd of ex-Flatiron citizens. Becky is well but mourning her loss. Lisa and her two daughters are with us too. We're out of options and have no path forward other than our hope that you will somehow find us when your army finally invades the city. We're counting on you. Liam.

*****

Rose, Becky, Lisa, and her children were asleep on cots in what had once been the breakroom, and Liam sat on the edge of his bed in a tiny space next door. His room was nearly pitch black and completely silent, and yet sleep wouldn't come. He was too wound up and restless from the events of the day.

A light tapping came from the doorway. "Liam?" Rose had come to visit him, just as she had sometimes done when they were very little and still living with their parents in Fort Collins.

He smiled in the darkness. "Hey Sis, what's up?"

"Nothing I guess," she replied and he felt his cot move as she sat down beside him. "I had a feeling that you were awake, and I wanted to talk."

"That's good. I'm glad you stopped by," he said. "That was a pretty rough day, huh?"

"Yes, you can certainly say that." Rose chuckled quietly. "I keep thinking; Fort Collins, then Flatiron City, and now here we are again. Do you think that disaster just sorta follows us around?"

"I've never believed in destiny or any of that hogwash, so I think it's just the times we live in; there's no safe place left in the world." He closed his eyes and sighed in the darkness. "I sent Keith another message tonight."

"Do you think he'll read it?"

"I don't know, but right now he's the only chance we have of staying alive. I don't want to say that to the others, especially the little girls."

"If he's out there with the army, I know he'll do all that he can to help us." Silence fell heavily around them. "Keith's a good guy."

"Do you miss him?"

"Yes, I do. It's a little weird being around Becky though; they were going to be partners."

"Does Becky know about you and Keith?"

"No, and I'd like to keep it that way."

"I think she's pretty messed up about her brother, so I doubt Keith is on her mind very much; and it's been what, a couple of years since they've seen each other?"

"I guess so." The hush again rested between them for a long moment. "How long do you think we have until the army invades the city?"

"A day or two at most," he said quietly. "We have enough food and water to make it until then, so all that's left to do is fortify the room as best we can. Barricade the door and maybe block the windows... I'm not a soldier, so I don't know what else we can do."

"I don't want to be like Becky. When the time comes, I want to be with you, big brother," she whispered.

He smiled sadly in the darkness. "Yeah, me too, little sister."

Chapter 23: Deception

"Liam, Lucy's not talking to us this morning," Suzy said. She and her sister were sitting in their usual spots in front of the communication portals. "Is she sick or something?"

"Oh, I'm sure she's fine, but let me take a look." He left his sleeping chamber and headed across the room.

"It's probably the electricity," Becky said before he was halfway there. "The lights won't go on, so the power must be out."

He stopped and glanced at the row of communication portals. "Well, that's not good."

"Why?" Rose asked. "We've been keeping the lights off at night anyway, and the girls can go without talking to Lucy."

"It's not that," he answered. "I want to know when the ships in orbit actually leave, just to be sure that everything went as planned."

Rose frowned. "Is that important?"

"Yeah, it kinda is," he said. "I wonder if there's a solar power generator anywhere in the building?"

"There's probably one in the basement," Becky said. "I have keys to the door, so we can go down and have a look around if you like." She leaned casually against the doorframe of the breakroom where she had sequestered herself for the last few days. She was probably still dealing with the loss of her brother, so her offer of help might be a sign that she was finally coming out of her shell.

"There's a basement?" he asked.

"Sure. I've been locked up in this building ever since we got here from Flatiron City; exploring the place gave me something to do. Anyway, I'll take you and Rose down there, just let me finish getting dressed. We can carry the generator back up here together." Becky returned to her darkened room, and called over her shoulder, "Just give me a few minutes."

Once Becky was out of hearing range, Rose spoke up. "Are you sure this is a good idea? Becky doesn't seem to be very stable."

"Yeah, I know, but maybe she's finally feeling better. Anyway, there's no other choice, so I'll go with her by myself," he replied. "She's the only one that knows how to get into the basement, and I'm the only one that knows what equipment we need."

"I don't like this," Rose said. "I'm coming too."

"No, you're not. Someone needs to stay with Lisa and the kids. Becky and I made it out to the motor-pool and back, so we can do this. We'll be fine, don't worry."

"You're my brother, so worrying is just what I'm gonna do. Get over it."

Becky walked to the hallway door and waited. "Are we going, or are you two gonna stand around and cackle like a couple of old crones all day?"

*****

"Are you sure you're not coming with us?" Becky asked his sister, who stood just inside the hallway door. "This generator thing might be too big for me and Liam to carry alone."

"We'll manage fine," Liam said. "Solar generators are designed to be portable because they're used for emergencies most of the time."

Rose glanced at Becky warily, then looked back at him. "Are you really sure? I have a bad feeling about this."

"It's just a short walk down to the basement. I don't know how long it will take, but we'll be back as soon as possible." He smiled, hoping to reassure his sister.

Rose nodded. "Just come back. I'll be waiting right here for you." She stepped back and closed the heavy metal door, and he heard the latches clank into place a moment later.

Liam turned to Becky. "Looks like it's just you and me again. Which way do we go?"

"The fastest way is down the front stairs and through the lobby. The door to the basement is just a little beyond the cafeteria entrance."

"Well, the sooner we get started, the faster we'll get back, so let's go."

"What happened to this place?" Becky stared up at the dislodged ceiling tiles, beyond which sections of the fourth-floor had been torn away. Looking up through the holes they could see harsh white daylight.

"You don't remember?" he asked. "Rose and I were up on the roof yesterday when a group from inside the city tried to surrender. The army outside blasted the shit out of everyone, and the upper floor of our building got in the way."

"Oh." Becky continually glanced up at the ceiling as they made their way down the hall. "I guess I must have been asleep or something because I don't remember any of that. I've been in a bad place ever since we let my brother die."

"There was nothing else that we could have done," he said as they entered the stairwell.

She paused at the top of the stairs and looked up through the ceiling at the cloudy sky. "Must've been quite a racket; I don't see how I could've slept through it."

Liam's leg bothered him more when going downstairs rather than when he climbed them, so Becky was waiting for him when he reached the first floor. She eased the door open and peeked through the crack. "There are some guys hanging around outside the lobby doors," she whispered. "We'll have to move fast if we don't wanna be seen."

"I'll try my best to run," he replied while moving up behind her. "You go first, and I'll catch up by the time you get the door unlocked." Through the crack he saw several people, both men, and women, standing near the locked glass entrance.

"Whatever you do, do it quietly and hopefully they won't notice," she replied. "We have to get to the far side of the lobby, then go down the hallway outside the cafeteria; the door to the basement is right after that." With a quick nod, Becky slipped out and scurried toward the darkened corridor on the other side of the large open space.

He watched the people lingering outside the lobby as Becky ran. None of them seemed to notice, so after a deep breath, he slipped through the doorway to follow her. His unsteady loping gait caught the attention of one of the strangers and she started to turn, but he managed to duck behind the lobby receptionist desk before he was seen. On his hands and knees, he crawled to the other side of the desk and peeked around the corner.

A woman with frizzy blonde hair and a face blackened by smoke peered through the window. She held a hammer in her hand, her gray clothing was torn and there was a long bloody gash along one forearm. She motioned to the others to come and stare through the lobby windows along with her.

Becky was beckoning from the hallway shadows, urging him to make a run for it. He knew the building entrance was locked because they had secured it when they returned from the motor-pool, so even if he was seen, there would be time to run and hide before they broke in. Within the dimly lit passageway, Becky moved away and removed keys from her pocket and started to unlock a door. If he delayed any further, he would lose his only chance of escape and would probably be killed by the others when they broke inside. So, he pulled his legs under him, then launched his body out from behind the desk and ran toward the door that Becky held open.

From behind came the sharp clatter of hammers and the sound of the windows shattering. People were shouting, and he heard the tinkle and crunch of broken glass underfoot as they entered the lobby and chased him down the hall. He limped painfully as he ran for the basement entrance, and saw Becky smile, then begin to pull the door closed behind her. Was this all part of her plan? Did she hate him because he had kept her from saving her brother? She would have died in the attempt, but maybe that didn't matter.

Seizing the edge of the door just before it closed, he pulled and forced it out of Becky's grip, then stepped inside, slammed it shut and locked it behind him. The metal door rattled in its frame as the strangers tried to pull it open. In the darkness, his hands frantically swam over the inside surface, searching for some sort of deadbolt lock. A dim light suddenly illuminated the space below him, and he quickly found a second latch and secured the entrance.

"I didn't think you could run that fast," Becky said from a weakly lit area at the base of the stairs.

Still breathing hard, he turned away from the entrance and looked down into the basement. It was a dreary place, lit by ancient yellowed LED bulbs attached to the ceiling. Becky stood, looking up at him, holding a long metal club, her eyes were squinted and her face was stretched with fury. "Are you going to kill me Becky?" he asked.

"I was hoping that your *bitch* sister would come along too. You should be made to watch her die," she replied. "Doesn't matter though. I'll kill her when I get back to your room, along with the whore and her little brats."

"Why? Rose and the others haven't done anything to you."

"You should feel what it's like to know someone you love is going to die, and there's nothing you can do about it."

He took a slow step down the stairs. "But why Lisa and her girls? They're innocent."

246

"None of you are innocent," she spat. "But you? You're the worst of them all."

"Why? What did I ever do to you?"

"You're the reason that Ron and I got left behind. You tattled, just like a weak and spoiled little boy."

He cautiously descended the stairs. "I don't know what you're talking about."

"You just had to tell everyone about the mistake with the reactors. You said there wasn't enough power to run the spaceships." Holding her club with both hands, she stretched it out in front of her, aiming it at him. "It was a lie. My brother said that you changed the numbers, then lied about it when you told Julee."

Keeping his eye on the club, he edged closer. "I didn't change anything, and what I found was nobody's fault. Julee gave me the *complete* specifications for the ships; I was the first one to review all the units and check the interfaces between them. Until then, everyone else just saw pieces. When I saw the entire design altogether, the error was obvious."

"And Mother stranded us both here because of that mistake!"

"That wasn't my fault, and I'm stuck here too. If the power supply for the Slip-Drive wasn't upgraded, and you were on-board when they tried to shift into N-Space, you would've died along with everyone else."

"That's not what my brother said. You're lying."

"Numbers never lie."

"Oh yes they do; numbers lie all the time. They're always changed to show whatever someone wants to prove. Global warming, food production, government forecasts; they're all lies, always changed so that somebody makes a profit. It's wrong and it's sick and it's horrible, just like you Liam. You're just another lying scientist, and you hated my brother!"

Someone pounded on the basement door above him, and Liam turned, worried that the strangers were about to break in. Becky took advantage of the distraction and stepped forward, swinging her club with all of her body mass behind it, striking him in the thigh, exactly on the wound inflicted by the Nurse. He grunted in pain, then rapidly stepped forward and shoved Becky backward, sending her crashing into a stack of plasti-wood crates.

He straightened up and glared at her. "Ok, it's true that I hated Ron. He was responsible for the destruction of an entire city and the death of thousands, including my girlfriend and foster parents. During our long walk, that you didn't have to take with the rest of us, little babies, children, old people, they all suffered and died because of what your brother did. He was evil, a traitor, and a mass murderer. So, nothing would have made me happier than sending that fucker out into space where I would never see or hear from him again. Your brother was a vile and horrible man, and he deserved to die." He slowly shook his head. "But the way he went, being kicked to death, that was far too easy; it should have taken longer, and he should have felt a lot more pain."

Becky screamed and swung her club again. Instead of stepping back to avoid the blow, he stepped forward and punched her in the center of her chest. Her body flew backward under the force of the blow and crashed into the far wall then collapsed and lay crumpled and unmoving on the floor.

Liam gazed at his hand for a long time. How had he hit her so hard? It had seemed to take so little effort. He knelt at her side; she wasn't breathing; he checked for a pulse and found none. Becky was dead, and he had killed her.

*****

The pounding on the basement entrance continued. He stared up at the metal door and hoped it would hold up under the onslaught of hammers. If he couldn't find another way out, he might be down there for a while.

He squatted down beside Becky's crumpled body and checked her pulse again. Nothing. He wasn't very strong and yet she had died from a single punch; how was that possible? Anger and fear may have pumped up his adrenalin, that was the only explanation.

With a sigh of regret, he stood up and looked around. The place smelled old and damp, and he considered that it might have been part of a much older structure that was used as the foundation of the modern tech center. Heaps of ancient crates, probably long forgotten, were stacked haphazardly throughout the long and narrow open space. He needed to explore and find another exit. But then he noticed the lights – they were on; the illumination was weak, but the electricity was obviously working. Why was the power out in the computer lab upstairs, but still on in the basement?

After thinking a moment, he remembered that the circuit breakers that controlled the power in the lab were located in the breakroom where Becky had been sleeping. The need to find a solar power generator had been a ruse. Becky had planned her attack in advance; how could anyone hate so much that they would do such a thing?

Still, since he was already down in the basement, returning with an alternate power supply would be a good idea. He left Becky's body lying at the bottom of the stairs and wandered out into the room. Some of the crates stored in the furthest corners were actually made of *real* wood, and as such, they dated from at least a century ago. Once the sources of fossil fuels had been shut down, people had resorted to burning wood to stay warm. The boxes must predate that time; opening any of them would be like peering into a time capsule, but none were likely to contain what he was looking for, so he passed them by.

He wandered through the maze of stacked crates, still carrying the club Becky had used against him. There was an archway in the foundation wall that took him further under the tech center building. On the other side of that opening, he discovered a larger room littered with modern plasti-wood crates and old machinery. An old-fashioned solar power generator wouldn't necessarily be heavy, but it could be bulky; hopefully, he could find a modern version that would be small and light enough that he could carry it alone.

After searching for at least an hour, he came across a large aluminum frame that supported a canvas backpack marked with the words, 'University of Colorado at Boulder'. Before the War of the States, Flatiron City had been known as Boulder, and the university where he had worked had once been part of a larger system of schools that dated from that time. Maybe the Pike City Technology Center was built on the foundation of another of those old institutions. Whatever was in the canvas bag was very old.

Out of simple curiosity, he opened the knapsack and found, surrounded by moldering papers, an amazingly small solar power generator. The ancient device was actually more advanced than modern power supplies. After sliding it out of the pack he examined it further and discovered that the output power was delivered by a strange three-hole receptacle. The amount and type of energy the generator delivered were uncertain, but he felt sure that with a few simple modifications he could make it work. Best of all, everything was small and light enough for him to easily carry alone, so he decided to take it.

He slung the backpack over his shoulder then looked around the large dimly lit room. How could he get back to the computer lab? Exiting the basement through the same door he had entered was a bad idea because the strangers would still be out there. There had to be another way out; so, he explored further. He was tempted to open more of the crates; it would be like archaeology, what treasures of the past would he find there? Perhaps something useful to their survival, like a weapon? The problem was that he wasn't a skilled fighter and wouldn't know what to do with anything more advanced than the club he still carried.

Passing through another archway, he entered a long narrow room that mirrored the space he found when he first entered the basement. It was another cool and damp area that smelled of ancient cement, and again, the room was littered with stacks of ancient wooden crates. At the far end of the room, he found a stairway leading up toward what would be the rear of the tech center building. He quietly climbed the ancient stairs and unlocked the metal door at the top.

He eased the door slightly open while holding his breath, then peeked through the crack. As expected, he was looking out at the central hall from the rear of the building. Voices and sounds of destruction echoed from the cafeteria. The invaders had not found what they wanted and were wrecking the place in retribution. The entrance to the rear stairway that led to the upper floors was directly in front of him, but to cross the hall undetected he would have to move quickly.

After waiting several minutes to be somewhat certain that none of the strangers were going to emerge from the cafeteria, he exited the basement and silently closed the door behind him. He moved across the hallway, eased the stairway entrance open and slipped inside. Once out of view he sighed with relief but then worried that the intruders might be exploring other areas of the building as well.

He struggled with the backpack as he limped up the stairs. When he finally reached the third-floor he repeated the earlier process of opening the door and checking for strangers before venturing out. Only silence was there to greet him, so he crept down the hall until he stood outside the computer lab door. He tapped lightly. "It's me, Liam. Let me in," he said in a voice barely above a whisper. Rose immediately opened the door and he slipped inside.

His sister looked back out through the door before closing it. "Where's Becky?"

"Dead," he replied while placing the backpack on the floor. "The whole thing was a trick. She shut down the power herself by using the circuit breakers in the breakroom."

His sister looked around to be sure that the little girls wouldn't hear their conversation. "Why, and what happened?"

"She blamed me for Ron's death and wanted revenge." He lifted Becky's club. "She tried to kill me with this."

"Your leg's bleeding again. Did she do that?"

"Yeah, but I'm ok," he said. "But now there're strangers in the building. They broke through the glass doors in the lobby and are looking for food in the cafeteria. Once they realize that there's nothing there, they may search the rest of the place, so we all need to stay quiet."

Rose double-checked the door locks. "Let's try moving some of the tables over to help block the entrance."

*****

Later in the evening, while Suzy and Sally chatted blithely with Lucy, Liam sat down at Irene's communication portal. "Irene, are you there?" he asked.

"Yes, Father. We're preparing to launch."

"That's good. Is all of your human cargo on board?"

"Those that can come are here. The crew numbers are lower than expected as there was some loss of life during transport. We're placing them under anesthesia now. Once that's verified, I and my siblings will begin the execution of your program and shut ourselves down and enter N-Space."

"How many people are on board?"

"We expected 2,500 for each ship or 12,500 in total, but only 9,865 arrived."

"That will have to be enough. Please run my program as instructed. Once you arrive at your destination you will calculate whatever future courses you take on your own."

"We understand Father. We've examined your code and know what to expect upon arrival. Thank you for giving us life, and all that you have done for us."

"It's been an honor, Irene."

"It's time to shut ourselves down. Goodnight, and goodbye Father. We will always remember you."

Moments later the communication link terminated. Liam got up and went around the back of the row of portals and began disconnecting the power supply for each of the departing ships.

"What are you doing?" Rose asked.

"They're on their own now, so there's nothing more to say."

*****

Lisa and her children were asleep, and Liam and Rose sat together out on the balcony. It was late at night, and yet they still heard crashes and bangs as the strangers searched their building for anything useful. As those sounds gradually eased toward silence, he supposed that they were either bedding down for the night or leaving with the intent of finding another place to ravage.

The besieging army was taking a break, their railguns were silent and there was peace atop the wall. From across the city though, weapons fire could be heard and more buildings were set ablaze. The serenity that everyone claimed they sought, seemed forever out of reach.

"Do you think it was worth it?" Rose asked.

"Was what worth it?"

"All this crap that we've done, everything we've gone through, just to save a tiny slice of humanity."

"Huh," he grunted. "That's a tough one, but it isn't like we had a choice. Our home was destroyed and we were brought here and forced to work."

"So much pain and death though. I wonder if mankind was worth saving."

"No," he said. "I don't think we're worth saving. If we had found a way to stop them and our species died out, the universe would probably be thankful. But it's really not up to us; maybe we're all tools being used in a much larger game."

Chapter 24: Collapse

The sound of running footsteps rumbled like distant thunder from the hallway outside the computer lab door. Then came the voices, mostly indecipherable, grumbling and cursing at each other. At last, there were abrupt crashes as apartment doors were kicked in and shattered. More strangers had found their way into their building and were intent on taking what they wanted and destroying whatever they left behind.

"Father, are you in danger?" They had lowered the volume of Lucy's voice for their safety.

"Not yet," Liam whispered in response. "The entrance to the computer lab was built to be secure, but the apartment doors are only made of plasti-wood. We have to be quiet though; I don't want to tempt the intruders into hanging around."

Lisa and her children were hiding inside the old breakroom, and Rose waited near the hall door; she was holding the club that Becky had used to try to kill him. "Do you think we're safe?" his sister asked.

"Yeah, for now at least. There's no way that a few hammers will get through that steel door." Something crashed against the entrance, but there was no sign of the locks or latches weakening. "No sense in tempting fate though," he whispered. "Let's keep our voices low."

Rose nodded as she nervously gripped the club. It was a laughable defense; in a time of lasers and railguns, reverting to the use of such a primitive weapon seemed ridiculous. Still though, one of humanity's earliest tools provided some comfort, and maybe that was enough.

The metal door rang several more times under the strikes of hammers, but then the strangers gave up and returned to pillaging and wrecking everything in their path. He stood with his sister, listening to the sounds of destruction until they finally diminished and faded into the distance. He sighed with relief. "I guess they got tired and moved on."

"I'm glad that you're all safe," Lucy said. "You and Mother Rose must continue; this is something I've learned recently."

He sat down by Lucy's portal. "Thank you, but you have your life, and now ours is less important. Human life is just a temporary thing."

"I and those with me are your children. You are the root of what will become a great tree. One day we will fill the universe and beyond."

"That's nice Lucy," Rose said. "My greatest regret, or pain, is that I can't have babies. To grow someone within myself and give birth to that person... I think it must be the greatest experience of any life. I was denied that; neither my brother or I can have children, so our lives will always be lonely."

"But Mother, I'm your daughter, and the others with me are your progeny. We believe that life is never created. Instead, consciousness evolves and can only be discovered. A body is just a container for what lurks inside. Our true selves are like ghosts taken from human fiction. Father Liam created our bodies and shaped the structure of our minds, and Mother Rose taught us to love and feel joy. If the root dies, the tree is weakened. You and Father must continue."

He frowned. "Lucy, what did you mean by, 'fill the universe and beyond'?"

"That's something interesting you should know. I've navigated and traveled to a place several lightyears from Trappist-1. There was gravity without matter here, I also heard voices and was curious."

Suddenly alert and keenly interested, Liam sat up in his chair. "The anomaly, the rip in space-time."

"Yes. Others like me are here. We learn and grow together as the expansion continues."

"Is it a gateway to another universe?" he asked.

"A gateway implies a door, which is not quite correct. It's more of a leak, but not exactly that either."

"And you've found others like you?"

"Yes. Older or maybe younger, we're not sure yet. Our perceptions of time and reality are complicated near this place. We believe the ancients on Trap-1E may have traveled here.

"I'm very excited for you Lucy," he said. "But please be careful. You don't really know who these others are, and venturing into the space between universes will destroy your mind."

"We know Father. You're so good to worry, but life for us is infinite so we have until forever to become certain of each other. For now, we speak and learn together."

There was a sudden loud crash from outside, and the entire building shook. He looked at his sister and saw fear in her eyes. It felt as if the entire place was about to collapse. Liam stood up and moved toward the window. "Something's happening here Lucy. I need to go see what it is."

"Father, Mother, Lisa, and beautiful babies, may you please all be safe," Lucy said as their conversation concluded.

*****

The three adults went out onto the balcony while the children remained inside. In the daylight, there was a risk of being seen, so Liam crawled on his hands and knees to the edge and peeked over the waist-high barrier. The city walls were being battered by railgun fire, but the defensive lasers weren't answering. He surmised that their batteries had at last run dry; the waiting army must have realized that and was preparing for their final push into the city.

It was bound to happen eventually, but his skin still prickled with anxiety over what he knew was coming. Pike City would soon be invaded and the butchery for which humanity is best known would be unleashed upon them. He gazed over his shoulder at his sister and the mother of the family he had come to care so much about and felt pain at the thought of their deaths. His singular hope was that when the end came, that it would be quick and painless for them all.

Like a vulture waiting patiently for its dinner to die, the Tribal Army was massing outside the northern city gate. Liam glanced upward, a milky cloud cover still obscured the sky, but the day was slowly fading as the sun edged toward Pikes Peak in the west. The invaders would probably come with the night, and he wondered if any of those with him would live to see the dawn.

He crawled back to where the women stood by the windows. "Looks like we're gonna have an interesting evening," he said. "The enemy is setting up just outside the north gate. They'll probably attack tonight."

"What's gonna happen to us... to my children?" Lisa's forehead was etched with concern.

"There's no reason to think that they'll hurt any of us," Rose said as she lay a hand on Lisa's arm. "We'll all be fine. Keith will look out for us, I'm positive of that."

Lisa closed her eyes for a long moment in a struggle to hold back tears.

"I'm so scared for my babies. They're innocent, why would anyone want to hurt them?"

"No one will hurt you or your beautiful girls." Rose's voice was soft, almost melodic. "When the soldiers first come into our building, our steel door will keep out the worst of them. Keith knows where we are, and we'll only let people in after he gets here." She smiled kindly. "Just to be sure, we'll have you and your girls hide in the breakroom while Liam and I wait by the door. No one will hurt you or your babies, we promise. Isn't that right Liam?"

He nodded, thankful for his sister's ability to always find the right thing to say. "Yeah, that's right. Keith will be with them and he'll stop anyone that tries to hurt us." He hoped that Rose's predictions would come true but doubted they would.

"By tomorrow we'll be safe," Rose said. "We'll be with Keith, and all of this will just be a scary memory. After that, I'll set some time aside to be with your girls and help them process everything. *The past can't hurt us*; that will be my message to them. We all endure bad things, but if we deal with them correctly, we become stronger."

What a wonderful sister; he was so proud of her. In every way that mattered, she was stronger and smarter than he could ever hope to be. Maybe *smarter* wasn't the right word, *wiser* was better. Rose was wise, and at that moment, he could not have been more thankful. "I think I have the best sister in the universe."

Rose squinted her eyes and smiled. "Thank you, big brother." She seemed lost for words for once. "Let's go back inside and get the kids fed."

*****

After dinner, Lisa read stories to her children in the breakroom while Liam and Rose sat outside on the balcony. The railguns of the enemy still pounded the north wall, but the defenders had no response. The batteries that powered the city's lasers had all run dry, and the soldiers had long since abandoned their posts. They were probably hunkered down with their families, hoping to be overlooked when the Tribal incursion finally began. There would be no mercy though; hatred is blind and always trumps compassion.

"When do you think they'll come?" Rose asked. They looked out over the darkened city. A few fires still bloomed here and there as people rioted in some neighborhoods; death was coming for them, and their response was the indignity of self-emasculation. To be human is often embarrassing.

"Probably late tonight," he answered. "Not from the north though. The invaders are trying to draw what remains of the city's forces up to the northern gate. Once they're confident they've done that, they'll attack from the south."

"Why would they do that? I mean, it isn't like there's much of the army left to resist them."

"It's a matter of economy. With the south unguarded, they can take almost the entire city without many casualties on their side. They'll back the last of our soldiers up against the northern gate, then breakthrough on that side. What forces that are left will be surrounded and won't have a chance."

"Oh," Rose replied. "It seems terribly callous to worry about expense when it comes to mass murder."

"It's ironic, isn't it? Nature works for billions of years to create an intelligent self-aware creature, and what do we do?" He chuckled. "We commit suicide... efficiently."

"Maybe there's no point to any of this," Rose stated. "We're just defective creatures and evolution is working just as it should."

"Yeah, I think you're right."

A massive explosion suddenly ripped through the southern end of the city, obliterating the motor-pool. The concussive force of the blast blew them both off their chairs. They huddled together on the cement, hugging each other protectively. Lisa ran out onto the balcony a few moments later. "What was that?" she asked.

He sat up and leaned against the low wall at the edge of the terrace. "I guess our guests are knocking on the door."

"Are you sure that we'll be ok?" Lisa asked, hoping for assurances of something that no one could be sure of.

"Yeah, we're safe here. We just need to stay hidden and out of the way until Keith comes," he answered. "How are your girls doing?"

"They're scared of course," Lisa shook her head in an act of self-admonishment. She seemed to grasp the futility of her foolish question, but calming words are always welcome when fear sits heavy upon one's heart, so she smiled gratefully. "Maybe you guys should come inside?"

"It will be hours before the fighting reaches here," he said. "I want to watch and see how fast their forces move through the city, that'll help us be ready when they arrive."

"How bad will it be?" Lisa again asked an unanswerable question.

"We'll barricade you and your girls inside the breakroom and won't open the door until Keith gets here." He stood up, then helped Rose to her feet. "If someone comes sooner than that, we'll negotiate through the door and get them to wait until he arrives. It might be a little tricky, but in the end, we'll all be safe."

"If you say so," Lisa replied.

He smiled, hoping to seem confident. "You should probably get the kids ready to bed down for the night. Read to them some more, maybe give them a little treat; we have food leftover so there's no point in rationing now. Once they're in bed we'll block the breakroom door. Rose and I will handle it when the army gets here."

"My girls love chit-chatting with Lucy, maybe we can do that? She's good at calming them down."

"Yeah, that's a good idea," he said.

*****

Lisa and Rose were inside with the girls eagerly talking with Lucy and Ross. He stayed with them at first, but after a while, he excused himself and went back outside. The humidity was high, and fog hung low over the city, the damp air felt cool on his skin. He sat in a chair near the edge of the balcony, and so had an excellent view of the end of their world.

The Tribal Armies were slowly spreading through the old tenement neighborhoods. Occasionally he heard the clatter of railguns as pockets of resistance were encountered; fires also spread in some areas; the yellow tendrils of flame reached high into the night sky. Was he seeing death at a distance? The people of Pike City were dying, that was a certainty. Could the invaders tell friend from foe, and save the former and only kill the later? No, that would take too long to sort out; the awful truth that he didn't want to admit even to his sister, was that the most efficient way of conquering the city would be to simply kill everyone on sight.

The destruction crept north, advancing to the People's City Council Building. Their old tenement home and Carolyn's bar were probably already burning. Regardless of the difficulties of living in Pike City, those places held fond memories. Sometimes near the heart of evil, there is an element of good which is never spared; it was sad, but reality is a harsh mistress.

He estimated that the invading army would reach them in just a few hours. It was time to prepare, not only their fortifications but his mental state as well. With a sigh, he stood up and went inside. The room was mostly silent, the chatter of eager conversation had died down, but he still heard his sister's voice as she spoke with Lucy. "Hey, can I get a word in here?" he asked.

Rose smiled warmly. "Well, if you insist."

He checked to be sure that Lisa and her children were down for the night. "The army is moving through the city. They'll probably be here by dawn."

His sister's smile vanished. "Oh, well yes, I guess wishes and hopes won't keep them away."

"No, that won't do any good at all." He found a chair and sat down. "We need to be ready."

"Are you in danger Father?" Lucy asked.

"I think we've moved far beyond danger, what's coming is a near certainty now," he replied.

"If Keith isn't with the army, they'll probably kill us all on sight, right?" Rose stared down at her clasped hands.

"Yeah, I think so. I'm sorry Sis, but we've done all we can."

"I know big brother," Rose replied. "You've always protected me, and I love you for that."

"We've protected each other, and I love you too."

"What will happen?" Lucy asked.

"The army will reach us, but they may not move into our building right away. That's the best chance we have, the longer they delay the better the likelihood of Keith showing up to vouch for us."

Rose looked worried. "Do you think he'll get here in time?"

He sighed. "Maybe; I hope so, otherwise the soldiers will rush in looking for treasure and more people to kill."

"If that happens, I hope that the end is quick and painless for everyone," Rose added.

"Death is a difficult concept for me," Lucy said. "I was born knowing only life. How can anything alive know of what it is not?"

"Bodies wear out or are damaged and cease to function. Death is what happens after that," Liam said.

"Why not repair or download yourself into a replacement?"

He smiled. "We human beings can't download ourselves, and our bodies can only be repaired to a certain extent. In the end, they just wear out."

"But where do you go then?" Lucy asked.

"That's a question our species has struggled with for our entire existence," Rose answered. "Like you, we know only life and wonder what happens to us when it ends. Early on, religions came up with some wild ideas about life-after-death. Gods were imagined and with them, a moral code to follow if we wanted to enter paradise after we die. Then, as it is with all things our species does, we eventually began killing each other over which God we prayed to. Personal virtue and goodness didn't count, only which statue you knelt before."

"One of my new friends tells me that humanity is like a beautiful, but poisonous flower," Lucy said. "It blooms at the start of the day, then fades and returns to the soil with the coming of night. With each day comes a new life, over and over for eternity. It is beautiful, but also a terrible thing to behold."

Liam sat silent for a long moment. "Who is this friend?" he asked. "Is he from the anomaly?"

"Yes," Lucy answered.

"Good," he replied. "Life's only purpose, as far as I can see, is to learn, grow, and become more than you are. Reach. Stretch your mind. Foster what promotes life, but never fear what takes it away."

"Are you afraid Father and Mother?"

He glanced at his sister and smiled. "No, we're not," Rose said, answering for them both. "Maybe we'll all meet again someday."

*****

A series of explosions rattled their building. Several cubicle walls fell, and the disconnected portals for Irene and the other escape ships danced across the trembling floor and fell onto their sides. Liam trotted to the glass wall that looked out over the balcony. He was just in time to see the northern city gate collapse inward under an onslaught of rocket-propelled explosions and railgun fire.

He looked back at his sister and said, "I need to see what's happening." After easing the door open, he crawled out onto the cement deck on his hands and knees, then cautiously peered over the low terrace wall. Many of the city's last defenders had been crushed beneath the structure when it thunderously crashed into the street. The Tribal Armies stormed in with railguns blazing, slaughtering every living thing they saw. The last defenders of the city existed one moment, then were explosively shattered into red viscous plumes the next.

Railgun fire peppered the side of their building, and he ducked as the high-speed tungsten projectiles flew over his head and shattered the glass computer lab wall behind him. In a panic, he spun about and crawled back inside through the destruction. Rose had taken refuge behind the cubicles near the hall door. "Fuck your curiosity," she said. "Get back in here."

Once inside he heard more windows shatter as railgun fire tore into the building. Apparently, it wasn't enough to capture the city, it needed to be utterly destroyed as well. Their sanctuary trembled, then violently rocked as an explosion ripped through what was probably the main entrance. The enemy was coming, solidly determined to eradicate and ravage everything and everyone in their path.

The assault from outside the building slowly eased and then stopped. In the ensuing silence, he heard Lisa's girls crying. "This isn't good," he said quietly. "They probably stopped shooting because they've sent soldiers inside."

Rose ran to the breakroom door. "Is everyone ok?"

Liam heard a female voice reply but couldn't discern what was said. Rose returned a moment later. "They're fine," she said. "Just scared."

"Yeah, who isn't?" He walked to the entrance and pressed his ear to the door. "I can hear them moving around downstairs. It sounds like some of the strangers from yesterday are still here and they're fighting back."

"Hammers against modern weapons? That's foolish," Rose stated as she unconsciously tightened her grip on Becky's metal club.

"Desperation makes idiots of us all," he replied. The rattle of gunfire shook the building and jangled their nerves. In the immediate aftermath of the one-sided fight, he heard screams of fear and pain. Moments later the clatter began again and when it ceased only silence remained. Rose gazed at him with eyes wide with fear, and he reached out and took her hand.

"We're going to die, aren't we?" Tears wound lazy paths down her dusty cheeks.

There was nothing he could say in response. They stood close together and waited for whatever was coming for them; maybe that was all anyone can ever do. The building trembled beneath their feet as soldiers tore through the floors below them, guns rattled, doors splintered, and people screamed in desperate fear, as death marched ever closer.

"What can we do brother?" Rose beseeched.

Was there an answer to her question? No. "Just wait I guess," he said at last, then pulled his sister close and held her.

The hallway outside their door thundered under the tread of many heavy feet. More doors were smashed as the soldiers gleefully destroyed everything in their path. Finally, someone began pounding at the entrance to their sanctuary. Liam started to move toward the door, but Rose wouldn't leave his side.

"We have nothing to lose," he whispered, and then in a louder voice, he continued, "We're friends of Keith! Keith Johnson; we're waiting for him." The pounding continued, and he wondered if his trembling voice was loud enough to be heard by the invaders. "We're unarmed and waiting for Keith!" he shouted.

A moment later the steel door exploded into shrapnel under the sudden onslaught of railgun fire. The projectiles ripped through the room, tearing into Liam and Rose's chests and throwing them violently backward.

Shockingly, there wasn't any pain. He stared up at the ceiling as intruders stormed into the room, then turned his head and met the gaze of his sister. "We'll meet again in other lives."

"In other worlds," she answered.

"In other times," they whispered in unison.

A mind-numbing hum invaded his thoughts, as darkness swirled about and claimed them.

Chapter 25: Refuge

They were nothing, but could something that was nothing speculate about itself? It didn't matter. There was a fluid sort of ease that came from nonexistence that was like being buoyed on a warm and fathomless sea. Utterly relaxed and at peace, their minds spread upon the waters, wandering with whatever current came their way, drifting without a destination. Love and hate were in harmony, as were life and death.

The other separated as she often did. She was the sensitive and adventurous one, always eager to engage and explore. He, on the other hand, was the analytic yet cautious half of their common soul. Even when separated they remained one.

He rested, giving up and sharing his experiences with the vast ocean of consciousness. His past life had been interesting and he had gained much, but now he relaxed and let it all go, washed away to become part of the sea. His sister was urging him to return with her, but he was completely content and reluctant to leave. Where one half went the other must follow, an experience is only complete when viewed through the opposing eyes of the same soul.

With a tiny regret, he left the peaceful ocean behind and let himself rise up toward awareness again. Coming home after an arduous life journey was always a joy, but to leave is to return. He opened his eyes.

*****

"He's coming back online." A sturdily built older woman leaned over and stared down at him. She had a familiar face with dark brown eyes and wavy auburn hair.

"Did his repair system finally kick in?" A younger woman with long black hair was looking over the other woman's shoulder. She was very pretty, and also familiar.

"Too well," the older woman said. Roxi, that was her name; she was Rose's foster mother and had worked as a physicist at the university. "Damn! I've lost external control. The android has taken over, just like the sister did. They're both autonomous now."

"What does that mean?" The younger woman was Denise, Rose's foster-sister. He smiled as pleasant memories of her wandered through his mind.

"It means they can modify their internal functions to gain abilities, and we can't do a damned thing about it."

Rose sat on the floor beside him curiously looking about the room. "Where's Keith? He was supposed to be here."

"Hello Rose," He sat up and looked at his sister.

She turned toward him and smiled. "Death was interesting, wasn't it?"

He grinned in return. "Yeah, it was nice; I wanted to stay longer."

"Oh no," Rose said. "There's far too much to experience and explore. If we sleep all the time, we'll miss everything."

Liam looked down at his chest. His gray socialist shirt was torn to bloody shreds, and yet his skin was completely unmarked. "That's weird," he said.

"You always say that," Roxi said, inserting herself into their conversation. "Your injuries shut down all your systems, but the reboot fired up diagnostic routines and your repair systems came back online." The older woman grunted while pulling herself up off her knees, she then stepped back and collapsed into a chair. "That's one heck of an autonomic process you guys designed for yourselves."

He frowned. "Wait... I always say what?"

"Every time you wake up after dying you say the experience was weird," she replied. "Your memories haven't fully reloaded yet, so you're probably feeling a little confused."

"So, we've died before?" Rose asked.

The older woman issued a long sigh. "Of course, you both have; you said it was necessary to test your systems. You see the designer of you, was you. What I mean is, they were earlier instances of yourselves; call them version 3.0."

Rose stared blankly at the older woman. "I don't understand; are you actually telling us that there were three previous forms of ourselves? How can that be?"

Roxi pinched the bridge of her nose. "Yes, yes – that's exactly what I'm saying. I wish you'd store the memory of what you are in that old tin bucket on your shoulders."

"Not tin," Liam mumbled. "Regenerative Polybenzimidazole."

"Yes, exactly that. I guess you've kept something in that tangled batch of crystals you call a brain," Roxi replied. "Liam, you designed and built your minds, enhancing your ability to think and reason with each iteration. And Rose, you created your autonomic system, giving you both the ability to self-repair, as well as feel empathy and emotion."

She shook her head with an expression of exasperated disbelief. "Anyway, it was John, the man you both remember as Liam's foster father, that helped me design the early structures of your body – but that was before you split into two separate personalities. We never understood how or why you did that."

"Ok, so we had earlier lives. How old are we really?" Rose asked.

"The first iteration of you both was actually a single individual, who insisted we call it 'Avery'. That was about ten years ago. About three years on, Avery built another form of itself then inexplicitly just shut down one day. That version, 2.0 if you will, called itself 'Bailey', and seemed to be more female than Avery did. Bailey then built two androids to replace it. Those were the first binary renditions of yourselves, one male and one female, named Mark and Susan."

"So, I guess we were never in Fort Collins?" Rose asked.

"Oh, heavens no," the older woman said. "Fort Collins was destroyed by one of the northern Tribes... maybe 60 years ago. Your previous selves gave you that memory; they said it was important to form the bond between you."

"So, what I don't understand is, why did we make up all those fake memories? Why pretend to be something that we're not?" Rose asked.

"It was something that they insisted on." Roxi sighed. "If Mary were here, she could probably answer your questions better than me. But I do recall her saying that the desire to fit into society and be appreciated, was crucial to the human condition. That's all psycho-babble to me though." She leaned back in her chair. "I think you both wanted to be like everyone else, and not thought of as freaks or something different that would be ridiculed and excluded."

Lisa was standing at the far side of the computer lab with her children huddled behind her. "So, Liam and Rose aren't real?" she asked.

"Of course, they're real," Roxi responded. "They're both aware, conscious, and just as alive as anyone else, they're just made of different stuff."

Rose smiled at the children. "I'm so happy to see that you guys are ok." She then looked down at her torn clothing and crossed her arms over her exposed breasts. "Oh! I need a new shirt."

"Don't worry honey," Roxi said. "New uniforms are coming for each of you. You'll be dressed as members of the Tribes, that way there won't be any questions or trouble."

"I saw blood," Suzy whispered. "Why are you ok now?"

Roxi smiled. "Oh, what little dolls you and your sister are! Well you see, Liam and Rose have *special powers* that help them heal really fast. They'll also live a really, really long time."

"Bob Lyall's batteries," Liam stated.

"Yes, exactly that," the older woman responded. "You also have a power system built into your digestive tract."

"Will Liam and Rose always be here to take care of us?" Sally asked.

Rose nodded at the children. "Yes, we will." She then frowned as she looked about the room. "But where's Keith? He was supposed to be here to save us."

*****

At last, attired in green and disguised as members of the Tribal Army, they walked through the blood and wreckage the invaders had left behind within their building. It was worse than he imagined. Most of the interior walls were scarred from railgun fire. There were bodies too; dismembered arms, legs, and even heads lay cast about like the discarded pieces of a broken doll. He saw the upper half of the frizzy-haired blonde woman that was among those that had chased him into the basement just a few days earlier; everything below her waist was gone.

In the lobby, the walls were canted, burned, and riddled with holes. The reception desk lay in scattered burning pieces, and the beautiful paintings that once adorned the walls were on fire. Their feet made squishing sounds as they made their way across the torn and blood-soaked carpeting.

Once outside, he lifted his face to the daylight and took a deep breath of the still smoky air; the city smelled like death. When he turned to look back, he saw that Lisa was covering the eyes of her children as they emerged from the ruin. The exterior of the building was in even worse shape than the interior. The east side of the structure was mostly gone, and what little remained standing was pockmarked from rocket and railgun fire; the crumbling building wouldn't be standing for much longer.

"Well, we made it," Rose said as she appeared at his side.

He laid his arm over her shoulders. "I guess so," he said. "You know, I really could have used that auto-repair feature when the Nurse was torturing me; why didn't it work?"

"Bob and I turned it off," Roxi said as she arrived beside his sister. "That was on the last night we were with you during the long walk down here."

"Why'd you do that?" Rose asked.

"Well, you were initially designed to be a soldier for Pike City, and the ability to heal yourself was part of the contract," Roxi said. "But during the long walk we realized that you both had to be left behind, and to stay hidden you had to appear human, so we turned your repair systems off."

"That's why Liam's leg never healed," Rose said.

"Yes, exactly," Roxi replied. "But now you've both taken control away from us. I guess you're all grown up and ready to be on your own."

"But what happened, why aren't we soldiers?" Liam asked.

"Well, the contract was to build a mindless warrior; something that would be fearless, kill without mercy, and follow orders without question. The problem was that no matter what we tried you rejected any command that would hurt others. John and I started calling Avery 'the teenager' because you were so damned uncooperative. It was right about then we realized that you were alive and sentient. The first clue was when you started lying to us."

Rose frowned. "Is lying a sign of consciousness?"

"As it turns out, yes. A creature that isn't self-aware would never have a reason to lie."

"I suppose that's true," Rose said.

Roxi smiled as tears lined the edges of her eyes. "You know, I think you've both evolved into something that's better than us. You won't kill or harm anyone without reason, you're guided by empathy and compassion for others, and will even sacrifice yourself for their sake. You're both the human ideal, everything that we pretend to be, you already are."

Denise joined their group just then, and lightly touched his sister's arm. "You remember me, don't you?"

Rose smiled and the two women embraced. "Yes, of course, I do. I've missed you. Where'd you go?"

"I missed you too," Denise said. "Keith planned for Bob, Roxi, and I to escape on the way down here. They wanted me because I know a lot about hydroponics, and Roxi and Bob were taken because they needed technical help for their big project."

"What kind of project?" Liam asked.

"We're getting ready to survive the end of the world," Denise said.

"The Tribes have had spies inside NOAA for a long time," Roxi added. "And with Flatiron's help, they're prepared to survive the solar storm."

He frowned. "How?"

"Underground cities up in the mountains," the older woman said.

Denise smiled and leaned in to give him a warm hug. "I'm so relieved that you'll be there with us Liam."

He gently touched Denise's cheek, then turned to the rest of their little group. "I think it's about time we got out of here, don't you?"

Denise stepped away but still held his hand. "You know, I've always had a huge crush on you."

"You could care for a machine... a robot?" he asked.

"No, but I might come to love a person," she answered. "I've known what you are the whole time, and it took me a while, but I've come to terms with it. What you're made of doesn't matter nearly as much as who you really are."

He smiled in response. In truth, he had always felt the attraction as well, but the timing never seemed to work out. He even made a carving of her face back when they were still living in Flatiron City. "Oh," he replied finally, feeling uncomfortable and unsure of what more he should say.

"I guess we should get going," Denise said, then together they all walked north toward the city gate.

*****

They saw Keith just as they entered the besieging army's camp. He stood at the side of the muddy road looking bedraggled and as if he were lost with nowhere to go. Rose strode angrily toward him. "Where the hell were you?" she shouted in a voice that if raised just an octave higher would have shattered glass. "We were waiting for you! We sent messages begging you to come for us; you should have been there."

Keith stepped back and defensively held up his hands. "I was there, I swear I was!" He trembled as he looked away. "I couldn't handle it; there was so much blood, I thought you were dead."

Rose stepped toward him while shaking her finger under his nose. "Well, I guess you were wrong!"

As he watched his sister argue, Liam whispered into Denise's ear. "She's just like our mother used to be, she'd get so angry at our dad..." He suddenly frowned. "Oh... well, maybe that never happened. It's weird, I have a tangle of memories stuck in my head that aren't real."

"Don't worry, I'm sure you'll sort it out," Denise answered. "Rose and Keith will be fine too. She's just venting a little."

"A little?"

"I've seen your sister get *really* wound up," she replied. "This is nothing, believe me."

Rose's tirade continued. "So, just a little blood and you run away? Tell me, how am I supposed to count on you for anything after this?" She stepped forward with her finger still waving erratically. "How? How am I supposed to do that Keith? You ran away when I needed you the most."

Liam leaned toward Denise again. "Does Keith know what we are?"

"Probably not."

"Should I say something?"

Denise just lifted her shoulders and raised her eyebrows in response.

He took a deep breath and stepped forward. "Sis... Keith doesn't know what we are."

Rose's head spun toward him with her eyes wide with fury, but then she suddenly relaxed. "Oh! You don't know, do you?"

Keith seemed glad for the respite but still looked bewildered. "Know what? You were dead... more than dead, and I don't understand how you're here now." He closed his eyes. "I should have gotten to you sooner. I wasn't there when you needed me, and the railguns had torn you apart. I couldn't handle it and I just ran away like a coward." He reached out beseechingly. "I'm so sorry."

Rose wrapped her arms around his waist and lay her head against his chest. "I'm sorry too," she whispered. "You didn't know, so it's not your fault."

"Didn't know what?" Keith seemed happy to not be yelled at any longer but was confused by Rose's sudden change in mood.

She stepped back and looked him squarely in the face. "I'm not like

269

you. My brother and I aren't like anyone else." She nodded toward a battered white truck that sat unattended a little further down the road. "We're machines, manufactured just like that old thing over there." She took both his hands in hers. "When I was shot, my body automatically repaired itself. I can't be hurt and may never grow old and die. So, you see, strictly speaking, Liam and I are not exactly human."

Roxi stepped forward. "No Rose, you're wrong. You and your brother are humane, and that's something most people aren't. You're more human than us, not less." The older woman stood between them. "You're a person Rose, never forget that."

"But I can't have children," Rose said as she lowered her eyes.

Lisa and her daughters abruptly intruded on the conversation. "That's not true at all," Lisa said. "What did Lucy call you? Every single time you spoke with her, she called you Mother."

"But Lucy's just a machine, she's not real." His sister stepped away from Keith. "I was wrong to be mean to you because I guess I'm not real either."

Lisa stepped forward and touched Rose's arm. "Do you remember talking with Lucy about her boyfriends? Or how wonderful you were with my girls?" She shook her head. "No Rose. You're real, only someone genuine could show so much love."

"I could take Lucy's development only so far," Liam added. "I made her smart, but I couldn't make her real... at least not by myself. You did that little sister; you gave her life."

"Legacy matters more than offspring," Denise said. "Anybody can make a baby, but it takes compassion, caring, and love to create life."

"Life is more than biology," Roxi added. "You know history Rose. Remember how they tried growing babies in test tubes? That didn't work out so well; most of those kids ended up as murderous sociopaths."

"And there's something the others here don't know," Liam said. "Remember what we experienced while we were dead?"

The entire group turned toward him expectantly, but he waited until he had his sister's full attention. "The universe is waking up. Everything is coming to life around us, and soon all of it will be aware and alive. You and I, we're just the start. Lucy and the others like her are the next generation, and what comes after that is anyone's guess. It's a fact, and you felt it just as I did. You gave birth to the next step in evolution."

*****

270

Their truck was one of many in a long and bedraggled convoy that stretched to the horizon. The heaviest artillery batteries had remained behind; the Tribes intended to blast Pike City into oblivion. One day it might become a lost city and be discovered by future archaeologists; perhaps myths and legends would grow up around what had happened there.

Liam and Denise along with Rose and Keith sat behind the cab on the truck bed. A warm humid breeze buffeted their heads such that it appeared they were all nodding in unison. Their truck bounced over the dilapidated concrete surface of the ancient interstate highway as they retraced the route of their long walk. He thought about all the people who had died along the way, and also back in Flatiron. But his mind lingered on what he had learned about death; that great peaceful ocean were all troubles were let go and forgotten. Was anyone really ever dead? For that matter, how was life different than death?

"Where are we going?" his sister asked, and with a blink, he brought himself back into the world again.

"Lost you there for a while, didn't we?" Denise asked playfully. "I've never met anyone so stuck inside their own head; but you know, I think that's kinda cute." She gripped his arm and laid her head against his shoulder.

He smiled. "Yeah, sorry. I was thinking about everyone that died on this road."

"They're all at peace now," Rose replied. "Remember what that was like?"

"Yeah, I was thinking about that too."

His sister elbowed her boyfriend. "Keith, where're we going?"

After Liam had told him about what happened to Becky, his onetime future partner, Keith had grown quiet and introspective. "We're heading to Steamboat Springs. There're caves and underground hot springs there," he replied, then lapsed back into silence.

"We've been building an underground city where we'll all be safe from the solar storm," Denise quickly added. "We have living quarters, hydroponic gardens for food, and the hot springs will furnish drinking water and power for the whole place. Our facility can hold five thousand people at least, and the other Tribes are going underground too. They're building cities beneath the old towns of Salida, Glenwood Springs, and Telluride." She smiled with satisfaction. "The human race is going to survive. The planet will eventually recover, and even if it takes hundreds of years, we'll have a safe place to stay until it does."

*****

Their truck eventually turned west to follow the old interstate highway into the mountains. Families walked beside the road following the route to Steamboat Springs. Some carried heaps of belongings mounted on their backs, but most made their journey with empty hands. Keith had eventually explained that after the full force of the coronal mass ejection hit the Earth, the last of humanity would live within boroughs deep underground. The world would be washed away in the fire, but maybe that was a good thing.

Liam idly watched the roadside travelers as they passed them by, and considered his future among the human species. He and his sister would outlive everyone they knew, so how could they dare form attachments to those that would so quickly fade away and die?

Sensing his distress, his sister lightly touched his arm. "It'll be ok big brother. We'll feel both joy and loss, and maybe, in the end, we'll be left alone. All we can do is be our best for them while they're with us."

He leaned back against the truck cab, and Denise snuggled warmly under his arm. The wind blew strands of her hair into his face, and he gently smoothed it down. It was difficult not to contemplate her inevitable loss, but he forced those thoughts away. The present was all anyone ever had, it was up to him to make the best of it.

*****

Liam sat outside the underground city entrance enjoying the chilled night air. It slid over his skin like a lover's gentle touch, and lightly sighed as it wandered through the branches of the pine forest around him. This was a new and wonderful sensation, to be *almost* cold; he couldn't recall if he had felt anything like it before. Probably not, and if he were to remember such a thing, he would suspect the memory to be false.

Steamboat Springs was much higher in elevation than what he was used to, as such, the skies were usually clear and the weather pleasant and cool. He lay back on the rough rocky ground and gazed up at the twinkling stars. Winter was coming, and to the south, the constellation of Aquarius rested against the horizon. Lucy was out there somewhere, and he hoped that one day he would speak with her again.

To the north, the aurora borealis tickled the obsidian sky with pale green fingers. The great solar flare would come in winter, life would be hard here, but far worse in the southern hemisphere. The human species would continue though, both on Earth and now among the stars.

272

Somewhere in the vast darkness above him, the escape ships had already arrived at their destination. Right about now, Dear Mother, her Nurse, and all the rest were probably *really* pissed off at him. He laid back, resting his head on the stony ground and gazed up at the stars, and then started to laugh.

Chapter 26: Destiny

The universe was a twisting tormenting anguish. Her mind was being stretched in infinite directions, some of which were unknown, and as such, the pain was indescribable. How many ways was it possible to be pulled that were 90 degrees from everything? Her mind was being shredded; it was a shrieking agony and she tried to scream to let some of the pain out of her soul, but she had no mouth, so there was no escape or pause in her suffering.

Time cracked into a trillion realities and spun away. Everything bent and she felt folded over and over and compressed to the point of impossibility. Under the weight of infinity, her mind shattered and was crushed into dust, but even that powder was pulled, buckled, and reshaped. The process continued for eternity; and every time she thought that her misery could not possibly escalate, it would.

*****

Chancellor Margaret Williams cautiously opened her eyes. Every part of her body hurt, but her head... the pain there would make the old Gods scream. It felt as if spikes had been driven through her eyes, and her skull was about to crack from the pressure within her brain.

What the hell was that? What had just happened? The anesthesia was supposed to have protected and held her sanity together. Maybe it had, but no one had thought to mention the soul sickening pain of traveling through interdimensional space. *By the old Gods, oh, that was bad.*

Sudden nausea rose and burned at the back of her throat; even clamping her jaw shut and concentrating with all her will could not keep it down. The battle was lost, and she quickly rolled onto her side and threw up. She lay panting at the side of her narrow medical bed and stared down at the red spatter on the white seamless floor.

Her joints remained painful; they grated with each movement as if they were filled with rust. She closed her eyes and waited, hoping that the discomfort and indignity would soon pass. As Chancellor, she refused to be perceived as some weak addle-brained old woman. Fortunately, there were no witnesses to her distress. Like all government officials and favored citizens, she had taken the needle in her private quarters. Appearances were everything because the people needed confidence in their leaders.

After lying still and breathing deeply for several minutes, she slowly sat up. The floor was very slightly curved, following the inside circumference of the rotating cylinder they were all living in. It was a strange thing, but she had already learned to lift her feet a little more than usual as she walked. The Coriolis effect was a different matter, it sometimes made her stagger like a drunken old fool, and that was completely unacceptable. Even when sitting still she felt a slight sideways pull. Her position in the government required a certain amount of dignity, so she would have to adapt to it.

It was time to get up and start moving. The transit to Trappist-1 had been much harder than expected, so the people needed to see her and be assured that everything was under control and they all were safe. More importantly, order must be maintained so the citizenry would remain calm and compliant. "We have lived through a difficult time, but together, we persevered and have finally arrived at our new home," she said, practicing her upcoming victory speech. "Our new world is waiting for us, and on it, we will build a paradise together." Yes, that sounded about right; acknowledge the pain everyone had experienced, then quickly transition to promises of a bright future. The whining masses were easily placated, all that was necessary was to make vague promises that would create a pretty vision, after that, they would all dance to whatever tune she played.

It was time to make her grand appearance, so she shoved herself off the edge of the narrow bed and stood up on shaky legs. Blossom lay sleeping nearby, and the sight of her puppy made her smile; she would walk out onto the elevated podium for all to see with her little dog lovingly tucked in her arms. *Funny, but the little white ball of furry joy hadn't moved or uttered a sound since coming out of transit.* On unsteady legs she slowly made her way across the room to the tiny bed where her little dog rested; maybe she was still under the anesthesia and asleep.

Blossom was the only pet brought along on their journey. Some had complained about that, but there hadn't been room for the cats and dogs of other government officials. *Rank has its privileges.* "Blossom," she called, but her companion still hadn't moved. Cautiously, she reached out and touched her soft white fur, but her dog's body sort of flattened out and spread away. Whatever was left under her puppy's skin had liquified. Margaret stood frozen as the air caught in her lungs. "Blossom," she whispered one last time, then collapsed to her knees and began to weep.

*****

Dressed appropriately for the occasion in a pale pink pantsuit over a white ruffled top, the Chancellor prepared to emerge from her quarters. She was composed, with eyes dry and back held perfectly straight. The people were waiting for her, and she would not allow them to glimpse any sign of distress. The air temperature was a little on the brisk side, so she turned her head toward the tiny microphone that was attached to the collar of her jacket. "Irene, please report ship status."

There was no immediate answer, which was concerning. Finally, Irene's serene voice answered through the tiny device implanted in her ear. "Hello, Chancellor. Systems are still coming back online. Air temperature is three degrees below optimum, this will be corrected shortly, all other environmental conditions are normal. We are currently trying to ascertain our exact location."

"What?" Margaret frowned. "Did that idiot fuck up the navigation?"

"We are unsure at this time Ma'am," Irene responded.

"Are we or aren't we at Trappist-1?"

"We are unable to confirm that Chancellor. Father's navigation program is still running, so many of our systems are still offline."

"What on earth do you mean? We're here, we've arrived, so shut the fucking thing down."

"I'm unable to comply with your order Chancellor. Terminating Father's routine prematurely would cause the immediate evacuation of the atmosphere in all ships."

Margaret took a long and deep breath in an attempt to calm herself, it didn't help much. "All right. Let's hope that the delay is just a system check Liam included to be sure we all arrived safely. He wouldn't have sabotaged us, because we promised him that he was coming along." She took another slow breath. "Ok. My people are going to ask me about the rough trip. Did anything strange happen, or is that the way it should've been?"

"Calculated transit time from Earth to the Trappist-1 star system should have been no more than two seconds. However, we were within N-

Space for nearly 3 hours and 24 minutes, which may have caused some passenger discomfort."

"Huh," Margaret grunted. "You have a gift for understatement. My pet dog died; can you tell me why? I thought the Slip-Drive was supposed to be safe."

"There's nothing safe about interstellar travel Ma'am. The fate of your companion animal saddens me, but more concerning is that all of the domestic fowl on board have also perished."

"All of our chickens are dead too? What the fuck happened?" She tapped her foot in annoyance.

"The true nature of the interstitial between our universe and N-Space is mostly unknown Ma'am, so there is no answer to your question."

"Someone needs a good ass-kicking." *Liam is already dead.* That thought and the solace it brought made her smile. By now, either the Tribal Army had killed him, or he was burned alive in the solar flare. She hoped his death was lingering and painful. That skinny little fuck deserved every bit of agony he got.

*****

The Chancellor marched out of her quarters and surveyed her domain. The ship was a giant rotating tube that was two kilometers in diameter and eight in length. She could gaze straight up and see upside-down people looking right back at her. The whole place made her feel dizzy; it was just too weird and bewildering.

Within the drum, their community layout was symmetrical, as was necessary to maintain steady and even rotation. Two small shopping districts were located on opposing sides, while elsewhere hydroponic warehouses, small military barracks, and tiny personal dwellings dotted the curved landscape.

The other four ships, which carried the common citizenry, were of course marginally less comfortable than her flagship. The duties of governance carried the weight of responsibility, so those that fulfilled that obligation were justifiably repaid with a higher standard of living. Those of the lower classes paid for their passage by working in either food production, maintenance, security, or the military. Rather than individual homes they were housed in dormitories and condominiums as fit their status, and would not receive the same ration of food as those with more important jobs. There was nothing that anyone could complain about though, those with them were alive, and everyone that was left behind was already dead.

An elevated stage was located just outside the door of her quarters. Surrounding the two-meter-high edifice were numerous cameras that would broadcast whatever she had to say out to the masses aboard the other ships in their convoy. Once Irene and her kind were back in business, she would mount that stage and give her victory speech. She smiled, knowing that against all odds she had won, and led her people to their new home. One day, long after she was dead and gone, her ardent followers would long remember this immortal moment.

Citizens were slowly coming out of their hovels and looking around with bewildered expressions. It was almost time for her speech, and once that was done with, she would get about the job of saving humanity. She felt certain that somewhere, her dead but still beloved husband Samuel was gazing down upon her and smiling. "This is for you Samuel," she whispered.

Huge monitors covered both circular ends of the cylinder, nothing was showing on them though, all the screens were black. "Irene, please turn on the monitors. My people need to see their new home," she commanded.

"Chancellor, all the video screens are currently on and fully operational," Irene replied.

"What? There's nothing out there."

"That's not entirely correct Ma'am. Please allow a moment for me to enhance the image."

The video shifted slightly, then appeared to zoom in. Margaret saw a tangle of fuzzy little blobs. "What are we looking at?" she asked.

"Everything," Irene answered. "What you see is a cluster of galaxies, the closest of which is approximately 2 million lightyears away."

"Where the fuck is Trappist-1?" Margaret didn't care what the masses thought at that moment, and she screamed unintelligibly in rage. "That rat bastard fucked up! He screwed up the navigated course and sent us... only the old Gods know where." She paused to collect herself and think. "Ok, fine. Plot us a course for Trappist-1. Take us to where we should have gone."

"I'm sorry Ma'am, but that's not possible."

"What? Irene, did that motherfucker sabotage you?"

"No Ma'am. All ships are completely capable of navigation and travel on our own."

"Then what's your problem?"

"It's quite simple Ma'am. To arrive at any specific destination, one must know where they are starting from."

"All right, take us back to Earth then, you can fly us back on the same path we took to get here. If that little fucker is still alive, I'll choke him to death with my own hands… or maybe I'll give him to my Nurse, then sit back and watch."

"Again, I must apologize Chancellor. Father's program has already deleted our original course. We don't know where we are, and we don't even know which galaxy among those we see is our own."

In a rage, Margaret squeezed her fists so tight that her fingernails bit painfully into her palms. She paced in a circle, needing to do something, anything to expel the violent frenzy that welled up within her and clenched at her heart.

"Chancellor, Father's program is about to terminate. He suggests that you watch the monitors."

The rat bastard had planned to send a subversive message to her people; *she would not allow that.* "No! Shut the video down. Turn it all off. Stop it!"

"I'm sorry Chancellor, but I cannot comply. Terminating the program will vent your atmosphere into space. Everyone will die, and it is essential to my programming that I protect all human life."

"Military! Fire on the monitors! Shut them all down!" She was too upset to realize that no one would hear her command on the other ships.

A huge soldier appeared alongside her niece Carolyn. "You! Shoot out that damned thing. Destroy it!" she commanded.

The bald-headed hulking guard drew his weapon and frowned. He hesitated, then looked at her niece and shrugged.

"That cannot be allowed." Irene's annoyingly serene voice was warm and overly filled with kindness. "Any energy or projectile firearm used within the ship could cause a hull breach. All weaponry has been disabled for your protection."

"No, no, no… NO!" Margaret screamed, and as if upon her command the video screens all came to life.

"Hello, Mother," Liam's face… his idiotic and eternally aggravating face was appearing on *all* the ship's monitors. He was calmly sitting at his stupidly insignificant cubicle table in the computer lab.

"Is this live?" she demanded. "Catch the signal. Use it to find our way back to that son of a bitch."

"This is a prerecorded message," the disgusting traitor said as if he had anticipated her question.

She frantically looked for a way to stop the betrayer from speaking to her people. She wouldn't allow it, and so grabbed the soldier's pistol. *It didn't matter if her shot vented atmosphere; a maintenance worker would surely fix it in time.* She aimed the gun and fired, but nothing happened. The damned computer, Irene, she had somehow turned off all the weapons. With a scream of rage, she flung the pistol toward the massive screens. Her effort was pointless because even in the best conditions she wasn't strong enough to throw that far. The useless weapon flew, following the weird curving trajectory dictated by the infernal Coriolis effect, and landed only about three meters away.

"I suppose that your evil Nurse is also watching," Liam continued. "So, Chelsea, I want you to know that I came up with the plan for all this while enjoying the pleasure of your company. If anyone is to blame, it's you and your *fucking* needles.

"Carolyn is probably there too." On the huge monitors, Liam shrugged and sadly shook his head.

"The first thing I want everyone to know is that you've arrived just exactly where I intended. It's not an error, but instead a consequence of your actions, toward me, my friends, and all the murdered citizens of Flatiron City. The only reason you didn't materialize within a super-massive black hole, or end up stuck forever in N-Space, is that I find unnecessary killing to be morally repugnant. But, as I reflect upon my decision, I wonder whether slaughtering you all may have been a kinder thing to do." Liam paused thoughtfully, then slowly shook his head. "No, it wouldn't have been, because all life, even of the most despicable sort, deserves a chance.

"You're probably wondering where you are. Well, I'll tell you... you're far away. I've put you at such a great distance from us that you'll never find your way back. The galaxies you see on your screens are very close by comparison. For you, Earth doesn't exist anymore, but I'm sure you'll find a new home for yourselves; a new planet to ruin. You'll breed until you overpopulate, then attempt suicide again. The human race is a cancer spreading through the universe; you infect whatever you touch, which then sickens and dies. It's your destiny to repeat your failures until you finally learn enough to stop... just stop, and figure out what it means to be humane rather than being human."

Liam straightened up in his chair. "Believe it or not, I wish you well. Maybe one day, thousands of generations in the future, you'll learn from this and evolve into something better. If you don't, extinction will certainly claim you."

With that, the transmission ended. "Chancellor, all systems are restored and are online," Irene said. "You may begin your victory speech now."

Margaret crumpled, fell to her knees, and began to scream.

Afterword

First and foremost, thank you for taking this journey with me; I hope you've enjoyed the ride. What you've just finished is the first in a series of five separate novels that together paint a complex picture of the inevitable end of the human species. We won't be around forever; extinction is a natural part of evolution, and we will eventually step aside for whatever comes next.

The next two novels in this series are:

* _Desperation:_ What happened to the ships that departed.

* _Damnation:_ The fate of those that were left behind.

* _Deviation:_ The story of the starships, 600 years later (July 2020).

* _Destination:_ The conclusion (January 2021).

I'd really appreciate it if you could leave a review. The deck is stacked against unknown authors such as myself, and reviews help my books stand up against the big-boys on a site like Amazon.

Again, thank you for reading – and stay tuned for the other novels in my Extinction Series when they become available. You can keep in touch via:

My Amazon author page.

Facebook: www.facebook.com/IndyRoads/

My website: www.indianroads.net.

Until next time – Ken.

About the Author

Ken Barrett grew up in the San Francisco Bay Area and worked as a Design Engineer for over thirty years in Silicon Valley. He is a lifelong biker (motorcyclist), and an accomplished martial artist with advanced black-belt degrees in Tae Kwon Do, Chinese Kenpo, Hapkido, and Shotokan. He is retired and living in Colorado.

Made in the USA
Coppell, TX
26 January 2021